TO634577

BOUND IN DARKNESS

Captivated

Devotion

Perception

Entrusted

Adored

Distraction

Forevermore

DEAD HEAT RANCH

Boots Optional

Betting on Grace

Overnight Love

Jared (a crossover novel)

DEVIL'S BEND

Chasing Dreams

Vanishing Dreams

HEROES & HAVOC

Wait for Morning

Beautifully Brutal

Without Regret

Never Say Never

Beautifully Loyal

Without Restraint

Tomorrow's Too Late

MISPLACED HALOS

Protected in Darkness

Salvation in Darkness

Bound in Darkness

OFFICE INTRIGUE

Office Intrigue

Intrigued Out of The Office

Their Rebellious Submissive

Their Famous Dominant

Their Ruthless Sadist

Their Naughty Student

Their Fairy Princess

Owned

PIER 70

Reckless

Fearless

Speechless

Harmless

Clueless

PRIMAL INSTINCTS

Chase (Volume 1-3)

Capture (Volume 4-6)

Claim (Volume 7-9)

THE JAMESONS OF COYOTE RIDGE

Hot Chocolate Wishes

Rough & Dirty

THE WALKERS OF COYOTE RIDGE

Kaleb

Zane

Travis

Holidays with The Walker Brothers

Ethan

Braydon

Sawyer

Brendon

Curtis

Jared

Hard to Hold

Hard to Handle

Beau

Rex

A Coyote Ridge Christmas

Mack

Kaden & Keegan

Trey

Rafe

Violet

STANDALONE NOVELS

Unhinged Trilogy

A Million Tiny Pieces

Inked on Paper

Bad Reputation

Bad Business

Filthy Hot Billionaire

RULE

NAUGHTY HOLIDAY EDITIONS

2015

2016

2021

BOUND IN DARKNESS

MISPLACED HALOS
BOOK THREE

NICOLE EDWARDS

***

COVER DETAILS:
Image: © demonburner | 123RF.com | *Design:* © Nicole Edwards Limited
INTERIOR DETAILS:
Image: © winwinartlab *(20193921)* | *123RF.com*
Formatting: Nicole Edwards Limited

 Formatted with Vellum

PROLOGUE

Friday, October 13, 2017

KAJ COURTENAY

"Son of a bitch!"

"Holy shit!"

"Tell me he's still alive, bro!"

I had to wonder about the last one. If sheer, endless agony meant I was alive, then yeppers. I was most definitely in the land of the living.

Had to be, right? Otherwise I wouldn't be listening to Obsidian's fool brothers ramble incessantly about whether or not I had succumbed to the lead shower I'd found myself in the middle of.

Not just one bullet. Oh, no. I'd never get that lucky. If memory served—and that was a bit iffy right now—there were at minimum three pieces of lead stuck somewhere in my torso. Likely in my lung since breathing was a bit more difficult than usual.

Oh, look at me playing the eternal optimist. Must still be kicking.

Fuck that. I was on fucking fire, every goddamn inch of me.

The blaze of agony had started somewhere in my chest and was now catching up with the rest of me. Good news... I could no longer feel my feet, so there was some relief there.

"Find Acadia!" Obsidian shouted, though who he was talking to I had no idea. "Right now!"

Breathe. Just breathe. In ... out ... in—

"I'm here, Obsidian."

Holy shit. Now *that* was the voice of an angel. Too bad I couldn't open my eyes to see her.

"How may I assist?"

Perhaps a bit more effort was required, because, heaven help me, I wanted to see her.

Try, try, try again.

Nope. Eyes won't work. What now?

Oh, right.

Thanks be to the Almighty, my sense of smell wasn't broken, so I turned my face in the direction of the soft scent of ... well, I didn't know what it smelled like, but it was the best thing my sinuses had ever pulled through them.

"I've got to get the bullets out," Obsidian grumbled, that deep, rumbling voice close. "He'll need blood."

Yes. Bullets out, blood in. *Good plan, big guy.*

"It would be my pleasure," the female intoned.

Heaven. I was pretty sure her voice was the sound made by all those harps in Heaven.

That lovely cadence drifted amongst the clouds currently filling my mind.

Not clouds, more like fog, growing thicker with every passing second. Perhaps I was hovering between Earth and Heaven, stuck in a state of limbo. Obsidian was down on the mainland while that female was drifting high in the clouds. If I was dangling somewhere in between, I was ready to follow her, wherever she was. Please and thank you.

"Where do you need me?" the angelic voice asked.

"Right there's fine," Obsidian responded.

I could imagine a halo ringing her head, casting a beautiful glow over her as she floated effortlessly on white, billowy— The image I was trying to conjure in my mind was obliterated by a blinding pain spearing my chest.

"Hey, Kaj. I can't promise this won't hurt," Obsidian stated.

More than this? Yeah. Doubtful. A grumble was all I could manage, the words in my head not being relayed to my mouth.

"Don't touch him until I'm finished." Obsidian's tone held an air of concern.

Who? Who was the big bastard talking to? The angel? No, I wanted her to touch me. Right now would be fine. She could carry me right off into the afterlife.

Surely this was the end for me. At least I was going out on a high note. Those demons might've nailed me where it counted, but I'd eliminated at least two dozen before I gave up the ghost. Proved myself to the male I'd come to consider a friend. A fucking angel, of all things. Never in my life had I thought I'd be cozied up to the feathered type, but hey, I was open-minded like that.

As the fire blazed through me, I briefly wondered whether someone would tell my father I was gone. Would Kardobahn mourn me? Yes, I decided. Perhaps we hadn't always been close, but I had a good relationship with my father and the new female Kardobahn had mated a few years back. There was no lingering animosity between us. Probably helped that, aside from being his oldest son, I was Kardobahn's *adighrielin*, the advisor to the vampire Alpha. To add another title to the list: leader of the Zenith. It had taken centuries, but I had finally proven my worth to my father. Surely that would mean something.

"Kaj, brother, I need you to take a deep breath."

The cold that raced over my skin said a deep breath likely wouldn't do any good. I was fading quickly, and truth was, I was ready. Not because I wanted to vacate my current life. No, I was content with how things were. Not necessarily happy, no. But I had no complaints. It had been a good life and I'd accomplished much in my five hundred-plus years on Earth. I was ready for the—

Mother.

Fucker.

The pain that lanced me took hold of my internal organs and … twisted, yanked, pulled—*Holy. Fuck.*—then jerked for good measure.

Good news was, my breath was soughing in and out of my lungs. Probably meant I was still kicking. Maybe.

Then there was another wrenching tug and the breathing thing…? Not all that important.

Ohfuckohfuckohfuckoh … fucking … hell!

I was aware of a piercing sound splitting the air around me. It coincided with the way my body splintered. Fire blazed through me as I was pulled in all directions, my insides churning, blistering as that inferno consumed me from head to toe. It went on for an eternity, then another until I was convinced I had died, but rather than go up, I was shot down to Hell, left to rot in the bowels of that fiery shithole.

"Breathe, Kaj."

The shrill noise halted, and I realized—sadly, mind you—I'd been screaming like a little bitch.

Lovely.

A soft hand swept over my forehead, once, twice.

The agony still ripped through me, but it was somehow bearable with her touch.

"He needs to feed," a male voice noted.

Obsidian. Still there. True friend he was. Minus the whole ripping-my-insides-to-shreds thing.

"I'll take care of him," the female replied, that lyrical voice my lifeline.

"When you need to feed," Obsidian stated, his voice directed elsewhere, "I want you to come find me." A strong hand pressed gently against my shoulder. "And you, my friend, will be good as new in no time. The bullets are removed, all four of them. Now you need to recuperate."

I gave a whole-hearted effort at opening my eyes. Not because I cared to see Obsidian leaning over me. No, I was interested in the female. The sweet, angelic female...

Before I could catch a glimpse of her, the darkness pulled me under.

Damn good thing vampires healed quickly.

That was my first thought when I came to in a dimly lit bedroom that was decorated in crimson and overlaid with swirly, silver doodads, an odd combination to the eye. Kinda made me nauseous.

At least the bed I lay on was soft, the comforter warm. The air smelled of cherry blossoms and the lightest hint of sandalwood, the combination going right to my head. A fire crackled in the hearth, warming the room and adding a weird ambience.

My attention was drawn to the door. It opened on a whisper, closed the same. My ears registered bare feet padding over hardwood, then drifting as they moved onto what I assumed was a rug.

"Perhaps you'll wake for morning meal this night," that sweet cadence relayed, filling the otherwise silent room.

It was in that moment I finally laid eyes on the female whose voice had lived in my dreams ever since I passed out earlier. She'd remained a fixation in my mind through the hours it took for the torment within my body to subside. Good news was, the pain was gone—mostly—and she was not. So either I was in Heaven, or she wasn't some angel who'd been sent to carry me home.

Honestly, I hoped for the latter. Lots still to do on this big hunk of rock.

I kept my lids low so I could watch as she set a tray down on the bedside table. She was startlingly beautiful. Dark brown hair piled high on her head and held there with some sort of colorful stick. The wisps that fluttered down around her face were a delectable contrast to her fair skin.

As though she sensed me, her head tilted my way and I saw her eyes for the first time. They were a translucent purple, and I was instantly reminded of amethyst stones, only her eyes were far more beautiful than any jewel. Radiantly incandescent. Was that a real thing? Yes, I decided. It was now.

"Oh, you *are* awake." The acknowledgment was communicated softly and without concern.

I continued to watch her. "Tired of me already?"

The soft smile that pulled at her exquisite mouth had a strange feeling erupting inside me.

Her gaze shifted from me to the meal she had produced. "I brought food in the hopes you would wake." She smiled softly. "In case you were hungry."

I gave the tray a half-hearted glance. I couldn't care less about food at the moment, although, now that she mentioned it, my stomach rumbled in direct conflict with my mind. How many hours had passed since I'd had my evening meal? What time was it?

Hating that I was flat on my back, I shifted so I could sit, but the female instantly stopped me, placing her small hand on my chest. My naked chest.

That touch had heat blooming through my entire body.

"Not yet. You need to feed first."

"I just fed," I said, my voice coming out raspy, as though I hadn't used it in a while.

Must've been a good nap I'd taken.

"And when might that've been?" she prompted

I turned my head, trying to find a clock. "Nightfall," I told her, though I absolutely had no intentions of going into specifics.

"What day do you think it is?" she questioned, standing tall and peering down at me with concern glittering in her eyes.

"Friday." I lifted a weak hand, waved it.

"Well, it is Friday, but I don't think it's the same Friday you're thinking of."

Frowning, I stared up at her, trying to figure out the riddle.

Before I could argue, she shifted her long, flowing skirt and positioned herself so she was perched on the edge of the mattress, body angled toward me while her legs were hanging over the side. There was a shocking grace to her every movement. She tugged the flaring sleeve of her dress back, revealing her delicate wrist. Her skin was so pale I could see the veins beneath.

I considered it for a moment. I rarely took from a female's wrist or her neck. As a rule, I fed from *cosrobols*, the blood whores who offered themselves up to me. They were provided by the Alpha, given to the Zenith to do with as they pleased.

Because I had no desire to get involved with one of them, I would take from the insides of their thighs, leaving marks that would not be visible to others. Not because I was ashamed that others would find out. I simply didn't want to see my mark upon them.

However, with this female ... I had the strange urge to mark her in more ways than mere puncture wounds upon her skin.

A fierce pain pierced my chest the moment I heard her blood pumping in her veins. Bloodlust? So soon? As my fangs shot out from the roof of my mouth, I realized I was starving.

"Take it," she offered, shifting her wrist closer.

With my eyes never leaving her face, I reached for her hand. Soft as powder, smooth as silk. I circled her forearm with my other hand, keeping her arm still as I penetrated her with my fangs. She didn't flinch as I drew from her, nor did she look away.

The second her blood slid down my throat, I felt the power within it. It infused me instantly, bringing to life the rest of my cells, as though they'd been dormant for weeks. My thirst didn't abate even as I drew more and more from her. Never did I close my eyes, fearful if I did, she might disappear.

By the time I'd had enough to tide me over, there was a strange roaring in my head. I released her from my lips, sealed the wounds on her flesh. And if I lingered a little longer than was appropriate ... well, I couldn't help myself.

"We were starting to worry you wouldn't wake up," she said as she lowered her sleeve over her wrist.

"I was due for a nap." I peered around, trying once more to find a clock.

Finding none, I glanced back at her, noticed she was frowning.

"What?" I asked.

"My lord, you've been unconscious for nearly five weeks."

Wait. Huh? Five weeks?

"Oh, fuck," I groaned, attempting to push to a sitting position. "Where're my clothes?"

"Please, my lord," she said softly, her gentle hand once more on my chest. "Your body needs to rest."

"I've *been* resting," I countered with a huff. "For five weeks, apparently. How much longer do I need?"

"With my blood in your veins"—she appeared to be calculating something—"I would say at least another month."

I watched her, noticing for the first time that there was an oddity to her. Not physically, but on a cellular level.

"You're not vampire," I stated.

"No, I am not."

"Nor are you an angel."

Her amethyst eyes lowered. "I am Fae, my lord."

Fae. As in the mystical fairies who were cast out of Heaven by the Almighty above? That Fae? I hadn't even known they still existed.

"We don't," she said, answering a question I thought had only sounded in my head. "Not outside of these walls. My kind has been relegated to serve the warriors and the *fiestreigh*. There are nineteen of us in total." Her warm fingers urged me back. "Now, please rest."

"Serve?" I relaxed into the pillow, realizing I would stay there all night just to hear her voice. "What does that mean?"

"Their blood and sexual needs."

I refused to acknowledge the dark, possessive rumble that sounded in my chest.

"Would you like me to leave, my lord?"

"What's your name?"

"Acadia."

Ah, I remembered now. The most beautiful name I'd ever heard. "And I assume you know mine?" I prompted.

9

"Of course, my lord."

I canted my head and smiled. "Then please, Acadia, do refrain from calling me my lord."

Her answering smile was the first of many that would slowly bring me peace.

I

KAJ

The sound of heavy footfalls had me looking up from my morning meal, a grin tugging at my mouth when I saw who it was and the dramatic way the male was making an entrance.

"Thank the good Heavenly Almighty we don't have to deal with that damn mating heat anymore," Blāz declared as his enormous body buckled and he flopped into the leather chair that had been tucked up beneath the table.

I peered down at the large vampire at the opposite end. Though I'd had some time to get used to the fact my males were back with me, I still found myself sending up a silent thank-you to the deity upstairs. To have gotten them back after I'd been certain they had met their demise was likely far more than I deserved, but I wasn't about to question the Almighty's reasons. They were here. That was all that mattered.

"You do realize there are five more warriors who've yet to mate," Kidel noted as he strolled into the room, pulled out a chair, fell into it.

"Yeah, but for now, they're not emitting that fucking energy." Blāz chuckled. "See what I did there?"

Considering the immense stress I was under, I welcomed the levity. As it was, I'd been going over and over *and over* the conversation I'd had with Michael a week ago. Only seven days I'd been pondering the archangel's request for me to resurrect the original vampire. Who, the male had so kindly told me, was currently riding shotgun in Oliver Calazans's body.

Oliver freaking Calazans. Obsidian's mate's brother.

For fuck's sake.

A ten-thousand-year-old all-powerful vampire soul smashed into a five-foot-seven-inch human. I couldn't fathom how that was even possible, yet I didn't doubt for one second Michael had pulled a stunt like that.

And while we both knew I couldn't really say no to the request, the archangel had still granted me time to consider it. Being familiar with Michael's thin patience, I figured that clock was quickly running out.

I pushed to my feet. "I need to talk to Mirakel."

"He's still back at Angel Central," Blāz stated. "Said he had something to take care of."

Blood needs, more than likely. For whatever reason, Mirakel had stopped allowing the Fae to come to his private quarters, though from what I knew, the male was continuing to feed from the same female ... whatever her name was.

"Thanks," Blāz said to the *heurosp* who delivered his morning meal.

"You're most welcome, sire."

Blāz rolled his eyes and pointed his fork at the male walking away, mouthing *sire*, and shaking his head. As a member of the Zenith, Blāz was used to being considered the upper echelon, but the *vestrahn* who regularly waited on us had never referred to us using any sort of honorific.

"He's spending quite a bit of time there," Kidel noted, as though he just realized Mirakel had been gone a lot.

"I think he's got a thing for Briony." Blāz grinned before shoveling eggs into his pie hole.

Yes, Briony. That was her name.

"She's a pretty one," Kidel said. "But the rumor is, she's never been with a male."

I cocked an eyebrow.

Blāz gasped as though that was a preposterous thought.

"What?" Kidel offered a sheepish shrug. "Males talk, too, you know."

Oh, I knew. They were a gossipy bunch, this one.

"I was about to head over," Huracān's deep voice boomed from the next room, where he reclined casually in a dinky leather armchair, ankle resting on the opposite knee, his iPad propped on his thigh. "Want me to track him down?"

"Whoa, dude. Didn't see you there," Blāz said. "Snazzy outfit. You got a hot date?"

Huracān rolled his eyes, focused on me. "Want me to send him this way?"

I took a moment to decide if making the trip over was worth it. From here, at least the echo of pain I felt in my chest whenever Acadia fed another male was bearable. When I was at Angel Central, it was brutal. Sometimes I thought she did it on purpose, choosing the exact moment of my arrival to open a vein to one of those greedy angels.

Not that I blamed her. I had taken to feeding from other females because I had no choice. Problem was, I was going to have to increase my volume. As it was, I was skipping a couple of days, and in order to be in top fighting form, I needed to feed daily. If I'd had a female vampire nearby, I would've opted to feed from her so Acadia didn't think I was trying to rub it in her face. That was absolutely not my intention. In fact, feeding in general had become an exercise in futility, something I wished wasn't a requirement for my mere existence.

But I couldn't avoid the place forever. We had too much shit to do for me to be hiding out from a female.

"I'll find him," I told the male. "I need to check in with Bijou, anyway." I peered down the table. "What's the word on the security?"

"I'm finishing up the controls for the cameras," Blāz noted. "We've got 'em installed, just need to sync, then I'll work with Reidar to get everything tied together. They've given us access to their exterior feeds already."

"Great."

"I'm telling you … those boys know what they're doing." Blāz spoke around a mouthful. "Can't say I'm not a little jealous." He smiled as he took a gulp of orange juice. "I wanna be them when I grow up."

The comment reminded me of Michael's request that we vow our loyalty to the angels, which I took to mean Michael wanted us to align our objectives, essentially work for them. As easy as I wanted to say that would be, I couldn't simply offer up an *oh, sure, of course*. I was, after all, the most powerful vampire, the one on the throne, so to speak. I had to take into consideration my entire race, not just a handful who would benefit most from a consolidation of strength.

Would those who trusted their Alpha to make smart decisions want me to pledge my allegiance to a faction of warrior angels? Probably not. The vampires were a very proud species. Rightfully so. We'd been placed on Earth to protect the human race, and we took our responsibilities seriously. Even the civilian vampires implanted in human communities had duties, whether it was contacting the tip line with sightings of demons or merely observing human behaviors that were conducive to luring demons to them. We were all playing a part.

Were the humans grateful? Of course not.

Hell, it took tremendous effort these days just to keep ourselves hidden from *Homo sapiens*, one of the many rules laid out by the Almighty. And what did we get for our efforts? The fucking humans found it amusing to dress up like some creepy caped crusader with fangs and call it a vampire. As if.

"Hey, Kaj? You good?"

Realizing I was standing at the table, I shook myself out of my wayward thoughts and nodded to Blāz. "I'll be back. Holler if you need me."

Rather than step outside and poof my ass over to the mansion, I opted to walk via the underground tunnels that wound through the mountain connecting Angel Central to the Lair. The tunnels had been dug out back when the angels had started building their new fortress many moons ago. Though they'd all but abandoned the house my crew and I now occupied, the tunnels had been maintained. The smooth concrete walls and floor did their job of holding back the earth, as well as concealing the titanium used to keep vampires and other supernatural creatures from popping in uninvited. While that was a nice security measure, it made getting out impossible, so once we started on the one-mile trek, we were pretty much relegated to the stroll. But we had the motion-activated gas torches along the walls to keep us company and provide light for those who didn't have the benefit of seeing in the dark.

Every few feet, a gas torch would come to life, brightening the path before another flared with a slight hiss. I continued with one foot in front of the other, breathing in and out in an attempt to clear my head before I saw my daughter.

I ground my back molars together as I recalled the conversation I'd had with the archangel.

"Kaj Courtenay, you are not only the Alpha of your species, you are the father of the female who shall mate the original vampire."

"Wait. Huh?" I stared at the archangel. *"My daughter is to mate the original vampire. Not to sound all Adam-and-Eve oddity or anything, but exactly how does one mate one to whom she is related?"*

"There are no direct descendants of the original vampire," Michael stated, as though that made all the sense in the world.

"No?" I motioned to myself. *"Exactly how did I come to be without the original vampire breeding?"*

Those strangely colored eyes remained on my face. *"The original vampire did not mate, nor did he breed."*

Okay, so clearly we were getting nowhere fast. *"You lost me."* I waved a hand. *"But it's all moot anyway. The original vampire is dead."*

"Quite the opposite. He is very much alive, merely ... preoccupied at the moment."

"Meaning...?"

"I've kept him hidden for his own protection."

"You?"

"Yes."

"For seven hundred years?" I got the feeling that didn't mean he was being locked in a cage somewhere. For one, Khari was far too powerful. He would've easily broken free. *"Where is he?"*

Michael took a deep breath. "Khari is currently in a human vessel."

Unable to help myself, I laughed. "A human vessel? The original vampire is sporting a human meat suit? Tell me, what poor sap is giving the male a ride?"

"You know him as Oliver Calazans."

My smile fell instantly. I stared at the archangel, slack-jawed and dumbfounded. "What did you say?"

"Do you really need me to repeat?"

That damn archangel had laid a whopper on me, and I had yet to figure out how to share the information without inciting a riot. So many were affected by the outcome of Michael's fate-weaving exercise—Obsidian, Penelope, Oliver, Bijou, the Fae—and yet the archangel didn't seem eager to spread the word.

Hell, just the thought of my daughter being mated to the original vampire, of all males, was enough to make me see red. Something instigated by the archangel, no doubt. As for Michael's reasons, I wasn't privy to them. Not surprising. The male who led us all around by the nose was selfish when it came to his secrets, parsing out only what he had to in order to get his way.

According to Michael, a ten-thousand-year-old vampire whose soul had been bouncing from one human vessel to the next for God only knew how many centuries was going to be my son-in-law, to use the human terminology. All the effort to shield the vampire had been because Bijou hadn't been in existence yet. Now she was, which meant Khari could be resurrected, his soul dumped back in his original body. Wherever it was.

But my biggest issue was the prearranged mating. I'd mistakenly thought we'd done away with that centuries ago. Unlike angels and humans, vampires didn't have predestined mates. There were no *amsouelots*, no destined souls.

No, vampires had our own unique method of mating: *mielix zan* was the term in the ancient language, which loosely translated to sexually imprinting. And we only did it once, if we were lucky to find our life mate at all. Which was why many vampires simply settled down with a mate who made them happy. We were similar to humans in that regard, wanting to couple because the endless days and nights were more bearable that way. As for *mielix zan* ... if and when we were affected, the option for mating anyone else went right out the window, as the humans liked to say.

I got the feeling Michael didn't understand that.

What if my daughter thought the male unworthy? It wasn't like I could simply force the mating upon her. I hadn't raised Bijou. Her mother had done that without a lick of help from me because the female had felt it unnecessary to mention she happened to be having my offspring. Twenty-six years later, Bijou popped up on my doorstep with a *hey, surprise! I'm your daughter*. I had known the moment I looked into her green eyes that she was mine, but that didn't make me a father by any stretch of the imagination. Had we developed a relationship since? Yeah. I liked to believe we had. It had taken effort on both our parts, but we seemed to be making it work.

Didn't mean I could resort to the old ways and pass her over as though she were a piece of property. The vampires had shed that tradition with the modern ages, and I was quite fond of the *select who you want to spend your time with* process. Even without the lifetime connection of *mielix zan*, I still believed in choices.

As I strolled through the tunnels, I tried to imagine the original vampire being trapped somewhere inside the body of Oliver Calazans.

How the fuck did that even work?

OLIVER CALAZANS

I strolled through the game room, pausing near the iron railing that overlooked the main floor below.

I did a quick visual sweep of the area, relieved when I saw no signs of Bijou. It meant I could sneak down for a bite since I'd purposely skipped the morning meal. Then again, I'd purposely skipped *every* communal meal for the past ... fifty days. Wow. Nearly two months now that I hadn't sat with my fellow ... with the angels for their twice-daily chow sessions.

Made me feel like a bit of a recluse, more in line with the guy who had been hog-tied and dragged here than the one who'd come to enjoy the sense of belonging I'd found with a bunch of holy motherfuckers.

However, there was no way around my bob-and-weave exercise. Ever since I'd witnessed Bijou feeding from Madok—that lucky bastard Fae with the magic blood—I hadn't been able to so much as look at her. It hurt too damn much to think about, so I'd gone back to my old, grumpy ways, hiding out when I wasn't in the war room using those fancy systems to hack whatever the angels needed access to.

With my path clear for the time being, I hurried down the front staircase to the main floor, strolled down the wide hall-way, over the fancy blue rug, past the weird lobby/living room that no one *ever* mingled in, then on to the kitchen, where I found Emily, the *heurosp* who'd just magically arrived with about a dozen others in the past month. I had no idea where they came from, but they'd integrated right into the day-to-day, helping out with the many goings-on at both Angel Central and the Lair.

"Hey," I greeted with a half-ass wave as I made my way to the pantry with the fancy opaque glass and the curly-cue etching that announced what was discreetly hidden behind it.

"Sire," Emily said softly, ducking her head.

"Oh, no," I corrected, gripping the knob and twisting. "I'm no sire. Just a plain ol' boring human."

Who couldn't feed a vampire, thus sending that vampire to bite the neck of a male worthy of her.

I shook off the thought.

"Shall I prepare you a meal?" Emily offered, her kindness exactly what I expected from those who worked in the mansion.

"I can get it." Last thing I wanted to do was put more on her plate.

"As you wish." She returned her attention to the few dishes that were in the sink.

I stepped inside the "pantry"—what mere mortals referred to as a decent-size bedroom—snagged a loaf of bread from one of the many shelves, grabbed the gallon jar of peanut butter, headed back out, then over to the complicated contraption they called a toaster oven. What happened to the good ol' spring-loaded thing that launched the toast high in the air when it was perfectly browned on both sides in like two minutes? This ridiculous thing had about fifty settings and took three times as long to make toast.

Resigned to spending a good portion of my twenties waiting for bread to brown, I tucked two pieces inside, began punching buttons, because toasting bread had been relegated to a fucking science and this thing had all the buttons to prove it. Once the heating coils were flaring red behind the little glass door, I tied the plastic bread bag off and replaced it in its home in the enormous pantry that had its own stairway leading down to a wine cellar fit for a kingdom.

When I returned, there was a fancy glass plate and a sterling silver butter knife on the counter beside the peanut butter.

I peered over my shoulder at Emily. I couldn't help but chuckle at the way she kept her chin tucked down as though I might not possibly be able to figure out she was the one who'd brought the utensils over. She was the only other person in the kitchen. How would I not know?

While I waited the remaining six minutes to toast bread, I turned around to face Emily, crossing my arms over my chest. "So, how's it going? You like it here?"

Pretty brown eyes lifted to meet mine. "I do, actually. It's quite pleasant."

"What did you do before?"

Her eyes quickly lowered. "That I do not recall. It was part of the agreement."

"Agreement?"

Her attention remained on her dishes. "Yes. Aside from recalling that this was a choice I made, to come here, I do not remember anything about my past."

Wow. That ... kinda sucked. Who would want to spend all their days living their life only to have their memories yanked away from them? Well, clearly Emily, since she'd evidently agreed to it. But still.

"Was it worth it?" I asked, wishing I could take the words back as soon as they were out.

"I... In my humble opinion, I believe it was, yes. This is an opportunity to serve my Lord and Savior; therefore, I find it quite worth it."

Well, then. Didn't I just feel like a dickhead.

"And you?" she asked. "How do you like it here?"

It was my turn to drop my gaze. "It's fine. I enjoy the work."

"As do I," she added, as though I'd suggested otherwise.

When she resumed her scrubbing of the dishes, I watched her. It was hard to pinpoint her exact age, but I had to assume she was somewhere in her mid- to late-twenties. In human years, anyway. Here in the land of immortals, age was irrelevant—quite literally just a number—so their physical appearance could belie their actual number of years since, like angels and apparently vampires, *heurosp* didn't age the same as humans.

But she was pretty in a sweet, innocent way. Long blond hair that she kept up in a ponytail, kind brown eyes, and a warm smile. Those were the things I'd noticed about her since her arrival. It was the sort of thing I noticed with most of the *heurosp* who wandered the estate taking care of the lot of them. For instance, Jeffrey: brown eyes, light brown hair, eager to take care of everyone. And then Phillip, who I suspected was the BMOC: dark brown hair, pale blue eyes, and a quick smile. I was pretty sure Jeffrey and Phillip were a couple, but I figured asking was a violation of their privacy. They seemed happy, whatever their relationship, and that was all that really mattered.

Ding!

Finally. Two days later, I had lightly toasted bread.

Turning back to my task, I slid out the pieces of crusty brown bread, slathered each with peanut butter, smashed them together, then returned the PB to the pantry where I'd gotten it. When I returned, there was a linen napkin, a perfectly ripened banana, and a glass of milk sitting beside my plate.

I peered over at Emily, noticed she was blushing sweetly.

"Thanks, Em," I said. "You're far too kind."

"You're more than welcome, sire."

Shaking my head at the title she used, I carried my plate and glass into the breakfast nook—though nook seemed to imply it was a small area and this one held a table that sat at least twenty-four people. It was used for meals that weren't eaten in the enormous dining room (think commercial cafeteria). Many times, I would see one of the *heurosp* having their meal in there, and I briefly wondered if Emily would've joined me if I'd asked.

I closed my eyes and sighed. No, I didn't wonder.

Because it wasn't my place.

I seriously needed to get a grip.

So I did, using both hands to tilt my sandwich up to my mouth. With my first bite, I groaned in pleasure.

Plop.

Peering down the front of my shirt, I sighed again.

"You dropped some."

My head jerked up to see Kaj passing down the hallway, his finger aimed directly at my shirt. The vampire offered a grin and kept on going.

I glanced down, shook my head at the melted peanut butter running in a river down the front of me.

If I had any luck at all, it was shit luck.

With a grunt, I lifted the sandwich to my mouth and mentally gave the shit luck the finger.

It replied by dropping another load of peanut butter.

Fan-fucking-tastic.

2

ACADIA

Alpha vampire radar.

Yep, I had it, and right now, it was homed in on the male who was circling back through the kitchen after going ... wherever he'd gone. The first time he passed, Kaj had been focused on Oliver's peanut butter fiasco, so I was given a reprieve. Thinking I was safe, I had remained right where I was.

Should've known better.

Now that radar was beeping loudly in my brain, seeming to grow louder the closer Kaj got. That was how it worked, as though we were tethered in some way. Part of it had to do with the fact that my blood ran in his veins, but I suspected there was something else that connected us, something deeper. Perhaps it was all the time we'd spent together back when I first learned of his existence, back when he'd suffered a near-fatal injury. After all, it had been during those six months that I had fallen in love with the male. That pure, unfettered love that would withstand time and tragedy, even if we were not together.

Not that I'd shared as much with him. Kaj had far more important things to worry about than me and my broken heart.

And it was most definitely broken. More so because I'd learned he was feeding from another.

Ever since he'd been injured during Eevuhl's attack on the mansion, Kaj had taken to feeding from one of the other Fae. And because he rotated through them, I couldn't quite place who it was. Not that it mattered. The Fae weren't the ones who had betrayed me. That had been Kaj. Initially, I'd been hurt by the disloyalty, then angry. Now that some time had passed, I was merely resigned to the fact the male and I were not destined to be together, despite what he had told me.

Then again, I was destined to be with no one. My ancestors had seen to that by defying the Heavens. Their punishment? Being relegated to the feeding tools for the warriors and the *fiestreigh*. Not much of a life, really, but on a positive note, I was free, to a degree. At least within the walls of this mansion.

Because I wished not to be a burden upon the Alpha, I got to my feet when I heard his footsteps, felt his presence growing stronger. I had been in the sunroom—an odd name for a room that never saw the sun—waiting for Obsidian to give me the go-ahead to visit Penelope and Ari'el. It was the highlight of my nights to spend time with the new mother and the blessed child. Had I known Kaj was coming for a visit, I would've remained in my chambers until I was called upon.

Anything to avoid running into him.

Unfortunately, molecular drifting wasn't an option

because I had been putting off feeding for days. I was now too weak to do anything more than the most basic of daily functions. And even those were becoming tedious.

Kaj appeared before I could make my way down the few steps to the kitchen. Our eyes met, held, and in that brief moment, I felt an echo of what we'd shared many moons ago, back when he'd been injured, and I'd been at his side, nursing him back to health. Seemed like a lifetime, though it had been not quite two years.

Ducking my head, I intended to hurry down the steps and through the kitchen, but my efforts were thwarted when my legs weakened, sending me tumbling headlong toward the floor.

"Acadia!"

Kaj moved faster than the speed of light, materializing directly in front of me, saving me from what could've been a nasty fall down the stairs.

The very instant my skin came in contact with his, I felt the fire bloom in my veins, the heat I'd been suppressing for as long as I could remember. It never failed—his touch lit me up from the inside out, no matter how much I pretended otherwise.

"When's the last time you fed?" he insisted, his voice like thunder rolling far off in the distance.

I attempted to push him away, I really did. Or that was my intention. I wasn't sure if he was simply too strong or I was too weak, but Kaj didn't budge. Instead, he shifted his weight, then lifted me off my feet.

"Kaj, please," I whispered, not wanting to cause a scene. There were *heurosp* in the kitchen, the evening meal being prepared well in advance of nightfall, as well as the standard daily chores getting underway.

His response was a grunt.

29

The trip from the sunroom up to the second floor felt like a millennium, though it had taken Kaj only a couple of minutes to traverse the distance. He didn't ask me where to take me, and I didn't ask where we were going. I had a feeling I knew, and when he paused outside my bedchamber, I realized I was right.

Part of me wanted to tell him I'd send for a male to take care of me, but I could see from his expression that would be a bad idea. According to what I'd heard, there was only so much a bonded male vampire could tolerate. And though Kaj seemed to be fighting this mating as much as I was, I was not about to push my luck.

"Open the door, Acadia."

His gruff words were spoken low and rife with demand. Enough that I pursed my lips and narrowed my gaze in defiance.

Of course, the door still opened behind me, pushed wide by his will.

Those beautiful eyes remained locked on my face as he strolled over the threshold, making his way deeper into the room, over to my bed.

"Thank you," I said kindly when he delivered me into my room, setting me gently on the edge of the bed.

Kaj didn't say a word, but his eyes spoke volumes.

My breath caught in my throat as I saw so many emotions flitter across his handsome face. He was, by far, the most impressive male I'd ever laid eyes on. Didn't matter the species, Kaj superseded them all. His black hair, those light green eyes, the hard angles of his face, high cheekbones, the perfect arch of his upper lip ... it all came together to form a devastatingly handsome male. Not to mention the air of danger that surrounded him, which only added to his sex appeal.

And truth was, I'd been infatuated with him since our first

meeting, the night Obsidian had removed the bullets that had riddled Kaj's chest. He'd been in so much pain that night, so I had remained at his side, watching over him while he healed. That night and the many that followed. As those minutes had ticked by, my love for him had been established, growing stronger and stronger until he'd shattered my heart into a million tiny pieces when he walked away.

For a brief moment, I wanted to tell him how much I missed him, how my heart physically ached whenever he fed from another, how I wished I could have him in my bed for one more night. I would tell him none of those things, though, because I knew, in the end, none of it mattered. We were simply not meant to be. The vampire Alpha and the lowly Fae did not a love story make.

"You must feed," he said softly, still holding my stare.

"I will."

He shook his head. "Now."

I nodded because I was in agreement. As soon as he left, I would call upon someone to come to me. It didn't make sense for me to ignore my health, and despite my black mood, I knew I had to pull myself together, move forward. After all, that was what Kaj was doing.

Kaj didn't turn away. Instead, he reached behind his head, grabbed the neck of the black T-shirt he wore, and pulled it off. He neatly set it on the bed beside me.

"Use me, Acadia."

My eyes instinctively dropped to his massive chest, to the thick muscles that padded his shoulders and arms, across his pectorals. I visually traveled downward, my gaze caressing every ripple of his abdomen, then onward to the stretched muscles that formed a V and dipped down into the dark jeans he wore. Many scars dotted his body, but they only added to his appeal. He was not a male who sat on the sidelines. He was in the trenches, fighting for the things he believed in, for what mattered most. It was one of the many things I loved about him.

"It's not a request," he stated firmly.

I met his stare, saw the same heat burning in his eyes that I felt igniting deep within my core. There was no denying the physical connection we shared. It had been almost immediate, from the very day Obsidian brought the injured male back. I still couldn't go back to where it had all happened, the Lair, as they referred to it now, the very residence Kaj now called home.

"I swear to you, I will not take anything in return."

The deep rumble of his voice sent a shiver down my spine.

And wasn't that the real issue here? I knew if I put my hands on him, if I drew from his energy, there would be no stopping for me.

"I can't, Kaj."

"You must."

I shook my head, and Heaven help me, a tear fell.

It was all too much.

KAJ

The sight of that single glittering tear sliding down her smooth cheek was enough to rip my insides clean in two. Made me want to drop to my knees, pledge my love and loyalty to this female for all of eternity. I wasn't the only one who'd been hurting as of late, and it pained me to know she was feeling it, too.

"Acadia." Her name fell from my lips as I swiped the wetness away with my thumb. "I assure you, I'm asking for naught. All I'm requesting is that you take from me."

I was lost in her purple gaze, the way the color shimmered with more unshed tears. It broke my heart to see her like this, knowing I was responsible for her pain. Not her hunger, no, but the emotional influx I could sense within her.

We'd been through so much together, yet there was more keeping us apart. Hell, I held the entire future of her species, not to mention my own, in the palm of my hand. All I had to do was resurrect an ancient vampire, and Acadia would be set free. Free to live without being enslaved to the angels, free to rule her race with fairness and certainty. I wasn't even sure she realized her status within the Fae, nor was I sure she cared, but that wasn't the point.

Another tear fell from her lashes, slowly trailing down her perfect face, breaking my heart all over again.

"I can sense your hunger," I whispered, my hand still on her cheek, my thumb stroking the soft skin. "Take from me, Acadia. I beg of you."

Her eyes lowered. "It's not fair to you."

"Who said anything about fair?" This was about necessity. I would deal with the aftermath, the need that would slay me. It was the least I deserved for all the pain I had caused her.

"I'll want more than you're willing to give."

I took a step closer, cupping her face with both hands. "There is absolutely nothing I will not provide you, Acadia. You are and will always be what matters most to me. Doesn't matter what stands between us."

"You don't mean that."

"I only speak the truth," I assured her.

"But you've fed from others."

I held her gaze for long seconds. "I did it so as not to burden you more than you already are."

Even as the words came out, I knew they sounded like an excuse, as though I was putting the blame on her. That wasn't the case.

Acadia's perfectly arched brows lowered. "You vowed not to feed from another."

True. I had. And I'd gone back on my word. I lived with that regret every moment of every day. Yet her happiness, her health, her very safety were what mattered most to me.

"I did," I confirmed. "And it pains me more than you know."

Another tear trickled from her lower lashes. This time I leaned forward, brushing my lips against her cheek to stop its descent.

I cupped the back of her head and held her to my chest. "You are my *nehadon*. Nothing will change that. My love will forever be pledged to you and only you. But I won't force this mating, *balisra*. You deserve more than that."

I wasn't sure what I expected in response, but for Acadia to place her small hands upon my chest wasn't on the list. Her touch was soothing, familiar. It woke parts of me that had been dormant for weeks now.

I released her as I took a step back, lowering my arms and opening myself up to her. I was hers in every way. Whatever she needed, I would provide. It mattered not what she was willing to give in return. For the rest of my days, I would ensure she never went without, even if that meant I had to. But I knew words meant so very little. Actions spoke louder, and I'd betrayed us both as of late.

We remained like that for the longest time, her palms flat on my chest, our eyes locked together. I could hardly breathe for wanting her, but I would refrain because no matter how long it took, Acadia would be the one to decide when we moved forward. *If* we moved forward.

No, I decided. I had it right the first time. *When*, not *if*, because once again, I was an eternal optimist. More importantly, I couldn't think of a life without her in it, and I refused to consider the remainder of my immortal life spent without her.

There was a slight flare in her gaze a second before I felt the pull that shocked my muscles, had me locking my knees. My cock thickened the instant she began feeding from me, the energy she drew flowing through me like an erotic wave before its exit. I dropped my head back, closed my eyes, and opened myself to her completely, giving her full access to every ounce of my being.

Her sudden inhale told me she hadn't expected that. Then again, I had yet to let her see my true power, the strength that I had as the most powerful vampire in existence. After all, being the Alpha wasn't merely a title bestowed upon me.

My cock throbbed behind my zipper, the damn thing begging for release. Ignoring it was impossible, so I squeezed my eyes closed as the sensation tore through me. My body shook, my muscles clenching to fight off the tremor. On the brink of a mind-blowing climax, I held off for as long as I could. And when it was all but inevitable, I placed my hands over Acadia's, holding them tight to my chest as I growled, the sound emerging from my chest and escaping on a rush of air. My cock kicked hard, still confined within the denim.

Acadia's sharp cry was what had me looking down. I watched as she trembled, as though my release ignited her own. Instinct had my fangs dropping, my eyes darting to her neck, to the pulse I could see beating there.

NICOLE EDWARDS

"Kaj!" Acadia jerked her hands from beneath mine before throwing herself at me.

I caught her weight with ease as she cupped my neck and pulled my head toward her.

"I need this, Kaj. I need ... I need the connection. Please."

Fuck.

A second felt like an eternity, but I didn't fight her. My upper lip pulled back from my fangs, and then I was piercing her vein, sinking into her as I wrapped one arm behind her back to hold her to me. Her body trembled. My chest pressed to her breasts as she curled her hands around my neck, feeding from my energy as I drank from her. Another release threatened as her blood disappeared down my throat in big gulps. I was desperate for her, always would be. Nothing could be done about that.

My free hand slid into her hair, tugging her head back so I could sink my fangs in deeper, my lips fusing to her skin. As I breathed her in, I came again. I couldn't stop it; the release barreled through me. The euphoria continued for an eternity as we fed from one another. It was a connection unlike any other. Another surge slammed into me, my release exploding from the head of my cock, this one stealing my breath and likely a large majority of my common sense.

Long minutes passed, but I came down from that mind-blowing high, retracting my fangs from Acadia's neck and sealing the wounds. Neither of us made a move to pull back, though, holding one another tightly. Acadia was kneeling on the bed, I was standing beside it. And though we had clothing between us, I was fairly certain this was the most intimate moment we'd ever shared.

I pressed my lips to her neck, breathed in her sweet cherry-blossom scent, content to remain just like that for the rest of eternity.

Unfortunately, Acadia was the one to pull back, albeit gently and only enough to meet my gaze.

"Only from me," she whispered softly. "I only want you to feed from me, Kaj."

Although my response was easily affirmative, I knew I had to take the opportunity to make the same request. If we were to move forward, this was something we had to get straight between us. Too much had happened of late. Too much was about to take place in the future. It was imperative the two of us get on the same page, or our fight to survive would be moot. Without her in my life, I knew nothing else would truly matter.

"Provided you vow to do the same, *balisra*." Before she could form a rebuttal, I shook my head. "They can and will be fine without you. I need this as much as you do. All of you in return for all of me."

Tears formed in her eyes. "You know I can't do that. If I don't fulfill my duties—"

"Trust me, *balisra*. That's all I ask, that you trust me. I'll talk to Obsidian, ensure he understands."

"No," she said quickly, hands falling away as she scrubbed the tears from her face. "I will speak with him. I must be the one to speak with him."

"Okay. And you'll tell me what he says?"

Her nod was subtle.

Forcing myself to release her, I grabbed my T-shirt, pulled it back on over my head.

"I'll be coming to you more often," I told her. "To feed. And what I need will make it impossible for you to feed others, Acadia. It's the way it's meant to be."

Another nod. Whether it was agreement or simply an acknowledgment of fact, I wasn't sure. However, it was more than I'd had an hour ago, so I would have to be content with it.

For now.

3

ACADIA

———

"So, tell me something," Kaj prompted the moment I stepped into his room.

"Well, good evening to you as well," I teased in response.

A smile pulled at his lips. "Good evening, Acadia. Tell me something."

I laughed, couldn't help it. "Whatever shall you like to know?"

While he formulated his question, I set the tray down on the bedside table, uncovering the eggs and toast I'd had prepared for him. It wasn't a steak dinner, but considering he was still on the mend—slow going, at that—I figured bland and light were the key. I was happy to see he had lost the gray pallor he'd been wearing for the past two weeks, ever since he awoke from his deep sleep. It had taken effort, but I'd managed to keep him in the bed for the majority of the time, save for his daily baths, which I had tended to in the bathtub at his request.

"Where's your family? Mother? Father? Are you close with them?"

I ducked my head, pretended to position the toast. "My mother and father are long since passed. I was orphaned. Now sit up so I can set your tray in your lap."

Kaj grimaced as he followed my instructions, positioning himself against a pillow, smoothing the blankets over his legs.

"Orphaned?"

I nodded. It was a tragic story, though I wasn't eager to go into the logistics. Being that the Fae had been found guilty of defying the Lord before my mother had conceived me, the pregnancy had been deemed illegal. My father had managed to hide my mother until she'd given birth. Upon the delivery, they'd been betrayed, my parents murdered. I wasn't sure who my saving grace had been, but some kind soul had taken me and delivered me unto the orphanage that cared for abandoned children of the Fae.

"And you?" I asked, wanting to redirect the subject to him. "Your mother and father?"

Kaj relaxed into the pillow as I set his tray over his muscled thighs. "My mother was murdered by a demon who'd been sent to destroy my father, the Alpha. He was able to get me out. He's still alive, living with his new mate and their two infant males."

"Vampires mate more than once?"

Kaj nodded. "We do not have predestined mates, and should a male not find his nehadon, he doesn't possess the instinct to devote himself only to one female."

Interesting. Why I thought vampires were like angels in that regard, I wasn't sure. I understood, of course, because Fae didn't have destinies at all.

"Do you see him often? Your father?"

"I work for him. I'm sure he believes I'm dead at this point."

"You should contact him," I urged.

Kaj shook his head. "Not until I can leave here. My mere existence puts all of you in danger. I'd prefer to keep that from knocking on your door."

Being that he was the son of the vampire Alpha, I understood his reasoning. While I wasn't versed in vampire history, I was aware of the fact the race was ruled by a single male.

"How long have you known Obsidian?" he asked.

I smiled. "Many lifetimes."

"How did you meet?"

"Michael came to the orphanage where we were being kept. I was but a teenager, as the humans say. Still young, uncertain of my future. Or whether I even had one. He made a proposition, one designed so that we could not refuse."

Kaj frowned, prompting me to explain.

"My ancestors defied God and were therefore banished from Heaven, punished upon Earth. Michael offered us the opportunity to atone for our sins by serving the needs of his warriors. At the time, he had yet to send Obsidian here to Earth, needing to ensure that they would be properly nourished. Evidently, he made a deal with God in that we would supply their blood, which both gave them strength and allowed the Almighty to monitor their whereabouts."

At times I wondered whether Michael had done so as a means of saving my race. Then he would do or say something to remind me I was here for one reason: to provide a direct line from Heaven to Earth, a means of tracking the warriors and providing them with life.

"Is he good to you? Obsidian?"

I nodded, settling into the chair I'd pulled over. "So very much. He has never treated us as his servants, never taken advantage. Nor have his brothers. As far as he's concerned, we're a part of his family, even if we have no freedom outside these walls."

I wasn't aware of how sad I sounded. Not until I felt a warm hand brushing my cheek. I peered up to see Kaj watching me intently, his fingers gentle as they swept over my skin. It was all I could do to keep my breaths even. His simple touch was more powerful than I expected. I figured it had more to do with the concern I detected than the actual brush of his skin against mine. I wasn't sure I'd ever seen that look on anyone's face before. Certainly not for me.

"I'm sorry," I said quickly, pulling away from his touch. "I mean not to bring down your mood."

"You could never," he replied, his arm retracting to the bed. "So if you feed him, I assume you feed from him as well?"

I shook my head. "Fae are fueled by energy produced by the soul. Which is the reason we provide ourselves in a sexual manner to the males. The sexual energy sustains us for much longer, though it's possible for us to maintain our strength without the heightened emotions."

"Have you provided these ... services to Obsidian?"

I studied his face momentarily, curious as to where this line of questioning was going. If I didn't know better, I would've sworn I sensed something possessive in his tone.

Of course, that was ridiculous.

"No," I told him. "He does not take from us in that way. He uses us solely for a blood source."

Obsidian was a noble male, one who seemed to understand the predicament we'd found ourselves in. Being that he'd been created for a purpose, to be used as a weapon in the war against Lucifer, he knew what it meant to serve for someone else's betterment.

"Why do you stay with me?"

I detected the insecurity in his tone, as though Kaj could not understand why someone would want to care for him.

"If you're asking whether it's my duty, the answer is no." I canted my head to the side. "I am not a servant to vampires. I am merely here because I choose to be. I happen to enjoy your company."

The smile he offered was one I found myself looking forward to. They were rare, which was why I'd made it my mission to pull more of them from him.

I tried to tell myself it was for his benefit, but I knew the truth deep down.

I simply liked to see him smile.

KAJ

I didn't know what I'd done to deserve this.

The care this female offered me was unlike anything I'd ever experienced. Even as the son of the Alpha, I had never received the regard of my father's status. I was a lowly servant, the right hand to the leader of the race as well as the Alpha's protector. Not since my mother had I known the sort of kindness Acadia was showing me.

Sure, I sensed she was truly concerned with my well-being, her need to nurture fierce, her protective instincts honed. However, I got the feeling she did not provide this level of care to just anyone.

Or perhaps that was simply wishful thinking, because Heaven knew I'd caught a glimpse of that possessive spark that continued to flicker within me. Every time I heard one of her stories, I wanted to

43

reach out, to hold her, protect her, assure her everything would be all right. And when she spoke of another male, my inner beast began to pace, baring his fangs and eager to rip out the throat of any male who'd had the pleasure of her touch.

Of course, I sensed Acadia would not be keen on me doing either of those things, but that didn't change my reactions.

Regardless, I was growing fonder of her every moment I spent in her presence. Listening to her voice was now one of my favorite pastimes, something I looked forward to whenever my eyes opened.

It was almost a shame I would have to leave soon, but it was inevitable. As soon as I was at full strength, I had to get back to Kardobahn. As it was, I was neglecting my duties to my father. The only reason I did not walk out of this mansion and make my way back to Seattle was because I knew the Zenith could handle things during my absence. Not to mention, I was no good to anyone in my current state. Despite the fact I'd been on the mend for weeks now, I felt no stronger than I had when I'd been shot. Something did not feel right, but I figured that was due to the nature of the injuries. Like Acadia continued to remind me, it took time to heal from the devastation my body had suffered.

I let my gaze slide over Acadia's beautiful face. She was a small female and her delicate features gave her an almost frail appearance. Of course, that was merely a visage. She was no frailer than I, and perhaps that was what attracted me the most. There was no denying her physical beauty captivated me. I'd never seen anyone more lovely. Her dark hair, her alabaster skin, and those lustrous amethyst eyes were quite the combination.

Not that I'd kept my perusal at neck level. Oh, no. The highly sexual beast within me was constantly admiring all the curves revealed by those form-fitting gowns she preferred. Today's preference had a bodice that cinched in her tiny waist and offered a delightful view of the swells of her breasts. The silk was purple and made her eyes darken, glittering in the simple light from the fire.

"Is something wrong?"

I narrowed my focus to her face, realized she had caught me staring. *"Just enjoying the view."*

The soft pink that infused her cheeks warmed me. Most of the females I spent time with weren't quite so ... what was the word? Feminine? Innocent? Yes, perhaps that was it.

"Is there anything I may get you?" she offered.

I shook my head, not looking away. In this moment, I had everything I could've ever wanted. Just being in her company was more than enough for me.

"Since you're choosing not to eat, perhaps you should feed," Acadia suggested.

Though I wanted to deny the offer, I knew I couldn't. If I wished to regain my strength, it was a necessity. More so than the calories I'd yet to ingest.

I nodded, watched as Acadia set her book on the bedside table before getting to her feet. My eyes tracked her as she stepped to the bed, then as she took the tray from my lap, setting it back on the bedside table. I stared unabashedly as she slid the silk sleeve back from her wrist, settled herself on the edge of the mattress. What I wanted to do was pull her over me, sink my fangs into her neck, hold her against me, feel the warmth of her skin against my own.

It wasn't happening, I knew, but it was a fantasy I'd come to enjoy.

"Kaj?"

My eyes focused on her face once more. *"Hmm?"*

"My wrist."

Right. Her wrist.

I hesitated before touching her, knowing the pleasure I would find simply by brushing my fingers on her skin. I'd learned to brace myself for impact, and I prayed she didn't realize just touching her brought my cock to a fully rigid state. Warmth infused me as I wrapped my fingers around her wrist, the other at her elbow, *bringing her to my lips. Her sweet scent intoxicated me, more so than even her blood.*

No sooner had I scored her vein than my body came alive. I held her delicate arm to my mouth, swept my thumb over her baby-soft skin as I drank from her. I liked that she watched me, even if I wished she didn't have to witness my body's reaction to her. Despite my pain, my cock hardened beneath the blankets, the light press of the sheets against the sensitive head not nearly enough friction. More of a nuisance, really, a stimulant I didn't need but couldn't ignore.

I groaned but didn't release her vein as I drew her life source into my body, prayed for the strength necessary to ignore the effects she unknowingly had on me.

When my hips began to gyrate, her eyes shifted lower. Those amethyst orbs cut back to my face, widening as realization dawned. I tightened my grip on her arm, refusing to let go, because if I did, I was going to bring myself to orgasm, and that was not appropriate considering the circumstances.

"Don't stop," she urged softly, her eyes locked on my face.

I wasn't sure whether she was referring to me feeding or my hips thrusting beneath the blankets. I had to believe it was the former, because there was no way this beautiful creature was suggesting I take care of myself in that manner.

When her breaths became heavier, the rapid rise of her chest drew my gaze downward. It was then that I noticed her nipples were hard, pressing against the thin fabric of the silk covering her. She was affected by me as well, and I wasn't sure what to do with that knowledge.

Acadia shifted closer, her wrist pressing more firmly to my mouth as her attention darted toward the lower half of me.

I didn't mean to do it, but I released her arm, sliding my hand beneath the blankets. I told myself it was to hide the rigid erection tenting the sheet, but I knew better. The dull throb in my cock was more than I could bear. When my hand brushed the hypersensitive head, I groaned, sealing my lips more firmly to her wrist.

"It's okay," she urged. "Keep going."

Again, I wasn't sure which she was referring to, but it no longer mattered. I fisted my cock as I fed from her vein. I stroked my erection roughly, attempting to ease the beast. In the end, it was the fact she was watching, her eyes locked on the movement of my hand beneath the sheet. As I began to pant, I freed my fangs from her, but didn't release her arm. I sealed the punctures with my tongue, then pressed my lips to her skin as I drove myself toward release, stroking myself to completion.

The orgasm came upon me with an intensity I didn't expect. My back bowed, and fire blazed through me, partially from the heat she generated within me but more so from the wounds I had yet to recover from. The combination of pleasure and pain was what triggered my release. My hips punched upward, driving my cock into my fist once, twice...

"Fuck..."

I was breathing heavily as I fought the darkness that threatened to take me under, the pain more intense than I expected.

"It's okay." Her fingers swept over my forehead, brushing my hair back. "Sleep now."

Though I wanted to clean myself, I couldn't muster the energy to do anything more. So I allowed my eyelids to lower, her beautiful face the last thing I saw before I gave in to the darkness.

4

MIRAKEL

J ust call me Mirakel Glutton for Punishment. No last name, of course. I hadn't been born into royalty; therefore, I was merely known by a first name ... and now my newest trait. Sounded better than Mirakel the Idiot, anyway.

I was certainly living up to it in a profound manner.

Proof was in the fact that I continued to seek out Briony rather than find another female to feed from. It would've made more sense to find one of my own kind. A quick trip into town would be all that was necessary for me to locate a sufficient blood source to quench the hunger that had intensified over the past couple of days. I'd purposely put it off for as long as I could, but refused to let it go too far. Nearly dying had been more than enough to remind me that biology wasn't something I could reject simply because I wanted to.

Now, as I strolled down the second-floor hallway of Angel Central, it took effort to put one foot in front of the other and at the same time to keep my legs from taking up a sprint. No doubt I was conflicted when it came to the particular Fae I was going to see. I wanted her, but I didn't want to want her. Made no damn sense whatsoever.

I paused at the door, lifted my hand to knock—

"Come in," the female called from the other side of the door.

Drawing in a deep breath, I turned the knob and stepped into the second-floor laundry suite. The place could've been a bedroom, as luxurious as it was. Twenty-five-by-twenty, creamy-taupe walls, LEDs recessed overhead, three washers and three dryers (also taupe) ran the length of one wall, and the opposite wall had dark brown shelving used to store blankets, sheets, towels, and God only knew what else. A couple of tables for folding and sorting stood at the far end of the room, and down the center of the space was a cushioned bench, you know, in case you got tired doing laundry.

Turned out, it was the perfect place when seeking a bit of privacy without having to deal with the intimacy of one of our bedchambers. I had learned my lesson, thank you very much. Having witnessed the female orgasm while she was feeding from me had been more than my feeble brain could handle. Hell, I'd dreamt about that very incident every night since, even saw it clearly when I closed my eyes.

Which is the reason I'd suggested this place. It was my way of ensuring we didn't get in over our heads. Of course, all these flat surfaces were as much a temptation as a bed, but I was choosing to pretend otherwise.

"M'lord." It was a pleasant greeting, one made without eye contact.

Rather than say her name, I grunted, proving my manners were lacking.

I closed the door and flipped the lock, ensuring no one would enter until I was ready for them to. If all went well, I'd be out of there in thirty minutes tops.

Exhaling heavily, I took a seat near Briony, but far enough to ensure there wasn't any unnecessary touching. As it was, I could smell her—a soft, sweet scent that went right to my head. Strawberries, I thought. She smelled like strawberries.

Fucking hell.

I probably should've started with some pleasantries. *Hey, how are you?* or *How've you been since I last saw you?* or maybe *You're looking pretty today.*

I said none of those things because my tongue got all twisted up when I was around her. I had no idea what I was drawn to, either. She was lovely, of course. More so than any female I'd ever seen, but I'd never been the sort to gauge my conquests by the exterior dressing. It was what was inside that mattered.

Then again, Briony was equally lovely on the inside.

Fuuuuck.

Without thinking, I shot to my feet and marched past her, beyond the last washing machine.

"I don't think I can do this," I grumbled, eyes locked on my boots to ensure I didn't look directly at her.

"I understand."

"Trust me, you don't."

"Is there something I can do to make this easier for you?" she offered, her voice so kind it made my heart pinch.

"Find me someone else," I muttered.

"Oh."

Yep, that was actually hurt I heard in her voice. And now I had offended her.

"I ... uh... That can certainly be arranged, m'lord."

Unable to help myself, I lifted my eyes to her. Today, she was wearing a pale pink gown made of silk that clung to all her delectable curves and pooled at her feet. While some of the Fae, mainly the males, dressed in modern trends, I had noticed a few of the females still opted for clothing that seemed better suited for a different time. These gowns Briony preferred were not of this century, I didn't think, and probably not the last, either. And while they weren't short and skimpy, they revealed every beautiful curve of her body as though she were wearing absolutely nothing at all.

"Don't go," I blurted when she got to her feet, hands clasped in front of her.

"If you don't want me, m'lord, I understand."

I planted my hands on my hips and tilted my head toward the ceiling. "Trust me, it's not that I don't want you."

The fact that I did was the real issue. I wasn't familiar with intimacy when it came to feeding. I'd never felt it before. Then again, I'd spent the majority of my life taking blood from *cosrobols*. Blood whores tended to be in great quantity in the larger clans. As a member of the Zenith, I'd had access to all I needed. When I'd been forced from the Seattle camp after Kardobahn's death, I had learned to take when opportunities arose, which generally involved a sexual encounter with a female vampire. But one-night stands equated to mutual pleasure, not intimacy.

Not necessarily ideal, but oddly, those had seemed far simpler than this. For some reason, I felt this strange connection to Briony, as though what I was taking from her was sacred.

"I apologize if I make you uncomfortable," she said softly, drawing my attention back to her.

"Let's just get this over with." Good to see I was still lacking with the manners. Great.

Briony took her seat on the bench once more, tugging the sleeve of her gown up to her elbow.

On unsteady legs, I circumvented the bench, coming around to the other side. Once more, I planted my ass on the cushion and did my best to breathe through my mouth. Her scent was too much for me.

"When's the last time you fed?" I asked, stopping myself before reaching for her.

"The last time I saw you."

Son of a bitch. I was not supposed to be happy about that. It shouldn't have made my dick hard to know I was the last to provide her sustenance, yet the damn thing hopped to attention like someone had given it physical attention.

"Then you'll feed from me first," I stated firmly.

It took a bit of rearranging down south, but I managed to throw one leg over the other side of the bench so I was straddling it, facing her. I then took off my T-shirt and briefly wondered if it would be rude to keep the damn thing over my face.

Of course it would, you dumb ass.

Yeah, yeah, fucking yeah.

I removed the cotton, balled it up, and tucked it between my thighs, hoping to keep her from seeing the steel rod gaining momentum in my jeans.

"I know of another way we can both feed at the same time," Briony said, her beautiful purple eyes trailing over my face.

Bad idea.

No matter what it was, I knew it would be a bad idea.

NICOLE EDWARDS

"Tell me," I said, dropping my eyes to the burgundy leather between us.

"It would be easier if I showed you."

Fucking fantastic.

I nodded, then held my breath when Briony turned so she was facing away from me, her legs hanging over the end of the bench. It was almost the same position we'd been in the first time I fed from her, back when I'd had her perched on my thighs, my arms banded around her. I had orgasmed that time, unable to hold myself back.

"You should move in behind me," Briony suggested.

No, I shouldn't.

Nope.

Nuh-uh.

I fucking moved behind her, the curve of her lovely ass pressed between my splayed thighs, that damn T-shirt doing not a fucking thing to stop my cock from thinking this was an intimate meet and greet.

Oh, but look at that. It got worse.

Briony leaned back against me, her back to my chest. To make it more comfortable for her, I had to shift closer again. Then move the fucking T-shirt.

Oh, yeah, I was going to Hell for this, no doubt about it.

I moaned softly when Briony drew her hair around to one side, revealing the smooth alabaster skin of her neck, that delectable scent of hers drifting right up into my sinuses.

She tilted her head to the side, providing me perfect access.

"How does this take care of you?" I asked, though I was surprised the words made any damn sense.

"When you're feeding from me, I simply need to link my fingers with yours."

Of course she did. Because *that* wouldn't be intimate at all.

Fuck, fuck, fuck.

Figuring this could all be over in minutes if I would simply vampire up, I leaned forward, then had to brush aside a few stray strands of her hair, which did not fucking help. Taking a deep breath, I thrust my arms forward so that they were ... oh, yeah, on her thighs.

Better and fucking better.

Closing my eyes, I leaned in and pierced her neck, no longer able to handle it. If I didn't hurry up, I was going to strip us both and sink inside her. More than just my fangs.

I did my best to focus on the blood I pulled into my mouth. Suck, swallow, suck, swallow.

Easy-peasy.

Ah, fuck.

Briony clearly wasn't aware of the war brewing in my fucking body, because she took my hands, turned them over on her thighs, then slid her much smaller fingers between mine. Her touch was as light as a feather, as soft as velvet. When she tightened her grip, I did as well, sealing our palms together.

I braced myself, and good thing, too. When Briony began siphoning my energy, my entire body jerked hard. It was all I could do to keep my mouth sealed to her neck.

I would later realize this was the absolute worst idea anyone would ever have.

I would also realize that I'd been wrong about the first few times I'd fed from the female. I'd thought those had altered me in unimaginable ways. Not like this, they hadn't.

It was in that moment, when Briony was sitting in front of me, my fangs buried in her neck, our fingers clasped tightly as she drew energy from my being, that the whole of my world shifted on its axis.

Because it was in that moment that my mind, body, and soul bonded with the female. A cataclysmic sexual imprinting, also known as *mielix zan* in vampire terminology.

Which, in the case of vampires, only happened once in our lifetime.

And could not be undone.

Which meant...

Yeah, I so did *not* want to think about that right now.

BIJOU COURTENAY

While Mirakel was fighting his battles just down the hall, I was dealing with my own.

As I peeked out my bedroom door, I prayed Oliver was not moving about. I couldn't sense him nearby, so I hoped that meant he was in the war room working. He spent a good amount of time down there, even during daylight hours when the rest of the *fiestreigh* were catching z's. I knew because I was constantly aware of where he was. It was the only way to avoid running into him, something I'd gotten relatively good at lately.

I glanced left, right, left again.

I let out a relieved sigh when I saw my father stepping out of Acadia's room, just two doors down from my own.

"I thought I heard you earlier," I called out, pretending I was out for an early-morning stroll, casually closing my door behind me.

Based on the look on his face, he had just fed. And the sight of his wet hair told me he'd also showered. I hoped that meant he was in a good mood, because there was something I wanted to talk to him about. Something important. And I could no longer put it off.

"I was coming to find you," he said, his green eyes brighter than usual. "Wanted to talk to you about … the … um … the training facility."

Training facility? Me? Really? Then why did I get the feeling he was avoiding a specific topic?

I peered up at him. "What about it? I didn't think it was completed yet."

"It's not. According to Obsidian, it's well underway and moving quickly. I've yet to see it, though."

"And you wanted what? For me to pitch in?" I chuckled. "Throw up a few walls? Slap on some paint?"

My father's smile was blinding. "No, sweet female. Not with the building of it. But I was thinking perhaps you'd be interested in training the new recruits."

How in Heaven's name did he think I was qualified to train fighters?

"Weapons," he said, obviously reading my mind. "Namely, firearms. You're quite good with a gun. Thought perhaps you could share some of that knowledge, teach safety as well as accuracy."

Fine, I would accept that because it was the truth. I'd learned to shoot at an early age, one of my mother's friends having run a human gun range near our house. I had spent quite a bit of time in those lanes, trying out various weapons, learning their abilities as well as my own. It was one of the few hobbies I had, probably the only one I still enjoyed.

Needless to say, my father's suggestion didn't sound like a

terrible idea. In fact, I'd been hoping to find something to spend my spare time on. I had far too much of it as it was.

"You don't have to answer right now," Kaj said, nodding toward the stairs. "Now what did you want to talk to me about?"

I smiled, then tucked my arm in his and continued down the hall toward the back stairs. "I was curious as to how you're settling in at the Lair. I heard Blāz got the shutter problem fixed and they got some furniture moved over."

"True and true. It's slow going, but we're getting there. Hoping to get all the security set up soon." He peered down at me. "Why?"

Okay. Go time. Taking a deep breath, I blurted out my request.

"I was wondering … *ifitwouldbepossibleformetomoveinover-there.*" I exhaled sharply. There. I did it.

"What was that?"

Of course he would make me repeat it. "Move in. Me. Over there. I was … just, you know, wondering."

As expected, Kaj stopped, turning to face me fully. "I thought you enjoyed being here?" He nodded toward the bedroom door we'd just passed. "You and Elizabeth seem to be getting along well."

"Yes, of course we are." Orianna's mother and I had become fast friends, sure. "But I don't have to live here to spend time with her."

His head tilted to the side as though he was attempting to read my mind. Then again, he probably was.

Crap.

"Look, I'm grateful they've allowed me to stay here, but I think I'd be better off…" *away from Oliver* "…with other vampires. And with you."

"You don't feel welcome here?"

I frowned. "I didn't say that." But it wasn't like I would tell him that I would do well with more space between me and the human male who currently resided in the room adjacent to mine.

"What's going on, Bijou?"

I unintentionally hurt Oliver. "Nothing." I took a step back, feeling a bit defensive. "It's just ... I..." This was not how I'd hoped this conversation would go. It was, of course, exactly how I'd seen it playing out, but still.

"Bijou."

"You know what?" I backed up another step, then one more, holding my hands up in surrender. "Never mind. It's fine."

Kaj stepped closer. "It's not that I don't want you with me. I just think you're safer here. At least right now."

How he could think that, considering the mansion had endured a devastating attack not too long ago, I wasn't sure. However, my father was a male who always had a reason, and right now, I wasn't interested in hearing it.

"Of course," I told him. "You know best."

"Bijou."

"Forget I asked," I said quickly. "I ... uh ... I've got something I need to do."

Without waiting for him to say my name again in that fatherly tone that somehow made me feel like I was ten years old, I spun around and hurried back to my room. I quickly closed the door and leaned against it.

Why had I thought that would be a good idea again?

Oh, right. Because I was getting tired of tiptoeing around the mansion in an effort to avoid Oliver. I knew he was doing the same, and truth was, I wanted to call him on it, but every time I started to, I chickened out.

I still remember the look on his face when he'd come to my

room and found me feeding from Madok. It wasn't like I had a choice. My options were extremely limited when it came to a blood source. Aside from seeking out one of my father's guards, I had only one other option. And Madok had kindly offered. The best part, I felt absolutely no connection to him. Not from a sexual standpoint, at least. As far as friends went ... well, yeah, I considered him one, but not like we were spending any time together.

Truth was, I missed Oliver. I had enjoyed the time we'd shared, whether it had been watching movies or playing pool, even swimming. But after what had happened between us that one night in the sauna...

My body warmed at the memory. If I closed my eyes, I could still feel the warmth of his tongue between my legs.

A chill shot down my spine, and I had to push off the door to keep from melting into a puddle.

If only I could go back to that moment before I'd pleaded for him to take care of the heat consuming us both, I would gladly walk away from him and tend to my own needs. Had I known it would be the death of what I'd considered a great friendship, I never would've allowed it to happen.

Unfortunately, time travel wasn't in my repertoire of skills.

Nor was altering the past.

Which meant I was going to have to figure out a way to move forward without Oliver in my life.

I only hoped he could one day forgive me for ruining everything.

5

REIDAR

The instant the shutters began their ascent, signaling it was safe to venture out of the mansion, I made a beeline for the front porch. I'd spent the entire day tossing and turning, attempting to sleep to no avail. It had taken forever, but finally, the night was upon us once again, and I had something to do.

Without waiting for Malak, my partner for the evening, I dematerialized, taking form in the empty streets of downtown Telluride.

"If I didn't know better, I'd think you were trying to hide," Malak said when he appeared at my side a few seconds later.

"Not hiding. Just needed to get some air."

Speaking of... I took a long inhale, let the cold, crisp air fill my lungs. I exhaled slowly, pivoted to get a good look at the area around us. No people strolling about, but that wasn't surprising. I knew if we headed back to the main drag, we'd find a few wandering around, mostly tourists willing to brave the ridiculous cold, taking in the sights of the small nowhere town.

"I know the feeling," Malak said as he began walking, forcing me to fall into step with him. "Mansion seems a bit crowded these days."

That it did, though we were understaffed with the warriors still out looking for their *amsouelots*.

I let my senses scan our surroundings, hoping against hope that tonight would be the night we encountered some demons. *Impietans*, shadow beasts, one of the *mesonneir*, hell, Lucifer could make an appearance, I didn't really give a shit. Right now, I was itching for a fight.

"You're twitchy," Malak noted.

Yes, I was. Very.

Partly because I was growing tired of this hide-and-seek game we were playing with the demons. Always seeking, never finding. Ever since Eevuhl was taken out at the hands of the Obsidian/Michael combo, the demons had been MIA. As much as I hoped they'd stricken them from Earth once and for all, I knew that wasn't the case. We weren't that lucky.

Which meant the demons were likely building their strength, gearing up for another battle.

But where? Where the fuck were they hiding?

At least we wouldn't be having the showdown at the mansion again. We'd made the place impenetrable, having been caught with our proverbial pants down the night Eevuhl had arrived unannounced. We still had no clue how the *trielair* demon had found us, but it didn't really matter, did it? Made no difference if he'd looked us up on Google or had a traitor whisper in his ear, he'd waltzed his happy, fucked-up ass right up damn near to the front door.

No longer were we merely relying on the *dhira* to keep us hidden. Now the demons, should they get the address, would have to work to get past our barriers, and unless they had some crazy skills, that wasn't happening.

"You doing okay?" Malak prompted. "I mean, since Winnie left?"

I exhaled heavily, kept moving forward, past one empty warehouse after another. "Yep. All good."

The last person I wanted to talk about was Winnie. Though I'd missed her for the first couple of weeks after she left, I realized it had been her physical presence I'd grown accustomed to. Having to listen to her rip me a new one every time we attempted to have a conversation was not something I missed. And while I couldn't interact with the female I'd once believed was my *amsouelot*, I had checked up on her via Facebook. She'd wasted no time integrating back into the human world, even started dating someone, according to her relationship status update. Who, I didn't know. Nor did I really care. I simply wanted to make sure she was doing fine, and it appeared she was.

"Well, if you ever want to talk about it..."

I glanced over at Malak as we ventured off the beaten path and into the trees. The path grew rocky as it ventured up the mountain. "Yeah? Maybe we could share a latte, too. Better yet, you could tell me about you and Raksa while we paint our nails."

The glare I received was the equivalent of *hell no*. In fact, I figured Malak would be more inclined to get mani/pedis than to talk about the male who was giving him trouble.

I couldn't help but smile to myself. Malak and Raksa thought no one realized they were ... well, honestly, I didn't know what they were. In a relationship? Fucking? Whatever it was, they seemed to be at odds right now. But try as they might, the two males weren't keeping it a secret. To their credit, they weren't trashing one another aloud the way Winnie had done to me, so everyone was respecting their privacy. As much as we could, anyway. Hard sometimes when the males were constantly having their heated conversations in public spaces. Almost as though they were avoiding being alone together.

"So no on the latte?" I taunted, continuing my trek, ducking under a thick evergreen branch.

A grunt was all I received in return.

"It's cool, you know," I told him. "Only thing I'd watch for is fighting alongside him. Not sure that's the best idea."

"There's nothing going on between me and Raksa."

Yeah, sure, okay. "Your biz, man."

And that was the real problem, I figured. I was stuck in the mansion watching everyone as they kept going like nothing had happened lately. Despite my best efforts to keep my nose out of everyone's business, it was hard not to notice all the happy-happy that was going on. Obsidian and Penelope, Eclipse and Orianna, Bijou and Oliver, Kaj and Acadia, and yes, even Malak and Raksa... Everywhere I turned, more couples were pairing up, laughing, smiling, joking. All while I was trying to figure out when someone had planted a bomb in my life and who'd pressed the detonator, the explosion ripping my seemingly content universe into fragments.

Of course, the others were likely trying to move past the literal explosion that had rocked the mansion, seeking solace in an effort to comfort themselves. My explosion was figurative, the demise of a relationship that never should've come to fruition in the first place.

I held up a hand when I heard voices. Malak went stone still, his eyes scanning the darkness.

Our efforts to search the mountain rarely resulted in anything other than stumbling on some unsuspecting humans out for a leisurely stroll or stealing a few minutes beneath the stars. But as the saying went, there was a first time for everything.

Letting my senses expand, I took in the scents in the air first. Animals, mostly small ones, had moved through recently. Humans, too. But there was no scent of evil or death like I'd been hoping for.

Shame.

We'd started searching the mountain in an attempt to see if Perfidious was hiding out there. It only made sense that he would stick around. It was exactly like the narcissistic demon to remain right under our noses and just out of sight. But one day, that demon's luck was going to run out, and we would find Asmia. And when we did, I hoped I was the one who got to send Perfidious back to his maker, the bastard.

Humans, Malak said in my head.

I nodded. Two males, one female. Probably sneaking off to get down and dirty where they thought no one was watching.

Unfortunately, I had no choice but to move closer. Both *impietans* and shadow beasts were drawn to humans, which meant it was possible they were loitering nearby, gearing up to go in for the kill.

Without making a sound, I moved forward, Malak on my six. We stuck to the trees, keeping out of sight while searching the night for evil.

Unfortunately for me, there was no evil lurking. Nope. Only stupid humans.

I saw the bright red tent first. As I moved around to the opposite side, I noticed the flames from what appeared to be a campfire. The humans came into view next, the three of them on a blanket near the fire, all still dressed, head to toe in winter wear, though specific parts of their bodies were unveiled. The two males were bookending the female, filling her from both ends and seemingly enjoying themselves as much as she was, if her urgent, muffled cries were anything to go by.

I glanced at Malak, signaled for him to go around.

It was too late for the image of the fornicating humans not to be burned into my brain, but I managed to avoid looking in their direction as Malak and I circled the pornographic camp-site, moving in an outward motion until we were convinced there were no demons lingering nearby.

Though I wished no harm to the humans, I hoped they had attracted something. It would've given me an outlet for this restless energy building inside me. At least when Winnie had been around, I'd had a way of unleashing it. At the very least, the sex between us had been good. Perhaps great, even. Not quite as kinky as I preferred, but I had no complaints.

I could not say the same for the status of this night.

PERFIDIOUS

I descended the steps leading to the lowest level of my humble abode, admiring the smooth stone walls, the gas lanterns that had been installed. It wasn't exactly a penthouse in the city, but I had to admit, I was growing rather fond of it. Probably had to do with the fact that it was private, no one around to annoy the shit out of me. Aside from my beautiful captive, that was. And she was not so much annoying as she was titillating.

"Good evening, gorgeous." I grinned, stepping out of the stairwell and approaching Asmia's cage. "Don't you look lovely today."

And she did, especially in the form-fitting red gown that clung to every curve. I was particularly fond of the way the neckline plunged low, revealing the perfect swells of her breasts, contained by nothing more than the silk. Because of the cut, I could see the hint of her nipples peeking out, beckoning me.

As I admired her form, the way she glided toward me, I unlatched the lock with my mind. Though I was still considering allowing Asmia into my bedroom, I had to admit, I did enjoy the idea of her caged down here for my enjoyment.

"You may greet me appropriately," I declared as I stepped into her cage, leaving the door open behind me.

"Good evening, my king," she said as she dipped into a lovely curtsy, her head lowering respectfully.

"How fare thee this evening?" I asked as she straightened.

"I am very well, my king." Her black eyes glittered with what looked like desire. "Better now that you're here."

As was I. "Did you sleep well?"

Asmia glanced over at the enormous bed she spent her days in. "Very well, my king. The only way it would've been improved would be to have slept in your arms."

I stepped up to her. "Kiss me, gorgeous."

"It would be my pleasure," she replied in a husky rasp.

I loved how sensual she was. Never hurried, never frantic. She started by lightly gliding her fingers along my cheeks, smiling back at me before her soft lips brushed mine gently, reverently. Only when I parted mine did she do the same, accepting me into her mouth. There was no hesitation in her as she licked at me, moving in closer, her breasts grazing my chest.

"Mmm." I pulled her into me, let her feel the arousal that was steadily growing. What I wouldn't give to push it into her mouth, to watch as she swallowed me down.

Yes, I was beginning to think it was time to kick things up a notch, to take her appropriately. These kisses were mere teases, something I looked forward to but knew wouldn't sustain me for much longer.

Of course, it wasn't some misguided sense of decency that held me back. Nor was it out of respect for the female. She belonged to me because I said so, and she agreed because I'd happily stripped her of her free will.

My restraint had to do with what was taking place outside the walls of my new kingdom. Those angels were still searching for Asmia, but they'd slowed their patrols drastically. Probably helped that they were focused on securing their compound since Eevuhl's attack.

And yes, that fiasco had caused a delay as well.

I had been shocked to hear the male had made an attempt to steal the unborn angel baby. Not so much to learn Eevuhl had met his demise in the process. That damn archangel wasn't one to tangle with. After all, Michael was the one who had slain Lucifer. And now Eevuhl could be added to the notches in that great sword of his.

But with Eevuhl gone, the *trielair* and their mission were no longer my problem. Thankfully, before the male had been sent back to Hell indefinitely, Eevuhl had relayed his change of guard to Lucifer, and I was officially in the role of leader of the shadow beasts, a coveted position that required very little effort. The first thing I'd learned about those damn demon dogs was that getting them to fall in line was like herding cats in a forest.

Didn't mean I wasn't up to the task. To hold up my end of the deal, I had already summoned the team leaders, requesting a weekly meeting for updates. The first of which would be taking place in a few days.

Reluctantly, I pulled my mouth from Asmia's, took a single step back, smiled. It would be nice to have this gorgeous female on my arm when they arrive.

I motioned toward the space directly in front of me. "Kneel before your king."

She was the epitome of beauty and grace as she moved toward me. After another brief curtsy, Asmia lowered herself to her knees, keeping her head bowed.

Oh, yes, my sweet fairy was almost ready. I'd been training her for the past few weeks, observing her reactions in an effort to see whether she was pretending. Considering I still held full control of her mind, her decisions weren't her own. However, her desires were. I could manipulate her into worshipping me, even offering up her body, but her desire to do so was still well within her control, even if I did have the ability to bend her to my will. From where I stood, Asmia was almost ready to take things to the next level.

Good thing for her, so was I.

I thought about the shadow beasts' arrival. Perhaps I should put her on an altar, claim her appropriately before those now under my control. After all, it was quite the feat to have acquired a creature as lovely as this one. For most, the Fae were merely a tale of tragedy in an otherwise tragic world. For centuries, they'd been thought to have died out. So the notion of having caught one of my very own ratcheted up my coolness factor by a million.

Yes. I liked that idea very much. I would put her on display before those who served me, giving them physical proof of my claim of being the king of this realm.

And if the shadow beasts proved worthy, maybe I would make it a weekly thing. What better way to instill loyalty than to show them who the true king was?

I peered down at my female and smiled. My cock roared to life, eager and aching.

Yes, perhaps it was time to shift tactics.

6

KAJ

"What the fuck are you doing?" I grumbled when I stepped into my bedchamber to find Blāz and two of the *heurosp* taking measurements.

"I've been tasked with fortifying your private quarters."

"Fortifying?" I watched as the *heurosp* dragged the tape measure from one end of the room to the other.

"For starters, we're taking down that wall"—Blāz motioned to his left—"so we can expand the space. Since this'll suffice as a panic room, it's necessary to give you the means to live in the event something happens."

"And what do you think's going to happen?"

Blāz shrugged. "Get that wall, would you?" he said to his helpers. "I figure you'll need a kitchen and storage for food."

"So you're prepping me for a doomsday event?"

The male smirked. "That's one way to look at it, sure. But we're also going to insulate the walls, floor, and ceiling with titanium. Then I've got this cool material that'll make it basically impenetrable."

"Perhaps I should find another room to sleep in temporarily."

Blāz smiled. "That's actually a fantastic idea."

I shook my head in disbelief. "It was a joke. Why can't you fortify another room, and I can move in there later?"

"Because this one is directly above your office."

"I don't have an office," I countered.

"You will soon."

Great.

"Which'll allow me to provide access from below. In the event you need to take refuge should something happen while you're working."

"Working? In an office?"

Blāz peered at me, eyebrows slowly lifting. "That's part of the role of Alpha, *phaal*. You've got documents to review, emails to tend to. Blah, blah, blah. You need a private space to take care of that."

No, what I needed was to be out in the field, getting my hands dirty with the Zenith. Not to be locked in this house for the rest of eternity.

"It'll take some getting used to," Blāz stated, as though he could read my mind.

"You don't say."

"Huracān told me this is priority," the male continued. "I'll do my best to have the work done during the night when you're tending to other business, but I can't promise you'll be able to stay here during the day. Construction and all."

Construction. Fucking great.

I turned to the *heurosp*. "Do me a favor. Have my things moved to another room."

"Of course, sire," the male said softly.

"You've got a week," I told Blāz.

The vampire barked a laugh, then sobered. "You're serious."

"I have shit to do, as you so kindly reminded me. I don't have time for this disruption."

"Perhaps you could stay with Acadia."

I narrowed my eyes. "That's not an option."

"Oh."

Before Blāz could launch into questions about my personal life, I spun around and headed for the door.

"I'll need you ready to go out with Mirakel," I told Blāz. "I'm sending him to the Dungeon. I want cameras installed over there so we can keep an eye on Darko."

Because of everything going on, I had put off addressing the traitor, but I had every intention of making that fucker pay for his deceit. However, I knew it had to be handled in a diplomatic fashion, and I was going to get a look-see as to what the vampire was doing.

"I'm ready when he is," Blāz called out as I stepped into the hall, then his voice lowered as he began barking orders at the poor *heurosp* who had been doomed to this task.

I strolled down the hallway, past the various rooms, only four of which were occupied since we had yet to fortify the ranks of the Zenith. At some point, I hoped all the rooms would be filled. God knew there were enough of them. Not nearly as many as the angels had built in the mansion they'd moved to. When they'd lived here, I figured the *fiestreigh* had been sharing spaces, probably two or three to a room if I had to guess.

That thought led to another. When the day came that Acadia moved in with me and we were mated appropriately, that small space wouldn't be nearly enough. Especially not if my female was open to having a family. I knew the Fae had been rendered infertile because she'd told me as much, but if Michael expected me to go along with the plan of resurrecting the original vampire, that was something that would have to be corrected. I wanted babies with the female if she was open to the idea.

Spinning back around, I strolled back to my private quarters, stuck my head in. "If you're going to accommodate me in the future, I suggest you add a couple of rooms to this space."

"Rooms?"

"Yes. Adjoining. With bathrooms."

Blāz's eyebrows lowered in confusion.

"If you're hell-bent on keeping me confined, you might want to account for the family I intend to have one day."

When those nearly colorless eyes widened, I smirked, then spun around and headed back down the hall. Let the male chew on that for a little while.

There was no sense going into a lengthy explanation, but the gist of it was, I had every intention of mating the female who owned my heart. No matter how long it took, I would wait until she was ready.

One day, though.

JANE

I knew I was losing it as I took in the unfamiliar surroundings, the strangers moving about the room, the weird machines connected to me via tubes in my arms, but I couldn't help it. The panic continued to rise, making it difficult to breathe.

Where was I? Who were these people? What were they doing to me?

Oh, God. *Someone help me, please!*

Clutching my chest, I drew in big gulps of air, but they didn't seem to make it past my throat.

"Honey, I need you to calm down." A firm but gentle hand curled around my wrist. "Take a deep breath. Yes. Good. Another."

The female looming over me sighed as though she was happy with the progress being made. I, however, felt no different. My chest felt compressed, as though there was a great weight upon it.

"Where am I?" I asked, not sure what was going on.

"You're in a hospital," the female with the kind eyes and gentle touch said as she patted my hand. "I want you to focus on breathing. That's all you need to worry about right now."

A series of approvals continued from the female as I inhaled, exhaled, managed to get my heart to calm.

"Now, can you tell me your name?"

My gaze swung back to the female. Name? I had no idea what my name was. I had no idea *where* I was or how I'd gotten here, either. In fact, I was hoping they could fill me in on what happened.

"It's okay," the older female wearing a loose-fitting maroon top and matching pants said. "Take a deep breath. We don't have to figure that out now."

"Where am I?"

"In a hospital," the female repeated, her concern evident.

"No, I mean, *where?*"

"Bellevue Hospital in Manhattan."

Manhattan? What was Manhattan? Where? *Where* was Manhattan, assuming it was a place? And if so, how did I get here?

"I'm going to step out," a younger female wearing a similar outfit to the other one, only in navy, said.

"We'll be fine. Won't we?"

Oh, she was talking to me. Not sure what response was necessary, I nodded, tried to relax against the pillow, ignoring the scratchy sheets and the strong chemical smell that permeated the room.

The door opened. One female slipped out; another appeared, this one wearing a white coat over a red silk shirt and black slacks. She was smaller than the female standing at my bedside, younger, too. Her dark hair hung over her shoulders, sleek and smooth. Her equally dark eyes were calm yet assessing.

A smile pulled at the stranger's mouth when she approached, but it didn't quite reach her eyes. "Good morning. My name's Dr. Chopra."

I stared at the female, confused. "Are you a healer?"

The female gave me an odd look but nodded. "I am. We're glad to see you've woken up."

Had I been asleep? For how long? And why?

The two females shared a quick look, the one at the bedside offering a quick shake of her head.

"How did I get here?" I asked the two females, feeling a

strange sensation in my chest, a tension of some sort that made it difficult to breathe again.

"You're having a panic attack," the older female said softly. "It's okay. Just breathe through it."

Panic attack? What was a panic attack? Would it kill me?

"How ... how did ... I get here?" I clutched my chest to stave off the tightness and pressed my head into the pillow.

"You were brought in by ambulance," the young healer explained. "You were found unconscious in an alley. Someone called the paramedics. They noticed you had a contusion on your head. Brought you here."

Contusion? What did that mean?

Oh, God. What was going on?

"Do you have any family you'd like us to call?"

I stared up at the older female, studied her face. Did I have family? I honestly didn't know. In fact, I didn't know anything.

"It's okay," Dr. Chopra said, her soft, cool hand gently settling on my wrist. "Right now, we only need you to rest. From the looks of it, you took a nasty fall, bumped your head. You've also got a broken ankle. I've had a few X-rays ordered, to make sure you haven't broken any other bones that we can't see."

Broken bones, contusions.

What the hell was going on?

More importantly, who was I?

ACADIA

———

"Well, good evening," Penelope greeted with a smile when I joined the female in the nursery.

"Good evening," I replied kindly. "I thought I'd stop in, check on our sweet angel baby."

The proud mother's smile grew immensely. "She's in a good mood this evening."

I peered over the side of the crib, my heart swelling at the sight.

"I hope I'm not intruding."

"Not at all," Penelope answered quickly. "Josie actually had to step away for a few minutes, and I was hoping to grab a shower. Would you mind watching Ari'el for a few minutes?"

"Mind?" I chuckled. "It would be an honor."

"Oh, you're a lifesaver." Penelope tugged the baby's little pants into place over her diaper. "She's dry and fed, so you'll get some playtime."

Playtime with a seven-week-old was exactly what I looked forward to. These days, Ari'el was staying awake a bit longer, her eyes wide as she took in her surroundings, every now and then a smile forming.

"Go," I urged. "And take your time. We'll be fine until you're finished."

"Thank you so much."

No thanks were needed, but I figured Penelope knew that. As it was, I longed for any minute I could spend with Ari'el. It was the closest I would ever get to having one of my own, and I was hopeful all the angels in the mansion would produce offspring, simply so I could get these rare moments to spend with them.

"Don't you look pretty," I cooed as I carefully lifted Ari'el from her crib. "Mommy dresses you so sweetly. It's probably a good thing Daddy doesn't pick out your clothes, huh? He tends to favor dark colors for his wardrobe. Not that you'd look bad in them, but you definitely look like an angel in pink."

Ari'el's eyes remained on my face as I spoke. I made sure to smile. Not that Ari'el necessarily knew the difference between a smile and a frown, but I wanted only to bring joy to the infant.

After settling into the white rocking chair in the corner, I got the baby situated in my arms so I could continue to talk to her.

"So where did we leave off, hmm? We were talking about Asmia the last time we were together, weren't we?"

I set the chair in motion, just a gentle forward-and-back movement.

"Well, I still remember the day she came to the mansion. She's the youngest of us, you know. So young. Which probably begs the question, how did she come about? To be honest, I have no idea. She doesn't know, either, which is the most bewildering part, I think. But there she was, on our doorstep, eager and willing to be part of our world. I learned later that Michael sent her to us, but where he found her is anyone's guess. You'll learn that about him. He doesn't share secrets often."

I continued to rock.

"Regardless of where she came from or how she got here, Asmia provided a radiant light that we all were drawn to. A sweet female with an enormous heart. And Taayin took to her right away." I smiled at the memory. "He never truly believed she was his *amsouelot*, but that was because Fae do not have a predestined mate. Not anymore. We belong solely to the *fiestreigh* at this point. But that doesn't mean we can't find love. I happen to know this firsthand."

My thoughts drifted to Kaj, to our recent encounters. Though we were still on rocky ground, I couldn't help but think our path had shifted directions once again.

"But that's been rectified. Your daddy made sure to take care of Asmia, protecting her. We haven't found her yet, but I have to believe she's still out there, and we will find her. We will bring her back. As for Taayin, I can't wait for the day he gets to see her again, when his heart is no longer broken. I wish I could foretell the future, but it's not for me to do." I brushed my finger over Ari'el's downy-soft hair. "They will both love you."

I had to wonder if perhaps they should allow Taayin in to see the baby. Perhaps Ari'el could renew his faith, bring him a bit of hope in what had become such a dark and dreary world for him.

"I'm going to visit him after this," I admitted to the baby. "I go down every day, sit with him. It's the least I can do. If I could bring her back myself, I would. Unfortunately, it's out of my hands."

As Ari'el's eyes began to droop, I began to hum softly, urging the sweet child to rest. And while she did, I gave myself a moment to pretend I would one day become a mother, one day have my own babe to hold in my arms like this. It was all I could do not to give in to the pain of reality. As much as I wanted to believe we'd paid our dues, atoned for the sins of our ancestors, that God was forgiving, I knew better than to hold my breath.

In the same regard, I never thought I would truly know love. And while I was hesitant to believe there might be a future with Kaj, I couldn't deny that I loved him, and I believed he felt the same for me. Considering I'd never thought a male would love me, it was more than I had before.

And yes, miracles did happen. I had to believe that Asmia was one of them. Otherwise, how would the female exist? The Fae had been infertile for centuries, which would make her conception impossible. Yet she was Fae, because I sensed it from the moment she came to the mansion. Plus, Asmia had provided life to the angels over the decades. Had she been something else, it wouldn't have been possible.

I had never thought to question any of it aloud, never mentioned it to Obsidian. I wasn't even sure the male was aware of the history of my species, of how we'd met our demise. If he was, he hadn't learned it from me. I'd told no one other than Kaj about what I knew.

Truly, I'd never trusted anyone fully.

Not before Kaj.

"Times are changing," I whispered to the sweet child. "Let's just hope it's for the better."

7

Friday, January 12, 2018

ACADIA

"I've been here for how many weeks now?"

I smiled, having expected the question. I'd had to leave Kaj to attend my other duties while he slept, and it never failed, whenever I returned, he greeted me by asking a question.

"Thirteen," I said easily.

"So why is it I'm not fully healed?" He grunted as he dropped his legs over the side of the bed.

That was a really good question. One I honestly didn't have an answer for. Even by my calculations, he should've been back to full strength by now.

I hurried over to assist. "You endured tremendous trauma to your body. It takes time to recover."

"You said with your blood I'd be healed by now."

I smiled, offering my arm as he pushed to his feet. "I said you'll heal more quickly. As I am not a healer, I cannot gauge how long it will take a vampire to recover from the injuries you sustained."

Sounded good, anyway.

He cut his eyes to mine. "I feel like an invalid."

"Well, I can assure you, you are not."

His response was a grunt.

"I suppose you are seeking a bath?"

Kaj shook his head. "I'd prefer a shower. I can't sit for another minute."

"I'm not sure that's wise. You have not been on your feet for quite some time."

"I'm taking a shower, Acadia. Argue all you want. I won't change my mind."

I suspected that was true. One thing I'd learned about Kaj was that he was stubborn. Though he appeared appreciative, I knew he wasn't keen on being taken care of. Perhaps that was part of the reason I enjoyed it so much. The surly vampire was a welcome distraction to my mundane life, and truth was, I looked forward to every minute I spent with him. Even if he didn't return the sentiment.

"Then I shall help you."

Offering myself as support, I assisted the vampire into the bathroom, then over to the shower. Though assist was embellished a bit. The male was enormous, and I knew if he had truly utilized me as a brace, I would've folded beneath his tremendous weight. Even in his current condition, Kaj was far stronger than I. Which was saying something, considering I had a wealth of strength thanks to my genetics. However, he outweighed me by at least one hundred pounds, and the additional weight was solid muscle.

Luckily, this guest room was one that had an open shower

concept. There were no obstacles in his path, making it easier to get him where he was insistent upon going.

"Why don't you use the facilities, and I'll start the water."

Another grunt.

I smiled to myself as I left him to go into the water closet before I hurried over to turn on the shower. I knew he preferred hot water as opposed to lukewarm, so I ensured it was steaming as it came from the multitude of shower heads.

Though it should've been an easy feat to perform such a simple task, I had to hold the flowing skirts of my dress up to keep them from getting wet. Why I bothered with my current attire, I wasn't sure. I blamed it on simplicity. My entire wardrobe consisted of floor-length gowns made of the finest fabrics. While I was most certainly cognizant of my appearance, I could not deny I was aiming for comfort mostly.

It also helped that I'd seen admiration on Kaj's handsome face when I caught him watching me. It gave me a thrill to know he found me appealing to the eye, even if he didn't say as much.

The sound of Kaj clearing his throat had me turning around. I instantly looked away when I realized he was nude.

"You've seen me before, female," he grumbled.

True, I had. But I tended to think of those times through the eyes of a caretaker, not necessarily a female. That wasn't all that easy to do, either. I was quite enthralled with the male. And yes, I was fascinated with his keen mind, but there was no denying his incredible physique played a large part in my fantasies.

Not that I would tell him as much.

"I shall get you some soap," I told him when I was confident he could stand on his own beneath the shower spray.

I hurried to the tub, retrieved the bottles I kept there for when he bathed, and brought them back to him.

"Kaj!"

NICOLE EDWARDS

He was propped against the tile as though his body had given out on him.

"I'm fine, Acadia," Kaj intoned. "Just leaning."

I breathed a sigh of relief. "I brought your soap."

His eyes opened, his head rolling on his neck as he peered in my direction. "As much as I want to do this on my own, I'm not sure how efficient I'll be."

I stared back at him, wondering what it was he was requesting.

"If you don't mind, I need you to wash me."

"Of course," I blurted, once more morphing into the role of caretaker.

My attention shot to the water, then down to my dress and back. "Kaj?"

"Hmm?" His eyes were closed once again.

"Would you mind if I remove my dress? I would hate to get it wet."

His eyes popped open and locked on mine. For a brief moment, I wondered if I had imagined the heat reflected there. A second later, I determined I had because he offered a single shoulder shrug.

"I'll be right back."

Hurrying over to the counter, I set down the bottles of soap and shampoo, then quickly removed my gown. It took effort because of the design, but I'd long ago gotten familiar with getting in and out of it. When I returned, I brought the bottles with me.

This time when Kaj's gaze settled on me, there was no way to misinterpret what I saw in his glittering green eyes.

"You're naked," he growled.

"Kaj..." I lowered my head. "I apologize if it offends. I do not wear undergarments beneath." And of course, I hadn't thought to wrap myself in a towel.

There was another growl, this one softer but no less potent. When I lifted my head, I noticed his fangs had descended, and he

90

was still regarding me with desire. But I also noticed his erection standing tall and proud from his delectable body.

"You're safe from me, female," he said, dropping his head back and closing his eyes. "But I cannot control the response of my body."

Resigning myself to getting this done, I joined him beneath the spray. I thought about my hair, the fact that it would undoubtedly get wet, then figured there was nothing to be done about it. With a quick tug, I pulled the pins that kept it up on my head and allowed it to fall around me, doing an efficient job of concealing my nakedness because the thick mass hung all the way to my waist.

I had the good sense to use a cloth, soaping it up and then sliding it over Kaj's skin as efficiently as I could, starting at his neck. While I applied the suds to his body, I took a moment to admire him. Being that his eyes were closed, I could do so unashamedly. He had lost weight since he arrived at the mansion, but he was still solidly built and strong. Though he wasn't at full strength, I would not underestimate his abilities. There was a wealth of power beneath the supple skin, his muscles flexing as I moved over them.

I was careful with his chest, though the exterior wounds had healed long ago. What he was dealing with now was the repair on the inside. Obsidian had mentioned he suspected there had been great damage done internally, but my blood was working to return him to as good as new. It just seemed to be taking some time.

When I had worked my way down his torso, I eased down to my knees and moved to his feet, working my way back up. His breathing was labored, and I worried that he was in pain, but I didn't dare speak. For one, I wasn't sure my voice would work, and two, I wanted to get this done as quickly as possible so he could get back to bed.

As I worked my way up his thick, powerful thighs, I peered up, and that was when I realized he was staring down at me, his bright green irises glittering, his fangs fully descended.

Realizing the compromising position I was in, I stood tall but continued to wash him, shifting higher on his thighs until I was at the juncture, sliding upward, cupping his heavy sac.

"Fuck." His head fell back as he hissed. "Acadia ... I..."

"Shh." I reached for the soap, then dropped the cloth, figuring it would be too coarse on his sensitive shaft.

When I took him in my soapy hand, his eyes opened and locked with mine.

"It's okay," I assured him. "I know it's been a while."

He didn't speak, his breath soughing in and out of his lungs as I used both hands, one to cup him, the other to stroke the steely length of his erection. We remained like that as I worked him. There was no pretense, as we both knew I wasn't doing this with cleanliness in mind.

"I'm going to come," he warned.

I nodded, then dropped my gaze to the thick stalk of flesh in my fist. I watched raptly, feeling him pulse in my hand. My grip tightened, helping him along.

When he came, it was with a dark rumble in his chest.

A sound that very nearly triggered my own orgasm.

KAJ

Restraint was a damn good thing to have in times like these. I knew firsthand because the temptation this female presented was unlike anything I'd ever known. I'd damn *near lost my shit when I saw her kneeling before me, peering up at me with those glittering purple eyes, her lips slightly open. The mental image of her taking me into her mouth nearly had me falling to the floor.*

Thank God for self-restraint, no matter how fragile.

"Leave me," I demanded as I fought to catch my breath, my cock still hard, still aching. Probably had to do with the fact I was still firmly in Acadia's smooth grip, her small fingers curled loosely around my flesh.

Concern and what looked a hell of a lot like anger glittered in those intriguing amethyst eyes when they leveled on me.

"Now," I insisted. "Go, Acadia."

I hissed when she released me, then watched as she stormed out, her long, silky hair down to her hips, swaying as she moved. I'd never seen her with her hair down, and I had to admit, I liked the look. She seemed more approachable that way.

I had to close my eyes as I relied on the tiled wall to hold me up. I heard Acadia's footsteps as she walked around the bathroom. I was aware of her getting a towel, the soft brush of it against her skin sounding in my ears. The whisper of silk as she retrieved her dress echoed back at me, and finally, she was leaving.

Only then did I open my eyes, my attention shifting to my spent cock. Only, the damn thing was still standing rigid despite the mind-obliterating orgasm.

Yep, it was safe to say I wanted her with a passion that knew no bounds. And had she not left me alone, chances were, I would've taken her right there in the shower, wounds be damned.

It took a few minutes to gather my wits, but I eventually shut off the water, then shuffled out of the shower only to find a plush towel waiting for me, draped over the towel warmer. Damn female. Why did she have to be so good to me? God knew I didn't deserve it. While she was attempting to take care of me, I was taking advantage of her. That damn hand job was proof. I should've insisted on washing myself, not requesting her to do so. But, of course, I had wanted to feel her touch, to see her hands as they moved over me. And I hadn't been lying. Efficiency wasn't something I was capable of, considering bending at the waist was damn near impossible. The pain in my chest was searing, a reminder that I was still healing, though I wasn't sure why the fuck it was taking so long.

As for the happy ending ... well, I hadn't expected it, nor had I done anything to prevent it.

It wouldn't surprise me if Acadia never came back. I wouldn't blame her, that was for damn sure.

I grunted as I attempted to dry myself, then gave up, tossing the towel onto the counter by the sink. I moved over, intending to brush my teeth, but stumbled, the pain in my chest blooming into a firestorm. It was all I could do to brace myself on the marble countertop, somehow managing to remain upright even as my vision dimmed.

"Kaj?"

I lifted my head, met those beautiful eyes in the mirror. "I'm sorry, Acadia."

"You have nothing to apologize for," she said softly, concern etched on her stunning face. "Aside from your rudeness afterward, that is."

A smile pulled at my mouth despite the agony ripping through my insides.

"We must get you back in bed."

I stared longingly at the toothbrush sitting in the little burgundy cup on the counter.

"Let me help you, Kaj."

It was then I realized she'd moved closer, standing directly behind me.

While I remained where I was, elbows locked, palms flat on the counter, Acadia turned on the water, wet the toothbrush, applied paste, then cut the water off. She passed the loaded brush my way, *then offered her assistance so I could stand. It was likely the most ungraceful attempt to brush teeth, but I managed with Acadia's help. When I was finished, she offered me a cup of water. I swished and spit, the cup being taken from my hand. Acadia then cleaned the brush, placed it back in its holder, and led me back to the bedroom.*

"Wait," she called out.

I exhaled my frustration. Getting horizontal was no longer a choice, but a necessity. If I didn't, I feared I would pass out.

Suddenly, a soft towel was swiped over my back, my ass, down my thighs. Acadia worked the cotton around to my front, successfully drying me. When she made a pass over my aching cock, I grunted, did my best not to think about her mouth on me.

And then I was finally in the bed, flat on my back, blankets pulled up over my hips.

Only then did I realize I was breathing hard, something my well-honed lungs weren't used to. The pain was a constant now, my muscles weak from exertion. I knew Acadia was aware of my discomfort because she was eyeing me with concern.

When she reached to fluff my pillow, I gently touched her wrist.

"I don't deserve your help," I said softly, trying to get comfortable as more pain ricocheted through my chest.

"I believe you do." Her soft hand curled over my bicep. "Now sleep, Kaj. I'll bring your morning meal shortly, and you'll also feed. Until then, rest."

Unable to help myself, I stared up at her, kept watching until I could no longer hold my eyes open.

Her face was the last thing I saw before I drifted off, and before I succumbed to exhaustion and pain, I sent up a prayer that her face would be the first thing I saw when I woke.

8

MIRAKEL

"Tell me, why is it we never had a club like this back in Seattle?" Blāz asked.

Figuring it was rhetorical, I didn't bother to respond as I maneuvered through the horde of bodies filling the space. The place was wall-to-wall packed with both humans and vampires, the air ripe with the scent of cheap perfume and sex, and there was no question where the latter was coming from. Everywhere I looked, there were fornicating bodies, humans being used in every manner possible. All as a means to conceal the fact the vampires were feasting on veins.

I had never understood the fetish of taking a human vein. It didn't provide sustenance, so what was the point?

Then again, until Briony, I had never known how erotic feeding could be. Since her ... well, I almost saw the appeal.

Almost being the key word.

As we moved through the space, I felt the eyes turning toward us, watching, assessing. Though the humans wouldn't understand what the draw was, the vampires were sensing who we were. It wasn't necessarily our size that had the males in the space judging us, more so the power they would pick up on. As members of the Zenith, we had more abilities than civilian vampires. We had to, after all, considering we were tasked with protecting the Alpha.

"I wouldn't even trust to drink out of a glass here," Blāz muttered.

I peered back over my shoulder to see Blāz's attention had been drawn to a pair of naked male vampires who were currently locked in a cage. They didn't seem at all disappointed by their inability to get free, either, having found plenty of entertainment with one another.

When I turned back to scan the space once more, I found myself nearly face-to-face with the vampire who owned this place. Or rather, the traitor.

"Well, well. Looks as though the Alpha's sent out his hit squad," Darko remarked, his black eyes locking on my face. "Where is he these days, anyway?"

I didn't bother to respond. It was all I could do not to wrap my fingers around the male's neck and squeeze.

As though reading my thoughts, Darko chuckled. "You have nothing to fear from me, warrior."

"I know."

That didn't seem to please the male who clearly believed all other vampires should bend the knee for him.

"So what brings you by?"

"Just checking out the local nightlife," Blāz stated, stepping up to my side. "Interesting place you got here."

"I happen to be fond of it." Darko's gaze bounced between us. "But I can't imagine it's a place you're interested in."

Oh, he had no fucking idea. I had great interest in it. In burning it down.

"Where's the wifey?" Blāz asked, his gaze dramatically swinging around the space. "It's been a while since I've seen Talia."

Darko's black eyes seemed to darken. "She's around."

Blāz chuckled. "She was always good at that, huh? Getting around."

I held out my arm to separate the two males. I wasn't sure why Blāz was trying to incite the bastard, but the last thing we needed was to have Darko tossing us out on our asses. We had a job to do, and as long as the male's eyes were on us, we wouldn't be able to get it done.

"Ignore him," I told Darko. "He's an asshole."

Darko's thick, bushy eyebrows remained low over his eyes as though he was trying to determine the fastest way to eliminate Blāz.

"We don't want any trouble," I continued. "Just here to check it out. Not many vampire hangouts around these parts."

"Oh, you'd be surprised." Darko's upper lip pulled back, his fangs flashing.

I didn't doubt there were plenty of underground hangouts. After I'd learned of Darko's intention of eliminating Kaj, I'd come to realize there were plenty of vampires who were willing to align with the likes of this asshole. In fact, had I not come when I had, chances were they would've succeeded in taking Kaj out right here in this very building.

"Well, feel free to hang out, enjoy the entertainment," Darko said with a snarl. "And please, do tell Kaj I hope to see him some-time soon. The last time he promised to stop in, he never showed."

Oh, he showed. And I had led him out through the underground tunnels.

"We'll be sure to let him know you said hello," Blāz said snidely. "I'm sure he's been thinking about you."

I fought the urge to smile. Kaj had been thinking about Darko. We all had. After all, planning the downfall of a traitor required the male's name to come up a time or two.

"If you indulge in the humans, just be sure to wipe their memories before you leave."

I inclined my head as though agreeing, then watched Darko make his way up the short stairs to the level that overlooked what was likely intended to be a dance floor. In reality, it was nothing more than an area for body parts to congregate. The last thing these people had on their minds was dancing.

"I'm going to need a distraction if you expect me to work my magic," Blāz said softly.

Turning to face him, I frowned. "What sort of distraction?"

"I don't know. Perhaps you could make out with one of the females."

"Not gonna happen," I growled softly.

I didn't bother to tell Blāz that it couldn't happen. Now that I'd imprinted on Briony, the mere thought of another female was enough to turn my stomach. Touching one would likely have me heaving up my evening meal.

Granted, that would likely be a distraction, but probably not what Blāz had in mind.

"Okay, fine." Blāz reached for my hand. "Take these."

Something small was passed over.

"Each one is a camera. We need the best view we can get, so I suggest there"—Blāz nodded toward the wall by the bar—"and there"—over to the main door—"and there." The last motion went to the wall behind Darko. "I'll put the last one in the cage."

I frowned. "In the cage?"

"Don't be a prude. It's not becoming." Blāz smirked. "Trust me. I've got it covered. Plus, I think it'll draw Darko's attention."

"What will draw—"

Before I could get the question out, Blāz snagged the arm of a scantily clad male vampire walking by.

"You. In the cage. On your knees."

The male's gaze raked over Blāz appreciatively before a smile turned up the corners of his mouth. "It would be my pleasure."

"Damn right it will." When the vampire sauntered off, Blāz turned his attention back to me. "Just get those cameras in place. When I'm done, I'll need to beat feet. ASAP."

Oh, hell.

BLĀZ

Sometimes you had to take one for the team.

And that was exactly what this male was about to do, because I damn sure wasn't going to be on my knees. Not in this nasty fucking place.

Sure, on the surface it didn't seem all that bad, but if you looked closely at the Dungeon ... yeah, never mind. I had no desire to take a close look at anything. And it wasn't that I was a germaphobe. No, it was more like I tended not to hang out with the dregs of society, and that was what I saw, no matter which direction I looked. Then again, Darko was here and that male was the lowest of scum. Fucking traitor.

"Did I say you could touch me?" I barked as I peered down at the vampire kneeling a few feet in front of me.

Those dark brown eyes glittered with interest, but I'd expected no less. It wasn't difficult to sniff out a submissive vampire. They weren't all that rare these days. Nor were they any sort of challenge.

Had it not been for the fact that we needed a distraction and right now Darko had his full attention on what I was about to do, I would've weaved my way straight for the front door.

Except we were there on a mission, and if we never had to step foot in this place again, it would be too fucking soon.

Because I wasn't an idiot, I slid a piece of metal into the locking mechanism to ensure I didn't find myself trapped in this shitty titanium-lined box. No doubt, one of Darko's tricks to keep vampires inside if he chose to keep them there.

Pretending to take a moment to get myself prepared for what was to come, I went for a stroll around the six-by-six cell, scanning the bars, the floor, the single wall on the back. I noticed the perfect spot to set my camera, but I knew I couldn't simply pin it in place without drawing some unnecessary attention. Instead, I turned around and leaned against the wall.

"Crawl over here," I commanded the male.

On all fours, the vampire cleared the distance between us.

"Put your hands behind your back," I instructed the male. "And don't move them."

I got a nod in response.

Much to my dismay, I noticed we'd garnered a small audience outside the cage. The only reason I didn't snap at the assholes to mind their own fucking business was because Darko had taken to watching as well, his female standing at his side, her eyes wide with anticipation.

"Open your mouth wide," I commanded, leveling the male with a stare as I blocked out the rest of the eyes on us.

The male's lips parted, his mouth opening.

"Wider. What do you think I am?"

Those dark eyes sparkled in anticipation.

With a sharp exhale, I made quick work of freeing my cock from my jeans. On a good day, I wasn't an exhibitionist. However, I couldn't deny I was in the market for a blow job. As it was, I didn't have many options when it came to interactions at the Lair. Not unless I wanted to get horizontal with one of the angels, and the truth was, there was only one who interested me.

"Don't. Fucking. Move," I growled as I guided my cock past those wide lips. "And don't use your fucking teeth."

Fuck.

Those lips wrapped around me tightly, sucking me in deep. The heat alone took me from semi-hard to steel in seconds. It was all I could do to keep myself upright against the wall as I closed my eyes and envisioned another mouth on me. This one belonging to a ridiculously sexy healer. What it was about Apollo, I didn't know, but from the second I'd been introduced to the male, I'd had some wicked hot fantasies about what it would be like to be pinned down by him. Or being the one doing the pinning. Either way, I didn't care which. Top, bottom. There was equal pleasure to be had, so I didn't necessarily have a preference.

Here, in this seedy brothel disguised as a nightclub, I didn't have the luxury of preference, so I welcomed those fantasies. Behind my closed eyelids, I could practically see those pale blue irises staring up at me as I thrust my cock deep into that luscious mouth. Thankfully, the mouth currently latched onto me wasn't all that bad. The male knew how to work me without using his hands, and I was all about helping him along, punishing the male's throat with hard, forceful thrusts.

All the while, I pretended Apollo was bringing me to orgasm. Apollo was sucking me harder, deeper, faster, taking everything I wanted to give him and then some.

It was all I could do to focus, to remember that Mirakel was somewhere in the club putting those damn cameras up. I had no idea how long it would take, but I hoped not too long, because those damn fantasies were pushing me closer and closer to the edge.

"Take all of me," I growled as I held myself still, my back settling against the wall so I could slide my hands behind me and work the last camera into the crevice I'd located.

The male before me pushed up on his knees and leaned forward, taking me to the hilt. When the vampire swallowed around the head, I groaned roughly.

"Suck me," I bellowed, finally getting the camera to stay put behind me.

With my mission accomplished, I held on for a few more minutes, scanning the interior for Mirakel. I finally found the male in the far corner near the door. A curt nod was all I received to let me know he'd completed his tasks as well.

Because I'd started the show, I figured I had to finish it. So when that head began to bob enthusiastically, I reached down and threaded my fingers in the thick black hair. Only I imagined the male was a blond as I began to impale that mouth. And when I came, I bit my lower lip to keep from shouting Apollo's name. I seriously doubted it would mean a fucking thing to anyone, but still. It was probably best I kept my infatuation to myself.

Shoving the male away, I quickly tucked my spent cock back in my jeans, righted my shirt, and headed for the door. I heard the click before I reached it, then smiled up at Darko as I pushed the door, and it came free.

Not this time, buddy.

The look I received could only be described as hatred.

Thanks for the good time, I mentally shot to Darko. *Let's not do this again, shall we?*

On that note, I followed Mirakel out into the night. I was eager to get home because, damn it to hell, now I needed a fucking shower.

KAJ

"Where's he going?" I asked when Blāz and Mirakel strolled into the house.

"Shower," Mirakel grumbled.

Ah. I didn't need more details than that. I knew Blāz, and considering where they'd come from, I had a relatively good idea what had transpired. The same thing that always did when the male got a minute away. Never one to ignore the opportunity to sate an urge, Blāz took the opportunities when they arose.

"Did you get the cameras installed?" I asked, making sure to specify where my curiosity lay.

"We did."

"Any problems?"

"None."

That was surprising.

"I did speak with Darko." Mirakel did not sound pleased by the notion.

"And?"

"He's a bastard."

I chuckled. "I agree. Anything noteworthy?"

Mirakel shook his head. "He asked where you were. Claims the last time you were supposed to stop by, you were a no-show."

"Was he bullshitting you?"

"Not that I could tell."

Which meant Darko had no idea Mirakel was the one who'd come and swept me out through an underground tunnel when Darko had laid a trap for me. We'd escaped, and if Darko was to be believed, no one was the wiser.

"Let's keep them in the dark, then." I got to my feet. "I'm heading over to Angel Central for morning meal. Care to come along?"

"I'm gonna hit the gym."

Which translated to: *I'm avoiding Briony.*

"I'll see you tonight, then."

Mirakel nodded, then headed toward the stairs to the second floor, probably to change, while I headed for the stairs leading down. I heard sounds coming from the room adjacent to the gym on the underground level, so I stopped and poked my head in. Huracān and Kidel were sparring, the two males looking fierce as they took out some of their aggressions on one another.

It was nice to see things getting back to the way they'd been. To the days before the world had gone to shit and the shadow beasts had started targeting the race. One of these days, I would ensure those assholes paid for what they'd done. It would take time and effort, but I would declare an all-out war on those fucking demons. If it was the last thing I did.

T wenty minutes later, after stopping to talk with a couple of the angels in the war room and a couple more who'd been chatting it up in the lower-level bar, I made my way into the dining room. The tables were mostly full, the *fiestreigh* having come in from their patrols for the meal before they hit the hay. I noticed Bijou and Elizabeth at a table near the back of the room, but what surprised me was that Acadia was sitting with them.

Figuring I could at least greet the females, I strolled over. Bijou was the first to notice me. The smile she offered was forced, indicating she was still upset with me after our last conversation, when she'd asked about moving to the Lair. It wasn't that I didn't want my daughter there, because I absolutely did. But right now, until we were able to get the residence fortified to ensure we could withstand any attack, I wasn't comfortable with her staying there.

"Ladies," I said, acknowledging all three with a smile. "Lovely to see you this morning."

Elizabeth peered up at me and smiled kindly, but like usual, she didn't say anything before returning her attention to her meal.

Unable to help myself, I placed my hand on Acadia's shoulder and gave a light squeeze. "I'd like to talk after."

She nodded in acknowledgement, and I took that as my cue to leave. I made my way around the tables, winding my way back to where Eclipse and Orianna were sitting. The male motioned me over, and I gladly accepted, dragging out the chair across from them.

"Is that...?" I leaned forward and studied what was on Orianna's plate.

"Cheez-Its," she said with a chuckle, then lifted the glass of yellow liquid. "And Mountain Dew. Breakfast of champions."

"She would eat this every day if I let her," Eclipse told me.

"I survived on this before I met him," Orianna explained. "And Phillip surprised me when he brought in cases of both a couple of days ago. I think he bought out Costco."

"Your doing?" I asked Eclipse.

"Nope. Not me. Phillip has taken a liking to my female." Eclipse glanced at Orianna, still grinning. "Perhaps I should keep a closer eye on him."

Orianna shrugged him off, playing right into his teasing. "Perhaps you should. I happen to be quite fond of him, too."

The soft growl Eclipse made was one I was all too familiar with. It was that of an overprotective male. Both vampires and angels were notorious for it.

"Good morning, sire."

I peered up to see Jeffrey standing at my side, a silver-covered plate on a tray.

Leaning back, I allowed the *heurosp* to set the items down. Before he disappeared, Jeffrey produced a pitcher of tea and filled the glass that had been set out.

"Thank you, Jeffrey."

"It's my absolute pleasure, sire."

I fought the urge to mouth *sire* the way Blāz had.

"You get any *vestrahn* hired yet?" Eclipse prompted.

Picking up my fork, I poked at what appeared to be beef stroganoff. "Not yet."

"If you don't mind me asking, what's the difference between a *vestrahn* and a *heurosp*?" Orianna asked.

"One's a vampire, the other a human," I informed her. "Aside from that, they have basically the same duties."

"Is there any reason why you'd want to replace what you've already got?" she asked.

"I have no issues with the *heurosp*. I simply prefer to employ vampires."

"That makes sense."

I lifted an eyebrow curiously.

Orianna smiled. "You want to offer jobs to your people. Can't fault you for that. It's what makes a good leader. You're looking out for the little guy."

I found it interesting that she could see that much, considering what little time I'd spent with her since Eclipse brought her to the mansion. Then again, I'd become relatively close to Eclipse during my stay there, and I figured mates talked about shit like that.

My gaze swung over to Acadia. At one time, we'd talked about anything and everything. Then again, I'd been laid up in a bed, unable to do anything else. So we had passed the time talking about family, friends. I'd shared more with her than I had with any other soul. She was simply easy to talk to, I figured.

My attention returned to the glass Orianna was drinking from.

"I have to say, it's a little disconcerting to watch you drink that."

Orianna pulled the glass from her mouth, peered at it, and smiled. "I can see that. Doesn't mean it's not serious awesomeness."

"I'll have to take your word for it."

Because, like plenty of other things I'd seen taking place within these walls, I had no desire to experience it for myself.

9

ACADIA

I had been pleasantly surprised by Kaj's arrival for the morning meal. And while he hadn't sat with us, it had been a comfort to know he was in the same room. Why? Well, I wasn't sure I could answer that. For whatever reason, I found myself missing his nearness despite the fact he'd been feeding from me for the past couple of days.

While I suspected that was his reason for wanting to speak with me, I looked forward to those few stolen moments we could be together.

Yes, I knew I sounded like a lovesick human, but it couldn't be helped. There was no denying my feelings for the male, even if we'd had a rocky go of it these past couple of months. Perhaps it was due to the fact I'd lived without him for the eighteen months he'd been gone. Having him back, seemingly for good, made me not want to waste another minute.

Of course, my pride didn't quite agree with me. He had hurt me, and a small part of me had a difficult time opening up to him again, fearful he would cause more pain when I wasn't looking.

"I'll see you both this evening," I said politely to the two females I'd shared my meal with.

"Have a good day," Elizabeth stated, her eyes twinkling.

I was so happy to see that some of the fog had lifted from Elizabeth's eyes. When Orianna's mother had come to the mansion, she'd been in a medication-induced fog. The human doctors had done their best to accommodate her pain by plying her with various opioids until Elizabeth could barely function. With Amethyst handling her care now, it seemed the healer had figured out a better way to manage her pain while still allowing her a chance to experience each day with some clarity. And to see Elizabeth joining us for the daily meals was such a delight.

"Thank you," I told the female before heading toward the kitchen.

I found Kaj standing beside the island, chatting it up with Jeffrey and Phillip while the *heurosp* prepared to clear the dining room once everyone was finished.

When I stepped into the space, his eyes lifted and settled on me.

I waited patiently while he finished his conversation, content to simply admire the male. He looked handsome in his black T-shirt and jeans. I half expected to see him wearing something more suitable for a man of his status. Then again, I knew he hadn't quite stepped into those shoes he'd been slated to fill, continuing to ride the line between his previous role as the right hand to the Alpha and being the Alpha himself.

No matter what he wore—a T-shirt and jeans or a three-piece suit—Kaj was the most handsome male I'd ever laid my eyes on. And that was saying something considering the beauty that surrounded me. The angels were designed to be spectacular; there was no doubt about it. Yet the king of vampires stole the show with little effort.

"If you'll excuse me," Kaj told the *heurosp* before sauntering toward me.

When he approached, I smiled up at him. "You wanted to speak with me?"

His smile was sexy. "I wanted to spend some time with you."

"Oh?" He held out his arm, and I easily slid mine through. "Where are we going?"

"I thought we'd go for a swim."

I chuckled. "Really?"

"Yes. Really."

Because I had no reason to decline his request, I fell into step with him. We strolled beyond the kitchen, through the front formal living space, then to the hall that led toward the garage and the entrance to the pool. Kaj paused to open the door for me, then held it while I stepped inside.

I was instantly hit with a wall of humidity, the scent of chemicals strong in the air.

Kaj took my hand, this time leading me around the Olympic-size pool with its eight lanes and over to the enormous hot tub that regally sat in the far corner.

"I do not have a swimsuit," I informed him.

"Neither do I." His smile was wicked.

"Then I guess we shall wear nothing," I teased.

"Sounds like a perfect plan to me."

There was a strange fluttering in my belly, something I

wasn't sure I'd ever felt. I found I liked the sensation because it was something akin to anticipation mixed with desire.

Kaj released me, then took a seat on one of the many chairs that lined the space. He quickly removed his boots and socks, then pulled his T-shirt over his head. His jeans were discarded next, and then he was standing there in a pair of silky black boxer briefs that hugged his muscular thighs nicely.

I felt my face warm, as though this was the first time I'd seen a male in this state of undress.

When he moved to stand behind me, I sucked in a breath as his warm fingers found the ties that held my dress together at my back. He didn't rush to undress me, his fingers sweeping over my skin ever so lightly as he freed me from the confines of the silk.

Before the gown could fall to the floor, I held it to my breasts, a hint of nerves giving me pause.

When I turned back, I was shocked to see Kaj strolling away from me. But there was nothing to fear, because he was simply retrieving one of the plush white towels that were kept poolside. He returned, holding it open as though providing me with a barrier to shield my nakedness.

Because I didn't have a modest bone in my body, I easily slipped out of the dress, then laid it over the back of one chair before taking the towel from his grasp. I was captivated by the hunger I could see sparkling in his light green eyes, though it was obvious he was attempting not to ogle.

With the towel loosely wrapped around me, I made my way to the stairs leading down into the warm water.

As I stepped down into it, I tossed the towel to the edge, keeping it from getting wet. I was sinking into the depths when the jets came to life, causing the water to bubble up around me, offering a hint of privacy, though I knew he could still see me if he wanted to.

I was surprised when Kaj kept his boxer briefs on, walking down the steps to join me. When he was thigh deep, he sank down until only his shoulders were above water. It was then he held out his hand to me, tugging me toward him as he maneuvered into one of the many contoured seats lining the outer edges of the oversized tub.

Allowing him to situate me on his lap, I relaxed against him, my back to his chest, the warm water easing the strain of the night.

"What did you want to talk about?" I prompted when we'd both gotten comfortable.

"I didn't." His arms slid around me, holding me against him. "I simply wanted to spend time with you. Just sit with me, Acadia. Let me hold you for a while."

How could I possibly deny him that when it was what I wanted more than anything else?

Here, alone with him, his strong arms banded around me, I felt complete and safer than I'd ever felt before.

It was then I realized this was the first time we'd done this since he returned to the mansion. Sat quietly, comfortably. No expectations.

Just the two of us.

At peace.

BIJOU

After assisting Elizabeth back to her bedroom and getting her situated in the new bed Amethyst had designed specifically for her needs, ensuring she could get in and out of it on her own, I made my way toward the game room.

Reidar, Blāz, Raksa, and Miklós were getting set up to play pool, so I plopped myself down on the leather sofa to watch.

"What brings you out so late?" Blāz asked as he moved around the pool table so he could take his position to break.

"Just trying to wind down," I told him.

"Not sure this'll help. I'm gearing up to kick some angel ass. Might get noisy when I make them cry."

Yep, that was what prompted the ruckus that followed. The angels took offense to the vampire's comment, coming back with their own taunts. For the next half hour, the four of them went head to head, two at a time, the next in line playing the winner. And true to his word, Blāz did kick some angel butt, eliminating his opponents one after the other, time and time again.

I'd gotten so caught up in their good-natured ribbing, I hadn't even noticed that Oliver was standing in the doorway leading to the hall, watching as he leaned casually against the door. While he focused on the others, I stared at him. For some reason, that darkness I'd noticed within him was more prominent, as though it was growing stronger. What was it, I wondered. I'd never noticed anything like it before.

Not that I usually got readings on people like that. Almost like an aura, only internal, as though it surrounded something hiding within him.

Oliver's eyes snapped to my face, and I started to look away but found myself trapped by his gaze, as though he was holding me there. Neither of us moved, eyes locked. My breath was lodged in my throat. There were so many things I wanted to say to him. Starting with an apology for the rift I'd put between us. My own selfishness had wrecked the good thing we had going, and I had lost the one real friend I'd had in a long time. Truth was, I missed Oliver, missed the times we'd spent together.

While I wouldn't necessarily say I was attracted to him, I was drawn to him, pulled in by something deeper.

As far as humans went, he was on the handsome end of the spectrum, even if he wasn't necessarily my type. Physically, at least. But I wasn't so shallow as to only look on the outside. No, with Oliver, it was about what was inside. He was funny, smart, and easy to be around. Even if he was standoffish to others, he'd never been that way with me.

"You want to play?" Blāz offered Oliver.

"No. I'm good." With that, Oliver stood tall, then turned and left.

I was tempted to follow him, to hash this out right here and now. Something kept me rooted to that damn sofa, though. Fear, perhaps. What if I apologized and he rejected me? Told me to get lost? I wasn't sure I could handle that from him. It was easier to remember the good times we'd had, to pretend we had simply drifted apart rather than risk him refusing to ever speak to me again.

A sense of longing overwhelmed me, but it wasn't for the male who'd left. No, I missed my mother. Had she still been alive, I wouldn't have hesitated to talk to her about this, get her opinion. I'd always looked to my mom for guidance.

"Hey, you okay?"

My eyes shot up to see Blāz bending over me, his expression reflecting his concern.

"I'm fine," I blurted, though I was anything but.

He obviously didn't believe me, but he nodded anyway, gave my shoulder a gentle squeeze.

"All right, children. What do you say we make this worthwhile?"

The voice preceded the male, and a second later, Apollo stepped into the room. The healer seemed larger than life, although Blāz, being the tallest in the room, stood a good three or four inches taller.

"What's at stake, Doc?" Blāz countered.

I watched as the two males locked eyes for a moment. Intimidation. That was what they were doing. Daring the other to up the ante.

Chuckling softly at the excessive testosterone being tossed around, I got to my feet. "I think I'll call it a day," I told them. "Good luck to you all."

More ribbing ensued as the five males began hassling one another, their voices booming through the open space. The sound trailed after me even as I made my way around the open area and down the hall to my bedroom. When I passed Oliver's door, I paused for a moment, considered knocking and telling him what was on my mind.

As was usually the case, I didn't, choosing instead to tuck my tail and move on.

One of these days, perhaps I'd get the nerve to settle this between us. And if not, maybe I'd simply move into the Lair and see how long it took anyone to notice.

Yes. That was likely the best idea I'd had in a long time.

KAJ

I wasn't sure how long we'd been in the hot tub, but I was content to remain right where I was for as long as possible.

With Acadia propped on my lap, my arms wrapped securely around her, I was at peace for the first time in a long time. In fact, the only times I'd ever been this content had been when I was with her. However, I'd never simply held her like this. Not unless we were in bed, succumbing to exhaustion, usually after an intense bout of mind-numbing sex.

But I wasn't after sex. Not this time.

No, I'd told myself I wanted to spend time with her. Didn't matter what we talked about or even if we talked at all. I merely wanted to be in her presence.

"I think we might prune in here," she finally said, her voice soft and relaxed.

"It's possible. Would you like to get out?"

She chuckled. "No."

"Me neither."

Her hand slid over my arm, gliding up and down over my skin. The lightest of touches that did so much to my body.

"I miss you, *balisra*," I whispered, pressing my lips to her shoulder.

"I miss you, too."

"I should probably get you up to your bed." It wasn't that I wanted to leave her, but the sun was inching higher in the sky beyond the protection of all those shutters and thick drapes, and we both needed our sleep.

"I want you to feed first," she said, her tone firm as her hand held my arm to her torso.

"Here?"

"Yes."

It wasn't like I wanted to argue. I needed to feed, and this was as good a place as any.

"And you?"

"I'm good until tonight," she said softly. "But I will come find you at nightfall."

"I want to touch you," I rasped against her ear. "Let me make you come with my fingers, *balisra*."

The sharp inhale and the way her body bucked against me told me she wasn't opposed to the idea.

"Spread your legs for me," I urged, sliding my hand over her thigh.

Acadia did as I instructed, her hand coming over mine as I slid my fingers over her pussy. Even in the water, I could feel her slickness, the way her body eased the way for my fingers to enter her. I took my time, grazing her clit lightly, teasing her as I pressed my lips to her shoulder, sliding higher. When she leaned her head back, baring her neck for me, providing me access to her vein, my fangs descended in anticipation. Still, I refrained, teasing her, building her higher. And when I plunged two fingers inside her, I pierced her neck.

She cried out, her body pressing into mine as I fingered her at the same time I drank from her. My cock was rock hard, but it had been since I joined her in here. It was the reason I'd left my boxers on. I had no intention of taking this further. Not yet. Not until my female understood I wasn't simply in this for the pleasure she brought me. I wanted to take care of her, to love her, to spend our eternity together.

Come for me. I pushed the words into her mind, loving the

way her body clasped my fingers as I urged her higher with the rhythmic press of my fingers.

"Kaj..."

God, I loved the way she said my name. That single syllable from her lips was the most erotic thing I'd ever heard.

Holding her in place with my mouth, I slid my other hand between her thighs and teased her clit relentlessly as I fucked her with two fingers. She shivered and moaned, pinned in place against me as I drank from her. I closed my eyes and let the erotic sounds drift in my ears, the sweet warmth of her body against mine, the way her pussy clamped down on me.

When she came, it was with a brittle cry that nearly had me coming myself. I staved off my release by focusing on bringing her down while I continued to feed. She settled against me, her breath raspy. Her hand came up to cup my face, holding me to her neck as I took more from her, but not too much. By the time I was finished, her breaths had returned to normal. After I sealed the wounds I'd inflicted, I shifted her so that I could find her mouth with mine.

I was lost to her. Completely and totally overwhelmed. I'd never felt anything like this before her, because she was my other half, the part that would make me whole.

"I love you," I whispered softly when I pulled back.

She didn't say the words back, but I didn't have to hear them. I knew how she felt, even if she was hesitant to tell me. One day, she would trust me enough to open up to me. And when that day came, I would be by her side for the rest of our existence.

"Let me get you up to your room."

Acadia nodded, then pressed her lips to mine once more. I knew it was her way of expressing what she wasn't ready to say. And I was more than willing to take whatever she was willing to give.

10

BLĀZ

"You can't beat me, angel," I told Apollo for the millionth time since the male had joined us in the game room.

For the past couple of hours, the other angels had slowly trickled out, one by one, until it was only the healer and me. From what I could tell, Apollo refused to give up, despite the fact he'd been beaten a dozen times.

Apollo took the chalk and rubbed it over the end of his stick as he moved around the table, studying the layout of the remaining balls.

"Perhaps I'm not looking to win," the male rumbled.

"No?" I stepped back to allow Apollo to move by me.

But the healer didn't stroll by. No, he made sure to brush the entire front of his body with his own. The heat that transferred between us was exactly what had been arcing since the male had stepped into the room. At first, I thought I had imagined it. Figured it had something to do with those fantasies I'd indulged back at the Dungeon, when that other male had been on his knees.

When Apollo didn't immediately move away, I pressed my hips forward. "What's your angle, healer?"

"Whatever you want it to be." The male leaned forward, taking aim at one of the stripes while he pressed his ass to my groin.

Yeah, there was no missing what he was getting at.

"What makes you think I'm interested?" I growled softly, placing my hand in the center of Apollo's back.

The male took the shot, missed, but he didn't immediately stand.

"Feel interested to me," Apollo countered.

Not liking the fact that Apollo was fucking with me, I quickly moved away, shifting to settle the fucking steel pipe that had grown between my legs.

"That's him," I told Apollo. "Not me."

The male's dark, rumbling laugh had my cock pulsing.

"I saw you with Elina earlier," I snarled. "Don't play me, healer."

Apollo stood tall, his broad shoulders squaring as he approached. "No one's playing here."

I recalled the way Apollo had been talking to the Fae earlier. The two of them had looked mighty cozy down in the infirmary when I had come through.

Not willing to back down, I faced off with the male. "I'm not sure I'm your type."

Those pale blue eyes raked over me. "You're definitely my type."

"So you swing both ways?"

Apollo met my stare head-on. "I tend to go after what intrigues me."

"Yeah, well, you're not *my* type."

Another laugh rumbled in the space between us, and I forced myself to back away. I had no desire to get into it with the healer. Last thing I needed was to cozy up to an angel. I had better things to do with my time, thank you very much.

Turning my attention back to the game, I lined up my next shot. Sank it. Then another. And another. I let my frustration fuel me as I put all the solids in the pockets, then followed it by sinking the eight ball. When I was finished, I put the stick back on the holder on the wall.

"It's inevitable," Apollo said, stepping up behind me, crowding me between his hard body and the wall.

"Only in your dreams," I retorted.

Warm breath fanned my neck when Apollo said, "Don't I know it."

"Notice I said *your* dreams, not mine."

"Whatever you have to tell yourself, vampire."

I knew my body was betraying me as I swayed on my feet.

"Whenever you're ready, the offer stands," Apollo rasped, his lips barely brushing my neck.

"I'm not sure you can handle me," I shot off, locking my knees to keep from falling.

"I'm willing to find out if you are."

Spinning around, I was nearly nose to nose with the male. I was a few inches taller, my shoulders broader, my body bigger, but there was something about the damn angel that made me feel small in comparison. I wasn't sure what it was, perhaps the dominating personality or the anticipation glittering in those baby blues. Whatever it was, I wasn't willing to bite.

Not yet.

"Same thing you told Elina earlier?" I snapped.

"Maybe."

I smirked, but it wasn't from amusement. "Perhaps you should go find her."

"Perhaps." Apollo stepped forward until our chests were pressed together. "But maybe I prefer a challenge."

Leaning in, I let my lips hover over the angel's. "Well, then, I hope you enjoy your hand."

It took all the control I had not to slam my lips down on the angel's. Instead, I skirted the sexy bastard, stepping to the side before spinning around and strolling out of the room.

I had no idea what game the healer was playing, but I had no desire to be anyone's second choice.

Didn't matter how fucking much I wanted to lay that angel out.

APOLLO

I watched as the vampire stormed out of the room.

I couldn't help smiling as I watched the male leave, admiring that big body as I imagined what he would look like naked.

Evidently, Blāz wasn't as easy as I had expected him to be.

Not that the male had given me any reason to believe he was. But I knew Blāz had no ties to anyone, no preference for any of the Fae he'd fed from during his stay there. Of course, I knew Blāz had only fed from the male Fae, which told me all I needed to know. And sure, I'd given it a shot, because why the hell not?

Granted, I hadn't realized Blāz had seen me talking to Elina earlier. That interaction had been completely innocent, but I hadn't felt the need to explain myself. Not when Blāz had clearly made up his mind. In fact, the conversation I'd had with Elina had been regarding her worries that one of the *heurosp* had come down with a cold. I had assured her I would check in with the human when I got the chance.

After placing the pool cue back in the holder, I went to reset the table so it would be ready for whoever came in there next. It was the unspoken rule within the house, and I was all for being a team player.

Funny that.

I hadn't considered myself a team player before I arrived there. In fact, I'd figured this would be one of the worst assignments I'd ever been on, but I quickly realized I'd jumped the gun on that assumption. The warriors and the *fiestreigh* had welcomed Amethyst and me with open arms, made my sister and me feel like part of the family from the day we arrived. I had managed to keep my distance for the first few days, but I soon realized it was futile. Those who resided within these walls weren't the sort to leave anyone out of the action, regardless of what it was.

So these days, I find myself sharing meals with the others, hanging out in the bar, even shooting pool a few mornings a week.

This morning, I had intended to get some shut-eye, but the moment I saw Blāz stroll through the infirmary on the way into the mansion, I was intrigued by the idea of the chase. Blāz could pretend all day long that he wasn't interested, but I had seen the way the male eyed me. Like I was dessert.

NICOLE EDWARDS

The fact of the matter was, I wasn't merely intrigued by the idea of the chase; I was intrigued by Blāz, period. I wanted to get to know the vampire. Not only in the carnal sense. Although that was definitely at the forefront of my mind. And I'd seen how those eerily colorless eyes glittered with heat when he looked at me. There was definitely attraction on both sides.

And if Blāz wanted to play hard to get...

I grinned.

I could certainly oblige the male.

For as long as it took.

B y the time I made it back down to the infirmary, the rest of the mansion had quieted, everyone taking refuge for the day.

I found my sister typing away on the computer at the small desk we'd set up outside the patient rooms.

"What're you working on?"

"Updating our inventory," she said absently. "What are you still doing up?"

"Been playing pool."

She spun on the small stool, smiling up at me. "Getting all settled in, are you?"

"Gotta pass the time somehow, right?"

"Oh, admit it, you like it here," she teased.

That I did. Although admitting it wasn't on the agenda. Instead, I offered her a smile. "How's Ari'el?"

Amethyst's blue eyes brightened. "She's precious. And healthy."

My sister had taken to the infant since the minute Ari'el came into the world. Then again, she'd always been that way, drawn to the babies she delivered. I figured that had to do with

130

the fact she'd always wanted one of her own but claimed it wasn't in the cards. Amethyst said she was married to her work, so there was no time for any other relationship, much less motherhood. I figured that had more to do with the fact she hadn't found her *amsouelot* yet. But he was out there, I knew. As for where, that was yet to be seen. Since we'd spent the past four hundred years focused mainly on Michael's warrior camp and the babies produced by the archsires and archdams, we hadn't really had much time to venture out. Now that we were here on Earth, I figured that would likely change things.

For both of us.

The doors leading to the tunnel swung open, drawing my attention. I fought the urge to smile when I saw Blāz stomping through them, a male on a mission.

"You and me. We need to talk," the male barked.

I was aware of my sister getting to her feet, then muttering something about going to do another count in the stock room before leaving us alone.

Placing my hands on my hips, I smirked. "Couldn't stay away, could you?"

"Fuck you," Blāz growled, moving closer until we were nearly toe to toe. "What is it you're after, angel?"

I held up my hands. "I'm as innocent as the day I was born."

"Innocent, my fucking ass."

I noticed the male had the mouth of a sailor, as the humans liked to say. Seemed he was rather fond of using the f-word to add flair to his vocabulary. Personally, I found it hot, though I couldn't say why that was.

"I told you what I wanted, Blāz. Whenever you're ready."

The sexy vampire stepped closer, his eyes narrowed. "No, you said the offer stands."

"It does."

The male's voice lowered. "And what offer might that be?"

Two could play this game. I leaned forward, closing the distance between our mouths. "Whatever you're willing to give me."

"You mean whatever I'm willing to take," Blāz countered.

I chuckled. "If that's how you want to play it, I'm game."

"You keep saying that."

"Because it's true."

"Prove it," Blāz growled.

"Don't mind if I do."

I knew Blāz was expecting me to be rough, which was the reason I held myself back. Instead of slamming my lips over his and thrusting my tongue inside him, I used a different tack. Canting my head slightly, I let my lips brush the vampire's. They were warm and softer than I expected. I nipped his lush lower lip, then licked the sting away as I slid my hand behind Blāz's head and pulled him closer. Our mouths fused for an instant, and just as I expected, he took over.

The soft growl that sounded in his chest was the prelude to what would likely be the most intense kiss of my existence. I was momentarily stunned when Blāz licked his way inside me, slowly, surely. There was no hesitation, no uncertainty. I knew exactly what he wanted, and I gave it back to him in spades.

The next thing I knew, I was pinned against one of the closed doors, the vampire's big body pressed against me, Blāz's hips gyrating as he ground against me. I hadn't expected it, honestly. The males I'd been with always looked to me to take the lead. That certainly wasn't the case here. Blāz had no problem taking the reins, and I had no problem handing them over.

Fuck.

Yeah, there I went using Blāz's favorite word.

The kiss ignited, tongues thrashing as I held him to me. What I noticed was that he never touched me. Not with his hands. He kept those down to his sides while his tongue brutally worked me over. It was shocking and oddly erotic for some reason, although I would've preferred the male's hands on me.

Then it ended abruptly when Blāz pulled out of my grasp, stepping back. Those odd colorless eyes met mine and held for the longest seconds of my life.

"Don't fuck with me, healer," Blāz hissed. "I don't appreciate it."

For whatever reason, I couldn't find words. My voice didn't work, so I simply stared back.

And when Blāz spun around and stormed out the way he'd come, I had to take a moment to gain my composure.

What.

The.

Fuck?

II

ACADIA

I hadn't meant to start something with Kaj.

Not that anything had really been started. That intimate moment we'd shared in the shower nearly two weeks ago was more like a flicker from a flame that burned out before it could roar to life.

That was how I would describe what was happening between the two of us. He'd been at the mansion for fifteen weeks now, getting stronger every single day, though he was still spending most of his time in bed, his insides healing slower than we'd all believed they would.

I wasn't complaining, of course. No, I was enjoying his company, spending all hours of the night with him. The only time I was away was during the daylight hours when I would retreat to my bedroom for sleep.

Which was where I was about to head now, albeit a bit more reluctantly than I figured was appropriate.

"Is there anything else I can get you before I retire for the day?" I asked after I had placed his meal tray out in the hall for the heurosp to retrieve.

"Yes," he said gruffly, his beautiful green eyes watching as I moved toward his bed.

"Anything," I offered.

"I'd like to feed."

I nodded. For whatever reason, he'd been refraining from feeding every day, rather skipping one, sometimes pushing it as much as two before he requested my vein. We both knew he would heal much faster if he fed more often, but I got the sense he was maintaining a polite distance between us.

Kaj adjusted his position in bed, his back against the pillow wedged between him and the headboard.

As I pulled my sleeve up, I perched on the edge of the mattress. I offered up my wrist, preparing myself for his touch.

Those long, strong fingers curled around my forearm, his gaze meeting mine. "I'd like your neck."

My eyes bounced over his face as his words sank in. He had yet to take from me in that manner, and I had assumed it was due to the intimacy it alluded to. Some males preferred it, but most were satisfied with the wrist. Easy, functional.

"Unless you're opposed to it," he said softly, his eyes boring into mine.

"Of course not."

He was still holding my arm, or I would've moved, would've attempted to find a position that would work for him.

Clearly Kaj had something in mind because he shifted over, providing room for me to join him. He tugged my arm, urging me to *climb onto the mattress with him. I felt a flutter in my belly as I got into the big bed, both curious and aroused by the idea of being here, like this, with him.*

After releasing his grip on my arm, he fluffed the pillow, then nodded with his chin. "Rest your head here."

A bit confused about the direction he was heading, I managed to recline on the bed, head resting on the pillow. I couldn't imagine this would be a comfortable position for him, but I wasn't going to say as much.

"Turn over on your side," he instructed. "Facing away from me."

Easing onto my side, I kept my back to him, tucking my hands beneath my cheek. I was aware of him moving, the mattress shifting from his weight. When he slipped in behind me, his front melding to my back, my breath halted in my lungs. Not from fear. No, what he triggered within me was in no way related to fear.

"Comfortable?"

I shifted my head once, the stick holding my hair in place pressing into my head.

"Here."

The next thing I knew, he was pulling the fastener free, my hair tumbling down. Kaj brushed the strands back from my shoulder, and a shiver danced down my spine. I liked when he touched me, though those moments were rare. Usually only when he was feeding, his hands curling around my arm to hold me still. But this touch ... it was different. And my body knew the difference immediately.

"Better?"

"Yes."

He moved closer, his body fully pressed against mine, his breath fanning my neck. I knew he was naked beneath the sheet, and part of me wished that luxurious cotton, not to mention my gown, wasn't between us, shielding me from his warmth. It was wrong to be wanting something from him, considering he was still healing, but as the weeks had progressed, I had been hoping something more might come from our constant interactions. The fact that I'd never experienced this sort of intimacy with a male was what prompted me to want to explore, to see where it might go.

Kaj's arm draped over my side, pulling me closer. I shifted to assist, and it was then I felt the hard ridge of his erection. The soft growl that rumbled in his chest had my mouth falling open, my lungs working overtime to drag air in.

As he pressed his lips against my neck, his arm slipped under mine, his hand curling over my shoulder to hold me.

"I'm going to bite you now," he whispered, the words a dark seduction in our current positions.

I tilted my head toward the pillow, offering myself to him.

When his fangs pierced my vein, I inhaled deeply, but not because it hurt. Quite the opposite, actually. I had never thought much about males feeding at my vein. It was a biological function that had to be tended to, one I was forced to provide. With Kaj ... this felt strangely different, and I figured that had to do with the fact I was attracted to him. More so than I'd ever been to another male.

He groaned even as he sucked, the muscles in his arm tensing. The feel of his lips on my neck had my skin tightening, my nipples pebbling. Every inch of me was sensitive, the lightest brush of air whispering over me making me tremble.

I found myself leaning into him, urging him closer. His erection pressed against my bottom, his hand curling around my breast. He was breathing harder through his nose, the air tickling as he drew on me again and again.

I wasn't sure what prompted me to do it, but I freed my breast from the silk of my gown, moaning when his warm hand cupped me. As he kneaded my flesh and took from my vein, I reached back for him, my hand gripping his hip. When he ground his erection against me, I levered my bottom toward him, wanting to offer the friction he needed.

His gruff moans had me growing warmer, my own soft moans escaping when he plucked my nipple with his fingers, his hips grinding. He fed from me as he tormented my body with the heat of his. Between my thighs, I grew slick, my sex clenching, reminding me I was empty despite the fact I longed to feel him moving inside me.

"Kaj..." My hand tightened on his hip as I urged him to find his release.

A deep, gravelly sound rumbled in his chest as he rutted behind me.

"Come for me," I urged.

The sound that escaped him was more torment than pleasure, as though he were desperate to refrain.

"Come for me, Kaj." It wasn't a request, it was a demand, and I sensed he knew that.

His arm banded tightly, the hand covering my breast squeezing firmly. Then his fangs slipped from my neck, his tongue swiped over the wounds as he continued to grind his erection against me.

"Acadia..." His hand slipped from my breast, sliding down my thigh as he yanked my gown up to my hips, his lips pressing against my skin as he continued to moan, the vibrations rocking me to my core.

I felt the sheet between us and wished he would abandon that, too. He didn't, though. He simply kissed my neck as he jerked his hips until thunder emerged from his chest and he came. I squeezed my thighs together, attempting to stave off the ache that had built in my core.

"I want to make you come," he growled, his hand sliding over my hip.

I parted my thighs, welcoming his hand.

"Can I make you come, Acadia?"

"Please, Kaj..."

He shifted, urging me onto my back as his hand cupped my sex.

"So beautiful," he whispered.

It was then I realized he was looking at my face, not what his fingers were doing between my legs. When he thrust one thick finger into me, my head pressed into the pillow, and I came in an instant. The orgasm exploded within me, the electrical current more powerful than anything I'd ever felt. He teased my flesh as I rode the wave. And when I came back to myself, my eyes opened to find he was still looking at me, the expression on his face one I'd never seen before. Perhaps wonder mixed with reverence.

I knew in that moment that what had transpired between us was more than sex. It was unlike anything I'd ever experienced with a male. A deeper connection had been developed.

And it was only getting started.

KAJ

What I wanted was to roll on top of this female, to mount her, drive us both to the precipice and over into the abyss. It was the same thing I'd wanted every time she'd come into my room for the past two weeks, ever since our one and only intimate encounter that day in my shower.

Despite the fact I'd just come, my cock was rock hard, aching with the need. Yet I refrained.

Truth be told, I wasn't sure where I found the restraint. For weeks now, my hunger for her had been growing. Not a steady rise, *either. No, this was an insurmountable pressure that threatened to weaken the fault lines of our tremulous relationship. From what I gathered, Acadia saw herself as my nurse, provided for me when I was otherwise unable to provide for myself. She took care of me day and night, waiting on me, feeding me, bathing me.*

And here I was again, having used her body to provide my release. I'd been selfish in my taking of pleasure, and that was the only reason I'd offered to do the same for her.

Okay, maybe not the only reason.

However, I couldn't help but think how she'd told me the Fae availed themselves to the angels in this manner. That bothered me more than anything, and I did not want her thinking I was taking because it was my due. No, what I wanted from her was more, yet I didn't seem to know how to relay that.

"Please stay," I urged when I suspected she would get to her feet.

"Are you sure?"

I'd never been more sure of anything in my life. What it was about this female, I had no idea, but I felt the connection between us. I'd sensed it the moment I opened my eyes all those weeks ago to find she was still with me, caring for me, healing me.

"I'm sure. Just let me clean up first."

Acadia was immediately on her feet, her gown sliding back down to cover all that delectable skin. I instantly wanted her to remove it so I could bask in her physical beauty for a while longer.

Rather than insist, I forced myself to my feet, made my way to the bathroom. The pain that bloomed in my torso was a familiar one. Despite the weeks I'd been here, I had yet to heal. Acadia was right, with her blood in my veins, I should've been at full strength by now, probably even back out in the world, returning to my duties. Instead, I continued to suffer setbacks, the pain still an insistent reminder that I was injured, each night the idea of a full recovery eluding me.

I shuffled my way to the sink, turned on the warm water, and grabbed a cloth from the shelf on the wall. I stared at myself in the mirror as I rinsed the remnants of my lust off my stomach. My mind drifted back to those few moments when I'd been at her vein, my body trembling with need, my cock throbbing with the urge to come. I could still hear Acadia's whispered words, her softly spoken commands. My body had belonged to her in those moments, and I wondered if she even realized it.

"Are you okay?"

My eyes shifted upward, seeing Acadia behind me in the reflective glass. I nodded because that was what she expected. As for whether that was the truth, I didn't know. Something told me I would never be okay. Not in any real sense of the word. Not after this ... the time I'd spent with her.

"May I assist you back to the bed?"

I could see her eyes moving over me, observing. I decided I liked the way she looked at me. There was a warmth in her gaze. Not only the heat of attraction. More. Deeper. As though she could see past the exterior to the male beneath.

Flipping the water off, I tossed the cloth into the sink, then snagged the hand towel and dried myself. I felt as though I needed to shield my nakedness, but I opted not to. My cock was still hard, still throbbing, but the damn thing didn't lead me, so it wasn't concerning. I could and would ignore it as I was apt to do around this female.

"Come on." Acadia held up her arm, allowed me to lean on her for stability.

When I stepped into the room, I realized she'd changed the sheets on the bed and now both sides were turned down, the pillows fluffed and awaiting two heads to lie on them.

"You still want me to stay?"

The uncertainty in her tone had me pausing, turning to look at her. My eyes scanned her beautiful features.

"Yes. Please." Forever, if you wouldn't mind. *Thankfully,*

those last words were only in my head, and I intended to keep them to myself.

Acadia kindly assisted me to my side of the bed, offered her strength as I eased into it. The blankets were pulled over my hips before she made her way around to the other side.

"Would you mind taking off the gown?"

I hadn't meant to say the words aloud, but once they were out there, it wasn't like I could take them back.

A soft smile pulled at her lips, and then she was working free the ties and buttons on the dress. I couldn't help staring at her as she revealed herself.

Once she was on the mattress, she slowly pulled the blankets up, covering her nakedness once more.

"Would you mind lying with me?" I prompted, holding out my arm, urging her to move in close.

The silk of her hair tickled my arm as she shifted, pressing against my side, her head resting in the crook of my shoulder. My arm curled around her back, pulling her closer, her warmth the only thing I cared about.

When Acadia rested her hand on my chest, I placed mine over it, wanting to hold her there, to ensure she didn't slip away as I drifted off.

And for the first time in years, I slept soundly.

12

KAJ

———

With the calendar rolling into March, I was starting to get restless. More so than usual.

I figured it had a lot to do with the fact I'd yet to fully integrate myself in the new role as Alpha of my race, choosing to come up with one excuse after another: Michael's request for me to pledge my loyalty, the insistence that I resurrect the original vampire, the notion of my daughter mating that ancient fanged creature. All those weighed heavily on my mind, making it impossible to address the important issues facing my race.

My main focus these past few days had been building my strength. When I wasn't spending time in the gym, I was at Acadia's vein, utilizing her blood for its potency. Not to mention, a reason to be in her presence. Though we had yet to consummate our newfound relationship, I had been working in that direction. Albeit slower than I would've liked.

But I wanted to think things were looking up in all aspects of my world. Hence, I'd been summoned.

Of course, I would've preferred my Fae had called for me, rather than Obsidian requesting my presence, but hey, I wasn't going to bitch. Right now, I needed something to focus on, and the male's current pet project was as good as any.

When Obsidian finally offered up an invitation to the new training facility, I eagerly accepted. Why the male had been so secretive up to this point, I wasn't sure, but I was eager to get a look-see and offer to contribute in any way necessary. Yes, another excuse to put off the inevitable. So what.

Now, as I stood within the walls of what looked to be nothing more than an enormous concrete box, I had to wonder what all the fuss was about.

"This?" I asked, peering over at Obsidian. "This is your idea of a training facility?"

The great expanse before me was nothing more than stone and concrete. A section of the mountain that had been dredged out, shored up, and cemented in so that it resembled a usable, albeit uninspired space. Where were the walls? The equipment? The tools necessary to create the next generation of warriors?

"Keep an open mind, vampire," Obsidian quipped.

Open mind. Right.

"How big is it?" I inquired.

"Roughly ten acres," the male answered. "So, in square feet, that's..."

"Four hundred thirty-five thousand, six hundred," Blāz noted. "Give or take based on your 'roughly.'"

Obsidian smirked. "Exactly."

"So, what? Half the size of Angel Central?" I teased.

Obsidian smirked. "We do what we can."

I studied the space. There were absolutely no windows because of its location within the mountain, which was crucial. No risk of attacks from the exterior, nor concerns we'd be incinerated by the sun by accident, something I was all too familiar with after the first shutter malfunction we'd encountered at the Lair. According to Blāz, we no longer had to worry, but I was skeptical. Last thing I wanted was to wake up dead.

Obsidian motioned me toward a table. "Miklós and Huracān finalized the blueprint early this morning. We are officially a go."

I scanned the sheet of paper covering the entire table. From the looks of it, they'd thought of pretty much everything. Workout space, equipment, and physical therapy rooms, a two-story weapons training area, mess hall, sleeping quarters with attached bathrooms, recreation room, separate locker rooms for males and females, including shower stalls and changing areas. Plus a—

"You're putting a pool down here?"

Obsidian grinned. "Of course. Olympic-sized with eight lanes. Pivotal to training, don't you think?"

Not quite the training I had undergone, but hey, when there was no expense to be spared, I figured there was no need to go medieval.

"Trainees will reside in the dorm." Obsidian pointed to a section on the page. "We can house fifty trainees at a time."

"Fifty?"

The male peered over at me. "Michael's rather optimistic. I'd prefer we keep the classes to somewhere in the vicinity of twenty-five max. But the extra space will allow the graduates a place to reside."

As for the size of the classes, I had to agree with him. When it came to building a powerful force, it wasn't about quantity but rather quality.

"We've also added classrooms, offices, and three gun ranges."

"What are your thoughts?" I asked Mirakel, who was currently skimming the blueprint.

The male looked up, neon blue eyes locking on Obsidian. "How long will it take to get it completed?"

"We've opted to bring the trainees in now," Obsidian explained, "put them to work. Time will be determined by their efforts."

I chuckled. "Building character early. I like it."

"If all goes well, we'll be up and running in four months. At least the basics, anyway."

If it were up to Michael, I knew we would've chiseled that number down to four weeks, but the archangel was rather ambitious, wasn't he?

"I have five males and two females I'd like to bring in for the first class," Mirakel told Obsidian.

"Of course." Obsidian glanced at me. "I assume you've spoken with Michael?"

"Briefly." I had yet to follow up with my answer to the archangel's request, but that didn't mean I hadn't thought about it endlessly. In fact, I could think of nothing else, including the long list of duties I was shirking as the Alpha.

"Apollo and Amethyst plan to have a clinic put in down here. They'll address any trainee injuries or illnesses here. No one will be permitted into either residence under any circumstances."

"What about meals?" Mirakel inquired.

"They'll have the equivalent of a mess hall. The trainees will be responsible for everything. Shifts will be outlined so they're frequently alternating between cooking, cleaning, assisting in the clinic, as well as their required training classes. By the time they've completed the program, not only will they be capable of fighting alongside the *fiestreigh* and the Zenith, they'll be successful in taking care of themselves."

"What about recreation?" Blāz inquired. "Or is it all work and no play?"

"You sound a lot like Apollo," Obsidian teased. "And yes, they'll have a rec room. Can't expect them to be working twenty-four-seven."

As much as we would've liked to, no, it wasn't feasible. Everyone needed time to decompress, and I figured the schedules would be aligned accordingly.

"And when they've completed their training, where will they reside?" Blāz asked.

"I figure we'll decide that once we've got a good read on their abilities."

I agreed. No sense planning for the future until we knew what the future would look like.

"If you're in agreement," Obsidian said as he turned to face me, "I'll let Michael know we're ready to start assessing. Like you, I'm not simply accepting them into the program because they've been bred to be warriors. I'd appreciate your males' help in weeding out those who don't cut it."

"We'd be happy to," I noted.

It made sense that Obsidian and I had become friends all those years ago. We had quite a bit in common, not to mention respect for each other. In this case, it was going to be absolutely necessary because two alpha males were going to butt heads when it came to final decisions. There was no getting around it.

"Would you mind giving us a minute?" I told the others.

Once my males filed out of the space, I tucked my hands in my pockets and began walking the length of the enormous area that would likely be the most state-of-the-art training facility to have ever graced Earth.

"Michael came to see me a few weeks ago," I told Obsidian.

"I heard."

He peered back at the angel. "Did he happen to mention what we discussed?"

"No." Obsidian began walking beside me. "It's not my business, and I informed him as much. Told him if it's regarding vampires, he's to leave me out of it. If you choose to include me, I expect you'll come to me."

Another reason I respected the male so much.

"Is there something you'd like me to know? Perhaps regarding Acadia?"

That pulled me up short. As far as I knew, Acadia had yet to talk to Obsidian. Though we'd interacted every day since our initial discussion regarding us feeding only from one another, she hadn't yet mentioned speaking to Obsidian.

"I'm not sure whether you're aware that Acadia's been with me since we were first sent down here," Obsidian said, resuming his stroll. "Fifteen hundred years she's been with us."

"I'm aware," I confirmed. "Believe it or not, I've learned quite a bit about Acadia during my time in her presence. The question is, are you aware of who she is?"

"Regarding her position within the Fae?" Obsidian nodded. "Yes."

"Is she aware of it?"

"Not that I know of."

I figured as much, although I wasn't sure that was possible. Then again, there were a few anomalies regarding the stories of the Fae.

"From my understanding," I continued, "Fae are ruled solely by their queen."

"That is correct. Back before they were cast out, their

queen was responsible for the decisions affecting their race. They've never acknowledged a king, even if the female was mated."

"Which means, if the Fae are released from their servitude, she would move into the role, responsible for her race." Or what was left of them, anyway.

"Correct. She would be the sole ruler."

Which was not an issue as far as I was concerned. I had no desire to be the ruler of the Fae. I had enough on my plate. However, I did believe that it made things a bit easier between us because that was the case.

"What brings that up?" Obsidian inquired. "Them being released from their duties?"

Great. This was the part I had least looked forward to. "Michael's asked me to do something. In return, he'll free the Fae from their responsibilities to you."

Another nod from the enormous angel. "Makes sense he would do that."

"He's also asked that I pledge my loyalty to you," I said.

Obsidian frowned. "In return, he'll free the Fae?"

"No. That's a separate request. He merely asked that we align ourselves with you."

Obsidian stopped, crossed his arms over his chest, and stared back at me. "And what's your opinion on the matter?"

I peered just beyond the angel. "It's not a pledge I'm comfortable making. You're talking about the whole of my race." I cut my eyes to the male's face. "Now, I'll gladly fight alongside you, but it's imperative the vampire race stand alone. If I fall within your rule, they'll have absolutely no respect for me as their leader."

"You've always been a proud species." Obsidian grinned. "And I agree with you in that regard. Which is why I wish I'd known about this request before Michael made it." The male's dark eyebrows lowered, as did his voice. "Kaj, I'd be honored to have you at my side. I'm aware of Michael's concerns regarding what's coming. And while he believes the *amsouelots* are no longer in danger, I disagree. Lucifer's not one to back down, even if he does have his eye on a different prize. But I do fully agree we're stronger together." He motioned toward the facility laid out before us. "Hence my decision to move forward. There are many things we can learn from one another, as can those who'll be fighting when we're long gone."

Despite the fact we were immortal, my thinking was along the same lines as Obsidian's. Because of our responsibilities, it was only fair to assume we would be taken out at some point. Just hopefully not for a couple more millennia.

"It would be my honor to fight at your side, angel." I smirked. "You're one of the few I trust implicitly."

"So you'll move forward with me? Not behind me or in front. Beside. Together."

I nodded. "Under one condition."

"What's that?"

"Provided Acadia will have me, I fully intend to mate the female, and I'll expect the boundaries to be respected by your males."

"I thought that was a done deal."

"Not quite. Unlike you and the humans, vampires don't have predestined mates."

Obsidian nodded. "I'm all too familiar with *mielix zan*, Kaj. And I know you've imprinted on Acadia. I also know you've been holding back."

"True. But strong as I may be, I can't defy it for much longer. And the last thing I want is to put your males in danger, but that's what it'll come to if I fully bond with the female."

A dark rumble came up from Obsidian's chest. "Trust me, vampire. That's the last thing I want, too."

"I need to speak with Michael," I told him. "There's still the matter of his other request."

"Care to share that—"

A flutter of sound came from behind me, drawing Obsidian's attention.

"Well, speak of the devil," I muttered.

Damn archangel always had the worst timing.

MICHAEL

"Long time no see." My gaze scanned both males, and I knew instantly that they weren't happy to see me.

What was new? I'd stopped expecting a warm welcome a dozen or so centuries back.

"My ears were burning," I told the males. "Figured I'd drop in, see what's going on."

While they sized me up, probably trying to determine how quickly they could get me back to Heaven, I turned to admire the beginnings of the new facility. Impressive. They'd made it much further than I'd expected, considering neither male had gotten back with me after my last conversations with them—Obsidian regarding my permanent residence here with them, Kaj regarding resurrecting the original vampire.

Based on the way they had their heads together now, I understood why.

"I'm going to assume we've come to an agreement," I told Obsidian.

"To a degree, yes. I'm moving forward with the training facility as we discussed. Although I'll only allow a minimal number of spots."

I had figured as much. I'd tossed out a number to get the male's head working, not because I truly expected the hands-on experience for fifty-plus angels. However, it did leave the ball in Obsidian's court, right where I had lobbed it.

"And the vampires?" I cut my gaze to Kaj. "Are you on board?"

"Mostly."

My nose curled. I was not a fan of that word. "Which part? Resurrecting the original vampire?"

"Huh?" Obsidian pulled off the dark shades that shielded his eyes, his keen gaze bouncing from Kaj to me, then back. "What the hell's he talking about?"

Chuckling, I cocked my head. "Didn't catch him up all the way, huh?"

The vampire's black eyebrows dipped low. "I hadn't gotten to it yet."

More like Kaj was putting off the inevitable.

I waved a hand in their direction. "Feel free to get him up to speed now."

"Original vampire? Khari?"

"One and the same," I called out as I strolled toward the empty space, pretending to admire their efforts.

A bit of grumbling sounded behind me, and I took that to mean Kaj hadn't intended to share the details with Obsidian. At least not yet. Probably had to do with the fact the human vessel the ancient male vampire was currently hitching a ride in was Obsidian's mate's brother. Or at least they believed him to be related. Although he wasn't. Semantics and all that.

While Kaj explained to Obsidian, I strolled through the vast space they'd dedicated to training. I'd known putting Obsidian in charge would be the right move. I could practically see the angels and vampires going toe to toe here, getting the hands-on experience necessary to fight alongside the most powerful beings in the known universe. Misplaced Halos, they were called. Honestly, I liked the term, though I couldn't say why. Perhaps that was what they could call this place.

"Are you shitting me?" Obsidian snarled.

I smiled to myself, ensuring the male did not see me. No sense poking the beast. Or was it bear?

No matter.

"My female's brother? He's the human host to the original vampire?"

Yep. Obsidian was handling the news about as well as Kaj had. No surprise there.

But unlike Kaj, I knew what was coming from Obsidian next.

Wait for it.

Three...

Two...

"You fucking knew she was my mate. And you put the vampire in her twin? What the fuck were you thinking?"

Spinning around, I kept my grin in place. "Technically, he's not her twin. They weren't even conceived by the same male and female."

Obsidian's brows slammed down. "What did you say?"

"I did what was necessary to protect the vampires. I won't apologize for it."

"So you manipulated humans?"

"In my defense, they're relatively easy to manipulate. Plus, the little boy had been abandoned by his birth mother. I merely gave him a loving home."

Although now that I thought about it, Oliver Calazans had never seemed all that happy. Perhaps I'd overestimated the family cohesiveness.

"Penelope's parents agreed to raise them as twins. They knew nothing of Khari." It still amazed me what humans were willing to do for money. No questions asked. And Penelope's greedy parents had been no exception.

"And what? You just want to pop him out of the human and ... what, Michael? How the hell do you resurrect an ancient vampire who's been riding shotgun in humans for centuries?"

Try millennia, I thought, but kept that one to myself. No sense adding to the tension.

"It gets better," Kaj groused. "Khari is to mate my daughter."

Obsidian threw up his arms and began to pace, huffing as he did. "This is bullshit, Michael. You've outdone yourself. Just when I thought you couldn't get any more underhanded than you already were."

I knew there was no reasoning with Obsidian. Telling the male that this was the only way I'd seen to keep the race alive would only be met with argument. And I didn't necessarily blame him. I had utilized various human vessels over the millennia, keeping Khari safe. And yes, I'd long ago defied the rules and identified who Obsidian's *amsouelot* was. I had bided my time, awaiting her birth, and the moment I'd learned of her existence, I'd done what I had to do to ensure Obsidian's path would eventually cross with Khari's.

Would I ever tell Obsidian as much? Nope. Nuh-uh. I had enough to atone for as it was. Did I think my deceit had contributed to the leak of the *amsouelots'* names? No. Of that much I was certain. However, I had yet to figure out who was behind it, but I wasn't giving up. Not until I nailed that bastard to the wall.

Ew. Bad turn of phrase. Humans and their strange idioms.

"What happens to Oliver when you extract the vampire?" Kaj inquired. "Will he have any memories of the first twenty-eight years of his life?"

"No." That part I felt bad about, but it couldn't be helped.

"So Khari will have those memories?" Obsidian asked.

"Correct."

"Fucking fantastic."

"I thought so," I said before I realized that was sarcasm.

More hands thrown in the air and finally Obsidian stormed out.

"That went well," Kaj grumbled.

"You were waiting in an effort to avoid that," I mused.

"It definitely could've been handled better, yes."

Maybe.

"Do you have an answer for me on the other?" I inquired, figuring since I had Kaj's attention, I might as well find out where we stood on the other issues.

"You're not going to like what I have to tell you."

Probably not, but I was all too familiar with that, too. It was rare that I ever got my way.

Not for lack of trying, mind you.

13

KAJ

After filling Michael in on my decision to support Obsidian as an equal, rather than declare to march to the beat of their drum, I had excused myself. Of course, the archangel had given me shit about my final decision on the original vampire, and I had not so kindly told him to shove it for a little while longer. As much as I wanted to resolve the problems for all species in one day, I knew it wasn't possible.

However, there was one situation I was prepared to resolve, and I knew I couldn't wait any longer. I'd spent far too many days sleeping alone when all I wanted was to feel Acadia pressed up to me through the daylight hours. Because she hadn't yet had the conversation with Obsidian that we'd discussed previously, I had to believe we weren't on the same page.

It was time we figured it out.

"*Phaal*, I think we might have a problem."

I spun around to face Huracān, who'd come jogging after me the moment I stepped into the Lair. "What?"

"It's ... Mirakel."

I narrowed my eyes, waiting for the male to continue. The concern on Huracān's face had me forgetting my previous plans of confronting Acadia in lieu of what was more pressing.

"Where is he?"

"The workout room."

Not sure how that could possibly be a problem, I propped my fists on my hips and waited for Huracān to get on with it.

"You should..." The male canted his head toward the back of the mansion. "Probably just need to see this for yourself."

I followed Huracān through the Lair, which was surprisingly busy. There were three *heurosp* in the kitchen, preparing what looked to be the morning meal, another who was tending to the floors, as well as Blāz and Kidel, who were sitting at the dining room table, fingers flying over their laptop keyboards as though they were in a race to finish first. No one looked up or paid us any mind as we strolled through to the door leading to the stairs that would take us down to the underground rooms. No sooner had we stepped into the concrete tunnel than I heard the sound. Loud clanks mixed with heavy grunts lured us in the direction of the workout room. When we got to the door, I stopped suddenly.

Mirakel was standing in the center of the space, a bar weighed down with God knew how many pounds in his hands. Eight hundred? Nine, maybe? He hefted it high in the air, held it there, then let it fall to the ground. Mirakel looked like he was trying out for the strongest male contest. And he was aiming to be the winner by a mile. I figured beneath that black mat, there was a sinkhole emerging.

Huracān nodded me inside but remained in the hall.

"Mirakel?"

The male's neon blue eyes shot toward me, chest heaving. He looked a little crazed, so I kept a safe distance.

"What's going on?" I prompted.

Mirakel shook his head.

"Something's bothering you." I motioned toward the weight on the floor. "Otherwise, you wouldn't be lifting the equivalent of an SUV."

As though cued, Mirakel's shoulders slumped, defeat overriding determination as he began studying the floor as though it held all the answers he was seeking.

I had no idea what to say or do, but I figured time was the answer, so I remained where I was, taking in the familiar space I'd spent too much time in lately.

We remained like that for a long moment before Mirakel went to his knees, dropping his head.

Oh, boy.

"I have failed you once more, *Phaal*."

Not by a long shot, I thought, but kept my mouth shut. No matter how often I told Mirakel as much, the male never seemed to take it to heart. As strong and powerful as Mirakel was, there was a vulnerability to him. It was due to his need to prove his worth to those he considered his superiors. Which, to Mirakel, was everyone he encountered. His view of himself was not the same as those who cared for him, but we'd long ago learned that dealing with Mirakel required patience and extreme care.

"Talk to me," I urged.

It was obvious something was bothering him, and I wanted to get to the bottom of it. For the past couple of weeks,

I'd noticed the tension in his shoulders, as though he was bearing a weight he wasn't strong enough to carry. Which was saying something considering the amount of weight he was capable of lifting.

"I have failed you," he repeated, his voice quivering with what was either anger or disappointment, I wasn't sure.

"What makes you think that?"

"I didn't mean for it to happen, *Phaal*. But I could've handled it better."

Okay, so now I was starting to worry.

"I have imprinted upon the female," Mirakel said softly. "Full-on *mielix zan*."

Only because I respected the seriousness in Mirakel's tone did I keep a straight face. What I wanted to do was congratulate the male, but I suspected that wasn't what the moment warranted. Suspecting I already knew the answer, I asked anyway. "Which female?"

"Briony. The Fae I've been feeding from."

Maybe congratulations weren't in order. It was one thing for a vampire to find his equal within the race. Something else entirely for a cross-species mating. Not that there was anything wrong with it, aside from the fact the Fae were, for all intents and purposes, incapable of mating because of their duties to the *fiestreigh*.

"And how do you wish to proceed?" I knew bonding with a female wasn't always simple. Especially not for vampires. Unlike angels, there were no destinies, no aligned souls. No, we were more animalistic in nature when it came to mating. And for us, it wasn't always a guarantee that the female would choose us. And when they didn't ... put it this way, life was lackluster at best.

"I wish not to scare her," Mirakel said softly.

"What makes you think you will?"

"I want her too much."

I smiled but kept it to myself. I understood that all too well. I'd been fighting my true nature for months now. I had yet to allow my inner beast free to bond with the female I desired.

It made perfect sense that Mirakel was working himself to exhaustion, making it impossible for him to claim the female as he wanted. It wasn't a foolproof plan, but it would buy him some time.

"Does the female know?"

Mirakel shook his head.

She would soon enough. Mirakel would be physically unable to feed from another without getting hostile. Biology be damned, once a male vampire underwent *mielix zan*, he would refrain from taking blood until it killed him, unless the blood source was the female with whom he'd imprinted.

Of course, it was possible. I had managed for those few weeks after the attack. Not ideal by any means, but doable. Especially when one was doing it to protect the one he loved.

"What do you need from me?" I asked, wanting to ensure the male understood I was here to help in any way I could.

"Nothing, *Phaal*. I will handle this, I assure you. But I must apologize for failing you."

I wanted to roll my eyes but I refrained. Mirakel was one of those pure souls, grateful for everything he'd been given and unwilling to accept that no one expected him to be perfect. His apologies weren't necessary, and they never failed to humble me, remind me of how far he had come from the boy he'd been when I found him all those years ago.

"You have not failed me, Mirakel. You could never. You are one of the strongest males I know. I trust that you'll come to me if you need my help."

He nodded.

"I'm going to Angel Central. To see Acadia. I'll return shortly. Stay here for now."

"Of course, *phaal*."

With a resigned sigh, I headed back toward the main floor of the Lair. I found Huracān pacing in what had once been a parlor and was now converted to an entertainment space complete with television mounted on the wall, dartboard, poker table. All the things the males requested for their downtime.

"What's going on?" Huracān asked, coming to an abrupt halt.

"*Mielix zan.*"

"Oh, shit." Huracān's eyes went wide. "Who?"

"Fae. Briony."

"Shall I bring her here?" the male offered.

I grinned. "If only it were that easy."

I went on to explain the Fae's role within the angel hierarchy.

"I'll talk to Obsidian," I told Huracān. "See how he wishes to handle this."

With a sigh, I resumed my original plan to go to Angel Central. I should've expected I would gain a travel companion, but Michael's appearance gave my heart a jolt, nonetheless.

"What do you want, archangel?" I snarled, continuing to march through the tunnels.

"It's my understanding you have a male who has imprinted upon a Fae."

"Miss nothing, do you?"

"Not if I can help it, no." Michael grinned, making time at my side. "You have the ability to free them, Kaj."

Yes, I knew that. But at what cost? I knew Michael didn't merely wish to bring the original vampire back for shits and giggles. There was an underlying reason, but for the life of me, I couldn't figure out what it could possibly be.

"I've already told you," Michael stated.

I shook my head. "Anyone ever tell you it's impolite to read minds?"

"Then why would I be given the ability?" He sounded sincerely perplexed.

"I don't have time for this conversation, Michael. I've got other things to tend to right now."

"I have it on good authority another of your males will imprint upon a Fae."

That was enough to get my attention. I stopped, head hanging as I pressed my hands to my hips. I took several deep breaths, then turned to face the archangel.

"Did you ever consider what will happen to the angels if the Fae are unable to feed them?"

Michael's brown-silver gaze shifted over my face. "I have those who are willing to support the war."

I waited for him to elaborate, because surely there was more to it.

"Angels," Michael specified. "In Heaven. Females and males who are willing to be called upon. It was my backup plan in the event my father chose to eliminate the Fae."

Those words drew a dark rumble from my chest, and I found myself stepping up to the archangel. The male wasn't quite as big as Obsidian, but he still had an inch or two on me. Of course, size didn't matter all that much considering the male could simply smite me if he so chose.

"Tempting," Michael said with a smirk, but it dropped quickly. "You have the ability to save their race, Kaj."

"I already told you, I'll align my alliance with the angels, but I won't vow to follow them. You of all people should understand why I can't."

Michael waved him off. "We're past that. You've told me your intentions. I'll respect them. As for the original vampire?"

I still didn't know where I stood on that. Probably wouldn't have been such a big deal except for the fact my daughter—

"He's already imprinted on her," Michael said, interrupting my thoughts. "If that matters to you."

Narrowing my eyes, I took a step back. "You're telling me Oliver Calazans and Bijou...?"

Michael shook his head. "No. The male you've interacted with is not the human. That's Khari. Once he emerges, you'll see what I mean."

"And where exactly does Khari go if the two are separated?"

"His body's been preserved. I'll take you to it."

Kaj's eyebrows shot skyward. "Here? On Earth?"

"Of course."

Oh, yes, of course. As if all this was just your average, everyday event. Resurrecting an ancient vampire who'd spent centuries encased in human vessels. No biggie.

I shook my head. "I have to speak with Obsidian. He deserves to know my intentions."

Michael seemed pleased to hear this.

"Not that I've made up my mind," I clarified.

That smile fell instantly. "He needs time to train, Kaj."

Confused, I narrowed my eyes on the archangel. "Who?"

"Khari?"

"For what?"

"For what's coming," the archangel said firmly.

"Which is?"

"Not for me to disclose."

Of course not. The male and his fucking secrets.

I sighed, then decided to ask the one question that had

been plaguing me. "And what happens to me when Khari comes back? I assume he'll take the role as Alpha."

"That is his role. The original vampire was created for that purpose." Michael's eyes narrowed. "Why? Do you want the job?"

Maybe. "Not really."

Michael grinned. "It's yours to have if you wish to fill those shoes, Kaj. Or you can step aside and let Khari assume his place."

I wasn't sure how I felt about that. Not that I'd done a damn thing to help the race since I'd assumed responsibility for them. But that didn't mean I wanted to step aside.

"It's not what you were meant for," Michael stated. "As you are now, you'll make a mediocre Alpha. But only because your heart's not in it."

How the archangel knew that, I wasn't sure. However, he had nailed it. No matter how hard I tried, I couldn't make myself fit into that role.

"Is that why it's so important to resurrect him?"

"No. It's imperative because he has a destiny to fulfill."

"Which means?"

Michael's eyes were locked on mine. "That's not for me to impart, vampire."

Of course not. That would be too fucking easy.

"I need time," I huffed, pivoting to resume my trek to Angel Central.

The voice that called out from behind me was deeper, as though spoken from a great distance. "I can give you no more time."

Had it not been for the fact he sounded remorseful, I wouldn't have stopped.

"While it is your choice, Kaj, there are devastating repercussions should you decline. Just know that without him, the vampires will not survive. Nor will the Fae."

Before I could ask what the fuck that meant, the archangel vanished in a flutter of wings.

Son of a bitch.

OBSIDIAN

I paced the hall beneath the mansion.

I would've been pacing my private quarters, but the last thing I wanted was to burden my *ereswa* with this bullshit. I knew Penelope would've gladly listened to me, likely offered good advice on how to handle, but I didn't want to lay this shit on her. Not until I had no other option. Namely because, for her, this would be personal. After all, the fucking original vampire was currently riding shotgun in Oliver Calazans.

What.

The.

Ever-loving.

Fuck.

How the hell did I tell Penelope that the male she believed was her brother was actually not related to her, but instead, the vessel for the original vampire, manipulated by Michael? No matter which way I twisted and turned the information, I couldn't make sense of the situation. Why Oliver? And why now?

The door to the tunnels opened, drawing my attention. I came to a stop, watching as Kaj appeared, looking as disconcerted as I felt.

"I was about to come look for you," I told him.

"Looks like I did the work for you." Kaj took a deep breath, exhaled heavily. "Mind if we find somewhere private to talk?"

"Office on the main floor? Or third-floor conference room?"

"Whichever has better booze," the vampire replied.

"Main floor it is."

As we fell into step together, I noticed the tension in Kaj's shoulders. "What's on your mind, vampire?"

"Every damn thing."

I knew the feeling. For the past few weeks, it seemed as though the world had gone topsy-turvy. Between the healers arriving, Eevuhl's intrusion, Michael inhabiting my body, Ari'el being born, Winnie leaving the mansion, Kaj moving in next door, the training center getting underway ... and now this shit with the original vampire, I felt like the weight of the world was now riding on my shoulders and my thighs were weakening from the pressure. Before long, I expected to be trying to dig myself out of a hole I'd unknowingly dredged in my wake.

From the looks of it, Kaj was feeling the same.

We walked side by side, neither of us speaking, though the unspoken words were louder than our footsteps.

Kaj was the one to break the silence when we passed the area where we were currently keeping Taayin. "I meant to ask, how's the male doing?"

Swallowing past the lump in my throat, I grunted. "Not well. We're still keeping him sedated, but Apollo's opposed to the continued treatment."

"I can't imagine it's healthy. But if it's in his best interest..."

Yeah, I wasn't so sure it was anymore. I'd originally agreed because I thought for sure we would find Asmia, bring her home, and all would be set to rights in Taayin's world. That hadn't been the case. Instead, we had lost her trail, and no matter our efforts, we were no closer to finding her than the day she disappeared. I couldn't help thinking Taayin would've found Asmia by now if we'd allowed him to beat down doors. Problem was, how much destruction would he leave in his wake? Enough to have us sent back to Heaven? It was highly likely. Which meant I really didn't have much of a choice.

The only positive in the whole thing had been Michael tethering Taayin's soul with Asmia's. It hadn't been an easy request to make, but it had been necessary. And because the archangel performed the miracle to ensure Asmia couldn't be claimed as a demon's mate—a convoluted and interesting twist because her soul was actually not in Heaven nor Hell—I now owed Michael. And in return, what did the archangel want? Oh, nothing much. Just to park his happy ass in the mansion for all of eternity and ride out the rest of our days alongside us.

Yep. That was the payment I had agreed to even though Michael had yet to take me up on it, and then shit like the original vampire popped up and I was once again doubting my decision.

Mostly.

"How're the *fiestreigh* coming with the updated security?" Kaj asked as he led the way up the twisting stairs to the main floor.

"More cameras have been installed, the new wall's been started, and the *dhira* has been reinforced." There were still additional measures I wanted to put in place, but I figured we could only tackle one thing at a time.

"Any news on whether Eevuhl's actually dead?"

That was the million-dollar question. As far as we knew, the demon was eliminated. But considering he'd simply shriveled up and vanished, there was still the possibility Lucifer had called him home in time to keep him alive.

"Unfortunately, we won't know. He'll either reappear somewhere or he won't."

I prayed for the latter. There were still two more we had to deal with—Aguhnee and Mizuhree—and Lucifer only knew where those two demons were and what they were up to.

Kaj peered back at me as we headed down the hall. "You think that's what Michael's worried about? Why he's adamant we focus on building our armies?"

Once inside the office, I closed the door, then proceeded toward the decanter on the table near the window. "I think Eevuhl's the least of his worries."

"So why the urgency? Why's he demanding I resurrect Khari? He said I have no more time to decide."

After pouring two fingers in each glass, I passed one over to my friend.

"Out of curiosity, what's holding you back?"

Kaj shrugged. "The unknown. Until a few weeks ago, I didn't know the original vampire still lived. Now he wants me to resurrect him."

"That's Michael for you." Perhaps I'd merely gotten used to the archangel's urgent demands. "But if it's any consolation, I think he has good intentions in delaying his requests. Bites him in the ass in the end, but I do believe he attempts to find other avenues if at all possible."

Kaj tossed back his drink, then strolled over to pour another. "And you're on board with it? We have no idea what it'll do to Penelope's brother."

"I'm on board with nothing," I told Kaj. "Hell, I'm only learning of this now. As for Oliver ... as much as I want to dig deep into that one, I cannot. I'm bound by my faith when it comes to humans, Kaj. I can only trust God's plan where they're concerned."

"Even with an archangel interfering?"

I nodded. As much as I didn't like what Michael had sprung on us, it wasn't my place to intervene. Although Oliver Calazans was believed to be Penelope's twin brother, it appeared he was not. And more importantly, he was still human, which meant I had no say in what happened to him.

Not that I was eager to share that with Penelope.

"Michael preserved Khari's body. Said he can take me to it."

I could hear Kaj's concern. "But...?"

"If we're going to do this, I'd prefer it be here. Where we can control the outcome."

"So you've decided to go through with it?"

Kaj turned to face me. "I fear my decision's selfish in nature, Obsidian."

"This is the favor, huh? The one where he'll release the Fae if you follow through?"

"Never easy, is it?"

Of course not.

I considered what this meant for all of us. Without the Fae to provide blood, we would be forced to seek an outside source. But more importantly, without the ability to keep us in His sight, it was possible God would recall us to Heaven.

"Michael has another option for your blood source," Kaj added, as though reading my mind.

"What might that be?"

Kaj took another long drink. "Something about angels in Heaven who are willing to be called upon."

Great. Another one of Michael's creations. If I had to guess, those were the offspring who hadn't been worthy of the fight.

So rather than be relegated to the *fiestreigh*, Michael had raised them to support the cause in other ways.

Seemed no matter how much I wanted to put my faith in Michael, the male always had an agenda that had me wavering in my viewpoint.

"He wouldn't elaborate," Kaj continued, "but he said if I do not follow through with this, the vampires would be eliminated. As would the Fae."

"Then it seems rather simple to me," I said as I tossed that information around.

"Does it?" Kaj sighed, poured another drink. "Because I'm confused as fuck."

I set my glass on the desk, then moved over to Kaj. I placed a firm hand on the male's shoulder.

"Together, we've got this, Kaj. Just know that I'm behind you. You risked your life for me and mine. I owe you. So whatever you decide, just know I've got your back."

"Even if it changes everything?"

I grinned. "Ever think maybe it's time for a change, Kaj?"

Based on the vampire's expression, it was a question he'd been pondering as well.

14

JANE

"Ah, good, you're awake."

I turned my head toward the voice, forcing my groggy eyes to remain open as the older nurse moved toward me.

"I just came to check on you before I leave for the evening," Trudy noted, gently closing the door behind her. "Are you feeling any better, Jane?"

That was what they'd taken to calling me. Jane. I wasn't sure where it came from or why, and I'd been too out of it to really care. Maybe my name really was Jane.

"Jane?"

A shrug was all I could muster. It had been a painful few days with one setback after another, the last of which was credited to my body's ill response to the pain medication they'd administered. After spending nearly twenty-four hours retching, I was too weak to do much of anything.

The older nurse smiled down at me. "It'll get better. I promise."

It was then I realized tears were trickling down my cheeks. I wasn't sure what caused them, though it could've been just about anything. After all, I was in a hospital, all alone, no family, no friends, no real name. I still had no idea who I was or where I came from, not even where I was going. When I really started thinking about it, my mind filled with dread at the thought of leaving this hospital and going out into the world.

"Shh." Trudy's gentle hand landed on my forearm. "You're safe here, Jane."

Safe? I wasn't sure I knew the meaning of that word. Had I been in danger before? Despite all the efforts to find a relative, no one seemed to be looking for me. Which begged the question, how had I been injured?

Trudy turned toward the rolling table at the head of the bed, grabbed a small white pad of paper and a pen. She jotted something down, then set it on the table that extended over the bed in front of me.

"That's my phone number. If you find you need someone to talk to, feel free to call me." The older female smiled. "It's just me and my cat, Gertrude, at the house, so you won't be disturbing anyone if you call."

I peered down at the neat handwriting, the numbers, and the dashes. I knew how to read, so at least I hadn't lost all my memory functions. Every time I opened my eyes and became aware of my new surroundings, I held out hope that my memories would return, that I would come to learn some things about myself. Perhaps I had a family, a mate, children. Maybe even a cat like Trudy had.

And every time I opened my eyes, I continued to be disappointed.

"All right, I'll leave you be. Remember, if you need anything..."

"Thank you," I managed, my voice but a rough whisper.

Another pat on my arm and then the kind female was leaving the room, closing the door behind her once more.

I didn't bother turning on the television. I had no interest in watching the fake families on television laugh or hearing about the gruesome things that humans were doing to one another. Seemed every time I caught a glimpse of the news, didn't matter if it was day or night, there was always something horrible taking place. Not necessarily where I was, but across this vast world. I couldn't help but wonder if I'd succumbed to violence as well. Was that how I ended up here? Someone had purposely harmed me? Based on the wounds I'd endured, the hospital staff seemed to believe that was the case. Evidently, so many broken bones and contusions weren't normal unless brought on by violence.

Of course, I couldn't answer any of the questions I'd been asked. Nurses, doctors, police officers. They'd all interrogated me numerous times, as though they were desperate to unearth my memories. And every time, I came up empty. My head seemed to be a big, black void of nothingness. As though I hadn't existed before I was brought here.

Now I was tired. Not at all eager for another dawn to come, for more questions my brain couldn't answer. It was easier to remain in the bleak fog that surrounded my mind, thanks to the medications they were pumping into me. Now that they'd purged the drug I'd reacted badly to, perhaps I could sleep.

As I closed my eyes and settled against the lumpy mattress, I blocked out all thought and attempted to focus on what the future held for me.

Unfortunately, that seemed as bleak and cold as the room I currently resided in.

KAJ

Too bad liquor didn't have the same effect on vampires that it did on humans.

Sure, it was a bit of a mood stabilizer, offering a semblance of relaxation, but I could've consumed the entire bottle and would've felt no better. Or worse, for that matter.

Granted, the conversation with Obsidian had helped. To know the male was behind my decision helped. Not in making it, but in knowing I would have support either way. Problem was, I knew there was only one answer, and yes, if we moved forward, this would change everything. Resurrecting the original vampire would ensure my race's survival, so Michael said, which was really the only reason behind following through, wasn't it?

Should've been, but I continued to think about the Fae. Releasing them from their servitude was equally important to me. The female I loved would be forever free, and that was honestly the only thing I could focus on. More so than knowing by bringing Khari back, I was ultimately sealing my daughter's fate. I tried not to think about the fact I'd considered another race above my own, but it was impossible to deny. The question was: how long could I put it off? There was a lot at stake, and I wasn't about to rush something like this.

One day at a time, I figured. When Michael got fed up, I suspected he'd let me know.

After leaving Obsidian, I headed up to the second floor, making my way to Acadia's room. Down below, I could hear the *heurosp* working away, tending to chores, making meals, keeping everything in order. Across the way, there was laughter coming from the game room, pool balls clacking, some wagers being made. Everything seemed almost ... normal.

It wasn't until I stepped up to Acadia's door that I realized there had been no echo of pain in my chest for the past week. Despite the fact she had yet to speak with Obsidian, I had to assume Acadia had abided by my request and had refrained from feeding the males in the mansion. Considering I'd fed from her daily—though we'd kept it completely civilized—I wondered if perhaps I'd taken more than I should have, leaving it impossible for her to provide to others.

I rapped my knuckles on the wood.

No answer.

I could feel her inside the space, so I let my senses scan within until I located her. Initially, I'd thought to do so as reassurance she was all right. When I heard the sound of water falling, I knew she was in the shower and that had my hand turning the knob, stepping inside.

Steam drifted from the bathroom along with the scent of cherry blossoms.

"Acadia?" I said softly when I neared the doorway.

I caught sight of her behind the clear glass wall that separated the shower from the rest of the space. It reminded me of the bathroom I'd used when I'd been healing, the one I'd had my first shower with her in. There had been no glass walls in

NICOLE EDWARDS

that one, but the view was still the same for me. And the reaction I had to seeing her was the same as it had always been. I was instantly hard, my body aching for hers.

I took the opportunity to admire her beautiful form, all those graceful curves. She was mesmerizing, her hair wet, clinging to her as it hung down to her hips.

And she was watching me as she stood there, her soapy hand sliding over her breast.

"Invite me in, *balisra*." I wasn't sure I'd said the words aloud as much as thought them, but the heat I saw flash in her amethyst eyes told me she'd heard me all the same.

"Please join me, *phaal*."

I stared back at her, shocked to hear her refer to me in that manner. I was not her Alpha, but she'd welcomed me as such.

The polite thing to do would've been to wait for her to finish, but I didn't want to wait. Not another minute. Hell, not another second. It had felt like an eternity since I'd held my female in my arms, and I was desperate to feel her against me.

While she continued to run her hands over her slick skin, I tugged my T-shirt over my head, let it fall to the floor. I toed off my boots, leaving them behind. One step forward, I began unbuttoning my jeans. Another and I was lowering the zipper. By the time I'd shed my clothes, I had approached the side of the shower, the glass partition no longer separating us.

Yet I waited.

Acadia's gaze slid over me, my body responding to the approval I saw in her eyes.

Mine.

"Yours," Acadia said softly, and again, I didn't know if I'd spoken aloud or projected the word.

Didn't matter.

Time seemed to slow as I took one step, then another, eliminating the distance between us. When I was within arm's reach, Acadia turned to face me, the spray of water slicking her hair back from her face.

"You are the most beautiful creature I've ever seen," I told her.

Her eyes glittered the way I'd come to love.

Whereas time had slowed when I approached, the moment my skin met hers, everything else faded, and time became nonexistent. The only thing that mattered in that moment was Acadia in my arms. Though the last time I'd held her, when we'd been in the hot tub, I had refrained. I was past that point now, unable to hold back anymore.

I pulled her into me, banding one arm around her waist, cupping the back of her head with the other, and bringing her mouth closer. I hovered there, my lips barely grazing hers. I was waiting for her to make the first move, needed her to eliminate that last breath between us. When she did, when Acadia's soft lips pressed to mine, her breasts crushing to my chest, my world splintered into fragments of light, the adrenaline flooding my veins.

All the time we'd wasted up to now coalesced into a single breath as I pinned her to the glass wall, crushing my lips to hers. Acadia's tongue fought with mine as I tried to inhale her, needing to feel her deep under my skin.

I slid my hands over her soft, smooth curves until I was cupping her ass. Keeping her trapped between my body and the glass, I lifted her off her feet. When her arms circled my neck, her mouth melding perfectly with mine, I shifted my hips so that my cock was pressed intimately between her thighs. Heaven Almighty, this was right where I wanted to be, her in my arms, warm and wet. If I could've frozen this moment in time, I would've done so.

"I need to be inside you," I rasped.

Acadia whimpered, a sound I knew to be approval of my understated request.

I lowered her onto me, pushing forward until my cock was buried as deep as her willing body would allow. I held her then, just like that, our bodies intimately joined in more ways than one. And I retracted my earlier statement. *This* was the moment I would freeze in time. It was both heaven and hell, the need building to impossible proportions.

No words were spoken, yet there was a wealth of conversation transpiring. So many things unsaid, so much emotion. It had been in a shower long ago when I'd first realized what she meant to me. A completely innocent encounter that had gotten out of hand. That had been the pivotal point for us, everything that followed building to this moment.

As much as I wanted to take her like that, slick-footed beneath the water, I feared the beast within would lose traction, so I decided to relocate. With her impaled on my cock, soap and water slicking her skin, I took her into the bedroom, gently eased her down to the mattress, not caring that I'd left the water running or that we were both soaking wet. I took care of the water, shutting it off with my mind, then willed the fireplace to come to life, providing warmth though I knew it wouldn't be necessary. The passion our bodies would generate would be enough to heat the entire mansion.

My heart took over, my need to dominate her overwhelming. It would be so easy for me to claim her once and for all. Once I did, our lives would forever be altered, and I wondered if she understood what that meant. It would forever tie me to her. My devotion would be unwavering. Nothing could come between me and my need for her. The only way she could be rid of me would be to send me far, far away or take my life. Otherwise, I would belong solely to her, my days dedicated to protecting and loving her.

I pulled back, staring down into her eyes, wanting Acadia to see my intention.

"Not yet, Kaj," she whispered, her beautiful eyes bouncing over my face. "For now, let's just have this."

It wasn't easy, but I managed to ignore the sharp pinch in my chest. I'd been holding off for her, and I would continue to do so for as long as she needed. Didn't mean I wasn't ready.

I growled low in my throat as my hips shifted back, then pitched forward, driving me deep inside her. I held her gaze for as long as I could, then tucked my head against her shoulder, the bed rocking with my momentum. My breath locked in my throat as sheer ecstasy consumed me, her body clutching me tightly. I slipped into her mind as I worked us both toward release, needing the connection, to feel what she was feeling.

It was then I noticed the tension she was attempting to hide, the fear of what would become of her once our mating was complete, but she was willing because she wanted me as much as I wanted her.

And it was her fear that helped me understand. I refrained from unleashing on her, held that part of myself back. It was inevitable, I knew. I would claim her as mine, but not until she knew I would move both Heaven and Earth for her.

"Kaj?"

I shook my head.

"I'm sorry..."

"Don't," I whispered against her ear. "Do not apologize, *balisra*."

I sensed her retreat. Not physically, because we were still joined. I was still moving inside her. Emotionally, Acadia shielded herself from me.

I lifted my head again, stared down at her. I found her hands, twined our fingers, and pinned her to the bed beneath me.

"Do not do that," I rumbled, holding her stare. "Do not retreat from me."

My hips began moving in earnest, driving forward, filling her as our gazes held. With our palms clasped, I opened myself to her, giving her full access to all that I was, letting her see into my mind, something that was now otherwise shielded from all.

Acadia inhaled sharply, her back bowing as my power flowed through our joined hands, her body absorbing the energy. I drove her to her first climax shortly thereafter, then rode the wave with her. As I stared down at the most beautiful female to have ever lived, I gave myself over to her.

"Kaj!"

"Come for me again, *balisra*." I pounded into her, the bed rocking into the wall, the pictures rattling.

And when I came, I threw my head back and roared, the sound bouncing off the rafters, rattling the chandelier overhead.

ACADIA

As I lay in Kaj's arms, I mulled over what I'd seen in his mind while we'd been joined so intimately. I wasn't sure whether he realized I'd been able to read his thoughts in that moment, but I had.

There was so much he was dealing with, all of it over-whelming even from a distance. He was worried about his males, Mirakel especially. But also Bijou, her request to move into the Lair, his refusal to allow her. And then there was the decision he was plagued with. That one had tripped me up momentarily. Whether he meant for me to find out, I was aware that he'd been given the ability to free the Fae from our servitude. Michael simply wished for him to bring forth the original vampire, and he would release me and my brothers and sisters.

I also knew he was going to go through with it. For me.

There was no denying the hope that flared in my chest. The thought of being free ... finally. I'd long ago stopped believing it was a possibility, giving in to the existence forced upon me. Now ... could it really happen? Could I be free to live as I wanted to? And if so, what exactly did that mean?

"What's on your mind, *balisra*?"

"You can't do it for me," I said softly, rubbing my hand over his arm where it was tucked around my chest.

"I can do anything for you." His voice rasped close to my ear. "And I will, Acadia."

It pained me to know he would base such a huge decision on doing what was right by me. As much as I wanted to be free, I would never ask so much from him.

"Are you hurt that I rejected you?" I asked because I had to know.

"I understand your reasons." His arm shifted, pulling me in closer. "And I vow to do right by you. I am yours, regardless. From here until eternity."

But I'd seen the desire in his eyes, the need to claim me. I'd almost given in, but something had held me back. Not some-thing. Me. I was holding myself back.

"I can't," I admitted. "Not until I know I can give you all I am in return."

Which meant I had to confront Obsidian, tell him what my intentions were. What that meant for my position within the *fiestreigh*. But before I could do that, I had to come to terms with what the repercussions might be.

"I get it. I do."

I pressed back against him, absorbing his warmth, letting it infuse me. I had missed this, the two of us close like this. Since his return to the mansion all those months ago, the sex had been a means of satisfying us both. This ... this was more, and I cherished this moment.

"Have you spoken to Obsidian?" he asked.

"I have not," I admitted, hating that I'd avoided him. "But I'm holding to my vow. I have fed no other since that day."

As for how long I could continue to do so, that wasn't known. I had a responsibility to the *fiestreigh*, and I took my duties seriously. If I were free, I could choose whether or not I wanted to support them. Until that time, I was bound by obligations forced upon me.

"I know you haven't, Acadia. I can sense it." He pressed his lips to my cheek. "Once I claim you, it won't be an option, *balisra*. If you give to another male or feed from one, it will push me over the edge. I will be a danger to every male within these walls."

I knew that. And perhaps I'd been hoping he would claim me so I didn't have to make such a big decision. It was actually an easy one to make, because I wanted nothing more than to belong to this male. However, it wouldn't change the fact I was enslaved by my duty to the *fiestreigh*. The real question was, if I opted out of my duties, what would become of me? Would God do as he promised?

"Do you know what we did to earn this punishment?" I asked Kaj, feeling the need to explain my hesitance.

"You never specified." His body relaxed as he pulled me against him, holding me gently but firmly.

"My ancestors defied God," I told him. "For centuries, we managed to remain hidden from humans. Almost entirely, in fact, back in the Old Country. Here, in the New World, things began to change. We began interacting with humans, similar to the way vampires do. Not fully immersed, but on the periphery. As long as we kept them from knowing what we were, it was fine. Then Calista, our Queen, she met a human male and fell in love with him. She was warned that it was against God's rules, but her love was so deep, so true, she decided it was fate that had intervened.

"Calista decided she was going to mate the human, but her people were against it. She couldn't be persuaded and figured the best way to gain acceptance was to get pregnant." I glanced back at him. "That was the reason God made us infertile. Calista found herself with child, but before she could give birth, God found out. The pregnancy was terminated upon her death. And because the Fae had welcomed the child despite the fact they had been against the mating, we were cast out. Our souls were banished from Heaven, and we were forced to forever walk the Earth. Upon our death, we simply wither and fade, forever trapped in the shadows, alone, unable to interact with anyone."

"So Michael intervened?"

"Yes. He offered us the opportunity to be the life source for his warriors on Earth. We're still not allowed in Heaven; instead, he made us indestructible. We cannot be killed; therefore, we cannot be forced to the shadows." I exhaled, then smiled. "In the beginning, I was terrified. Upon meeting Obsidian, I'd expected him to be a hard male. It didn't take long to realize he wasn't forcing us, but rather embracing us within his family."

"Would you have left if he released you?" Kaj inquired.

"No. I don't know anyone who would, either. Though we have no real choice, Obsidian has never made us feel that way. It's an illusion, mind you. I know that, but I wouldn't trade this family for my freedom."

Until Kaj, I had never really understood how bound I was. As long as I was enslaved to the warriors, I would not be free to be with him. No matter how much I wished it so.

"I'm going to free you, Acadia," he said, brushing my hair back from my shoulder before he planted his lips there. "And I'm going to claim you as mine."

I turned to face him, cupping his beautiful face as I scanned his hard features. "I'm already yours. Nothing will change that."

"Then help me, *balisra*. I need you at my side."

"There's no other place I'd rather be," I admitted, at the same time praying it was where I would one day be allowed to be, but essentially knowing it was out of my control.

As well as his.

15

Friday, February 2, 2018

ACADIA

When I opened the door to Kaj's room, I was surprised to find it was dark.

Well, mostly dark. The fire was blazing in the fireplace, which offered enough light to see by, the golden glow licking along the walls and the furniture near the hearth.

My gaze settled on the bed first. No Kaj.

Then the bathroom. Nope. Just as dark as the room.

Frowning, I stepped inside, easing the door closed behind me. "Kaj?"

"Good evening."

His voice came from the direction of the fireplace, on the oppo-site side of the room from the bed.

"Is everything all right?"

"Come join me, please." The tension I detected in his tone gave me pause.

Was he in pain? Was he upset? I didn't know him well enough to decipher his mood, but it wasn't like it really mattered what was bothering him; I had a strange desire to fix whatever it was.

I made my way over, taking in his still form. He was sitting on the thick-cushioned love seat I often sat on when he was resting. He patted the spot beside him.

I looked at the cushion, up to his face, back to the cushion. It wasn't difficult to understand what he wanted from me, but what I didn't know was why. Was he planning to tell me he was leaving? That he no longer needed my assistance?

As for why those were my first concerns, I wasn't quite sure.

Confused, I met his stare. "What's going on?"

"I want to talk to you."

That didn't sound good.

Then again, he had been acting a bit strange since the morning when he'd fed from my neck while I'd been in his bed. Though he had fed from me three times since then, it had been from my wrist while he was sitting on the edge of the bed. As though he'd been bothered by what happened between us.

As for me, I only remembered how good it felt when he touched me, even more so when I'd slept at his side through the day. That was the first and only time I'd spent in his arms, and there was no denying I was hoping for more. That wasn't his plan, though.

"About?" I prompted as I resigned myself to the conversation, easing onto the seat, though not getting comfortable as I angled my body toward his.

His green eyes glowed in the firelight as he stared at me.

When he placed his hand on my cheek, I started, surprised by the touch. But before he could pull away, I reached up and held his fingers to my face.

"I'm sorry," he said softly.

"For?"

"What happened the other morning. I was completely out of line."

The other morning. When he brought me to orgasm after finding his own. He thought he was out of line? How? I'd practically begged him, hadn't I?

"Do you regret what happened?" I asked, holding his gaze.

"It was inappropriate."

"That doesn't answer my question."

Once again, he remained silent.

"I enjoyed what ... what's been happening between us," I admitted, needing him to know I wasn't offended or put off.

"I took advantage of you."

I almost told him that this was merely part of my duties, but I got the feeling that would not go over well. Nor was it even remotely true. What was happening between us was more than that. At least from my side. I definitely didn't see our interactions as something I was bound to. No, more like wanted to do.

His hand was still on my cheek, but then the other lifted. When he had my face between his palms, Kaj pulled me closer. I leaned in, then waited as his lips hovered over mine.

"I don't see it that way," I assured him. "This... I want this, Kaj."

He seemed surprised by my admission, his body remaining still, his eyes continuing to caress my face.

I waited him out.

"You've given me numerous orgasms, yet I haven't had the pleasure of your kiss."

Not sure what to say to that, I rested my palm on his thigh, letting him know I was okay with this.

When he kissed me for the first time, I felt the sensation

throughout my entire body. Fingers, toes, they all tingled from the exquisite feeling. His lips warm against mine, his breath soft, the tension between us coiling, drawing me into him. And when he pulled me closer, his tongue sliding over my lower lip and then into my mouth, I moaned softly.

He was a gentle yet dominant male, and his kiss reflected as much. Kaj maintained the control as he explored me, his tongue moving alongside mine, his hand sliding around to palm the back of my head as he leaned in to meet me halfway. Warmth pooled between my legs, desire unlike anything I'd known before tightening in my core. Never had I wanted a male as much as I wanted Kaj. And that was even before kissing was on the table. Now ... well, truth be told, I didn't engage in a lot of kissing. It wasn't necessary to do with males to sate baser urges. In fact, it felt far too intimate, which made this moment all the more potent, I supposed.

I'd actually been disappointed when he retreated after that amazing morning we'd had in his bed. Part of me had expected things to progress after that. Before now. I was more than willing, more than ready to see what might transpire between us if he would simply let his guard down some.

"Balisra," he whispered against my lips. "I want to feel you beneath me. I need to be inside you. Is this wrong of me?"

"Not at all." God, no. Mini explosions fired off inside me, the tingling between my legs proof my body was eager for the same.

"Will you bathe with me?" he asked, pulling back and looking at me.

"Of course." Although I wasn't sure I could wait that long. I wanted to feel him inside my now. Here. On this sofa. I wanted the warmth of his naked body covering mine, the hard length of him pressed against me, his arousal filling me, stretching me. It was what I dreamt about during the daylight hours, what I fantasized at night when I was taking care of him.

"Keep looking at me like that and we won't make it to the bathroom," he growled softly.

"I'm okay with that, too."

Another growl rumbled in the air as he took my hand and got to his feet. He was slower than usual, which gave me pause.

"Are you in pain?"

He winced. "It's nothing."

"Kaj."

I stood my ground, staring up at him, studying his face as though that would tell me what was wrong. I knew he wouldn't tell me because he didn't want to appear weak. He would never appear that way to me. He was a fierce male, a strong, powerful male.

"I want you to feed," I told him.

"After the bath."

I shook my head. "Before. Or no bath."

Kaj smiled, and it almost reached his eyes. "Bossy female."

"Concerned," I corrected as I motioned for him to sit back down.

"From your neck again," he said, as though that was the only way he was willing to do it.

"You can have any vein you'd like, Kaj. I am yours in whatever way you need."

His eyes heated, the desire glittering. It spoke to the female within me, the one who craved every intimate part of him.

"Now sit."

Kaj eased back onto the small sofa, wincing once again. His pain concerned me. I needed to talk to Obsidian. See if he could do something. Perhaps we'd missed one of the bullets?

As I looked at him, I decided on the best way to do this. And opted to straddle his thighs, a move that seemed to surprise him.

"I have nothing on beneath this robe," he said.

It sounded like a warning.

"And I have nothing on beneath this gown."

"Take it off, balisra."

I nodded, then leaned forward so he could work the zipper on my back. When the gown gave, I held it to my chest as I got to my feet once more. As he watched, with the firelight at my back, I let the silk fall to the floor. His eyes took a slow trip down my body, and I could feel the rake of his gaze like a physical caress. My skin prickled, my nipples pebbled, and my sex grew wet.

I allowed him time to peruse, and when he finally held out his hand to me, I placed mine in it. Once I was situated, straddling his thighs, I reached for the belt on his robe, unwound it, and slid my hands beneath, revealing all his smooth, warm flesh.

"You'll be the death of me, female."

Though he'd meant it as a tease, I shivered as unease trickled down my spine. The thought of something happening to him... It was too much to bear.

Sliding my hips forward, I trapped his erection between our bodies, then eased my upper body to his, ensuring he had access to my vein.

"Feed from me," I urged.

There was no hesitation before his fangs penetrated me, which told me more than he probably realized. His body was weak, and he needed blood, but he'd been holding back.

In an effort to keep him at my vein, I slid my hand between our bodies and curled my fingers around his erection. As he sucked, I stroked. Slowly, leisurely. I wasn't trying to draw his orgasm out; I simply wanted to offer pleasure as he fed. When I thought he was going to release me, I loosened my grip. When he sucked more, I stroked firmly. Kaj clearly understood what I was doing because he settled in, his arms banding around me as he resigned himself to feeding.

It was in that room, on that little love seat, in front of that warm fire that I felt myself fall for the male at my vein. I'd never fallen for anyone before, didn't think it was in the cards for me.

Clearly that was because I'd been waiting for this male.

Kaj.

And time would prove that he would be my one and only love.

KAJ

T hough I attempted to ignore it, pain shot through my torso, fierce and hot. I'd suspected something was wrong before now, but I'd been hoping time was what I needed to heal completely.

As much as I wanted to believe Acadia's blood would suffice, I knew better. Her blood was potent and pure, but it wasn't doing the job of healing me, which I took to mean something was wrong.

Seriously wrong.

And now, as I released her vein, sealed the wounds, the flickers around my vision grew more intense, my head becoming fuzzy.

"Acadia..."

I felt her move, her hand falling from my erection. Her face was close to mine, the only reason I saw the concern because my vision was dimming.

"Kaj. Talk to me. Kaj?"

Her words drifted to my ears, but they were muted, as though I were underwater. Unable to hold my head up, I let it fall to the cushion behind me, my eyes closing. Yes, something was definitely wrong.

"Kaj!"

That was the last thing I heard as the pain consumed me, dragged me to a suspended state. I was conscious, mostly. But I was drifting in and out, my breaths labored, body weak. The pain ratcheted up, burning in my chest, making it difficult to inhale, exhale.

"Acadia..." I said her name not as a cry for help, more so because I loved it. I loved her.

I'd come to accept it as fact after she'd spent the day in my bed, curled up against me. I had remained awake while she slept, content to hold her in my arms, to feel her chest rise and fall. During that time, I'd also accepted that I had forced her into this, abused the assistance she had been offering. She hadn't signed on to accommodate my sexual needs, merely my blood needs. And I had taken advantage of her.

Which was why I wanted to talk. Perhaps she would forgive me, allow me the opportunity to start over, to show her I wasn't a selfish male. Not usually, anyway.

I was aware of her moving off me, but my eyes wouldn't open, my arms falling to my sides. My body was useless, overwhelmed by the agony blazing through my insides.

A soft rustle sounded in my ears, and I figured Acadia was getting dressed.

Then there were more sounds: a door being opened, heavy footsteps on the floor. I was jolted, a groan slipping out of my throat as I fought to hang on to consciousness. Strong arms slid beneath me, and I was lifted. My body was no longer controlled by my brain, though. In fact, the pain was drifting off, as though I was separating from it entirely. My brain flickering in and out, the world slipping away.

The last thing I was aware of was my back meeting the bed, my head eased onto the pillow.

And Acadia's sweet voice pleading with me to stay with her.

· · ·

When I came to, I kept my eyes closed, let my senses scan my surroundings. I was in a warm room, a soft bed beneath me, blankets covering my lower body.

Breaths.

I heard her breaths first. Soft, rhythmic, slightly elevated as though she was worried.

"Acadia?" The word came out broken and hoarse.

"Kaj." There was relief in her tone. "Oh, God. Kaj."

A soft hand touched my biceps, then silk slid over my chest when she rested her head there.

It took a couple of tries, but I managed to get my arm to work, my hand shifting so I could touch her, brushing her hair back.

"How long..." I swallowed, my throat bone dry. "How long have I been out?"

"Three days."

Holy shit.

As I remained like that, Acadia's head resting on my bare chest, I kept my eyes sealed shut, gave my body a good mental once-over, checking in with the various parts to ensure I was still in one piece. I was content to say there was no more pain. Not the agony I'd been plagued with, anyway. Discomfort and soreness had taken their place.

"What happened?"

Her head lifted; her hand fell away. I tried to open my eyes but couldn't.

Something touched my lips, and I realized it was a straw. Greedy for fluids, I drew from it. The chilled water coated my throat, relieving me quickly, taken away only when I stopped drinking.

Acadia's head returned to my chest, my hand once again settling on her hair, the need to touch her greater than I expected. A sense of calm washed over me as I succumbed to sleep once more.

16

MIRAKEL

———

Although I'd managed to keep my distance, I knew I could no longer put off feeding. It had been too long as it was, the lack of blood making my brain logy, my muscles weak.

At least I had the good sense to find neutral ground. This time I opted for the infirmary, for one of the empty patient rooms. That was where I was now, sitting in a hard plastic chair that I feared was going to buckle beneath my weight. The other choice was to pace the room, and since that would mean I had to exert energy, it was a no-go.

A knock sounded on the door a second before it opened, Briony's beautiful face appearing.

I forced my gaze back to the floor.

"You summoned?" she said softly.

Was it my imagination, or was there a hint of disappointment in her tone? It was enough to have me lifting my gaze, observing her as she stepped into the room and closed the door behind her.

This morning, she was wearing a velvet gown the same color as her eyes. It cinched in at her waist and flared at her hips, the heavy skirt brushing along the floor as she moved. I'd never seen anything more beautiful in my life.

"Where would you like me?" she asked, her words curt.

I swallowed hard, met her gaze. "Would you prefer I find someone else?"

I meant the words to come out as an accusation; instead, they sounded tormented, even to my own ears.

Clearly Briony heard the vulnerability I'd meant to hide because her face instantly softened. "No. Of course not."

I'd actually considered asking one of the other Fae, but in the end, I knew I couldn't go through with it. The mere thought of taking from another female... It made my gut churn violently.

I nodded toward the hospital-type bed that filled the space. "Would you mind sitting up there?"

She didn't speak, simply positioned herself on the edge of the mattress, her legs dangling down, her small feet peeking out from beneath the hem of the skirt. God, she had lovely feet. Her toenails were painted the same color as her gown, and I wondered if she always did that.

Scooting the chair closer to the bed, I ignored the violent screech of the metal on the tile as I got close enough that she wouldn't have to stretch.

Though I wanted nothing more than to take her neck, I knew I wouldn't survive it. I'd managed to keep away from her for so long, I feared that I would go too far given the opportunity. And Heaven knew I wanted her with a ferocity that defied logic. She certainly wouldn't understand it.

As I was reaching for her hand, I noticed she was trembling. The sight had me panicking, pushing the chair back against the wall, giving her space.

"I'm sorry," I blurted as I shot to my feet. "I don't mean to scare you."

"What?"

I nodded toward her trembling limbs. "You're scared of me. I can sense it."

Briony stopped the shaking by placing her other hand firmly on her wrist. "No. I'm not. It's..." Her eyes lowered. "I've put off feeding a little too long."

"Since when?"

She whispered a response I couldn't hear, which was saying something considering my keen senses. Then again, they could be failing since I'd waited longer than I should have to feed myself.

"When, Briony?" I demanded.

"Not since you," she whispered.

Five days. The same amount of time I'd gone.

My inner beast wanted to shout his pleasure of knowing she hadn't fed from another, but seeing her in her current state worried me. The problem was, I knew I couldn't handle feeding her until I'd refueled myself. If she took from what little energy I had left, chances were good she would kill me.

But what if the same were true for her? Could she really handle feeding me?

I couldn't take that chance. I would rather die than harm her in any way.

Turning to face her, I snagged the neck of my T-shirt and yanked it over my head. I forced my knees to lock as I came to stand before her. When I took her hands and lifted them to my chest, I watched her eyes widen.

"What—"

I pressed her palms to my chest and held them there, meeting her gaze.

As though her body recognized what she needed to survive, I instantly felt the pull as she siphoned my energy from me. Barely a minute had passed when I felt my knees weaken, but I held firm, closing my eyes as I battled the mind-numbing drain. Damn good thing, too, because I could feel the room spinning, knew I was going to hit the floor any minute now, and I would much rather not see it coming.

"Mirakel?"

I felt Briony pulling away, or trying to. I kept her hands firmly on my chest, needing her to take from me. It was my duty to provide what was necessary for her. She was my *nehadon*, even if she didn't understand it. I knew. And this was what I lived for.

A sharp scream pierced the air seconds before I hit the ground. Thankfully, it was only a knee that jarred into the tiled floor as my leg gave out. Then the other.

Briony's hands fell away because I could no longer keep them there as I fell over, my shoulder meeting the cold, hard floor, then my cheek.

The last thing I thought before the world disappeared: *Fuck, that hurt.*

APOLLO

I came to an abrupt halt when I crashed through the door to the patient room to find Mirakel laid out on the floor.

"What happened?"

Briony's eyes were wide as she knelt beside the enormous vampire, her hand brushing his hair back from his face. "I don't know. He was supposed to feed from me. Then he insisted I feed from him." She nodded, as though I could see what happened next.

"When was the last time you fed?" I asked her.

She shrugged.

"Briony, I don't have time for this shit. When?"

"Five days," she muttered.

"And him?"

"The same, I think."

I sighed. "You do know it's not advised to feed another when you're not taking care of yourself, right?"

She didn't answer, but I hadn't expected her to.

"Step back," I commanded.

Briony was up on her feet and moving back to give me room. With ease, I slid my arms beneath the male and lifted him off the ground. I wasn't as gentle when I dumped Mirakel onto the bed. Not because of his weight. More so because I was tired of seeing shit like this. It seemed to be a recurring thing around this place for whatever reason.

Well, I knew the reason. It wasn't difficult to deduce that the male vampire had bonded with the female Fae. It was the easiest explanation as to why he would put off feeding. And considering Briony's reputation around this place, I had to admit I respected Mirakel a bit more now. He was doing right by the female. Mostly.

"What can I do?" she asked softly.

"You can feed," I snapped.

"Okay."

Apollo's eyes shot to her. "I was being facetious, female. You can't feed from another male."

Her red-gold eyebrows shot lower. "I most certainly can."

I sighed. "I don't think you understand what's going on here, Briony."

Her hands went to her hips. "Then enlighten me, healer."

I knew beneath that innocent facade was a backbone of steel. Had to be considering what the Fae had endured over the centuries.

"The male has bonded with you."

"He *what*?"

"Bonded. *Mielix zan*. Imprinted. It's a vampire thing. If you feed from another male right now, he's going to come out of this and go ape shit." Although I kind of wanted to see that, considering the male was down for the count.

Then again, I had no interest in stitching up another because a bonded male vampire had torn through someone else.

"Okay, here's what I'm going to do." I quickly took Mirakel's pulse, then turned back to Briony. "I'm going to bring in blood and force-feed it to him if I have to. That should tide him over enough to wake him up. At that point, you're going to feed from him. Then in an hour or so, when you're both a little more stable, he'll feed from you."

She nodded, but I wasn't sure she'd heard a thing I said. Based on the way those amethyst eyes were locked on Mirakel, she was still trying to process the fact a vampire had bonded with her.

When she didn't say anything, I stepped out to retrieve the blood. When I returned a minute later, Briony was standing beside Mirakel's bed, brushing his hair back from his face. While there was still concern etched on her pretty features, there was something else. Approval, maybe? Hope? I had no clue, honestly.

It didn't take much to get the blood bag prepped and the tube pressed against Mirakel's lips. I started the process by squeezing the bag, allowing several drops of blood to hit the male's tongue. That seemed to do the trick because Mirakel's head turned as he sought the source of the nourishment, his lips wrapping around the tube like a straw.

Damn good thing Amethyst had insisted we start storing Fae blood as a backup. She was brilliant in that regard, always thinking ahead, and that was why we now had numerous bags stored in a refrigerator in the storage room.

"Here." I urged Briony to take the bag. "When he comes to fully, which he will in a minute or so, I want you to make sure he finishes this."

"Okay."

"And when he asks, which he will, assure him that this is your blood."

"Is it?'

I cocked my head to the side. "Yes. I'm not an idiot."

"Oh."

Yeah, it was clear she had no idea how this whole bonding thing worked. But since this truly wasn't my area of expertise, I didn't feel the need to explain it to her.

"Like I said, I want you to wait an hour after he finishes that. Then you can feed from him. And the cycle can begin all over again."

She at least had the decency to appear sheepish.

Leaving the two of them to it, I stepped back out into the hall. I strolled over to the computer, pulled up the number to the Lair, and snatched my cell phone from the table. Punching in the digits, I hit the call button.

"What?"

The voice that sounded on the other end was familiar, and it drew a smile out of me.

"This is Apollo. I wanted to let someone know that Mirakel's over here taking up space in one of my beds. He passed out from lack of feeding. It's being taken care of, in case you care."

"Fuck you, Doc. We care."

I chuckled, enjoying the fact I got a rise out of Blāz. Then I hung up, wondering just how long it would take the vampire to storm his way into the infirmary and give me another piece of his mind.

I honestly hoped it didn't take long. As it was, it had seemed far too long since the last time we went toe to toe.

BLĀZ

S tand. Sit. Stand. Sit.

I had alternated the motion repeatedly for the past

two minutes, my feet not quite giving in to the idea of going to the infirmary.

Damn doc. What the fuck?

I peered into the parlor, where Kidel and Huracān had taken up a game of darts. For a brief instant, I considered telling them about Mirakel, letting one—or both, hell, I didn't care—haul their happy asses down to the infirmary to check on the male.

But no.

Oh, hell no. My body had other ideas, and for some fucked-up reason, it thought I should be the one to head over.

I peered down at my crotch. "No," I told the damn appendage that was starting to rise in anticipation.

"Who're you talking to?"

My head snapped up in time to see Kidel looking at me like I'd lost my damn mind.

Then again, I was almost certain I had. Totally fucking lost it.

"No one," I muttered. "I'll be back."

Kidel nodded, then turned his attention back to the game.

Fucking hell.

Once again on my feet, I headed for the underground tunnels. I had to adjust my stride as I fought with my idiot cock. The damn thing was thick and proud, as though what was at the end of the tunnel was his best friend in all the world.

Fucking dumb ass.

"Just go in there, check on Mirakel, come back. Easy-peasy. Don't look at the doc. Don't talk to the doc. Don't even fucking think about the doc."

I growled.

Easier fucking said than done. Ever since the Kiss Heard

Round the World, I hadn't stopped thinking about Apollo. Not for a minute. And here I was.

No way to ignore the way Apollo had taunted me on the damn phone. I'd known instantly what the doc was up to.

"In case you care," I muttered. "Why the fuck wouldn't we care?"

Damn needling asshole.

Why me? Why did Apollo have to go and notice me? It was bad enough I had spent the past few weeks thinking about the damn angel, fantasizing about him. That had been hard enough. It was like Apollo knew, and now he wanted to push me.

I saw the doors leading into the residence up ahead. I squared my shoulders, shifted my hips, and strolled forward. After placing my palm on the wall, letting the laser scan my retina, then instructing the door to open to satisfy the voice recognition, I took a deep breath and fought the urge to mow down the doors.

I managed to make it through without ripping off any of the hinges, even maintained a steady, even pace.

The angel had his back to me, but I wasn't fooled. No way Apollo didn't know someone was coming up on his six.

"Wondered how long it'd take you," the doc muttered before turning to face me.

Those pale blue eyes raked over me without an ounce of discretion.

Tonight, the angel was sporting a pair of black scrubs, which, I had to admit, were damn appealing on him. His blond hair was brushed back from his face, the shadow of a beard coming in, the scruff only a tad darker than his hair. He looked good enough to fucking eat.

No.

No, he did not. I wasn't here for a meal, damn it.

"Where is he?" I barked.

Apollo hooked a thumb over his shoulder, indicating the farthest door. I headed that way, pretending I didn't find it hot the way the sexy angel filled out those scrubs.

Rather than stroll into the room, I peeked in the rectangular window in the door. I saw Briony first. The pretty Fae was standing at Mirakel's bedside, her eyes locked on the enormous male laid out on the bed.

I was considering what my next move was when I felt the warmth of a body at my back.

"They're doing fine," Apollo whispered near my ear. "Couple of idiots ignoring their biological needs. But they'll survive."

But would I? I wondered. My body reacted instantly to Apollo's nearness, the gruff sound of his voice.

I didn't bother to turn around. "So why'd you call me?"

Apollo pressed up against my back, full-on heat contact, and I thought for a minute my knees would buckle.

Fuck. Ing. Hell.

Oh, not to worry, though. That damn angel banded one arm around me, keeping me off the floor as he backed us both into the room across the way.

No sooner had we stepped into the darkened space than I spun around and slammed the angel into the wall, our mouths crushing together. Heat pierced every molecule as the doc's tongue thrust against mine.

Fuck, he tasted good. Like mint. And sex.

Heaven help me.

What was it about this damn male that undid me? I didn't understand it. For two hundred seventy-nine years, I had never let another male get to me like this. Then again, my body had never reacted quite to this extreme, either. It was as though there was some magnetic force bringing us together. I was the damn magnet and Apollo a piece of sheet metal.

As was always the case, I kept my hands to myself, refusing to give in to the urge to touch. Tasting was enough. If I got my hands on him, God only knew how far I'd take it.

Granted, Apollo didn't seem to have the same problem. His big hands were gentle yet firm as they pushed beneath my T-shirt. Apollo's fingers spread wide as he spanned my stomach, my chest, back down, around. When Apollo cupped my ass and jerked me forward, I groaned low in my throat. The kiss was brutal, and there was no doubt my lips would be bruised when this was over, but I couldn't stop myself. I didn't want to stop.

"Touch me," Apollo demanded.

"No."

As though daring me to stop him, the healer reached for the button on my jeans. Our mouths separated so I could watch what he was doing. Even in the nearly pitch-black space, I could see clearly, watching as those deft fingers released the button, then the zipper. When Apollo thrust his hands into my pants, I groaned again.

"Fuck," I hissed, turning so my back was to the door. Otherwise, I would've been a puddle on the floor.

That big hand curled around my cock, stroking oh so gently. The male was fucking with me, no doubt about it. Be that as it may, I didn't even think to stop him.

Apollo worked me up, down, up, down. Enough friction to make my head spin, but not nearly enough to send me over.

As I focused on breathing, I let my head fall back against the wall, the sensations consuming me, overwhelming.

"I want to feel you inside me," Apollo rasped, his voice a dark rumble against my ear.

"Never gonna happen," I bit out, though I knew it for the lie it was.

The healer chuckled softly, and then in one swift move, he spun me around, my chest crashing into the door. Apollo's hand never stopped moving on my cock, stroking firmly, confidently.

I felt Apollo's body against mine, a delicious weight that held me in place while the male worked me closer to orgasm.

"It'll happen," Apollo stated, his lips brushing my earlobe. "Don't doubt that for a second."

I placed my palms on the wall and pushed back against the heavy weight holding me. I made no attempt to push Apollo away. No, this was the simple need to be grounded in this moment.

"Fuck," I cried out, my cock twitching and pulsing as my release neared.

"Come for me," the healer demanded. "Let go for me, Blāz."

I wanted to refuse Apollo for the sake of it, but even I knew that wasn't possible. I wanted this too much, even if I had no room in my life for this.

The male's other arm banded around me, sliding up my shirt, his palm splayed flat. It was the warmth that seared me that did me in. Well, that and the amazingly good hand job the doc was giving me.

My hips bucked, driving my erection into that fist, and a second later, I was flying, my body bursting apart as my cock kicked hard. Thank fuck for the male holding me up because my knees buckled from the pure pleasure that pierced me from head to toe.

When it was over, I couldn't move. That didn't seem to matter, because Apollo was holding me there, his arms firmly wrapped around me as though he'd known what would happen.

"One of these days..." Apollo whispered, his lips trailing down my neck.

For a brief moment, I felt the scrape of his fangs, and a strange sensation washed over me. I wanted to know what those would feel like piercing my vein. I'd never fed another soul in my life, never planned on it. But right here, right now ... I almost wished it so.

Luckily, my common sense returned along with my strength. I pushed to my full height, pulling away from Apollo, tucking myself away, and righting my jeans.

"Never happen, healer," I growled before storming out of the room and making a beeline for the Lair.

17

KAJ

"What are you looking at?" I asked as I approached Kidel on Wednesday evening.

The male sat back in his chair and motioned toward the screen. "These are the four cameras Mirakel and Blāz managed to set up at the Dungeon."

Leaning in, I quickly skimmed each of the four scenes. It took less than a second because they weren't depicting anything other than an empty space.

"It's early yet," Kidel said as though he could sense my frustration. "But this morning, after the club closed, Darko stayed for a while. Another vampire arrived, and they talked for a good half hour."

"About?"

The male frowned. "That's the problem. Either the audio's bad on those cams or they're blocking it somehow. I can't hear a thing."

"But you should?" I strolled to the chair at Kidel's right.

"Yeah." Kidel's fingers began moving over the keys swiftly. "I may have to go in there myself, take a look."

"Take Huracān if you do." No way was I sending only one in. Last thing I cared to do was set up one of my own. I didn't trust Darko as far as I could throw the bastard.

"Will do. I figured I'd give it a couple of days. Don't want him to get suspicious."

I leaned back to give the *heurosp* room to set my meal in front of me. "Thank you."

"My pleasure, sire."

When the female disappeared from the room, I peered at Kidel. "Any update on when we're getting *vestrahn* in place?"

I got a shrug in return. "Blāz is supposed to be working on that."

I picked up my fork. "Supposed to be?"

Kidel's gold eyes swung toward me. "I mean no offense, *phaal*, but we're spread a bit thin right now. With only four of us, it's slow going. Blāz is prioritizing the panic room." The male smirked. "That's what he's dubbed the project. I'm dealing with a few bugs in the exterior security and working with the *fiestreigh* to fortify theirs and ours. Not easy when I can't see a damn thing outside these walls. Huracān's lending his muscle, going out on patrol with the angels."

"And Mirakel?" I inquired when the male didn't include him.

"I think he's doing his best to be invisible."

Ah. Right. Mirakel was doing his best to hide from Briony.

"You know Apollo had to give him a blood bag early this

morning. Evidently, he'd put off feeding too long. So did Briony. From what I heard, Mirakel passed out."

Fuck.

Although I wanted to push that issue aside and pretend it would fix itself, I knew better. For one, Kidel was right. We were extremely short-staffed. While it had always been the five of us, we hadn't been the only ones who made up the Zenith. But without a trustworthy pool of soldiers to choose from, I was hesitant to staff an army. Not to mention, I didn't have anything for them to do aside from the obvious.

Which meant I needed to get my ass in gear.

"I need help," I told Kidel.

The male's eyes shot to my face once more.

"What?" I smirked. "Never thought you'd hear me say that?"

Kidel chuckled softly. "Actually, no."

"Well, it's true. I've delayed long enough. It's time we get with the program."

"Whatever you need me to do."

"We need to figure out what my father was tending to, and I need to pick up where he left off."

No sooner were the words out of my mouth than Blāz sauntered in. His eyes were bloodshot, his black hair mussed, at least two days' worth of beard growth on his face.

"You look like shit," Kidel offered.

Blāz nodded, then dropped into a chair at the opposite end of the table. "Evening to you, too."

Kidel peered at me as though looking for help.

"We were just discussing our next steps," I told Blāz. "It's time I sit in the Alpha's chair. I've put it off long enough."

That seemed to surprise Blāz.

"I'll admit, I have no fucking clue what comes first."

"I do." Blāz waved a hand at me. "Lemme grab my laptop."

NICOLE EDWARDS

With that, the male shot up from his chair and vanished.

"Need I say, I think we're in trouble now," Kidel mumbled.

Probably. Of the five of us, Blāz had worked closest to Kardobahn regarding his daily endeavors. So if anyone knew the lay of the land, it was he.

I was finishing off my pancakes and eggs when Blāz reappeared, his laptop in hand and a set of Beats over his ears. Without saying a word, he got to work, eyes focused on the screen in front of him.

Okay, so when I said *we* needed to figure it out, clearly Blāz thought I meant him. But whatever. I knew that Blāz would take the task and run with it. Then again, I had no idea what would come next, but I figured I would let it be a surprise.

"I'm going to chat with Mirakel," I told Kidel. "Then let's meet up before dawn to see if we can come up with a plan on moving forward."

"Of course, *phaal*. I'll let the others know."

After tossing back the rest of my lukewarm coffee, I made my way down to the workout room, figuring it was a safe bet Mirakel was already down there. Sure enough, I found him reclining on the bench, hefting an overloaded bar up, down, up, down.

"How're you feeling?" I prompted when I stepped into the space.

Mirakel set the bar on the pegs and inched out from beneath it. He was on his feet in an instant, towel in his hands.

"Better," he said, his eyes clear.

"I heard you nearly starved yourself again."

Those neon blue eyes dropped to the floor. "I'm sor—"

"Look. I get it," I interrupted. "And I sympathize with where your head's at right now. But we've got things to do and I need you."

Mirakel's gaze slammed into mine. "Of course, *phaal*. Anything."

"First off, I want you feeding daily. Every morning before you retire to your room. If I find out you skip even one day, I won't be pleased."

The enormous male nodded.

"Second, I want you to work with Huracān. Let's get those recruits here. To the training center," I clarified. "We're under-staffed, and the only way to change that is to start from scratch. Bring those five males and two females in. Let's get their training underway. You and Huracān will lead the effort on that front. Working with the *fiestreigh*, of course."

Another nod.

"I expect you to check in with me every morning. After you've fed. I don't want to hold your hand, but I do want to make sure you're taking care of yourself."

Had I given the instruction to any of the others, I knew I would've been met with resistance. That wasn't the case with Mirakel. The male wanted structure, always had. And these past few weeks ... hell, ever since Kardobahn was killed, had likely been hell for him. Because I had thought they'd been killed, too, I had taken off in an effort to find safety, slowly working my way back to the angels for refuge. Now that I was here, now that we were finally in a place to start rebuilding our regime, it was time I took the reins.

"I'm going to talk to Briony. I'll request she not feed any of the others until we figure out how to move forward."

I knew it really wasn't my place, but right now, it had to be done. I couldn't afford to be down even one vampire, certainly not Mirakel. And eventually, it wouldn't matter anyway. Not when I freed the Fae indefinitely. I figured now was not the best time to relay that little detail to Mirakel, though. Not until I had a sit-down with Michael and figured out the terms.

"Thank you, *phaal*," Mirakel said, bowing before me.

With a renewed sense of purpose, I set forth to take care of the most pressing things. I expected once those were out of the way, the rest would fall into place.

I could only hope sooner rather than later.

OLIVER

"Hey, guys, I think I might have something," I called out to the males currently congregating at the nearby desks in the war room.

"What's up?" Miklós asked, spinning in his chair to peer back at me.

I tapped a few keys, sending the image on my computer screen to one of the monitors on the wall. "Looks like you've got an influx of demons converging on a small town in Texas."

All eyes shot to the screen, then a few shifted back to me.

"Where'd you get that?" Kandarie asked.

"I set up an algorithm to monitor traffic cams in and around the locations you've pinpointed as possible places for the *amsouelots*," I explained. "It sends me an alert when there are four or more figures in one place, provided they're lacking a heat source."

"Holy shit," Reidar muttered as he moved to stand on my right. "That's fucking brilliant."

"Not too bad for a human," someone teased.

I grinned. "I had to work on it a bit. Kept getting alerted to college frat boys who'd stayed out in the cold too long."

Someone chuckled.

"Someone needs to alert Aphotic and Decebal."

"Already done," I informed him. "Just wanted to let you know in case someone needs to send in the cavalry."

"We're whole right now," Reidar explained. "All the *lieterras* are out with their respective warrior. As are the *ladeares*. So Aphotic's got sufficient backup. As long as he knows what's coming his way, he should be good."

I nodded as I watched the image play.

"What else are you watching?" Miklós asked, rolling his chair over and propping an elbow on my desk. "Looks like you've got the *impietans* covered. Any tricks up your sleeve regarding shadow beasts?"

"I've started putting something together, but I need unique factors to focus on."

"Demon dogs," someone stated. "Only they roam in human form."

"Not helpful," I answered. "But I have hacked into all the cams in the area. I've entered Asmia's physical description in the event she happens to be out and about."

"Doubtful," Reidar grumbled. "If I were Perfidious, I wouldn't let her out of my sight."

Yeah, that was what I figured, too, but it didn't hurt.

"Maybe we should hit up Bijou. She's probably got the most experience with shadow beasts. Maybe she can give us some pointers."

I didn't look at Miklós, hoping the angel wasn't including

me in that *we*. I wasn't sure I was up for a conversation with her.

"I'll call her. See if she can come down here," Reidar said.

Ever so helpful, that one.

While I attempted not to listen to the one-sided conversation, I focused on the various screens flipping across my monitor.

"She's on her way down," Reidar noted. "I'll have her sit with you for a while. See what you can come up with."

Great.

Probably too late to fake a migraine. Or an aneurysm.

Since I just ate, couldn't use that excuse, either.

While I waited for the inevitable, I toggled over to the web browser and found the tab I'd opened to do a search on vampires. It wasn't that I'd expected human lore to have what I was looking for, but I'd made the effort. And no, I hadn't found a single thing to help me regarding whether or not a vampire could truly survive on the blood of a human. Nothing beyond the standard bullshit myths made up by humans.

Hitting the small X that would close the tab, I quickly flipped back to the cams I was monitoring and just in time, too.

"Hey. I'm here. What's up?"

I squeezed my eyes shut as her voice drifted through me. It was like a sucker punch every time I heard her speak. The sweet lilt of her voice was enough to have my heart rate elevating, my palms sweating. It was stupid, I knew. I'd managed to successfully alienate her for the past few weeks, and now it seemed we'd passed the point of no return. It wasn't like I could approach her and apologize for what I'd done that night in the sauna. Hell, I couldn't even think about that incident without my body hardening.

"You wanted some information on shadow beasts?"

Forcing my eyes open, I turned my head but didn't look up at her. I couldn't. Seeing her was too painful.

With a few clicks, I had a screen open to a blank Word document. I pushed back my chair and stood.

"If you could jot down any notable factors, that'd be great."

"Oliver?"

Ignoring her, I raced out of the room, down the hall, and up the stairs. I had no idea where I was going, but I figured when there was enough distance between us, perhaps my legs would stop moving.

I had to wonder if New York would be far enough.

18

MICHAEL

———

Keeping my physical form shielded, I made my way through the mansion.

Initially, I'd dropped in to check on Ari'el, but after spending an hour with the child, I figured I would get a lay of the land. Now that I was waiting for decisions from both Obsidian and Kaj, it seemed the two males were avoiding me. Which meant I wasn't being summoned, and I'd run out of excuses to pop in. If I stayed too long, I knew I'd be ushered out, so I figured the best way to see what was going on was to go undetected.

Too bad I was bored out of my gourd.

I had already whispered through the war room, watching the males work. I didn't know how the hell they didn't lose their minds being cooped up like that all the time. Then I followed a couple of the *heurosp* around to check their work. Like always, those humans didn't miss a beat. If they made the floor any shinier, I'd have to wonder if it was glass.

The vampires weren't any better. Those males were laser-focused on something, but I didn't stick around long enough to figure out what their objective was. The healers were the same. Their schedules were alternating so that one of them was on at all times, the other snoozing. When I stopped by the infirmary, I found Amethyst working away on the computer. What she was doing, I didn't know, didn't really care. They were here because Obsidian had requested their presence, and truthfully, I was grateful to know they were taking such good care of Ari'el. Amethyst had taken quite a liking to the child, which put my mind at ease.

After that, I found myself drifting. All seemed hard at work, and I had no one to eavesdrop on. No one worth paying attention to, anyway.

Which was how I ended up here in the third-floor living room with Zeus and Aphrodite. The canines were smarter than they looked. Both had detected my presence almost instantly, forcing me to shimmer into existence or risk them alerting the angels.

Now, as I fluffed their furry necks, I waited.

For what, I had no idea. Perhaps for Kaj to come in and tell me he was ready for the resurrection. Or for Obsidian to hit me up to drop all those future warriors in his lap. Maybe Penelope to ask me to babysit. That was my preference. Though I'd made sure to keep tabs on the baby, I hadn't spent nearly enough time with her. Didn't matter that I'd held Ari'el in my arms every single day since she arrived in this world. It would never be enough.

For some reason, that made me think about Acadia and Kaj. Those two had found their way back to one another, though they seemed to be taking their own sweet time making up for lost time. I thought for sure I had sealed their fate when I'd intervened while Kaj was healing. Tossing in another bullet after Obsidian had effectively removed the others hadn't been an easy feat. But it had worked, keeping Kaj with Acadia longer than he would've been otherwise. Not that I intended to let anyone know the part I'd played in that.

In the end, Kaj had healed and had left anyway. Honestly, I hadn't expected the Alpha to stay gone for so long after that. Granted, I also hadn't expected the devastation that had transpired when those damn devil dogs had eliminated Kardobahn. If I had any idea it was going to happen, I would've gladly put a stop to it. But, no. Lucifer kept his intentions close to the vest, and I usually learned about my brother's latest path of destruction as it was going down.

Of course, I had interfered a bit after that. In my defense, it had been necessary. Kaj had made numerous attempts to get in touch with Acadia after his departure, but I had intervened, ensuring those calls never went through. It had been imperative that the male learn of his daughter first, so I had delayed his attempt to reunite with the Fae. Again, I hadn't expected it to take a year and a half to get him back here, but in the end, it had worked out. Acadia seemed to forgive Kaj, and thankfully, neither one of them had figured out I'd had a hand in holding them together or in keeping them apart.

Luckily for me, many things hadn't been figured out by the angels and the Fae. The parts I'd played over the centuries had been great as I moved the pieces around on the board, lining them up where I needed them. One of them being Asmia, who shouldn't even exist because her species wasn't capable of reproducing. Yet no one seemed to question how she'd come about. I suspected there was some curiosity, but the questions had never arisen, and I hadn't felt the need to disclose my hand in the matter. Until the time it was necessary, I intended to keep that secret, as well as the many others I harbored.

As I appeased the dogs, I let my senses spread through the mansion. I detected some unrest with the human male known as Oliver Calazans. That was normal, I figured. Considering Khari had found his mate, it was only a matter of time before something prompted the vampire soul to seek what he was desperate to claim. Unfortunately, he couldn't do that within the human's body. As for how he would go about making his presence known, I wasn't sure. Since it hadn't happened in the past nine thousand years since I had tucked him away, I didn't even know what to expect.

Perhaps I needed to find a hobby. Something to keep me busy while the angels and vampires were choosing to ignore me. Or better yet, maybe it was time to push a few buttons, get things moving in the direction I needed them to go.

Despite my desire to let things play out as they were meant to, I knew we were running out of time.

ACADIA

I managed to make it another night.

I had successfully avoided the *fiestreigh*, though it had been touch-and-go when I'd learned Gryffyth had

BOUND IN DARKNESS

been seeking me out. Luckily, he'd found Ziana to tend to his blood needs, and I'd been off the hook.

Now, as I sat in my bedchamber, avoiding the morning meal to ensure no one else managed to corner me, I knew I needed to confront Obsidian. It was becoming too difficult to avoid everyone, and I was at the point where the idea of feeding any of the other males didn't sit right with me.

A knock sounded on my door and I looked up, fearing one of them had found me.

Allowing my senses to scan the other side of the wood, I breathed a sigh of relief when I realized it was Kaj. The door opened a second later, and the male stepped into the room.

He looked good. Healthy and strong.

He also looked determined.

When he closed the door behind him, I got to my feet, wanting to greet him appropriately. Since he'd left my bed that evening, I'd been looking forward to reuniting with him.

"What's wrong, *balisra*?"

I shook my head, forced a smile. "Nothing. Why would you think that?"

Kaj canted his head to the side. "You can't hide from me."

Technically, I could. If I truly wanted to, I could've shielded myself from him. It was one of the many powers the Fae had. It was the very reason we'd managed to go undetected in the world for so long.

"I was hoping to find you downstairs," he said softly, taking my hand and leading me to the small seating area in front of the fireplace.

When he took a seat, pulling me into his lap, I went willingly. "I wasn't hungry."

A soft growl was his response. "I also know when you're not being truthful."

Of course he did. But not because he had heightened

senses. I had never been able to lie to him. Even when I had wanted him to believe I no longer cared about him, I hadn't been able to hide my true feelings.

Leaning my head on his shoulder, I relaxed against him. "What kept you away so long?"

His lips brushed my forehead. "I assume you're not referring to today."

I smiled. "No. Not today. When you left. After you healed."

Kaj exhaled heavily, settling into the cushion. "After I found Kardobahn's camp destroyed and thought I lost my males, I went into hiding for a bit. I thought about coming right back, but worried the shadow beasts would catch my scent and follow me here. Just when I thought it was safe to make my way here, Bijou showed up. How she found me, I still don't know, but I figure a higher power had a hand in that."

Probably. I knew Michael manipulated things to suit his needs, and based on what I'd learned by reading Kaj's mind regarding the original vampire, it was highly likely he'd set that in motion.

"My focus was to protect her," Kaj explained. "At the same time, get to know her. I always planned to bring her back here because I knew she'd be safe, but I had to bide my time. Even though I knew without a doubt she was who she said she was, I didn't trust her right off."

"You don't trust easily," I whispered.

"No. I don't." Kaj exhaled. "But I made every attempt to get in touch with you. None of my calls were returned."

This time, I lifted my head, peered into his eyes. "I never received any calls while you were gone."

He held my gaze. "I swear to you, *balisra*, I tried. I hated that I couldn't return to you, but I never meant for you to think I'd abandoned you."

And I had. I had believed that Kaj had simply written me

off when he'd walked out the door. It still pained me to think about. He had broken my heart when he left, and try as I might, I never could understand his reasons. But I'd never truly understood what his life entailed, either. We'd been confined to that bedroom most of the time. The things we'd shared were about our pasts, not the present or the future. So I had never fully understood who he was.

"But I'm back now," he said, once more pulling me against him. "And I'm not going anywhere, Acadia. As long as you'll have me, this is where I intend to be."

As much as I wanted to tell him I wanted us to be together, there was still that underlying fear of what would happen to me if I did. There was no way to ignore the reasons I was here. I had a duty, and there was always the risk that the Almighty would eliminate me if I defied them. Though my heart belonged to Kaj, my body wasn't my own to give freely, nor was my heart.

"I'm going to order food to be brought up," he said softly. "Then we'll eat, take a bath if you'd like."

"Will you stay with me today?" I asked, sliding my hand over his chest. "I don't want to sleep alone."

"I wouldn't want to be anywhere else, *balisra*."

I knew deep down that he meant that, and it soothed me in many ways.

If only I could soothe him by settling his mind, assuring him that I would forever belong with him.

It was the only thing I wanted, and it was the one thing I knew I couldn't give.

19

ACADIA

I had spent the past three days watching over Kaj as he slept, praying he would heal now that Obsidian had truly removed all the lead that had been lodged in him. After the incident when Kaj had passed out from the pain, I had sought Obsidian, insisting he do something. It was then the male offered another exam, one that alerted him to the fact he had indeed missed one of the bullets.

With Obsidian's assurance that he would heal fully, I had remained in the bedroom with Kaj, refusing to leave his side. I couldn't imagine what I looked like now, after three days of ignoring myself completely. The only time I slipped away was to use the bathroom and freshen myself up a bit, but I had avoided showering because I didn't want to leave Kaj for that long.

A soft grunt sounded from the male as he shifted, rolling onto his back.

I leaned onto the mattress, watching him closely, praying he would finally open his eyes once more.

"Balisra..."

"I'm here," I whispered. "I'm here, Kaj."

A smile tilted his lips seconds before his eyes opened, his head turning toward me. "You're here."

Was it wrong of me that I enjoyed the relief I heard in his tone?

"I never left," I told him.

As though he just realized where he was and perhaps remembered what had happened, his eyes scanned the space around him.

"What happened?"

I went on to explain about our conversation on the sofa, him passing out, Obsidian coming in, finding and removing another bullet.

"That explains it, huh?"

I frowned. "What?"

"Why I feel like a new male."

Relaxing for the first time in days, I exhaled heavily, then realized a tear had fallen, the wetness rolling down my cheek.

Kaj turned back to me, his hand lifting, cradling my cheek as he swiped the tear with his thumb. "Do not cry, balisra."

I forced a smile. "I'm sorry."

"Do not apologize."

"I was worried about you."

"I was, too," he said with a soft chuckle.

"You need to eat and you need to feed," I told him.

"First, I need a shower," he rasped as he pushed himself up. "I've been in this bed for days."

"May I assist you?"

"I would be honored if you would."

I briefly wondered if he recalled the conversation we'd been having prior to this setback. The one where he had apologized, believing he had taken advantage of me during our time together. I wanted to bring it up, to assure him that I was here in a capacity other than as his nurse, but I refrained.

It only took a couple of minutes to get us both beneath the hot spray. Kaj was sturdier than I'd expected him to be, and I considered that a good thing. In fact, I was sure he was in much better shape than before Obsidian had worked that second round of magic. I hadn't expected the relief it brought on, but it was so much, I actually swayed on my feet.

"Come here, Acadia."

When Kaj held out his hand to me, I took a step forward, allowed him to pull me into him. Our naked bodies pressed together as he wrapped his thick arms around me, holding me close. I rested my head on his chest and returned the gesture, ringing his waist with my arms. In that moment, I let myself cry, hoping the water would conceal my tears.

"You need not worry about me," he whispered, his words spoken softly over my head. "You've taken good care of me."

Perhaps. But that didn't change the fact I'd spent the past few days worried he would succumb to those injuries and I would spend the rest of eternity without him.

Kaj shifted, forcing me to lean back. His finger curled under my chin, urging me to look up at him.

His green eyes glittered with health and warmth, and yes, I saw heat in there, too. His body was coming to life as we stood beneath the water, and mine was answering the call. My relief that he was all right was soon overshadowed by the heat our bodies generated when in such close contact. And when Kaj reached for the bottle of soap on the ledge, I took a step back, watching him as he poured a generous amount into his palms before requesting I turn around.

Not sure what his intentions were, I did, giving him my back. To my relief, he pulled me against him, his arms coming around, soapy hands beginning their leisurely stroll over my skin. He started with my shoulders, down my arms, my hands, back up. When he moved on to my chest, my breaths became labored. When he moved down to my breasts, I was panting. He teased and fondled as he caressed me so gently it was all I could do to remain on my feet.

Minutes passed as he paid attention to every inch of me, getting more soap when the suds had been washed away. He kneeled behind me, working down the fronts of my legs, then up the backs. Kaj cupped my bottom, lightly teasing between my legs, cleaning me intimately before moving higher. By the time he was standing tall, I was once again swaying, my muscles loose, my body aching for his.

Then it was his turn. While he soaped up, an endeavor that was not quite as reverent but equally provocative, I watched. His skin glistened as water sluiced over him, running in rivulets down his chest, his thick thighs. I wanted to offer to assist, but couldn't quite focus, so I settled for observing. His erection was thick and heavy as he lathered himself, the suds briefly shielding him before being washed away.

"I want to make love to you," he rasped.

I swallowed, my heart expanding, my belly fluttering. No one had ever made love to me before. It was something I'd read about in fiction books that Obsidian brought in. The idea of two hearts bonding as one, two bodies joining in a dance as old as time.

Once we were both rinsed, the water was turned off, towels were retrieved, bodies were dried. Then I took his hand and led the way to the bedroom. I was the first on the bed because I wanted him to know I was willing and eager. This wasn't him taking advantage of the situation, this was me offering myself to him.

When he joined me, it was to cover me with his warmth before his mouth found mine. We remained like that for long minutes, my hands exploring him while our tongues mated.

And while my body grew more insistent, my desires raging out of control, I could've been content to stay just like that for the rest of my days. During the time we'd been together, Kaj had become important to me.

Enough that I realized and accepted that ... I was in love for the first time in my life.

KAJ

lthough I had been intimate with females before, never had it felt like this.

Perhaps that was because I felt more alive than ever before. I wasn't sure it had anything to do with my near-death experience so much as it related to how I felt when Acadia was with me. With her, every touch, every taste was significantly more intense, a joining of more than mere bodies.

I wasn't sure when it had happened, or even how, but I had fallen for the female. No, amend that. I had imprinted on her, my soul claiming her as my own for eternity. It was what we referred to as mielix zan, an affliction that affected males of my species. I had bonded with the female, and there would never be another who could take her place in my life.

As I held myself over her, I wanted to mark her with my scent, to infuse her with my venom, to tie her to me for eternity.

I couldn't, of course.

For one, Acadia wasn't aware of my feelings for her, my needs. She was caring for me, and yes, I got the feeling she had developed some affections for me, but as for whether she was willing to bind herself to me for the rest of our existence, I didn't know. And I didn't think now the appropriate time to ask.

No, right here, right now, our bodies were eager to merge, and I was content with that. I'd spent weeks worried that I was making assumptions about desires that weren't there. However, she had corrected my thinking when I apologized. And here we were, my body finally mending appropriately, my heart still belonging to her even if she wasn't aware of it.

"Make love to me, Kaj," she whispered, her mouth separating from mine as she kissed down my jaw, my neck.

I closed my eyes, drowning in the sensual onslaught as her hands and lips caressed. As much as I wanted to slide into the warm haven of her body, I knew I needed to feed first. It was the only way to ensure I could satisfy her. My own needs were secondary, but my strength was failing because I'd spent too much time in this bed.

I hated to do it, but I shifted off her, rolling to my side and pulling her against me, her back to my chest.

"I need to feed," I whispered, kissing her neck as I brushed her hair away from that delicate column.

Acadia leaned into me, her body forming to mine. She tilted her head down toward the pillow, giving me the access I needed.

As desperate to taste her as I was to feed, I kissed and licked her skin. "I'm going to be inside you before I'm done," I warned.

"Yes ... please, Kaj. I..." She shifted again, her ass grinding against my groin. "I want to feel you inside me."

I growled low in my throat as my fangs shot down from my jaw. I dragged one sharpened point over her skin, licked her. When she moaned softly, I pierced her vein. Her blood was so potent it shocked my system instantly. I drank from her, my hand moving to her breast, cupping her, plucking her nipple as my body roared to life, my strength returning.

My hips began a slow grind. When she lifted her upper leg, my erection slid between her thighs, seeking the heart of her. Together, we adjusted so I could penetrate even as I fed from her vein. My fangs remained lodged inside her as her hand slid down, guiding me into her heat. My lungs ceased to work for a brief moment as the slick walls of her pussy enveloped me.

"Kaj..."

My name on her lips had me refocusing. I drank her down as I rocked my hips, the head of my cock throbbing as I sank inside her.

I continued to feed even as I rolled over her, mounting her from behind. My hips were rolling on their own, pushing me inside the heavenly heat. Deeper, deeper still. I refrained from pulling out, loving the way her pussy clenched around me, milking me as I sought all the pleasures her body could offer me.

As much as possible, I focused on feeding, taking from her vein while I gently rocked, careful not to tear her flesh in the process. I maintained a smooth, gentle rhythm for as long as possible. And when it became too much, I retracted my fangs, licked the wounds to seal them before I let myself go, my hips retreating before slamming forward. I growled as the sensations ripped through me, the silky heat of her overwhelming my senses.

I took her then. I did my best to maintain a steady pace, to treat her with care even as my hips jerked forward.

"More, Kaj ... please."

When Acadia shifted, her hips pushing back against me, I realized what she was requesting. Making love didn't necessarily mean being gentle and sweet; it was more a state of mind. And here, in this room, with the fire warming the air, the scent of her arousal, the softness of her body beneath mine, I made love to her in the way we both needed.

As minutes ticked by, positions changed. I dislodged long

enough to roll her onto her back so I could see her beautiful face. I drove into her again, watching as her eyes closed, a brilliant smile pulling on her mouth.

"Yes..." Her knees lifted, squeezing my hips as I drove us both higher.

When she came the first time, her body pulling taut, her sex strangling me, I wanted to roar my approval. Instead, I focused on sending her over again.

More shifting, different position. Acadia on top, riding me, her smooth hands braced on my chest as she took control, driving me to insanity with the exquisite pull on my cock. Minutes passed as she took what she needed. When she orgasmed again, I flipped us so she was beneath me once more. This time, I draped her legs over my forearms and let myself go. My hips were like pistons, fast and furious, as I clung to her, the electric current starting at the base of my spine and working its way up and out. My balls drew up tight, my cock pulsing as my release barreled through me. And when I came, it was with one final punch of my hips and a roar loud enough to rattle the chandelier dangling above the bed.

Careful not to suffocate her, I rolled, taking her with me so she was draped over my sated body, my cock still lodged inside her.

"I'm not done with you," I told her. "Just need a minute."

Her laugh was so sweet, my body reignited, my cock pulsing inside her once more.

Acadia moaned as she gyrated her hips, the friction sending heat to my extremities, bringing life to those recovering nerve endings.

"I'm not done with you, either," she whispered.

And she went on to prove it.

For hours.

20

MIRAKEL

Fucking treadmill.

One would think the designers of those damn things could figure out how to make them powerful enough to keep up with a full-grown male vampire.

Okay, fine. Perhaps they weren't aware that there *were* full-grown male vampires, so whatevs.

Thanks to my quick reflexes, I managed—barely—to keep from breaking my neck when I all but exploded the motor on that damn thing. And now, as the belt limped along while I held firm on the side rails, I was stuck with nothing to help rid me of this abundance of energy that had kept me confined to this room for the majority of the night and into the day.

I glanced at the clock on the wall.

Twenty minutes until I had to meet with Briony.

What I wanted to do was tell her I couldn't make it. However, that was my brain talking. The rest of me was all about the meeting, desperate for even a small glimpse of her.

And yeah, yeah. I knew it was wrong. *Mielix zan* was not something to be avoided unless you were a recluse and never saw anyone. I'd gone and imprinted on the female, and she had no freaking clue what that meant. As it was, I was grateful she'd yet to feed another male. Heaven help us all if I couldn't manage to keep my distance if and when that happened. It was part of the reason I'd restricted myself to the weight room, hoping all the stone and earth between me and her would be enough barrier to prevent me from feeling it should it happen.

Of course, I'd been called to the carpet and rightfully so. Because I'd been so caught up in my own problems, I had ignored the very reason I was here. Thankfully, Kaj had kindly realigned my priorities, and I was back where I needed to be.

Snagging a crisp white towel from the rack, I wiped my face and the back of my neck. What I needed was a shower, then maybe half a dozen sandwiches. Perhaps then I'd be calm enough to go to her, to feed without losing my shit. Even the thought of touching her again was enough to keep my cock in a semi-hard state all the time. Didn't matter that I'd worked that fool out a good half a dozen times every single day just to keep it from getting pissed at me. Asshole still saluted me at all hours.

As I made my way up the stairs into the house, I kept my head down, slipping through the parlor to the hallway leading up the back way to my room. Last thing I wanted was to have a conversation with—

"Hey, Mirakel!" Blāz shouted.

I grunted in response, taking the stairs three at a time. I rushed down the hallway, listening to the male's voice behind me.

"Yo, dude! I just wanted to let you know—"

Desperate to get away from him, I slammed through my bedroom door and came to an abrupt halt.

"—that Briony's here to see you."

Yeah. She was definitely there. And she was most def seeing me because her glittering purple eyes were in the process of caressing my bare chest.

I grunted again, holding my position in the doorway as I considered the ignorance of walking into that room and closing the door behind me. It was a testament to my desperation that I would even think it was an option, *b-t-dubbs*.

This morning, Briony was wearing emerald-green robes that hung from her narrow shoulders, resting gently against her full breasts, tied with a matching sash around her tiny waist before dropping all the way to the floor, covering her feet. Her red-gold hair was pulled up once again, pinned in place to reveal her delicate neck.

As usual, she looked absolutely stunning, and I was pretty damn sure it required no effort on her part. She simply was beautiful.

"I'm sorry to bother you," she said softly, bowing her head slightly. "One of the *heurosp* said they would be occupying the laundry suite, and I figured after what happened in the infirmary ... I thought it more appropriate if I came here."

Not appropriate, no. *Temptation* was the word I would use.

"Briony..." I took a deep breath, gripping the hand towel in my fist. "I think it's best—"

"Please don't send me away."

Her urgent tone had my words dying in my throat. "What?"

Those amethyst eyes scanned my face. "I know you don't like to be alone with me—"

"I like it too much," I corrected, though I wasn't sure what the fuck was wrong with me.

"Uh…"

Yeah. Exactly. Uh.

"You like being alone with me?"

Could she seriously be that naive? Part of me had thought her innocence was faked. Similar to the *cosrobols* I usually fed from. Those females were always pretending, doing whatever was necessary to please the male they were offering themselves to. But Briony … she seemed sincerely confused that I could possibly want to be alone with her.

Because I wasn't going to let her go until I explained myself, and hopefully found a way to let her know I couldn't do this anymore, I closed the door behind me.

Just call me dumb ass. It was, after all, my new title.

"Mirakel?"

I closed my eyes because the sound of my name from her lips was too much.

"I thought you wanted to find someone else," she said softly.

Feeling like a resistance band pulled to its maximum, my eyes flew open, and I pinned her with my stare. "Does it look like I want someone else?" I snapped, reaching down and crudely gripping the hard-on that tented my shorts.

Considering how innocent she was, I expected her to shudder, perhaps back away.

When her eyes lowered, it wasn't to shy away. Oh, no. That female's gaze raked over my crotch for long seconds. And while she was doing that, someone stole every ounce of oxygen from the room.

Fuck.

"I need a shower," I rumbled, glaring at her as I stormed across the room to the bathroom, ignoring the steel beam tenting my shorts.

Without bothering to close the door, because, come on, I

was a glutton for punishment, I flipped on the water. I then kicked off my shoes, stripped off my socks, then my shorts, tossed the towel, and stepped into the enormous glass shower, pulling the clear door closed behind me. The water sprayed over my head as I tipped my face up, brushing my hair back. When I brought my head back to level, I opened my eyes to see Briony standing in the doorway.

Watching me.

Like I was a fucking matinee.

Holy. Fuck.

"Turn around, female," I demanded.

"I'd prefer to watch."

It was the first time I'd heard anything remotely assertive come out of her mouth. Fuck me, but I liked it.

"Then watch." With my eyes on her, I gripped my cock in my fist and stroked.

It was enough to capture her attention, her eyes slowly drifting down and lingering as I worked myself with my hand. Her mouth opened slightly and right before my fucking eyes, the female's little pink tongue darted out to lick her lower lip.

"Briony..." This was not a good idea. Not just not a good idea, it was a royally bad one.

Clearly she'd called my bluff and now I was stuck holding my dick. Literally.

"For fuck's sake," I grumbled, releasing myself and grabbing the shampoo.

With my eyes closed so as to limit the temptation, I went through the motions. I washed my hair, my body, then rinsed myself off, all while my cock pulled a bob and throb between my legs.

I flipped off the water, snagged one of the thick towels from the warmer just outside the shower stall, then wrapped it around my hips.

"I think we need to postpone this," I informed her as I strolled back into the bathroom, doing my best not to breathe in her sweet strawberry scent.

"Why do I bother you so much?" she asked, her voice trailing behind me.

"I don't know." Total lie. Not like I could tell her I'd bonded with her in the way only a male vampire could: with total abandon and absolute disregard for all others who existed within his orbit.

I paused at the door. I'd come over here intending to open it and usher her out. Now I couldn't seem to lift my arm to grip the knob.

I inhaled sharply when soft hands came to rest on my back. My body drew up tight, that single touch nearly enough to set me off.

"Briony ... I'm warning you, love."

"Warning me about what?" Those hands moved over my skin, as though she were memorizing every muscle.

"Keep that up and you'll find out."

My heart was pounding, the sound magnified in my ears as my blood hummed in my veins. The need to touch her, kiss her ... fucking claim her ... was more than I could stand. And if she didn't stop...

Heaven help me, if she didn't stop, I was terrified I was seconds away from letting my dumb handle take over.

BRIONY

Mirakel was the absolute most stunning male I'd ever laid eyes on.

And in all my years, I had seen quite a few males.

Well, parts of them, at least.

Most wouldn't believe that I had never been with a male before. Not in a romantic sense, anyway. Oh, wow. And now my naiveté was showing. *Romantic sense?* I didn't think males and females tended to think along those lines these days. Everything had gone ... *casual* as of late. Yes, that was a good word for it. Friends with benefits, no strings attached, casual sex. All terms used by the populace who were having sex before marriage.

Regardless, I was still a virgin, and I doubted anyone would've guessed that about me. Then again, if they knew nearly all males reacted similarly to the way Mirakel did around me, perhaps it was a bit more believable.

I wasn't sure what it was about me, but males tended to view me as something fragile, innocent. Untouchable. Likely the reason I was untouched. They didn't mind feeding me when necessary, nor did they have a problem drinking from my vein. However, not a single one had ever wanted me ... *that* way. Not the way I knew Mirakel wanted me.

Truth be told, I'd never wanted a male before him, either. Not like this, with a deep-seated desire that remained even when I wasn't near him. None had ever stirred such crazy things inside me, made me do things such as have an orgasm while feeding. Yet, with him, I'd done so on more than one occasion.

As for the reason I was here in Mirakel's room ... well, that was entirely selfish on my part. I remembered vividly how difficult he'd found being around me, and I knew it wasn't because I repulsed him. No, quite the opposite. According to the healer, the vampire had imprinted, and while I didn't know what that entailed, nor what it might lead to, I found I was intrigued by the notion.

Hence, I was here. I'd come to Mirakel's room this morning in an attempt to push him, to see if he would give in to what was plaguing us both.

And here I was, taunting the beast because I knew deep down that was the only way he was going to give in. He was a noble male, far too polite to take me the way he wanted. But I'd seen it in his beautiful eyes. The heat, the need, the passion. And perhaps I was out of my mind, but I wanted to experience it.

"Briony, what are you doing?"

His voice was dark thunder, rasped out of his lungs as though he was hanging by a thread.

"Wanting you," I admitted, leaning in and pressing my lips to his back.

His sharp inhale spurred me on. Without fear, I trailed my lips up his long spinal column, loving the way the muscles in his back flexed as though he could hardly contain himself. Because of the drastic difference in our heights, I couldn't reach all that high, but the broad expanse of his back left plenty for me to linger over.

"I ... you don't want this. Trust me, love. You—"

An animalistic growl sounded when I nipped him with my teeth.

Before I knew what had happened, I found myself pinned

to the bedroom door, Mirakel's enormous body surrounding me, those neon blue eyes brightly lit as he stared down at me.

"I want this," I assured him, reaching up and brushing his jaw with my fingertips. "More than you know."

"We can't."

"Why?" I was tired of the evasion. If Mirakel didn't want me, he was going to have to tell me as much.

His head lowered, and I felt his warm breath fan my cheek. I turned my head to the side, bringing my lips closer to his.

"Tell me," I urged.

As was his nature, Mirakel didn't respond. I'd gotten familiar with the strong, silent vampire over the past few weeks since I'd started feeding him. He was a male of few words, but those he did speak were more than enough to send that desire pulsing through me.

My hands trailed down to his neck, lower to his chest. I pressed my palms against him, felt the rapid thump of his heart.

"You don't know what you're asking for."

I met his eyes. "Then show me."

Once again, he moved so fast I was barely aware of it until my hands were lifted above my head, pinned to the door in one of his big fists, the other cupping my face, his thumb tilting my head back. It was an aggressive move, but there was such gentleness in his touch. As much as he was trying to scare me, I sensed he didn't want to hurt me.

"Do you know how old I am?" I prompted.

His head pulled back slightly, eyes narrowed as though I'd just asked him to solve for pi.

"One thousand, two hundred forty-seven." I held his stare. "Do you know how many males I've been with?"

The look in his eyes said he didn't want to know the answer to that.

"Zero, Mirakel. I have never taken a male inside my body."

The dark growl that sounded was so deep I felt it resonate through me.

"I want to be with you. I want to know what it feels like to have your hands on me, your lips. Your tongue. I want to feel you move inside me."

Another tortured sound escaped him.

"If you don't want me, I understand," I said quickly. "But if you're holding off for another reason … please don't."

I could feel the tension coiling in his body, could sense he was struggling with what he wanted and what he thought was right.

"If nothing else, let me feel your mouth on mine," I told him, the words barely a breath of sound between us.

His gaze bounced over my face, then settled on my lips. I was still pinned to the door, his hand banded around my wrists, his knee pressing between my thighs, his chest so close, but not quite touching.

It felt like forever as he battled whatever war plagued him, but when Mirakel's head lowered, his lips brushing so lightly against mine, I couldn't help but moan as I tried to lean into him.

His grip on my chin tightened. "Let me be in control. It's the only way I'll survive this."

I tried to nod but my head wouldn't move, so I whispered my acquiescence.

Mirakel's lips were softer than I'd imagined they would be, yet firm at the same time. They were like a feather at first, but then he leaned in, his head tilting slightly as he pressed them against mine. Not sure what he wanted me to do, I remained still, shifting to align our mouths. When I felt his tongue slide over my lower lip, I opened to accept him. When he licked his way inside, I met his tongue with my own, sliding lightly against his, my insides coiling tightly as I let him teach me what was necessary to please him.

What started slow and gentle grew wings and took flight when Mirakel released my hands and cupped both sides of my face as he sealed his mouth to mine and thrust his tongue inside, an insistent exploration. My body grew warm, a distinct heat building between my legs as my arousal peaked. It was a heady sensation that threatened to weaken my knees, but I managed to remain upright, not wanting to do anything that would cause him to stop.

Unfortunately, that was exactly what he did, jerking away from me as he stumbled back.

"What's wrong?"

It was then I realized his eyes were glowing, a brilliant light emerging as though he was lit from within. I didn't know much about vampires, but I'd never heard of this before. It intrigued me, but also made me hesitant.

"If you know what's good for you, you will leave. Right now."

His guttural tone had me staying right where I was.

As much as I wanted him, I wasn't about to push him in a direction he didn't want to go.

Nor would I cave because, Heaven help me, I wanted him more than I'd ever wanted anything.

Which meant Mirakel was going to have to make a final decision. And I wasn't leaving until he did.

21

OLIVER

———

I couldn't sleep.

I knew that on the other side of those closed shutters, the sun was rising in the sky, brightening and heating the Earth, but I was trapped inside, all the exits sealed and locked to ensure the safety of those who would be rendered to ash by the sun's deadly rays.

Honestly, I couldn't remember the last time I'd seen the sun. Months, for sure. Did I miss it? No, not really. Then again, I'd been living in Vegas before I relocated here, and I'd been drawn to the nightlife there. I hadn't been avoiding the sun, per se; I'd simply grown accustomed to sleeping during the day. I couldn't help but wonder if Penelope missed it. Because she was now an angel, my sister could no longer slip out to watch it rising or setting simply because she wanted to.

That instantly made me think about my niece. Could Ari'el go out in the sunlight? Since she was the offspring of two angels, I assumed not. I smiled as I thought about the precious child. Having never been around a baby before, I found it both awkward and awe-inspiring to be in her tiny presence.

I glanced at the clock. Maybe Penelope was down in the sunroom with Ari'el. For the last couple of weeks, she would bring the baby down after everyone had gone to bed, sitting in the dimly lit room. Probably wanting some peace and quiet as well as to get out of the confines of her private quarters. I understood the need to move around, to be out in the open. Sometimes I felt as though I was trapped, unable to go forward or back, stuck in one place both physically and mentally.

Yes, getting out of this room was ideal.

Pushing myself off my bed, I snagged a robe, pulling it on over the cotton pants and T-shirt I wore, slid my feet into moccasins, and headed out. From below, I could hear the sounds of the *heurosp* cleaning up after the morning meal. It wouldn't take them long, and then the day shift would move on to cleaning the floors, dusting, and polishing the furniture. It was their routine. The night shift tended to the glass on the windows as well as taking care of the things that needed tending to outside while catering to all who lived beneath the roof, which required a significant amount of effort, which explained why there were so many of them.

I headed for the back of the house, past Bijou's room, beyond Elizabeth's, to the stairwell that led down.

When I hit the main floor, I heard the whisper of voices as the *heurosp* diligently worked.

And as I'd expected, Penelope was sitting in the sunroom, Obsidian at her side, his big arm stretched along the cushions at her back. They were both peering down at Ari'el, so much love shining on their faces. I briefly wondered if my parents had ever looked at me and Penelope like that. Probably Penelope if I had to guess. She would claim otherwise, but I knew the truth. I hadn't been their blood child, but rather one they'd adopted. I'd often wondered why they'd even bothered, because they had never seemed all that interested in me.

Not to mention the timing of it. They'd attempted to pass me off as Penelope's twin, for fuck's sake. My sister still believed that was the case, and I had never felt the need to tell her otherwise. It wouldn't change a damn thing, so what was the point? I'd caused her enough pain and frustration over the years. And though I was responsible for most of that pain, the majority of that frustration, I'd never truly wanted to hurt her. So I kept that secret, pretending as my parents did that I was part of their family.

But what I never understood was why they wanted two babies when they could've easily given one all their love and attention. Perhaps good ol' Mom and Dad were as selfish back then as they were now. Made sense that they'd want more than they already had.

"Hey."

My head shot up at the sound of Penelope's voice.

I smiled, moving up the few steps leading into the oversized room. "Hey back. I thought maybe I'd catch you down here."

Obsidian leaned in, pressed a kiss to Penelope's cheek, then ran one finger over Ari'el's before he got to his feet. When he passed me, he gave my shoulder a firm squeeze.

"Can't sleep?" Penelope asked, patting the cushion beside her.

"It's becoming a trend," I admitted.

"Want to hold her? If nothing else, it'll help you relax."

Though I still found it awkward, I welcomed the opportunity. I wasn't sure why that was, either. I'd never been fond of kids, didn't matter their age. But from the moment Ari'el was born, I'd been drawn to her.

It took me a minute to get situated, but then Penelope passed the sleeping baby to me, positioning her in my arms so she was secure, all while making sure Penelope didn't accidentally brush me so as not to cause herself undue pain. Evidently, when an angel mated, there was all sorts of weird shit that went on, including making the touch of the opposite sex painful. I hadn't known that little fact when I'd practically assaulted my sister months ago, my anger having been prevalent at that time. Since I'd learned of the strange phenomenon, I'd made a point to ensure I didn't hurt her.

Of course, I didn't have to avoid Ari'el. She was merely a child, her future mate perhaps determined—again, something I'd learned about angel destinies, blah, blah, blah—but not sealed, so for now, I could safely hold her in my arms. The first time I'd held her, I had nearly freaked, fearful I would injure her in some way. Since then, I'd realized the baby merely needed warmth and security, and my arms could provide that.

"I still can't believe how perfect she is," Penelope whispered, softly touching Ari'el's puffy cheek.

I continued to stare down at my niece, not sure what to say. I knew my sister wasn't using the term literally, but I could see the perfection the same as she could. Her little nose, the tiny, almost nonexistent eyebrows, pursed lips, and smooth, rounded cheeks. Unlike some people, I couldn't tell who she resembled. She had black hair like her father, but her mother's coloring. And yes, all of it came together perfectly to create the sweet angel.

I had no idea how long I remained like that, but voices in the kitchen drew my attention. I looked up to see Bijou had come in. She was talking so animatedly with Phillip, I almost smiled, but managed to refrain.

"How are things with you two?" Penelope asked, her voice so soft it barely registered.

"We haven't talked in ... a while," I admitted.

"I'm sorry. I know you two have become friends."

We had, and perhaps that was what I missed the most. I'd had someone to spend time with, to talk to. She had been interested in me on a personal level, and vice versa. These days, I felt completely alone. The job with the *fiestreigh* helped because it kept my mind occupied for a good ten hours of the night, but there were still too many hours left when the metaphorical darkness would creep in, threatening to strangle me.

My attention shifted back to Ari'el, and I smiled, couldn't help it. I lifted her higher up my chest, pressed a kiss to her forehead, before passing her back to her mother.

"I think I'll turn in," I told her. "Thank you for this."

"Anytime you want to see her, Oliver. Anytime."

I nodded, then studied my sister's face for a moment. She was no longer the same girl I'd grown up with. My sister was now a mom, a wife. An angel. But I didn't think those things had changed her as much as I'd originally thought. No, I was pretty sure my sister had changed long ago, and I'd been so wrapped up in my own anger, my own sense of betrayal that I'd never noticed.

My loss, that was for sure.

"See you tonight," I told her.

"Sleep well, Oliver."

Yeah, probably wasn't going to happen.

But like I had for the past few weeks, I would pretend.

After all, it was the only thing that got me through the long nights and even longer days.

BIJOU

I watched Oliver leave the sunroom, head hanging low as he made his way down the hallway to the back stairs. He seemed different to me. Where I'd previously seen life, now only exhaustion resided. Though it had been but a few weeks since our falling-out, it felt like an eternity, and that familiar ache intensified in my chest.

It was my chance, I knew. An opportunity to confront him, to tell him I was sorry for everything that had happened, and ask him to forgive me.

His footsteps sounded in the stairwell, then on the floor above me, moving down the hall to his—

Before I knew what I was doing, I vanished my corporeal form, then resumed it on the second floor in front of his bedroom door. Oliver started, his head jerking upward, eyes wide when they landed on me.

"I'm sorry," I said quickly, then realized it sounded like I was apologizing for startling him. "Not for this. Well, yes, this, too. But more..." Inhale, exhale. Slow and steady. "I wanted to apologize for my actions of late."

Oliver's dark eyebrows lowered. "Actions?"

I waved in the direction of the pool. "You know, when I made you ... do what you did."

His laugh was strong but lacked any amusement. "You

didn't *make* me do anything, Bijou. What happened... It was a mistake."

Ouch. No denying that hurt.

However, I had to agree with him. Not because I hadn't wanted it to happen. Or because I didn't secretly wish it would happen again. But what transpired between us had set the course for the destruction of our friendship. And that was my fault. I had pushed him that night, begged, pleaded. He probably believed I would've done that regardless of who I'd been with, but that wasn't true. I had wanted Oliver that night, had seen it as an opportunity to bring us closer.

It had been wrong of me, I knew that now. Oliver hadn't wanted to take our friendship to another level, and I'd assumed he would if I simply made a move. Lessons learned.

"Can you forgive me?"

His eyes raked over my face. "Nothing to forgive."

Not sure what I was doing, I took a step forward. "I'd like us to be friends."

"We are friends," he countered.

"I want to be friends like we were before. Not the kind who avoid each other."

"I'm not avoid—"

I held up my hand. "Let's not pretend. It's a waste of time for both of us. I'm apologizing to you, Oliver. I owe you that much. If you don't want to be friends, I get it. I totally do."

His mouth opened, closed.

I waited, hoping he would say something to clear the air between us. I could tell he had something he wanted to say.

When the silence grew painful between us, I offered a smile. "Anyway. That's what I wanted to say. I'm sorry. Really sorry, Oliver."

Stepping to the side, I moved around him and started toward my bedroom.

"Hey, Bijou?"

My heart leaped into my throat, and I managed to turn around. "Yeah?"

"You wanna catch a movie? Like, maybe Saturday morning?"

When I smiled, I felt it brighten every cell in my body. "I would like that, yeah."

His smile was dim, but it was genuine. "I'll come find you. Say eight o'clock?"

I nodded, then watched as he opened his door and slipped inside.

It was a start, I reminded myself as I followed his lead, going into my own room.

Definitely a start.

Making my way to the closet, I quickly disrobed, pulling on my pajamas. I then headed for the sink and went through my daily routine of washing my face, brushing my teeth. Face lotion came next. Hand lotion to follow. When I got into my bed, I snagged the last bottle of lotion from my bedside table, slathered my feet before slipping beneath the sheets. I willed the lights off and lay in the dark. I considered starting a fire in the hearth, decided against it as I pulled the blankets up to my neck.

I thought back to the conversation I'd had with Oliver a few weeks ago, when I'd asked about his parents.

"My mother ran off with a younger man," Oliver explained. *"My father buried himself in work. It was rare we saw either of them after they split. I take that back. We rarely saw them before that, either."*

"Do you see them now?" I waved my hand. *"I mean, before you came here."*

"No. My father calls from time to time, though."

"Do you talk to him?"

"Every once in a while. He's more interested in giving me shit, telling me how I've fucked up my life."

"Does he know you're here?"

Oliver shook his head. *"Thinks Penelope and I are still in Vegas. It's not like he'd come visit, so I don't have to worry about him showing up there."*

"I'm sorry."

"Don't be. It's not like I miss him."

"I miss my mother," I admitted, surprised the words had come out.

Oliver shifted on the sofa, turning so he was facing me more fully. *"I heard what happened to her."*

I focused on my hands, clasping and unclasping in my lap. *"They killed her."*

The pain burned in my chest when I thought about how my mother had died alone in our house, the shadow beasts having sensed her, following her from the grocery store. I had been out with friends that night, hanging out, having fun. All the while, my mother had been suffering at the hands of those demons.

"How did you find Kaj?" he prompted.

"My mother kept a journal. I found it in the wreckage of the house. She'd tucked it under her mattress, and I guess it had fallen out when they ransacked the place."

Now, as I lay in the darkened bedroom of the mansion, I thought back to that journal. I hadn't intended to violate my mother's privacy, but by then, a month had passed since her death, and I'd been missing her so much. I had been staying in a motel, trying to figure out where I would go next, what I was going to do. I'd had nothing at the time. Nothing more than a human driver's license that worked to allow me to function within the human world.

That night, I had been crying, clutching the journal because it was the only thing I had left of my mother. When the tears had finally dried on my cheeks, I opened the book, flipped through the pages. On the very last page, I saw my name. It had been a note for me. As though my mother had expected one day I would find the journal. I could still see those words on the page, my mother's fastidious handwriting. The note had told me how much she loved me, how proud she was of me. It had broken my heart all over again, knowing I hadn't been there to save my mother.

But it was what came after that that I would remember for always: *I've never told him about you, and for that, I am forever sorry. But your father's a good man, a proud man. If he knew about you, he would've wanted to be a part of your life. I hope one day you'll find him. While your conception was an accident, I've never seen it as such. From the moment I learned of you, I wanted you with all that I was. My biggest regret is not allowing him to know. Should something ever happen to me, Bijou, know that you can turn to him. He will take care of you. He's that kind of male.*

I remembered being angry at the time. My mother had spoken so highly of the male who had fathered me, yet she hadn't told Kaj about me. To this day, I didn't understand, and I had never bothered to ask Kaj.

One day, maybe.

The next night, I took my backpack, which had everything I owned, and my mother's car, and went in search of Kaj. Little did I know that my entire world would change again when I found him. At the time, I hadn't put two and two together. Not once had I connected the dots.

Imagine my surprise when I finally realized that my father was the direct descendant of the royal family. By the time I found him, my father had become the Alpha vampire.

PERFIDIOUS

S hortly before nightfall, I crawled out of my warm bed and made my way down to Asmia's cell.

I could see through the bars that my sweet fairy was asleep in the big bed, her lithe body covered by all those blankets.

Freeing the padlock with my mind, I opened the door and stepped inside. I moved over to the bed, patted her arm.

"Good evening, gorgeous," I greeted, watching her face for signs of distaste.

"Good evening, my king," she rasped softly, her lids cracking open, a smile forming on her luscious mouth.

Nope. No signs that she wasn't completely content to be at my beck and call. The mind control was still working.

"What brings you to me this evening?" she asked, shifting to her back as I pulled the blankets down, revealing her beautiful naked form to my hungry gaze.

"It's time to prepare you for our guests' arrival."

Her eyebrows dropped an inch. "Prepare?"

"I've got an important meeting this night," I informed her. "And it's imperative that you're there with me."

"It would be my honor, my king." Asmia slowly sat up. "What shall I do to prepare?"

I motioned for the exit. "I've got everything you'll need in my chambers."

I'd sent Sirius out last night to retrieve the items that would allow my female to pamper herself in preparation for the ritual I intended to perform. While I'd intended to send Sirius on his merry way, there was no denying the demon was still useful. Since I couldn't leave Asmia, I needed someone to tend to my shopping and various errands. The male didn't seem keen on the idea, but he didn't have much of a choice in the matter. As far as Lucifer was concerned, Sirius was a minion to be used and abused by the *mesonneir*. And since I still held the glorious title, I wasn't above using my status to get what I needed.

"Come now." I motioned for her to get out of the bed.

Asmia moved with grace, her long legs sliding over the edge of the mattress, her elegant feet lowering to the floor. I snagged her silk robe from where it hung over the bedpost, then helped her into it. Though I preferred she be naked at all times, I wasn't keen on giving Sirius a peek at her. Not yet. Not until the ceremony. Until then, she was for my eyes only.

At that point, every demon in residence would see her beauty as I claimed her as my own.

And at that time, Asmia would get her first glimpse of what I truly was.

After all, it was the demon who would be taking her as my own.

22

KAJ

———

"What exactly am I looking at?" I asked Blāz.

The male had insisted he have an hour of my time first thing tonight to go over something important.

That was how I found myself in what appeared to be an office. Oddly, it was set up in much the same way Kardobahn's had been. The room had one wall of dark wood shelves lined with books varying in size and color. A navy rug with some intricate, old-world pattern lay in the center of the space. A wall of windows seemingly brought the outdoors in, though there wasn't anything to see thanks to the *dhira* the angels had erected. There was a fire going in the hearth. The Courtenay family crest hung above the mantel. And of course, there was an enormous mahogany desk with a burgundy-leather executive chair that was surprisingly comfortable if I did say so myself.

A black leather blotter sat on top of the wood beneath the fancy Apple MacBook I found myself staring at, a Mont Blanc sitting on a legal pad off to the side.

Blāz pointed over my shoulder at the screen. "This is the email account we use to contact the Alpha."

"Who's we?"

"*We*," Blāz said with a chuckle. "The common folk."

Right.

Squinting, I stared at the number reflected by the inbox. "Does that say ... two thousand?"

"Two thousand, four hundred and seventy-nine to be exact," Blāz agreed. "And believe it or not, I've been going through them for the past week. I've managed to tackle a good thousand, but they're coming in fast."

As though his comment triggered the sync, another four popped in. As I skimmed the names of the senders, I was saddened to say they weren't junk email or spam. I scanned several of the others. Nope, none of the *Sexy woman seeks handsome man,* or *The last diet you'll ever need,* or *CBD is your best friend,* lingering for me to delete. All looked legit from where I sat.

Legit and more than a little daunting.

It wasn't like I knew how to answer someone's request to mate. Just mate. Why the hell did they need my permission?

Or the announcement about an upcoming birth, my presence requested at the welcoming ceremony.

"What exactly am I supposed to do with these?"

"Answer them."

I jerked my attention to the male standing beside me. "I'll

be here for the rest of my goddamn life. I can't reply to all these."

Nor could I be at all these places to oversee and welcome. Fuck.

My gaze shot to the keyboard, thinking about the hunting and pecking that would take place just to type out a good evening.

Blāz chuckled. "I agree."

Thank God.

"Which is why I'm suggesting you hire an assistant."

I peered back at Blāz once more. "An assistant?"

The male nodded. "I was actually thinking Bijou would be good."

I shook my head. "Not Bijou. I've already asked her to help with firearms training."

"Then we bring someone in from the outside."

"Yeah?" I chuckled. "A stranger? You want to bring a stranger here?"

"Kardobahn had help," Blāz noted. "A lot, in fact."

True. I rarely interacted with my father's staff, but I'd seen them flitting about. Unfortunately, they'd all been slaughtered during the attack.

"And how do we do that?" I asked. "How do we find vampires willing to work for the Alpha?"

"Easy." Blāz leaned over, twisting the laptop toward him, then tapping on the keys. He turned it back. "These are job boards."

I stared at the screen. There before me were dozens of postings for jobs, each with various wording that humans would likely not understand but that would make perfect sense to vampires. A few were even in the ancient language.

"Give me the go-ahead and I'll start tossing up some postings. I've got a couple out there already seeking *vestrahn*, though we've yet to receive any responses."

That didn't sound good. "Why not?"

"I was probably a bit vague. Now that we've settled in, I know more of what we need, so I can be more specific."

We needed everything. Butlers, maids, chefs. As much as I appreciated the *heurosp* who were temporarily assisting, they weren't vampires, which meant their loyalties were not to us. And ultimately, I wanted to provide for my people, give them opportunities they might not otherwise have.

I turned the computer, then got to my feet. "Have at it. Hire yourself an underling while you're at it. Probably wouldn't hurt to get some legal counsel on the payroll. Someone who knows vampire law inside and out."

"Understood." Blāz dropped into the chair and flexed his fingers, his face splitting in a wide grin.

"I'm heading over to the training center," I explained. "Mirakel and Huracān should be arriving with the first seven we'll be moving through."

"Seven? That's a good number."

I wasn't sure about all that, but I was eager to get this underway.

"If you need help, find Kidel," I told him. "And all interviews will need to be done elsewhere. I don't want anyone brought in until they've been vetted completely."

Blāz didn't look up, his fingers still flying over the keyboard. "Got it, boss."

Confident we'd be bringing in a few newbies in the near future, I left him to work and made my way to the training center. My phone buzzed as I stepped into the space. A quick glance told me the trainees had arrived. I shot a note to Obsidian to let him know, then headed to the rear entrance, which would eliminate the need for entry via either residence, essentially reducing risk to those who lived on the premises. It wasn't exactly easy to get to, considering it wound through the mountain, but it would suffice.

I could hear the sound of vehicle doors opening, closing, footsteps on pavement. I waited inside, legs spread wide, arms crossed over my chest.

A few seconds later, the exterior door swung open, Huracān leading the pack, stepping through the doors first, and offering a quick nod before moving toward me. All seven trainees had black hoods over their heads, each one with their hand on the shoulder of the one in front as they shuffled forward.

"You may remove the hood," I announced when they'd all stopped. "Then line up, side by side."

I watched as they each discarded the face covering before lining up shoulder to shoulder.

I considered each one, recalling the information Mirakel had provided when we'd gone through the selection process. Five males and two females, ranging in age from twenty-six to twenty-nine. In vampire years, they were considered young. But that was what I wanted. Impressionable and moldable worked better when it came to building the ranks of our future warriors. They still had a ton to learn, more so from experiences than books, and learn they would. I'd been surprised to find the females listed, but not at all disappointed. Having a daughter of my own, I fully supported females having the ability to fight for what they believed in and being prepared to protect themselves and others.

"Welcome," I said gruffly.

No one spoke.

Good. They'd obviously listened to instructions.

"As you know, the first seven days you're here are your trial period. Should we deem you incompetent to complete this

275

program, you'll be sent home to your parents so you can endeavor to do something else with your lives. The fastest way to be kicked out of here is to disrespect anyone you come in contact with. That means one another. I will not tolerate bickering between you. This is not a contest. We're not here to determine who's faster, stronger, smarter. You wouldn't be here if we didn't think you were capable. Now it's your turn to prove yourself."

Of course, I wasn't naive enough to believe they wouldn't have altercations. I simply wanted to put it out there in the hopes they might opt to keep the peace because I'd deemed it necessary. However, I would not kick them out for acting like ... the young they still were. To a degree, anyway.

I paced down the line, looking from one face to another.

"At some point in the near future, we'll be receiving twenty additional trainees. Angels. If any of you have a problem with that, I want you to step forward."

No one moved.

Good for them.

"This is not meant to be fun for you. You will be working your asses off every night. I expect you to give one hundred fifty percent. If anyone's unable to do that, I want you to step forward."

Still no movement.

So far, so good.

Just to ensure they were listening, I said, "If you know who I am, I want you to step forward."

All seven took one step forward.

The rear doors opened, and Mirakel stepped inside, then dumped seven duffel bags onto the floor.

"Tonight, you'll spend your time getting settled in and familiar with the facility. The first thing you'll notice is that it's not complete. That's intentional." I smirked. "We're leaving the hard work to you. Consider it a character-building exercise. And because you will be living here, we'll leave it to you to determine how to go about doing that. Tomorrow evening, when I return, I will expect to find an outline of steps you'll be taking in order to accomplish your tasks. In the meantime ... well, I suggest you get down to business. Congratulations, and remember, you will earn your right to remain here. This is not a privilege. Don't ever forget that."

After nodding to Huracān, I glanced at all seven once more before turning and strolling out.

I was interested to see which of them broke first. Because I had no doubt, at least one of them would. Within the first forty-eight hours.

ACADIA

I wasn't sure what had gotten into me, but from the moment my eyes opened, I felt the need to do something.

Sure, I had a bit more time on my hands right now because I was purposely avoiding the *fiestreigh*, shirking my duties to feed them. I was, however, continuing to feed Kaj, and as he promised, he was feeding more often than was usual. Most males fed once a day to maintain their strength, but they didn't require much because of the frequency. That wasn't the case with Kaj. He was seeking me out twice daily and drinking longer than was usual.

Not that my body couldn't handle it. He was, of course, returning the favor, and his energy was far more potent than any I'd taken in quite some time. Not since Obsidian had I felt that sort of power flow through me.

And while I was getting plenty of face time with Kaj, I didn't want our only interaction to be sexual in nature or even about feeding. Couples did more than spend their time in bed, and if we were going to pursue this, it was important we did something outside the bedroom.

Which was why I had asked the *heurosp* to prepare lunch for the two of us and then requested one get a message to Kaj. Now I was in the fourth-floor attic awaiting his arrival. Initially, I'd thought to have the windows opened to bring the outside in, but due to the low temperatures, I had forgone that idea. Instead, I'd had the ceilings decorated with white lights, which I thought to mimic stars, and our meal would be consumed on a blanket on the floor.

Yes, maybe I'd stolen the idea from the internet. I simply typed in first date ideas and got a million to choose from. It seemed there was no limit to the human imagination. If they could think it up, they'd already done it, photographed it, and posted it for everyone else to learn from. Of course, my options were limited since Kaj and I couldn't leave the residence due to safety concerns at the moment, so I'd gone the practical route. Hence, the picnic in the attic.

"Acadia?"

The abrupt sound startled me, but that didn't last long. The sound of Kaj's voice brought warmth to my chest, settling me quickly. "Over here."

"I'm sorry I'm late. I was dealing with—"

Kaj appeared, looking striking in his dark jeans and a black

278

Henley. The male rarely wore anything that wasn't of the midnight variety, and I found it suited him.

"What's this?" he asked, propping his hands on his hips and peering around.

"I thought we'd have lunch together."

His gaze made its way back to me. "This was your idea?"

I nodded. "I wanted to do something ... different, something to surprise you."

"I like different."

Kaj glanced at the blanket, then at his booted feet. A second later, he was toeing off his footwear and joining me.

As he lowered himself beside me, I felt a strange swarm of anxiety bubble in my veins. Despite the fact I was one thousand five hundred and fifteen years old, I'd never been on a date before, and I figured, as far as terminology went, that was what this was. Back when Kaj and I were getting to know one another, we were always in his room. I knew he preferred privacy, as did I, so this seemed a suitable solution to hiding out in one of our rooms and risking things turning sexual. Granted, I wasn't opposed to the idea, but it wasn't my underlying reason for summoning him.

Needing something to do with my hands, I began parsing out the chicken salad sandwiches and the chips, having opted for simple. Of course, there were four sandwiches—three for Kaj, one for me—and it didn't take much time to divvy them up.

"Acadia?"

"Hmm?"

"Are you nervous?"

I smiled shyly. "Is it obvious?"

He chuckled.

"I've never been on a date before," I admitted.

His expression sobered as though he was reading into the reasons why that was.

"I hope I'm doing this right," I added quickly, not wanting to bring any unnecessary tension.

"Everything you do is right, *balisra*."

I didn't know about that, but I was happy he seemed pleased.

"I heard your trainees were coming today," I prompted, hoping to get on a safe subject.

"Arrived a couple of hours ago. Seven of them."

"How are they doing?"

"I think they're a little shocked. The training facility is bare bones right now. Obsidian wanted to leave the building to them."

"Oh, wow." I smiled up at him. "That'll be interesting."

"They're young. They can handle it. Builds character."

"True. How long do you think it'll take?"

"To build? Or to build character?"

I laughed. "The former."

"A few months. Obsidian's bringing in twenty trainees. With all hands on deck and ten hours a night … they should have it done by summer."

"Just out of curiosity…" I picked at the crust on the bread. "Who's going to be feeding the trainees?"

"Michael's loaning us angels."

I frowned. "Angels?"

Kaj took a bite of his sandwich, chewed. "He said they've been bred for this."

So what did that mean for me? For the Fae?

An inexplicable fear eliminated my appetite as I considered what that meant. I was only there to provide sustenance for the warriors and the *fiestreigh*. If they didn't need me anymore—

A gentle hand landed on my arm. "Acadia, we're keeping the trainees separate for a reason. It'll take some time to build trust, and until then, we prefer to keep the *fiestreigh* separate. For your safety."

I swallowed hard, holding his steady gaze. "Okay."

"There are a lot of things in the works," he continued. "And with more vampires coming on board, we'll need the Fae. Until we have a blood source of our own, that is."

I nodded.

"You're spread thin as it is. You said so yourself. And with you out of the mix, plus Briony..."

I frowned. "What's wrong with Briony?"

His gaze shifted to his sandwich, and he smiled. "It's come to my attention that Mirakel has imprinted on the female. It's safer if she is not providing for the other males. I requested she take a temporary time-out from her duties."

Oddly, that news made me smile. Why, I wasn't exactly sure. Briony was a special female. I'd always thought so. Sweet, innocent. And I was fairly certain she intimidated the males because of it. It was no secret that she had never availed herself to the males. Or the opposite. Which was a rarity. Especially considering the female's age.

"That certainly explains some of the tension," I told him. "I've noticed Mirakel's been coming over and they've been hiding out in the laundry suite."

Kaj laughed. "The laundry suite?" He took a sip of water. "He probably thought it was safer that way."

"Safer?"

"Less intimate, I guess I should've said. Then again, I would have no problem getting you naked in the laundry suite. Or any other staff-only room."

I was grateful for the dim lighting because my cheeks were burning from my blush.

"So what exactly does one do on a first date?" I prompted, forcing myself to eat. "I read about ideas on the internet, but..."

"Good question."

I locked eyes with his. "You've never been on a date?"

"Not in the traditional sense, no." His gaze shifted to his sandwich. "I've always been employed by my father. Dating wasn't conducive to protecting the Alpha. So I saw no reason to pretend otherwise."

I thought about Bijou and, in turn, Bijou's mother. "Have you ever been in love?"

"No." His beautiful green eyes lifted to meet mine. "Not until you, that is."

Another blush warmed me. "What about Bijou's mother?"

"It wasn't love." He reached for a second sandwich. "It was a mutual attraction. I met her on one of Kardobahn's trips. He would insist on interacting with the race, so from time to time, he would travel. The Zenith went with him, of course. One night, I met a female working in one of the reception halls."

"What was her name?"

"Alya." He took a drink of water. "I remember thinking she had kind eyes. Honest eyes." His lips thinned. "Safe to say, I'm not a good judge of character."

"Why's that?"

"Her kind, honest eyes didn't bother to tell me she was pregnant."

Oh. "Perhaps she didn't want to burden you."

Kaj's dark brows lowered. "Burden? Bijou's my blood. I hardly see that as a burden."

"That's not what I mean," I said quickly. "You said it yourself, it was a mutual attraction. Perhaps she knew you weren't looking for more than that."

He nodded. "Perhaps. Doesn't change the fact she kept something vitally important from me."

I agreed. It didn't. But since the female wasn't alive to explain her reasons, I didn't feel it was my place to dissect them.

"Well, I'm glad Bijou found you."

His face relaxed. "I am, too." He smiled. "I just wish I'd been around to see her grow up."

"Do you wish for more children?" I asked, managing to force the words past the lump in my throat.

Kaj's eyes lifted to mine, held firm. "*Balisra*, the only thing I wish is to have you for the rest of my days. Should we be blessed with young, then so be it."

I couldn't look at him. The fact that I would never have children was a pain I couldn't deal with. God had made the Fae infertile. Those who were here in the mansion were all that remained of my race. And though we were immortal, there would not be any more to carry on our lineage.

I flinched when Kaj's warm hand curled beneath my chin. He had moved closer.

"It will all work out in the end, *balisra*. Trust me on that."

Leaning into him, I nodded. I did trust him.

But I also knew what the Almighty was capable of. And some things were simply not meant to be.

JANE

L ying in the hospital bed, I stared up at the television. It claimed to be a previously aired news update, but I had no frame of reference to know whether the stories they mentioned were relevant to me or not. Did previously aired mean recently? Or was it from a year ago? I'd yet to figure out the whys and hows of my surroundings, and those I was interacting with hadn't offered much, either.

This was day six for me. That was all I knew. Six days into a life I couldn't remember, one where I didn't have a name or a family, no shelter, no means of getting to and from. Despite the fact I'd been told I was found injured on the street somewhere, I couldn't remember that, nor could I remember being brought here. The hospital room I resided in was the first and only deposit in my memory bank.

I probably should've been grateful that the nurses and doctors, as they called themselves, had started referring to me as Jane. Simple name, not flashy. I wasn't sure it suited me, or even how they'd come to decide on it, but it would do, I figured. At the least, it seemed to make everyone else more comfortable to have a way of referring to me.

According to Dr. Chopra, I had suffered a concussion, which she said likely contributed to the amnesia, as well as a plethora of broken bones, including my left foot and ankle, right thigh, right elbow, and the pinky finger on my left hand. Not to mention, my nose and some sort of tear in my hip. None of which they'd figured out until they did extensive X-rays. Dr. Chopra had determined either I had a high threshold for pain or I possibly suffered from a disease that didn't allow me to feel it.

I wasn't sure about anything other than the fact I was now confined to this bed for an undetermined amount of time. Dr. Chopra said we would take it one day at a time, but we wouldn't be discussing discharge until I was able to take care of myself.

For some reason, that had settled my nerves. Having thought about being released into the great big world had caused undue anxiety and triggered another of those panic attacks.

Didn't mean I wasn't thinking about what I would do when they did let me leave. Whether it was in a few days or a few months. Where I would go once I left the safety of this place was anyone's guess. Trudy, the kind, older nurse who had seemingly befriended me, had told me there was a shelter I could seek. She'd even given me a card with the name of a church, but told me I didn't need to worry about it yet.

Easier said than done.

As I scanned the television channels, I felt a little better. At least I now had some frame of reference, even if it was all based on fictitious television. There were still some things to be learned from sit-coms, or so they were called.

I knew I would need a job, probably something close, since I didn't have a method of transportation. A place to rest my head would also be a necessity.

Panic would've set in at this point, but the medical staff was pushing something into my IV along with the pain medication, something that would help me relax, they said. It kept me calm. Mostly. There was still fear because I had no idea who I was, and the more I thought about it, the worse my panic became.

Breathe.

In ... out ... in.

My gaze strayed to the television, and I picked up the clicker, tapped the button to change it to something more upbeat. Sleep was elusive, but I was catching up often. The problem was the stories my mind was telling while I was asleep. I wasn't sure if they were real or a figment of my imagination, thanks to all the television. The only thing I remembered when I woke was the stench of death and the unbelievable heat that seemed to consume me. Nothing ever appeared in my dreams, not that I could remember, anyway. It was as though I was locked somewhere, kept in isolation.

I sighed when Ray Romano said something to his wife, Deborah, on the television. I smiled in an attempt to force the fear to the back of my mind.

According to those currently responsible for my care, there was no sense in dwelling on it now.

The question I had was, how long before I did have to worry about it? What then?

23

Thursday, March 1, 2018

ACADIA

———

I awoke in Kaj's bed only to find the male was nowhere in sight. Evidently, he'd slipped out of the room while I'd been resting.

Not that I was surprised. It had been four and a half months ago that he'd been injured. During that time, he hadn't spent a single minute outside of the room. Now that he was healed, it seemed he didn't want to spend any more time than necessary in there.

Of course, he could've had the decency to wake me.

Fine. I probably needed the rest. After all, he was taking a lot out of me these days.

The thought made me smile. More like I was giving him a lot more of me these days. Every time I turned around, we were falling *into one another, the majority of our time spent horizontal unless we were in the shower. Then it was vertical sex and that ... well, there was something to be said about sex in the shower.*

Forcing my weary body out of the bed, I considered the gown I'd discarded this morning when I'd joined him in bed.

Probably be best if I went to my room to shower and change before I went in search of him. If I had to guess, Kaj was spending time with Obsidian. The two males were catching up now that Kaj was back to the land of the living, as he liked to describe his forward motion.

I hurried to pull my gown on, then slipped out of the room and down the hall. I could hear others moving around the mansion, getting up for the night. Doors were open as I headed down the hall, the rooms being cleaned by the heurosp *now that they were vacated.*

I couldn't wait for the new residence to be completed. As it was, it was still in the planning stages. But from what I'd seen, it was going to be a palace to rival all. No more sharing spaces for us. No, we would each have our own private spaces, and I looked forward to that. It was a pain to share a bathroom with two other females. It had been almost nice to be sharing a space with Kaj.

Hurrying into my room, I was glad to see Aasfa and Dahlia were already moving about. It meant I would have the bathroom to myself.

After a quick shower, I dried my hair, doctored my face with a hint of makeup, and pulled a clean gown from the closet. This one was one of my favorites. The burgundy velvet offset my coloring quite nicely. Not to mention, the bodice was one that accentuated my waist and my hips. I couldn't help wondering what Kaj would think of it.

Once dressed, my hair pinned up off my neck, I set off to find Kaj. Before I could make it to the first floor, I ran into Khalon, one of the male soldiers who made up the fiestreigh.

"Good evening," he greeted kindly, his eyes shifting to the floor bashfully.

"Good evening," I greeted in turn. "Has everyone finished evening meal?"

"No. They're still down there. I was ... actually, I was coming up to find you."

I didn't need to ask him what for. There was only one reason the males sought me out.

But the thought of feeding him... For the first time since being paired with Obsidian and his angel soldiers, I did not look forward to my job.

Not that I had the luxury of shirking my duties.

"Shall we find some privacy?" I offered, forcing the words past my dry throat.

"I don't believe anyone's in the office," he said, motioning toward the opposite end of the hall.

Nodding, I pivoted and led the way, my steps slow, sluggish. I actually felt as though I was walking toward my own death, not simply heading off to do what I'd done millions of times over the centuries. And it was Khalon of all males. He was one of the most polite, most considerate within the household. He'd never made any advances toward me, never suggested anything sexual. I should've been relieved.

I wasn't.

When I stepped inside, I made my way over to the desk, Khalon right behind me. He took a seat in the high-back executive chair, and I perched on the edge of the desk, pulling my sleeve back to offer my wrist.

As though he didn't sense anything out of the ordinary, Khalon please'd and thank you'd me before taking my wrist to his mouth. His fangs pierced me a second later. While he fed, his eyes remaining down, I fought the strange emotions that were churning inside me. For the past four and a half months, ever since Kaj had arrived, I had fed no one but him. This felt like something of a betrayal of the male I'd grown close to over those weeks.

A sound in the hall had me turning quickly.

Kaj was standing in the doorway, one hand on the jamb, the other rubbing his chest as though he was in pain. Our eyes met, held, and I could see the torment in those lovely green eyes.

Something churned in my stomach at the thought of him seeing me like this. It had never felt like an intimate thing, not even when there was sexual interaction, because it was a means to an end for us. I required their energy to survive, and they required my blood. A give-and-take.

But right now, right here, Khalon taking from my wrist felt like the most intimate thing I'd ever done, and the thought of Kaj witnessing it...

I was seconds from halting the male still feeding from me when Kaj stood tall and masked his expression before disappearing.

Knowing I had to go after him to explain, I urged Khalon along, then excused myself before he was finished. I felt a tad guilty for leaving him there, staring after me as though he'd done something wrong, but getting to Kaj was all that mattered.

KAJ

I needed to go.

Clearly I'd overstayed my welcome, and I needed to get back to the life I'd abandoned when I'd been injured. Kardobahn and the Zenith were likely worried. Or more aptly, they were pissed, thinking I truly had abandoned them.

Until this moment, the thought of leaving Acadia was one I ignored, putting it off, telling myself I could stay a little longer. I wasn't back to one hundred percent, though I was close, so I could take a little more time.

Evidently, I was the only one who wanted me to stay.

The instant I'd felt the pain in my chest, I thought I was having a relapse, that Obsidian hadn't removed that final bullet, or maybe there was another. But the pain had been different, and there'd been a strange pull that dragged me out of the dining room and up the stairs. I had followed that invisible line only to find myself standing in the doorway, watching the female I loved feeding another.

The agony I'd endured in that moment had surpassed even the worst of those bullet wounds I'd sustained all those months ago.

Because I had nothing here that belonged to me, I wasn't exactly sure what I was doing. I didn't need to pack, and I already had my cell phone on me. Taking a deep breath, I turned to face the door, resigned to going downstairs and thanking Obsidian for his hospitality. Before I made it to the door, it flew open, and Acadia came racing in. Her hair had fallen from the pins holding it up, and for a second, I thought I would lose what I'd eaten. Had she...?

"Kaj. I'm..." Her eyes widened as she came to a stop.

At first, I wasn't sure what she looked so shocked by, but then I heard it. I was growling, an animalistic sound that escaped me. The thought of another male taking what belonged to me... It was all I could do not to storm out of the room, find that fucker, and rip his head from his body.

The door closed, clearly willed so by Acadia.

"Did you let him fuck you?" I snarled.

She jerked back as though I'd slapped her, and a hint of regret went through me.

"How dare you?"

I stepped forward. "How dare I? You were the one in that room with that male, Acadia. Not me."

Her shoulders squared, and her expression shifted from stunned surprise to outrage. "Because that's my duty, Kaj. That's why I'm here. Or did you forget that?"

"Or do you mean, did I think I was special?" I shouted. "Of course I didn't." Oh, I totally had, but now I knew the error of my ways.

"Then why are you upset?"

"I'm not," I lied, and I knew she could see right through me.

"Then maybe you should stop growling," she countered.

Yep. That was me. Still doing that.

Fucking fantastic.

"What do you want, Acadia?"

She stared at me for a long moment. When she finally nodded, her shoulders squaring, her chin tilting up, I knew I was not going to like what came next.

"I came to apologize," she said softly. "It was not my intention for you to see that. Unfortunately, it is my responsibility to feed the males within this residence. It is my sole purpose for being here. And while I've been able to avoid it since your arrival, it's not something I can escape indefinitely."

Now I felt like an ass.

A very possessive, very pissed-off ass.

"I don't expect you to understand," she continued. "But this is the sad reality of my existence. I figured you understood that. Now that you've healed, now that you're up and about, I have no reason to continue to hide out from them."

"You've been hiding?"

Her beautiful purple eyes lowered to the floor. "Ever since you arrived. I've managed to get away with it because I was caring for you."

I cleared the distance between us, curled my finger beneath her chin, and forced her to look at me. "Tell me you hated it."

Her gaze bounced over my face. "Every second."

Another growl escaped me as I jerked her toward me, my mouth finding hers. I needed to mark her, to claim her, to ensure every male within fifty miles knew she belonged to me. That she was off-limits to anyone but me.

Before I knew what I was doing, I had all but ripped her gown from her body as I did the same to my own clothes.

If it hadn't been for the fact Acadia was holding on to me so tightly, I would've been appalled by my behavior. Instead, I had a single-minded focus.

I didn't even bother moving us to the bed. Instead, I took her to the ground right there and mounted her.

"Acadia..."

"Please, Kaj."

Her fingernails dug into my back as I rocked my body into hers, filling her.

"Mine," I growled, marking what was mine as I rubbed myself against her, ensuring her skin held my scent.

I could smell that other male on her, and I hated it with every breath I took. So much, I found myself lifting her wrist to my mouth and piercing her vein alongside those wounds that were already healing. I needed to rid her body of that male's scent.

"Kaj!" Acadia's body clamped down on me, her climax triggering mine.

But I didn't stop there.

Couldn't.

I pulled out long enough to flip her over and take her from behind. This time, I pierced her neck with my fangs, not so much drinking from her but ensuring my scent was everywhere.

She came again, her hips meeting mine thrust for thrust.

More shifting as I flipped her back over so I could watch her. This time, I knelt between her legs, my fingers curled around her thighs as I impaled her, pulling her toward me with every brutal thrust. This time when I came, I pulled out of her, spraying her stomach, her breasts. It was dirty and messy but so fucking necessary. I was out of my mind. I knew it. She probably did, too.

But I couldn't stop.

Once more, I plunged into her body, curling my arm beneath her and holding her to me as I chased one more release for us both. When she cried out my name, I slammed into her, dragging out those sweet moans until I thought my head would explode.

"Acadia ... balisra..." I threw my head back and roared, the sound more feral than any that had ever come out of me.

As much as I wanted to apologize for taking her that way, I couldn't.

This was who I was. What I was.

And it only made sense that she knew it.

24

KAJ

ours later, I was still thinking about the "date" I'd had with Acadia.

Never had I really thought about the fact we hadn't gone on a traditional date. Then again, our lives weren't all that traditional, were they? Me being the Alpha of an entire species, her being part of an angel faction sent to Earth to protect humans.

But that didn't mean Acadia didn't deserve that sort of courting. She'd put forth the effort, and now, as I walked into my private quarters, I decided I would, too. She deserved far more from me than my alpha male ego insistent upon dominating her. The question was, what would she enjoy? During the time we spent together back when I was injured, we whiled away hours upon hours talking. Mostly about facts, though. Her upbringing, mine. Our responsibilities. Never had I asked many personal questions.

Of course, that didn't mean I hadn't picked up on things. I happened to know she loved chocolate cake. As in, she would have it for evening and morning meals and every one in between if it were appropriate. I knew she gave herself pedicures and manicures because she enjoyed the solitude, although she could've easily had someone come in to do it. Also, her favorite movie was *Casablanca*, though I'd never understood the fascination.

Hmm.

The sound of a throat clearing had me spinning around. Blāz was standing on a ladder in the corner of the room.

"What the fuck are you doing?" I asked, glaring at the male.

"Sorry, boss. Didn't expect you back so soon."

"Please fucking tell me that's not a camera."

Blāz snorted. "No. Absolutely not. Heaven knows we don't need to see what you do in your private space."

I was thinking more about the fact I was not going to have anyone sneaking a peek at my female during those rare times Acadia came to me.

"Didn't I leave my room so you wouldn't be bothering me with this shit?"

Blāz smirked. "Didn't help that you took up rez in one of the rooms I'm including in your suite."

For fuck's sake.

When Blāz didn't continue, I motioned him to get on with it.

"I won't bore you with the details, but we're relatively close to being finished with the basics."

"The basics?"

"Yep. Next comes the demolition and rebuild."

I rolled my eyes.

Blāz stepped down from the ladder, then folded it quickly and carried it toward the door. "We've got a lot to do in the coming days."

"How long's this going to take?"

"As long as it needs to. Like I said, you are the Alpha, and since we've got the means to do so, we'll ensure you have a safe escape should it be necessary."

"Safe, meaning what?"

"Everything, *phaal*. It means everything." His voice lowered respectfully. "Where I'm concerned, we shall ensure you are never compromised the way your father was. Within the confines of these walls, you will be safe from any and all threats."

"Including the sun?" I asked, meaning it as a joke.

"Yes."

"And in the event of a fire?"

Blāz smirked. "Never underestimate me, *phaal*. Your safety is my utmost concern."

With that, the male pulled open the door, offered a one-handed wave, and slipped out.

It took a minute to remember what I'd been doing before the interruption. When I did, I grabbed the phone on the small desk, dropping into the seat, and hit zero.

"Yes, sire? How may I be of assistance?"

"I'd like to take Acadia on a date. A movie date. In the theater."

"That can easily be arranged, sire. Are there any specifics?"

I rattled off a few things, then asked Phillip to send someone to my room. I wanted to handwrite the invitation and have it delivered to her. When the male agreed, we disconnected.

After jotting my request in a manner that was readable,

then handing it off to the *heurosp* who arrived, I had just enough time to shower and change before meeting Acadia in the theater.

Feeling like a youth for perhaps the first time in my life, I found myself smiling as I strolled into the bathroom.

An hour later, I was walking through the clinic at Angel Central. I didn't stop to check in with the healers, though I heard Apollo speaking, then a male responding. Amethyst offered a half-hearted wave from where she was seated in front of a computer screen.

I continued out of the infirmary, down the hallway. I passed the various storage rooms, the war room, which was still buzzing as they tied off the night's patrols. On to the recreation room/bar. There were several people hanging around, including Eclipse and Orianna, who were sitting side by side on one of the sofas, as well as Malak, who was behind the bar, and Raksa, sitting on a stool.

Up the stairs, into the house. The *heurosp* were busy preparing the morning meal, while Obsidian and Penelope were in the sunroom talking to Aphotic and Stygian. I was surprised to see the brothers, but I didn't stop to chat. I wasn't about to be late for my date.

The dining room doors were open, and I could see several angels and vampires, even a couple of humans, already seated, including Bijou and Elizabeth. On the far side of the room, Oliver was sitting alone, his gaze locked on my daughter.

I shook my head at the obvious affection the male had for Bijou. If only he knew what was in store for him. Admittedly, there was a twinge of guilt that scurried through me. I knew Oliver's fate, yet I hadn't shared the details with anyone other than Obsidian.

Because I wouldn't be doing so now, I pushed the thought to the back of my mind as I continued on. Through the kitchen, past the small formal seating area, down the wide hallway toward the front doors. Then up the stairs to the second floor. The doors to the library were open, but no one was inside. To the right, I could hear the clack of pool balls and the rumble of conversation. To the left … that was the direction I was heading, right after I picked up my date.

I went left, then hung a quick right down the hall to Acadia's room, where I stopped and rapped my knuckles on the wood.

For some reason, I swiped my hand down my shirt to smooth out the wrinkles, though I was fairly certain I'd never done that before. Ever. I stopped before I checked my hair. That was just stupid.

When the door opened, my jaw promptly unhinged, my eyes caressing the beautiful female who appeared.

"I thought I was going to meet you," she said softly.

I smiled. "I thought this more appropriate. Are you ready?"

"I am."

I offered my arm, then curled my hand over hers when she slid her arm through.

"Two dates in one week," she said softly as we made our way back down the hall, to the right this time and down to the theater.

"We're making up for lost time."

Her laughter made my chest puff out like I'd done something spectacular. Truth was, Acadia was the spectacular one, and I was going to ensure she realized it. This was something simple that we needed, alone time, together. As a couple.

Phillip was standing at the theater doors, holding one open for us.

I nodded at the male, then led the way inside. The overhead lights were on, the screen dark, and on the left side was what appeared to be a concession stand, stocked with every kind of candy known to humankind. As well as a popcorn machine that was getting a workout.

"Would you care for anything?" I asked.

"M&M's," Acadia said quickly, as though she'd had those on her mind.

"Popcorn, sire?"

"Absolutely. And sodas."

"I'll bring them right down. Please take your seats."

So I did, leading Acadia down to the second row, which appeared to be the most popular based on the way the cushions looked to be more worn than the others. I held on to my female's arm as she took her seat. When she was situated, I moved to the adjacent one. Phillip wasn't far behind, delivering two popcorns—complete with their own red and white bags that announced what they were—and two soft drinks in red cups with clear straws.

These angels didn't play around.

"The movie will begin shortly, sire. Would you like for me to remain?"

"No. We'll be fine on our own. Thank you, Phillip."

"It is my absolute pleasure," the male said with a deep bow. "If you need anything else, simply press the button and we'll be right in to assist."

I disappeared, and a moment later, the projector overhead came on, the movie filling the screen.

Acadia giggled. "*Casablanca*? You remembered?"

"I remember everything, *balisra*." And it was true where she was concerned.

The lights dimmed, and a minute later, Acadia was captivated by the movie, and I divided my attention between the screen and the most fascinating female I'd ever been blessed with meeting.

Yes, we would be doing more of this, I decided.

Maybe I could talk the angels into putting in a bowling alley.

ACADIA

A s the credits began to roll, I found myself smiling. I would likely continue to reflect on this night as one of the best in the history books. Two dates in one week. And one of those had been my very first official date.

"I heard a rumor," Kaj prompted, drawing my attention to him as the screen faded to black, the lights brightening though it was still dim in comparison to the rest of the mansion.

I turned my head to the side, smiling over at him. "About?"

"Someone mentioned that humans like to make out in movie theaters."

I chuckled. "Do they?"

Kaj shrugged. "It's what I heard." He scanned the dim interior of the theater the angels used for recreation. "Though I'm not sure I can see the appeal."

Chuckling, I got to my feet and stepped over so that I was in front of him. When I moved closer, he held out his arms like he had expected me to sit with him. Once I was settled on his lap, I stared at his profile, running my fingers through the silky hair at the nape of his neck.

"Perhaps we should give it a try," I offered, knowing that had been his intention.

"Yeah?" His smile was ridiculously sexy. "Then perhaps you could start by putting your mouth on mine."

Oh, I could definitely do that.

Twisting my upper body, I pressed my forehead to his, inhaled that musky scent that was his and his alone. Our lips lingered apart for long seconds, that tease that would spark the flames between us. I still remember the first time he kissed me, how soft and smooth and warm his mouth was, how insistent his tongue became as it licked into my mouth.

A soft growl rumbled in his chest as Kaj's hand came around to cup my neck, his thumb brushing over my cheek as he eliminated the distance between our lips. I leaned into him, let myself get lost in the warmth of his mouth. He tasted both salty and sweet thanks to the refreshments we'd enjoyed during the movie. It made me want to devour him whole.

I was aware of a soft whirring sound and the recliner dipping backward. My body fell into his as his tongue mated with mine. His hand slid lower, his palm flattening on my chest, warmth seeping into the bare skin there. He didn't move lower, but my body didn't seem to mind. His touch alone was more than enough to fan those embers into a full-blown bonfire.

"Kaj..."

"Tell me, *balisra*."

"I ache for you," I whispered against his mouth.

Another dark rumble.

I had learned how to draw those out of him long ago, and it didn't matter how often I heard those seductive growls, they always affected me the same. I felt like I was the most precious thing in his world when I was with him. Didn't matter if he was riding the hard edge of desire and taking me fast and hard, or times like this, when he seemed content to merely linger and tease. Those eighteen months he was gone were pure hell on me. The life I'd envisioned with him had been ripped right out from under me.

My anger had been justified, I knew. But I was also aware that our time here was fleeting. I'd almost lost him once due to the injuries he had sustained. Then I'd lost him because of distance and time. Another attack had come at us, and my relief in knowing he hadn't been critically wounded despite how dire the situation had been had kept me sane even as he'd taken the vein of another.

But those hardships were behind us, and I was tired of waiting, not willing to risk losing another minute we had together. After all, no one knew what the Almighty had in store for us. He could easily erase my very existence tomorrow if he felt it necessary.

Now that Kaj was here, now that he was settling in because he wanted to remain close to me, I'd allowed myself to open up to the possibilities once again, and though I truly feared what the future might bring, I decided I could no longer allow that fear to hold me back.

"What's on your mind?" he said softly, pulling back, his hand returning to my cheek.

"You."

"What about me?"

"I'm glad you're here," I admitted.

"As am I, *balisra*. As am I."

His mouth returned to mine, a bit more insistent this time. His tongue delved between my lips, and I met him with eager ambition. Though the theater wasn't the most private place, right now it was ours. This was a milestone for us, a pivotal point in our relationship, and I wanted to explore it, to create a moment in time that we could both remember fondly for years to come.

"May I do something for you?" I asked.

When he pulled back this time, his eyes were brighter, a delicate light seeming to be coming from within.

"What did you have in mind?"

"You'll need to sit the chair up."

He did, the recliner slowly lifting, the footrest going back down.

Emboldened by the desire I sensed within him, I took the reins of the moment, easing down from his lap until I was kneeling on the floor.

He gasped, clearly recognizing my intent.

As I stared up at him, my fingers worked free the button on his jeans, then moved to the zipper.

With his help, I managed to ease them down his thighs, trapping his knees in the denim.

"Lower," I insisted, my voice rougher than I expected.

I tugged until the denim gave, sliding out from under his thick thighs and onward to bunch at his ankles. It was then that I positioned myself between his legs, forcing his knees wide so I could reach his heavy erection.

I wanted to feel him in my mouth. Before him, I'd never known that this was something males enjoyed, but we had explored together, and I had learned so many things about his body, the things he enjoyed, what would make him groan long and low.

This was one of those things.

Gripping his rigid length in my fist, I lowered my mouth to the bulbous head. I licked him first, then opened my mouth wide to take him inside.

"*Balisra*... Fuck."

There had been moments when Kaj would grip my hair roughly, tugging as I bobbed over him, and other times when he would fist the blankets to keep from reaching for me. Here, in the darkened theater, his hands gripped the leather armrests as he held himself there while I worked my lips around him.

Taking him in my mouth was such an intimate thing for me. It formed a connection between us, one where I sought to give him pleasure, and he was forced to endure. When I took him like this for the first time, the reactions of my body had surprised me. I was as turned on by what he allowed me to do to him as he was because of the sensations.

"Ah, fuck ... *balisra* ... your mouth ... so fucking sweet."

Those lewd words probably should've offended, but I enjoyed them immensely. I loved when Kaj lost himself, as though he had no idea how to rein in what he was feeling. I was in full control, which was a heady feeling in itself.

Working him with my lips, my tongue, my hands, I leisurely took him deep in my mouth, licking and sucking. I could feel every ridge, every vein, and the pulse that beat beneath the surface. I had learned I could feed from him like this, too. If I were to place my hands on his thighs, the energy I could siphon was exorbitant because he was unhinged. That alone gave me more power.

Not that I would do that now. I was content to focus on his pleasure.

"Acadia..."

That was his way of warning me he was close. I'd known it based on the flex and pulse of his sex in my mouth, the way his hips jerked forward to thrust in deeper when I lowered my mouth onto him again and again.

I reached out to him with my mind: *I want to taste you on my tongue.*

The thunderous growl that shot up from his chest had my

sex clenching, a programmed response because I knew he would return the favor when I was finished. Kaj had been known to spend hours with his head between my thighs, his mouth on my sex. My inner muscles squeezed as I thought about the pleasure he would give.

"*Balisra* ... I'm so close." His hand gripped my forearm as though he needed to anchor himself. "So fucking close ... ah, fuck ... just like that."

His breaths rasped in and out of his lungs as I worked him, hollowing out my cheeks because I knew he enjoyed the suction. I tightened my grip around the base of his erection, squeezing more firmly as I stroked in tandem with my ministrations.

His thighs tensed, which was the only warning I needed before his hips jerked roughly, his hand tightening on my arm. I felt the pulse of his thick shaft seconds before he growled long and low in his throat. I swallowed him down as he ejaculated, then licked lightly as I cleaned him.

When I lifted my head to look up at him, his eyes were glowing more brightly, a sense of peace relaxing his hard features. He looked at me with such awe, I felt it deep in my soul.

Then again, I felt him there, too.

As though we were entwined somehow, two halves of a whole.

25

KAJ

———

This female had always had the ability to rock me to my very core. From the very moment I laid eyes on her so long ago.

During our initial time together, the dance was a slow one, a journey initiated by chance and sealed by circumstance, gaining momentum with every passing night. At first, I felt guilty, but Acadia assured me it was mutual.

Although I had most definitely been the one to instigate our interactions back when I first came to the mansion, over time, as I grew stronger, the tide had turned. Eventually, because Acadia requested it, I had offered myself up to her sexual exploration and given the same in return. I would be the first to admit I hadn't been inexperienced before her, but I hadn't been nearly as experienced as I'd given myself credit for.

Then again, I'd never been with a female whose pleasure was my sole motivation. With Acadia, the only thing I wanted was to give her that riotous release over and over again.

"Privacy," I grumbled as I reached for my jeans to pull them up my thighs. "We need some. And we need it now."

We were still in the theater, my body temporarily sated by her exquisite ministrations. But it was my turn, and what I wanted to do to her required more space than this recliner would offer.

Peering up at Acadia, I saw her eyes were glazed with passion, an expression I was used to seeing on her face. I'd never expected her to be as forthcoming with her desires as she was. The females I'd lain with previously had been self-serving, always looking to receive before they were willing to give. That wasn't the case with Acadia. I had to take the reins if I wanted to return the favor because she was content to continue for as long as I would allow.

Great as that was, there were times when a male wanted nothing more than to bury his face between the thighs of his female and make her cry out his name.

This was one of those times.

Once my jeans were righted, I reached for her, lifting her off her feet and into my arms. Her soft giggle stirred all those crazy emotions within me, and I was grateful there wasn't a great distance that had to be traveled to get her back to her room. Easy enough to will the door open, close it behind us. Over to the bed, on it.

Oh, yeah. Right where I wanted her.

I lay out over my sexy Fae, finding her mouth with my own, her arms wreathing my neck. I loved when we were this close, almost didn't matter that we were both fully dressed.

Of course, that was the work of a moment, but rather than will our clothes away, I took my time undressing her, peeling that sexy fucking gown down her absurdly beautiful body. Beneath, she wore nothing, and I fucking loved that, too.

"Spread those pretty legs for me, *balisra*."

Acadia lifted up onto her elbows, watching as she did as I requested. She'd always been right there with me, eager to see what I was doing to her. I figured that added to the eroticism, something else that intrigued me. Acadia had never been a shy lover. It was her interest in exploring that had the ability to do me in.

As I kissed my way up the inside of her thigh, I felt her eyes on me, so I ensured she could see my tongue sweeping over her smooth skin. There wasn't any hair on her body, and that had been a pleasant surprise the first time I saw her naked. To know there was nothing to hinder the friction of my hands or my mouth spurred me forward. I kissed high up on her thigh, then dragged my tongue over and down, gliding to the heart of her.

Acadia moaned, her stomach muscles tightening as I focused on her clitoris, licking my way around the tiny bundle of nerves, circling before drawing it between my lips.

"Kaj ... yes ... that. Do more of that."

Who was I to deny her anything? I spent long minutes worshiping her with my tongue, bringing her to the brink, and letting her ease back down. I bestowed the same attention that she'd given me in that theater. I wanted her to come, but not until I'd gotten my fill. Not that I would ever get enough of her. I could've spent hours, hell, nights right here, my face buried in her pussy, my tongue working her into a frenzy. This was heaven for me, right here with my sweet fairy writhing and moaning.

"I want you inside me," she rasped.

"Patience, *balisra*. Not until you come all over my face."

Another of her strangled moans sounded in my ears as I

suckled her clit, thrashing it with my tongue. I remained like that, taking my cues from her soft pleas. When she finally came, my name ripped from her throat, I felt like I was the king of the universe.

Getting rid of my clothing took a bit more work, but as I stripped, I watched her, admired the curves of her body, the smoothness of her alabaster skin. She was true perfection in my eyes. Once more, I found myself wanting to claim her. I longed for the day when her skin would forever hold the imprint of my scent, her veins filled with my *sonavex*, the secretion I would pump into her bloodstream to mark her as mine and only mine.

All in due time, I knew.

For now, I simply wanted to be one with her.

Once I was naked, I crawled over her. I snaked my arm beneath her back, brought our mouths together, then rolled so she was atop me.

"Sit on me, *balisra*. Take me inside you."

Acadia's mouth hovered over mine as she reached between us, guiding my cock to the slick heat between her thighs. I held my breath as I breached her entrance, pushing inside. The tight clasp of her pussy had the air expelling from my lungs in a rush. The feeling exquisite, just as it was every time I was inside her.

I shifted my hands behind my head and watched as she sat up. Her breasts swayed as her hips began a perfect grind over me. Up, down, forward, back. She knew exactly what she needed, and I loved that she was willing to take it. I remained like that, observing, admiring, as she took us both higher and higher. I didn't move to take over until she'd brought herself to orgasm. Only then did I reach for her, shifting so that she was beneath me, my body laid out over her. I ground my hips to hers, burying myself as deep as I could go.

"I love you, *balisra*." I felt the need to tell her as much. I didn't say it nearly enough, but like the dates we'd been on, I realized it was necessary. I never wanted Acadia to question how I felt about her. She deserved all of me. Not only my body, or the energy source I could provide. She deserved everything I had to give and then some.

I gripped her hip and angled my cock, driving into her slow and deep. The clasp of her pussy held me suspended in that ethereal place that I never knew existed until I met her. Somewhere between overwhelming ecstasy and pure, unadulterated bliss. I clung to that sensation as I rode her. When her nails dug into my flesh, I increased my pace, put more power behind my thrusts until the bed was rocking. I fucked her harder, faster, deeper, taking everything she offered and giving the same in return.

"*Balisra* ... I'm going to come deep inside you."

She moaned, her body rocking with mine, a perfect counterbalance until our breaths rasped out of exhausted lungs, our bodies tangled and racing to the precipice.

"Kaj!"

Her orgasm, the way her body locked down on me, was what sent me over. I slammed my hips forward, burying myself as deep as physically possible, and let myself go.

"I love you, *balisra*." I knew I would be telling her that for as long as I lived.

She didn't say the words back, but I didn't need to hear them. I knew. I knew deep down that Acadia loved me. Something kept her from speaking the words aloud, but she would when she was ready. Until then, I would simply continue to tell her what she meant to me.

This female was all I had ever wanted and the only thing I would ever need.

She was my very heartbeat.

MIRAKEL

After the last time Briony came to my room, told me what she wanted, and stared at me as though I could simply nod and agree, I had seriously considered keeping my distance. After all, I'd sent her away, neither of us satisfied with the outcome.

Of course, that was two days ago, and turned out, it wasn't physically possible for me to stay away. Sure, it had something to do with my blood needs, but not as much as I pretended. Since I'd learned the healers had started storing blood on site, I actually had another option, though I tended to pretend it didn't exist.

Unfortunately, I knew I had hurt Briony when I'd ushered her out of my room after she had been so candid about what she wanted from me. And that meant it was up to me to apologize.

So there I was, standing outside her bedroom door, hand raised to knock. I'd been there for a solid ten minutes, plenty of time to get my thoughts in order, but I felt as jumbled and chaotic as I ever had since she walked away from me the last time.

The problem was, I didn't know how to salvage this. Briony had been honest about what she wanted, and I'd been a coward.

Suddenly, the door swung wide and Briony's beautiful face appeared.

"Are you going to stay out there all morning?"

There was little warmth in her tone, which told me she hadn't forgiven me for my asshole-ish-ness.

Yes, that was a word. And I was the king of it, thank you very much.

Taking a deep breath, I lowered my hand to my side. "I came to apologize."

"Save it."

Ouch. I deserved that. I did.

"Briony..."

"Don't 'Briony' me," she snapped. "I put myself out there, Mirakel. I told you how I felt and you—"

I cut her off, nudging her into the room and closing the door behind me. I had no desire for the entire mansion to hear our conversation.

"First of all," I stated firmly, "you did not tell me how you felt. You told me what you wanted."

"And the difference is?"

"One pertains to your feelings on the matter, and the other is simply sex."

Her amethyst eyes widened.

I stepped around her, scanning the room. It was the first time I'd been in here, and I found it oddly comforting. It was a female's room. From the white velvet drapes hanging from the ceiling to the floor, concealing the shuttered windows, to the white shag rug peeking out from beneath the bed. Even the furniture was a brilliant white. The color in the space came from the jewel-toned pillows and throw blankets, the emerald-green bedding. It reminded me of the female herself. Unassuming to most, yet full of life.

"I don't know how to do this," I admitted, turning to face her.

"Oh." Her eyes widened. "I didn't realize... We could learn together."

I grinned. She thought I was inexperienced. Wouldn't that be a thrill?

"That's not what I meant. I'm not a virgin, Briony. I'm three hundred and eighty-two years old. I've had numerous lovers in my lifetime, and I'd always expected I would have many more." I met her gaze, held it. "Then I met you."

Her face softened. "Meaning?"

"What do you know about the mating habits of vampires?"

She shook her head. "Nothing."

"Vampires mate for life. When a male finds his *nehadon*, there's no one else for him. Ever. It's a phenomenon known as *mielix zan*. It loosely translates to a sexual imprinting."

"I didn't realize you had a mate." She looked sincerely apologetic.

I moved toward her. "I don't." I stopped when I was peering down at her. "But I have imprinted. Which means I've found my mate."

Based on the glimmer in her eyes, I suspected she knew where this was going.

"You, Briony."

"So the healer was right?"

I frowned. "What?"

"Nothing." She smiled.

I took a deep breath. "I can't control my nature, nor can I change it. And that puts you in a precarious situation. Or more accurately, the other males in this mansion. I know what your duties entail. I know you feed the males within this residence. I get that. But I can't tolerate it—not even the *idea* of it— because I've bonded with you."

"And you regret that?"

I frowned. "No. Of course not."

"Then why do you continuously push me away?"

"You deserve better than me, love. So much better."

"But what if I don't want better? What if I want you? You haven't given me that opportunity."

Okay, so I had imagined a dozen ways this would play out, but the many times I'd fantasized this convo in my head ... that had never been what I heard coming from her mouth.

"I don't know the first thing about bonding," she said softly, stepping forward, her eyes still locked with mine. "But I won't know if you don't give me the chance."

"Is that what you want?"

"I don't know. But I figure it's worth exploring, don't you?"

My gaze dropped to her mouth. I remembered how good she tasted, how perfectly she'd fit against me when I kissed her that first time in my room. Two days ago. That was all it had been, but it felt like a millennium.

"I won't lie," she stated. "I haven't been saving myself for anyone. But in that same regard, I've never encountered a male I wanted the way I want you. I don't know what that means, but I know we'll never know if you keep pushing me away."

Heaven help me.

"I don't want to push you away," I said, my voice so low I wondered if I'd merely thought the words.

"Then don't." She placed her hands on my chest.

I covered them with my own, continuing to hold her stare. "Forgive me, Briony."

"There's nothing to forgive."

But there was. So much. I wouldn't be an easy male for her, I knew. I was highly sexual, my needs intense. It was a character trait unique to vampires. She deserved better than that, but the bonded side of me wasn't capable of releasing her. The mere thought of another male touching her, kissing her... It was enough to make me mental.

Easing down to my knees, I peered up at her. "Forgive me, Briony." I knew I'd said it once, but I couldn't move forward until she accepted it.

Her soft, cool hands cupped my face, her eyes glittering. "There's nothing to forgive," she repeated. "But if that's what you need, then yes, I forgive you."

I leaned forward, my arms moving around her, holding her as I pressed my face to her abdomen.

"I never want to hurt you. But I fear I will."

Her arms curled around my head. "I'm far stronger than you give me credit for, Mirakel. Perhaps you should give me the chance to show you that."

Yes. A chance.

I wanted that.

With all that I was.

"Mirakel?"

"Hmm?" I pulled back, looked up at her.

"Let's explore this together. Just the two of us."

"I'm going to want more than you can give."

Her smile was radiant. "You don't know that."

Oh, I knew, all right.

How else did I explain every other person in my life abandoning me? I'd never been wanted before, and I'd learned over the centuries not to get my hopes up.

As much as I wanted to think otherwise, I found it difficult to believe now would be any different.

26

BIJOU

A movie.

That was what was on the agenda come morning.

Which meant I simply needed to get through the next eight hours, and I was home free.

Of course, being immersed in the middle of the chaos known as the training center wasn't exactly how I'd hoped to spend my evening, but when Huracān asked me to stop in to meet the new recruits, I wasn't able to refuse.

"The good news is, they've figured out how to bed down for now."

I peered around the bunks that lined one solid wall. Two narrow beds, one set atop the other, were positioned like fence posts for as far as the eye could see. Okay, maybe not that far. If my quick math was correct, there were thirteen bunks—twenty-six beds—in total, with roughly ten feet between each. And like what I'd seen on television, they were taking their cues from the American military. Each mattress had a puke-green bedspread pulled tight with perfect corners on the ends and a single white pillow at the top.

"Will they have more privacy eventually?"

"Yes," Huracān replied. "We'll have two to a room. They'll share a private bath."

"And the females?" I asked, noticing there were currently five standing in the long line of angels and vampires.

"We'll be placing the outlier with one of the duets, provided they all last that long."

I cut my gaze to him. "I assume that's not a gender bias, Huracān."

He chuckled. "Not at all. Hell, I suspect the males will ring out before the females."

"What about meals? How are they dealing with that?"

"The *heurosp* have agreed to feed them until they have the kitchen in order."

By *in order*, I took that to mean built and accessorized, because as it stood now, there weren't any walls, no appliances, not even running water.

"Mind if I talk with them?" I asked.

"Be my guest. I'm going to assist with the building material that was delivered this morning."

As the hulking vampire walked away, I headed toward a group of trainees who currently had their heads together and were peering down at a notebook.

"Evening," I greeted, stopping a few feet away.

Six pairs of eyes lifted, and suddenly two of them snapped to attention, backs going ramrod straight, hands at their sides, chins up.

"Stand down," I said with a chuckle. "Treat me like you would any of the Zenith."

"But you are the Alpha's daughter," one of them countered.

"And you are going to one day be working for the Alpha. I think it's safe to say we'll be in close contact for the duration. Might as well become friends."

During that brief conversation, the other four had taken up similar positions, though they clearly hadn't realized why they were doing it. And when the first two relaxed their shoulders, so did the others.

"How about we start with names?" I prompted. "My name's Bijou. Call me Bijou. What may I call you?"

The trainees blurted their name as they moved down the line: Romer, Sariel, Berk, Engel, Koray, and last but not least, Jayke.

Not that I would remember their names. Not immediately, but I suspected as we got to know one another, I wouldn't have an issue. Of course, noting whether they were angel or vampire was much easier for me than their family-given honorific. As a vampire, I could sense my own kind. They had a unique scent. Angels ... well, they were masked, which was how I could detect them from humans. Always protected, that lot.

"What are you starting on?" I inquired.

Sariel, an angel, motioned toward the notebook. "It's imperative we have our living quarters and feeding facility constructed first."

Smart. I completely agreed.

"We've decided to work on the kitchen first," Romer (vampire) noted, motioning toward the rows of bunks. "For the time being, we have our sleeping arrangements. Not ideal, but livable."

I turned and surveyed the space. "If you had your living quarters erected, it would give you more privacy from noise, right? In turn, you could run twenty-four-hour shifts on the rest. That way, you're not working on top of one another, plus you're covering more ground by not wasting even daylight hours."

Romer glanced at Sariel. "That's not a bad idea."

Sariel nodded. "I agree. Plus, we're looking at simple walls for the sleeping quarters."

I was surprised to see the two working so well together. Then again, they were just getting started. I figured with time, their individual personalities would start to come out. The leaders would move to the front and likely clash heads, hindering progress, while others would hold grudges.

Hopefully they'd make some progress before that happened.

"Hey, Bijou?"

Turning, I saw Blāz strolling toward me. He smiled brightly, his nearly colorless eyes glittering merrily. "Mind giving me a hand? I need to interview a female. Thought you'd like to take a trip."

Out of the mansion? No way could I pass that one up.

"Of course," I told him, trying to tamp down some of my excitement. I turned back to the trainees. "Well, good luck to all of you. I'll be around, so if you have any questions ... I'll do my best to help out."

The two vampires—Romer and Berk—bowed before me, making me blush.

Knowing better than to wave them off, I offered a clumsy curtsy in return, then fell into step with Blāz.

"I will never get used to that," I told the male.

"It's nice to see, though."

Yeah, maybe.

Still uber-weird.

. . .

"Next time, I'm driving," I told Blāz as the male steered the Escalade toward town.

"You don't like my driving?"

"This is not driving," I countered. "This is cruising."

The male chuckled. "Your father would castrate me if anything happened to you. Since I've grown quite fond of my anatomy, I'll stick with cruising."

"Where are we meeting her?"

"Coffee shop." His eyes remained on the road, even when we emerged from the angels' *dhira*, offering clear visibility.

"Seriously?" I fought the urge to clap my hands in glee.

I couldn't recall the last time I'd been to a coffee shop, but I could smell it now. The poignant aroma of espresso, the sweetness of all the fancy things they poured into their fancy drinks.

"Her name's Leilana," he said. "The female we're meeting with."

"What position are you interviewing for?"

"The personal assistant to the Alpha. According to her resume, she's fully qualified."

"And what makes someone qualified to be the PA to the leader of a race?" I inquired because I enjoyed talking to the male.

"Killer typing skills, for one."

"And what exactly are we looking for in this candidate?"

"Think about the assistant as being the go-between. She'll be the face of the *kirlesgun*."

The face of the current regime. Made sense. "So we're looking for someone well-dressed and well-spoken?"

"Her attire's not as important because we can work on that. However, her ability to communicate clearly is crucial, yes."

"Do we know anything else about her? I assume she'll be

residing within the Lair." It only made sense that we knew her history.

"I did a background check. Free and clear."

"No marks at all?" I peered over at him. "So she's managed to remain clear of humans?"

"I know, it's a shocker, right? But yep. She implemented a school system within her clan, and she's focused on educating the offspring mostly."

Sounded very noble.

"How old is she?"

Blāz's eyes cut to mine briefly. "One forty-five."

So, still very young in the eyes of the vampire community. Probably a good thing. Not too jaded from history.

"And her feelings on the current *kirlesgun*?" I asked.

"That was the first thing I asked her." He grinned. "She and her family were staunch supporters of Kardobahn, and they support Kaj though they would prefer to get to know him better."

I understood that. My father had yet to make a name for himself as the *phaal*. Then again, he'd been too busy running for his life to have time to make an impact. Now that we had settled somewhat, I hoped that would change in the near future.

"What would you like me to do?" I asked as Blāz flipped the turn signal and steered the SUV into a parking lot lined with stand-alone stores, including Books & Beans. I assumed that was our destination, and my mouth watered with thoughts of a cappuccino.

"Preferably lead the interview," he said, motioning for me to get out.

I stepped out into the cool night air and inhaled deeply. I couldn't remember the last time I'd been outside, but it was glorious to be beneath the stars, the crisp air slipping into my nostrils, the scent of coffee drifting toward me. When I joined Blāz at the front of the vehicle, I noticed he was tucking in his shirt, adjusting the weapons he had beneath the suede jacket he wore.

"You look beautiful," I teased.

He offered a smirk, then gestured for me to walk before him. Our keen senses scanned our surroundings as I led the way to the glass door of the coffee shop. A tinkling overhead signaled our arrival, and we were instantly greeted by a couple of employees manning the coffee bar at the very back of the shop. Warm air billowed our way, along with the delicious scent of coffee.

I was just about to ask how we would know who we were looking for when I caught the scent of a vampire nearby. I scanned the various seating areas and located the female sitting in a small section blocked in by short bookshelves.

The female's eyes lifted as though she, too, had caught our presence.

"I have to have coffee while we're here," I whispered to Blāz. "We can introduce ourselves, then I'll get us something."

"I'll get it," he countered.

"Scared to be left alone with her?" I joked.

"You have no idea," he rasped.

I actually found that interesting since I wasn't sure Blāz had ever met a stranger. He was likely the most outgoing of all the males who worked for my father.

Oh, yeah. This was going to be fun.

ACADIA

When Kaj asked me to join him for a walk-through of the new training facility, I was surprised but not at all disappointed.

Now, as we stepped into the din, I smiled.

Angels and vampires alike were scattered about, working diligently on their tasks. A few were chatting softly, a couple of them had headphones on their heads, more were moving to the beat of the music drifting out from a set of speakers set up on a table.

"How long have they been working on this?" I asked, sliding my hand in his when he offered it.

"This is their first full day together. The angels arrived just before dawn, the vampires a couple of days ago. On Thursday."

The enormous space spread out before us was brightly lit with various forms of lighting, none of which were coming from the inserts in the ceiling, which had yet to be connected to power.

As we neared, I noticed Huracān talking to two young males, using hand signals to exaggerate whatever it was he was explaining to them.

Heavy footfalls sounded behind us, drawing us both up short. Obsidian strolled over, his eyes shielded by those dark lenses, but I could tell he was taking it all in, likely determining what was different from the last time he was there.

Out of habit, I offered a slight curtsy to the male when he approached. It wasn't that I'd always been formal with him, but right now, I felt the need. Probably had everything to do with the fact I felt as though I was abandoning him and had yet to explain myself.

"How're they doing?" Obsidian asked, his question directed at Kaj.

"Just got here myself." Kaj caught Huracān's attention, motioned him toward us. "Perhaps we can get an update."

The enormous male strolled over, a wide grin on his rugged face. "Greetings. You just missed Bijou. She stopped in to check it out."

"What'd she think?" Kaj inquired.

Huracān smirked. "She didn't say, but the vampires sure took notice of their princess."

I smiled at that. I could see how these trainees might be intimidated to have royalty in their presence. However, I'd had the pleasure of talking to Bijou, and the female was rather approachable. More so, the longer she was here.

"Thought I'd give my female a tour," Kaj said, his hand squeezing mine lightly when he said *female*.

For whatever reason, that made my heart skip a beat. After last night, the movie date, the erotic encounters afterward, Kaj had remained in my bed until nightfall. When he awoke, I was already awake, lying in the darkened room, watching his face as he slept. No sooner had he caught sight of me than he moved over me and gave me a grand wake-up with his body. Afterward, he slipped out to give me time to shower and get ready for the night. When I came down to join the others for the evening meal, he was there waiting for me, securing a table at the back of the room.

Needless to say, I was enjoying this time with him. It felt strangely different than before. I had always expected to be utilized for my blood, sometimes engaging in sex because it offered the energy that would fuel me for longer periods. Never had the males made me feel like I was simply a tool at their disposal, but there'd never been any real intimacy, either.

Except with Kaj. He'd always been different with me. In the beginning, when I was nursing him back to health, he was hesitant. Then, when he returned this time, we'd endured the *gathenya*, seeking one another out to quench that over-whelming need. Now that things had settled, it was as though we were coming into our own.

"So, what do you think?" Huracān asked Kaj and Obsidian. "Bijou gave them the idea of getting their private rooms built so they could work in shifts, filling the full twenty-four hours with work."

"Bijou did?" Obsidian glanced around. "That's a brilliant idea." Obsidian smirked at Kaj. "Didn't get her brains from her father, huh?"

Kaj chuckled. "Certainly not."

"Their objective this night is to get all the walls for the sleeping quarters erected, insulated, and Sheetrocked. Tomorrow they'll move on to tape and float, painting. Perhaps by Monday, they'll be starting their shifts."

I watched as a group of trainees carried in lumber from an exterior door. As Fae, I could sense which were vampires and which were angels. They varied in all sizes, shapes, and color-ings. These were likely the most formidable of their species, born and bred for this particular purpose—protecting humans or providing backup to those whose sole responsi-bility was to protect humans, as was the case with the warriors.

As I watched them, I thought back to all the times a new male would come to the mansion, joining the *fiestreigh*. It was rare they came in multiples despite Michael's best efforts to reproduce males who were as formidable as the warriors. The other Fae and I had been there to welcome them in, to help them get situated, as well as to offer them the life source necessary for them to remain on Earth.

"How often will they feed?" I asked, recalling Kaj mentioning Michael had allocated angels to perform those duties.

"Daily for now. The angels come as soon as the sun goes down and it's safe for them," Obsidian noted. "As long as we keep our numbers low, we'll have a one-to-one ratio for feeding. Once they've completed their task, they return to Heaven."

It felt strange that Michael would've opted to utilize angels instead of Fae. Though I knew we didn't have the numbers to handle an additional twenty-seven who needed blood, I still had concerns as to what that would mean for me and the others. Would Michael one day replace us? Send us into the shadows for all of eternity? After all, there was nowhere else for us to go. And if we weren't needed any longer...

"Acadia?"

The deep cadence of Kaj's voice drew my attention from my thoughts. "Hmm?"

"Are you okay, *balisra*?"

Shaking off the negative energy, I stood a bit taller and smiled. "Of course. I find this place fascinating. I'm sure once it's completed, it'll be even more impressive."

"That's the plan," Obsidian agreed. "Now, if you'll excuse me, I need to check in with Reidar. I've got someone coming to relieve you, Huracān."

"Thank you," the male said. "I figure we could work in four-hour increments so as not to ignore our duties."

I listened with half an ear while the males chatted briefly before dispersing.

All the while wondering exactly how much things were changing for us.

Question was: was this for better or worse?

27

ACADIA

———

"Who were you talking to?" I prompted when Kaj ended his phone call and joined me on the small love seat in his room.

"My father."

My eyes shot to his face as I tried to discern his tone, more specifically, the concern I heard in it.

"As I suspected, he thought I was dead."

"I assume he was happy to hear that isn't the case."

Kaj nodded, his gaze locked on the cold fireplace before us. "He needs me back there."

Although I'd known this day was coming, I couldn't deny the

ache that bloomed in my chest. The thought of Kaj leaving, of not seeing him, was more painful than it should've been, considering I hadn't deluded myself into thinking this was a forever thing.

"When will you be leaving?" I inquired, not looking at him as I spoke.

"I told him I'd be back in a week."

A week. That was all the time we had left together? I wasn't sure whether that was good or bad. Would it hurt less if he went back now? If I weren't subjected to six or seven more nights of him sleeping beside me? Or could I find a way to make enough memories in that time to tide me over for eternity? Neither seemed satisfactory as far as my sanity went, but it wasn't really my decision, now was it?

"Acadia?"

"Hmm?"

"Look at me, balisra."

I forced myself to look over, my heart in my throat. I could see the pain in his eyes. He didn't want to leave me any more than I wanted him to go. But behind that, I could see his resignation. His duty was to his father, and mine was to the warriors. We came from different worlds, and others expected things from us.

Kaj leaned toward me, his big, warm hand curling around my cheek, his fingers settling under my hair, his thumb stroking gently.

"I don't want you to go," I told him, though I hadn't intended to lay that at his feet.

"I don't want to go, either."

But it was going to happen regardless. We both knew it.

"You could come with me," he whispered.

No, I couldn't. But he already knew that. My duties were here, my life here. And even if I was willing to go, it wasn't an option. If I were to walk out of this mansion, I would be stricken from existence, cast into the shadows, neither alive nor dead.

Kaj scooted closer, his fingers sliding deeper into my hair as he *cradled my face and urged my mouth to his. I went without question because this was the only place I wanted to be. With him for as long as time and destiny allowed.*

What I really wanted to do was run to my room and bury my head in my blankets, cry for the injustice of it all. But I knew it wouldn't change anything, and the thought of wasting what precious time we had left hurt almost as much as the idea of never seeing him again.

To be fair, I thought things had changed between us. After he'd witnessed me feeding Khalon, after he'd taken me to the floor and all but claimed me as his own, I had entertained the idea of being Kaj's forever. Deep down, I'd known that wasn't an option, but for a while, it had been easy to pretend. For the past month, he'd kept me close, and I had stayed willingly.

His lips brushed mine softly as he inched even closer. "Let me hold you, balisra.*"*

"Make love to me," I pleaded.

A soft growl escaped him, one that had a way of igniting my insides, warming my entire being. And when he shifted his weight so that he could move over me, I reclined, welcoming his body against mine. For long minutes, his mouth fused to mine, and I got lost in the sensation of his kiss. Time seemed to stand still as our hands wandered, clothing began to slip away until we were skin to skin.

And when he settled between my thighs, his erection pushing into me, I welcomed him into my body as I had so many times. He made love to me then, slowly and leisurely, neither of us rushing, satisfied to let the sensations linger, the heat build into a conflagration that consumed us both.

As he cradled my face, I curled my fingers around his hand, holding him to me as I kissed his palm. Tears dripped from my eyes unbidden.

"Oh, sweet love," he whispered. "Don't cry."

I sobbed and attempted to force a smile, but it wouldn't form.

My heart was breaking, and though he was still with me, I felt as though he were a million miles away already.

His focus shifted, his hips moving faster as he drove us both to the precipice and then over.

I wanted to tell him I loved him, but the words were merely that. Words. They wouldn't convince him to stay because he had more pressing things to deal with, and the last thing I wanted to do was hurt him more than he was already hurting.

It pained me to know that the week would soon be over and he would be leaving, but I vowed to cherish every last minute with him, and when he walked away, I would keep him locked deep within my heart for eternity.

It would have to be enough to know that I'd been loved once in my never-ending existence, and I needed these memories to sustain me going forward.

KAJ

I lay in the darkened room, my arm looped around Acadia as she slept.

Nearly six months had passed since I arrived here, and so much had changed within that time. Perhaps not for others, but for me. I had fully recovered from my injuries, my body stronger than before because I'd fed from Acadia all this time.

The mere thought of returning to my previous existence, feeding *from the* cosrobols *day in and day out, did not sit well with me. I couldn't fathom putting my mouth on another, biology be damned.*

But I would because that was what was expected of me. My life was not my own any more than Acadia's was her own. My duty was to the Alpha. Regardless of what my heart wanted, I couldn't stay here.

"Why aren't you resting?" Acadia whispered, her lips brushing my chest as she shifted in my arms.

"I'm content to hold you all day," I assured her, shifting to watch as she moved over me.

Because I didn't want to miss a moment, I willed the bedside lamp on despite the fact I could see clearly in the dark. The artificial light allowed me the ability to connect with Acadia visually, and that was as much of an aphrodisiac as her hands moving over me.

"Take me inside you," I rasped, sliding my hands up her thighs as she straddled my hips.

Acadia lifted, her small hand curling around my erection and guiding me into the haven of her body.

I groaned as her slick heat slid over me, her tight sheath welcoming me.

Once I was seated deep within her, Acadia leaned forward, her palms flattening against my chest. I quickly covered hers with mine and held her to me.

"Take from me," I urged.

Her eyes met mine, and a second later, my back arched as she drew her strength from my body. My cock kicked as the pleasure consumed me. It was as much mental as it was physical. Knowing I could be the life source she needed was a pleasure all its own.

She rolled her hips forward and back, stroking me with the smooth walls of her sex. I watched as she rode me, her hair swaying around her shoulders, falling over my chest, tickling my skin. I would miss this most. Not necessarily the sex, but the connection we shared. This was more than mere physical pleasure. It was two beings coming together as one. I was whole for the first time in my life, complete in a way I knew I would never be without her.

We stayed like that for the longest time, her body recharging from the energy she took from me, mine maintaining a strong, steady pulse as the erotic pleasure coursed through my veins. And when it was my turn, I repositioned so that I was behind her, my cock finding its way inside her once more. I pierced her vein as I rocked my hips, driving deep. I had no idea how many times either of us climaxed, but I knew it wasn't nearly enough to sustain me forever.

I retracted my fangs, sealed her wounds, then rolled over her so that she was beneath me, her beautiful eyes peering up at me. I drove into her again, my hands sliding over hers as I pinned her to the bed and rode her for long minutes, my hips pumping, my heart soaring. This was as close to Heaven as I hoped to ever be. Right here, with this female. She was my heart, my very reason for breathing. She brought me back from death, and I would never forget her.

Not even if I lived forever.

28

BIJOU

"Perhaps you could tell us a little about yourself," I prompted when I joined the interviewee after Blāz slipped away to place our order.

"I'm an open book," Leilana said with a smile that registered all the way to her eyes.

As far as first impressions went, I found the female to be a bit on the ... hesitant side. As though she wasn't exactly comfortable leaving the safety of her clan to venture out into the human world. Not that I considered that a bad thing, per se, but it was rare to encounter a vampire who wasn't well-versed in human interactions. However, Leilana's eyes continued to scan the room as though she was waiting for the older female scanning the cookbooks to do a running dive on top of her.

Regarding appearances... Leilana was pretty in an understated manner. She was on the petite side, her blond hair pulled back into a sleek ponytail, the end draped over her shoulder. Her eyes were a radiant blue, her lips a soft pink. She had minimal makeup on, and the outfit she wore looked better suited for an elderly human than a one-hundred-forty-five-year-old vampire. I had to wonder if she wore the bulky clothes to cover herself up rather than embrace the lush figure she clearly hid beneath.

But I wasn't here to judge her on her fashion sense or to make assumptions about her self-view. This was a job interview, and I'd do well to remember that.

"Tell me about your family," I said, because it was obvious the female needed a more structured request.

"I still live at home with my mother and father. In Tennessee. My two younger sisters reside there as well. I have two older brothers, who moved to New York to assist the clans in that region. I'm close with my family, I guess you could say. We have a good relationship."

I had to wonder whether Blāz had done background checks on all family members or if he'd kept it restricted to the female before me. Even knowing what little I did about the male, I couldn't imagine he hadn't been extremely thorough in his investigations before setting up this meeting.

Luckily, said male strolled our way carrying one large ceramic mug and a bottle of water. When he passed over the coffee cup, I smiled up at him, offering a thanks. He then cracked the lid on his water and dropped into the chair at my side. He looked bored and more than a little uncomfortable, but I couldn't imagine why.

"We were just talking about her family," I explained.

He nodded as though he couldn't care less about that. When he peered back at Leilana, he said, "And your skill set?"

Way to get right to the point, Blāz.

He smiled, clearly acknowledging the words I'd projected in his head.

"I'm proficient in computers," she said quickly, her eyes not quite meeting Blāz's.

I watched the two as Leilana continued to explain how many words per minute she could type, how she'd been trained in shorthand dictation. It wasn't what the female was saying that caught my attention, however. No, that was reserved for the way Leilana was watching Blāz. Mostly when the male wasn't looking, as though she was too nervous to meet his gaze head-on.

Not that I blamed Leilana. Blāz was an incredibly attractive male. From the brush-cut black hair to that enormous, incredibly built body, Blāz definitely drew the eyes of females. I couldn't help wondering what he thought of Leilana.

Then, as Blāz began rambling about computer crap, I tried to imagine the pair of them as a mated couple. They would probably have beautiful offspring, I thought. Blāz with his nearly colorless irises—a rarity for vampires—and black hair, combined with Leilana and her bright blue eyes and blond hair. The male's features would likely eclipse the female's as far as coloring went.

Oh, what the hell was I doing? These two were not going to be a couple. They were both employed by the Alpha. Or they might be, as was the case with Leilana. But that was just like me to ferret out their happily ever after. I'd been doing that for as long as I could remember. Didn't matter who I was with; if they were single, I was constantly trying to pair them up.

Probably had a lot to do with the fact I'd thought I had found my own happily ever after with Reve. Then, as soon as he found out I was related to the Alpha, the male had turned his back on me, proving exactly how high he held me in his esteem.

Huh. I realized that was the first time I'd thought about Reve in … weeks? Months? I wasn't sure, but I didn't appreciate him bearing down on my conscience right then.

As I sipped my cappuccino and listened to Leilana and Blāz slip into technical computer terms, I realized for the first time that I had moved on from Reve, from the past I'd left behind when I found my father and we moved to Darkness. Despite the issues I was having with Oliver, I was, in fact, happy. Mostly. There were still plenty of times I missed my mother so much the ache in my chest took on a life of its own. But I was still able to function, forming relationships with those at the mansion.

"Bijou?"

I jerked my head toward Blāz. "Hmm?"

"Is there anything else you'd like to ask Leilana?"

Setting my cup down, I considered the female as I gathered my thoughts.

"Say you learned of a threat against the Alpha," I prompted. "What would you do with that information?"

Those bright blue eyes widened. "I would promptly bring it to the attention of the Alpha or his guards."

"And if the threat came from one of your family members?" I asked, playing devil's advocate.

"It would matter not," the female said resolutely. "A threat, no matter who it might come from, cannot be ignored."

Good answer, though I wasn't convinced the female would betray her family that way. I got the feeling Leilana would want to do right by her Alpha, but I wasn't so sure she would.

"Do you have an issue being in the presence of a large number of males at one time?"

"It's not something I'm accustomed to, no. However, I would not have an issue with it."

"Are you capable of defending yourself?"

"In what manner?"

"Against a threat. Should someone corner you, do you have the ability to defend yourself?"

"If you're asking whether I've been trained for combat, then no."

"Are you opposed to learning basic self-defense?"

"Absolutely not. I believe it would be of benefit to me."

Another good answer.

I nodded at Blāz, then reached for my cup. "That's all I've got."

Blāz picked up the conversational baton and gave Leilana the opportunity to ask questions. The female only had a few: should she be selected for the position, would she have the ability to keep in contact with her family? Would she need to acquire a vehicle to perform her duties? And last but not least, would she be able to bring her personal possessions with her if she were hired and asked to move into the residence of the Alpha?

Yes, no, and of course were Blāz's easy responses.

While they concluded with pleasantries, I finished my coffee and longingly looked at the counter, wondering if I should get another to go. Probably not, I thought. I knew the repercussions of too much caffeine.

However, I was curious as to whether the *heurosp* would be open to installing an espresso machine at Angel Central. Or better yet, at the Lair.

Yes. The latter because no matter what my father said, I still wanted to move in there. For some reason, I felt as though I was meant to be amongst my own kind. It wasn't that I was capable of predicting the future, but I got the strange feeling something big was coming.

Something that was going to rock the foundation of my very existence.

I just didn't know what or when, but I expected it would be sooner rather than later.

KAJ

After leaving the training facility, I brought Acadia to the Lair. I couldn't recall her visiting since we moved in, and I was eager for her to get acclimated to it. If I had a say in the matter, she would be residing there with me in the near future.

"This is my office," I told her as we stepped into the room.

It looked exactly the same as earlier, except no Blāz behind the desk working at the laptop.

"This is lovely," she said, releasing my hand as she began moving about the space. "We used this as an entertainment space when we resided here."

"Seems more suited for it," I told her. "Considering the size."

"I think this works nicely as an office for you. Plenty of space for you to relax if you do not wish to work, plus it's private."

She paused before the fireplace, and I had an image of her laid out on a blanket before the flames, her body covered in nothing but my flesh, moving beneath me as I brought us both to climax.

I cleared my throat.

I wasn't sure what had come over me, but I'd been hard and aching ever since I left her bed. Didn't seem to matter that I had her that evening; I still wanted her now, and I feared my need for her was going to interfere with my good intentions. I wanted nothing more than to court her appropriately, to take her on dates and share small talk. But the more I thought about her, the more I wanted to feel her bare skin against my palms, her pussy gliding over my cock.

The door at my back closed on its own. I peered at it, then over to Acadia.

She had turned to face me, the flames flickering behind her in the hearth, the glow backlighting her.

"I don't have to read your mind to know what you're thinking, Kaj."

Smiling, I moved toward her. "And what am I thinking?"

"The same thing I am."

"Elaborate, *balisra*."

"That we would both feel better if we were skin to skin right now."

"You have not fed yet tonight."

"I have not," she agreed.

"I would like to avail myself to you now."

I saw the flash of desire in her eyes, felt the answering call within me. My cock was already thick and hard behind my zipper, eager to feel her in any capacity. Of course, my mind drifted to our encounter in the theater, to the way she had been on her knees before me, my cock tunneling into the blessed warmth of her mouth.

"Let me look at you, *balisra*. Take off your gown."

Without hesitation, she began unhooking the ties at her back, her breasts straining as her arms were pulled back. When the bodice loosened, I followed the path of the silk as it slid down her curves to pool at her feet.

"Have I mentioned how much I love that you're naked beneath your gowns?"

"You have not."

"I think about it endlessly." I took another step closer, stopping when there were a few feet between us. "I think about hefting those heavy skirts up and sliding into you from behind. Or pulling you onto my lap so you can ride me while everyone else has their evening meal, oblivious to the fact that I'm moving inside you."

Her nipples hardened into pretty points.

"Let your hair down."

Acadia raised her hands to free the clips holding her hair atop her head, and I admired the way her breasts lifted with the movement.

My gaze cut to the desk. More accurately, the leather chair behind it.

Holding out my hand for her, I waited until she closed the distance between us, then twined our fingers and led the way over.

I turned the chair to the side, then pivoted to face Acadia.

"Take my cock out, *balisra*."

Our eyes remained locked as she worked open my jeans, freeing my erection from the denim, her smooth fingers trailing over my sensitive flesh.

"Have I mentioned I'm quite fond of your bossiness?" Acadia teased.

"Is that so?"

"Yes."

With my jeans shackling my ankles, I eased into the chair, then motioned for her to turn around. Acadia rotated toward the fireplace, and I gripped her hips, pulling her down into my lap.

"No, not yet," I whispered when she went to adjust my cock between her legs. "I want to touch you first."

Acadia leaned back against me when I positioned her knees over the arms of the chair, spreading her wide.

Perhaps it was an afterthought, but I had the sense to lock the door with my mind, ensuring no one walked in on us. As much as I fantasized about taking her in public places, I wanted Acadia all to myself. The thought of anyone seeing her like this was enough to have a growl rumbling in my chest.

I slid my arms around her hips, then tucked my hand between her thighs, teasing the folds of her sex with my fingers.

"I love touching you like this," I mumbled as I slowly stroked her. "Having you naked like this. I could spend the rest of eternity with you in my arms."

She moaned softly when I pushed one finger inside her, her pussy clutching me tightly.

I kissed her shoulder, her neck, fingering her flesh until her juices were coating my fingers.

"I crave you," I whispered. "Doesn't matter when or where, I never stop wanting you."

Her soft moan spurred me on.

"Do you want to feel me inside you?" I nipped her earlobe.

"More than anything."

It was a testament to my impatience that I couldn't refrain from taking her right then and there. The fact that she encouraged me by grinding her ass against my groin was almost too much for me.

I hated that I had to remove my hands from her soft flesh, but it was necessary. I lifted her up and pulled her back so my cock was between her thighs. I could not see down her torso, but I didn't need to. Her fingers curled around my shaft as she guided me inside her. When the head was pressed firmly to her entrance, I lowered her onto me, inhaling sharply as her body clutched me snugly.

Once she was seated atop me, I offered her my hands. She linked our fingers, which worked twofold. It gave her the ability to lift and lower herself on me while at the same time she absorbed my energy. Relaxing into the plush leather, I opened myself up to her, giving her every part of myself, unleashing my full power so I could fuel the female I loved.

As it did so often when we were like this, time stood still as she rode me, milking my sex with her own as she drew the energy from my body. It was an exquisite sensation to be used like this, to know that I was giving her what she needed while at the same time we were as close as two beings could possibly be.

Her movements were unhurried as she worked herself over me. Up, down, up, down.

"Tell me when you need more," I urged, gritting my teeth as my orgasm built within me.

"I always need more," she whimpered. "Kaj … please … I want you to take me."

A guttural sound erupted from me as I shifted forward. Acadia got her balance as I wrapped an arm around her middle, our fingers still clasped. I remained lodged fully inside her as I stood, urging her to lean over the desk. When she did, she released my hands.

"Hold on, *balisra*."

I growled low in my throat, driving my hips forward, filling her. I was rougher than I intended because I was desperate. Those few minutes in the chair had been a tease, and my inner beast was eager to dominate her.

Gripping her hips firmly, I held her in place as I impaled her, my eyes locked on her shoulders, the way her long hair fell down around her face as she rocked forward and back, taking me deep within her. Her pussy squeezed me tightly seconds before she cried out my name. That was the first of several orgasms I forced upon her, holding back for as long as I could.

When I came, it was with her name on my lips, the release ripped from me, shattering my body and mind at the same time.

But it wasn't enough.

I pulled out, grabbed her hand, and tugged her toward the sofa. I had the mind to assist her onto the cushions before I mounted her like the animal I was. No sooner had her back relaxed against the leather than I leaned over her, slamming my hips forward, impaling her on my cock.

"Feed from me," I demanded.

Acadia's palms went to my chest. When she began siphoning from me once more, my back bowed, and a growl escaped. My hips took on a life of their own as I pushed deep, retreated. Faster, harder, deeper. My need for her was its own entity, and I couldn't seem to stop. I came several more times, my release answering the call of hers. It wasn't until she pulled her palms from my chest that I took a deep breath and became the single-minded beast. I couldn't claim her yet, though I wanted it more than I wanted air. So for now, this would have to do. I would take her as often as I could and be satisfied with that.

"Mine," I growled low in my throat, meeting her amethyst gaze. "You are mine, Acadia."

"Yours," she rasped, her hands sliding up my arms as I braced myself over her, slamming in deep again and again as though it might help in some way.

This time when I came, it was with a snarl, my teeth gritting tightly to hold in the beast who was desperate to mark her for all eternity. I spilled myself inside her and cried out her name when she orgasmed once more, her nails digging into my forearms.

She was everything I had ever wanted, more than I knew I deserved.

And one day ... one day very soon ... I would mark her as mine and show her what it meant to be complete for the first time in our lives.

PERFIDIOUS

Now that I had shed my human husk, I felt powerful. More so than I had in a long time.

Of course, my demon form was far more advanced than those little minions Eevuhl had brought back with him all those months ago. Aside from the fact my skin was slick and red, and I had two horn-like protrusions on my head, I had a body indicative of a human. Two arms, two legs, a thick cock. Needless to say, it wasn't all that difficult to fill out the human husks when necessary, my body fitting perfectly within whatever body I chose.

However, in this form, sensations were heightened, not muted by the skin of the humans I wore to blend. It had been eons since I'd traipsed around, naked in a sense, but it felt good. It felt right.

The question was, how would Asmia react to my true form? She'd yet to see me because I'd wanted it to be a surprise. Hence, I was currently sitting on my throne in the elaborate cave I'd had dug out of the mountain, the shadow beasts gathering before me down below. I'd purposely kept distance between myself and them, ensuring they understood my rightful position above them.

"I'm glad you could come," I addressed the males and females. "I felt it imperative we get right to the reason you are here. Beginning this night, you'll be answering only to me. As you've probably heard, Eevuhl is no longer of this Earth, having been eliminated by the archangel Michael."

There was some grumbling going on, but I ignored it.

"This night, you will pledge your loyalty unto me. Some of you are likely curious as to why you would do that. Most of you don't know me. In time, you will come to. But as a way of proving to you that I am worthy of your obedience, I'd like to introduce you to my queen."

I held my arm out, motioning for Asmia to join me. Sirius had brought her forth and kept her contained behind my throne in an effort to ensure the shadow beasts did not see her, as well as ensuring Asmia didn't see me. As I mentioned, I wanted it to be a surprise.

Standing tall, I stepped down from my throne, turning to the side so I could see the Fae's eyes when she took me in for the first time.

357

"Come here, my queen," I called out as she stepped toward me.

As had been the case for weeks now, Asmia showed absolutely no emotion when her eyes slid over me. She didn't appear aware that my appearance had drastically changed, nor did she seem concerned. Perhaps I should consider loosening the reins on the mind control simply so I could get a reaction out of her.

Not yet, though.

Right now, I had something else in mind.

Taking her by the shoulders, I urged her out in front, giving the shadow beasts below a glimpse of the Fae I had obtained.

As expected, a ruckus erupted, most of the demons likely eager to get their hands on her.

Unfortunately for them, she wasn't theirs for the taking. Asmia belonged only to me.

Stepping up behind her, I brushed her long blond hair back, then freed the sash that was holding the blood-red robe closed. I then pulled the silk from her shoulders, allowing it to fall to the floor, revealing her in all her glory to those who would be envious of me.

"If there's ever any doubt in your minds who's the king here on Earth, you should know, I obtained her on my own. Stole her away from those pesky angels without help." I smiled down at them. "But more importantly, I know of others who are there for the taking. Provided you do right by me, there's nothing to say you will not have your very own Fae."

That incited the masses, a round of hisses and growls sounding from the demonic beasts.

"Our objective is to eliminate the vampires. That's your sole purpose here. From what I've seen, you've made great strides, but we're not there yet."

I slid my hands around Asmia, cupping her full breasts in my palms.

"Consider this your motivation," I announced, pulling Asmia back against me. "And you, my dear, sweet queen, are going to know what it's like to be claimed once and for all."

"It would be my pleasure, my king," she said, her voice crisp and clear as it rang out, the response of the shadow beasts exactly as I'd expected.

29

OLIVER

It had been a long time since I had been on a date.

Granted, this wasn't really a date. It was more like a mutual outing for friends.

Try telling my heart that. That damn organ was doing the jitterbug in my chest, the shimmy and shake so strong they had my stomach churning nervously.

Even now, as I sat in the leather recliner beside Bijou, some chick flick playing on the screen, I could hardly keep my eyes from straying over to her. The only thing that stopped me was my not wanting to make this awkward. I'd never met a woman...err...*female* like Bijou. A woman implied she was human, but that was not the case. She was vampire, an entirely different species that I hadn't even known existed until she appeared at Angel Central.

And I thought coming to terms with living with angels was difficult.

Then again, I'd often heard stories of vampires because they were commonplace for humans in terms of storytelling. So perhaps I hadn't been quite so shocked that they existed. More like ... relieved?

Strange word to think, but it was an apt description.

It did not, however, explain why I had this strange fascination with her. Or this irrational idea that one day I could feed from her and she from me. That wasn't feasible because I was human. Hell, I didn't even have fangs.

But that didn't stop my overactive imagination from attempting to conjure it up.

"Are you okay?"

I jerked when a soft hand touched mine. My eyes shot to that touch, then over to Bijou. She was watching me curiously.

"Yeah. Why?"

"You ... hissed."

I frowned. "I did not hiss."

Bijou chuckled. "You actually did."

I realized she hadn't pulled her hand away. Nor did she when I flipped mine over. My breath slammed into my ribs when she linked our fingers, our palms touching intimately. At that point, the movie disappeared entirely. At least for me. The only thing I was cognizant of was how soft her hand was, how warm her fingers were. As I stared at our joined palms, I felt a warmth deep inside me, as though a glacier had been melted, replaced by ... sunlight.

It was an eerie feeling, I had to admit. Almost as though she had unlocked a part of my soul, cracking me wide open.

I'd felt a similar feeling when I'd been with her in the sauna. That night, when I'd buried my tongue between her thighs and brought her to orgasm in an attempt to ease her from the angels' freaky mating heat. As much as I'd wanted to take her then, to sink into the heavenly warmth of her body, I had run away from her, locked myself in my room, and banged out my own orgasm with my hand.

Yet that connection I'd felt with her then returned now. Heat replaced the ice in my veins, and I could've sworn something was coming alive inside me.

Bijou's eyes shifted to me as though she felt whatever was emerging.

"Oliver?"

Her voice was distorted, as though I was hearing it from underwater. For a moment, I was confused. We were in a theater, not the swimming pool.

"Oliver!"

My body jerked hard, sending me back against the chair. Everything went fuzzy.

"I'll get help, Oliver! I'm going to get help."

I focused on her words, her panic registering, but I had no idea what was going on. My body was trembling ... no, make that vibrating. More like a volcanic eruption.

My mouth opened to tell her I was fine, but no words came out. There was a twisting within my body, as though something was attempting to get out. There was no pain, just a sense of ... emergence.

I was seconds from panicking when suddenly my eyesight cut out on me, the room going black. All sound faded and then...

. . .

W hen I awoke, I was in the infirmary, the bright lights overhead blinding me before I could stop my eyelids from lifting.

Fuck me.

I slammed them shut and exhaled heavily.

"Oliver?"

"It's me," I said, not bothering to open my eyes. "Could you shut off the lights, please?"

A second later, I noticed the darkness behind my closed lids, so I made another attempt at cracking them open. Slow and easy … yep. That worked. The room was dark except for a dim illumination coming from behind my head and the one from the machine standing beside the bed.

"What happened?" I asked, searching until I found Bijou standing near the door, her thin arms crossed over her chest, black sweater hitched just above the waistband of her jeans. I should not have been checking out her belly button, yet…

"You had a seizure," a male voice said.

Apollo. Yay. Just what I didn't want, an angel doctor poking and prodding at me.

"Have you had them before?" the doctor asked.

"Nope. Never. Maybe too much popcorn."

"Popcorn won't cause—"

"It was a joke, Doc."

"Ah. Gotcha. But no seizures before?"

"No."

"Can you tell me what happened? Did you notice anything just before you seized?"

I thought back to sitting in the theater, holding Bijou's hand. That strange sensation inside me, like something was trying to emerge.

"Nothing happened," I blurted. "I was just sitting there and ... well, you know the rest."

"Perhaps it was the screen," Bijou offered. "Hasn't that happened before? Certain lights triggering seizures in humans?"

"I suppose it's possible," Apollo agreed.

Except there hadn't been any strobes going on. Not unless I counted the ones in my head at the time. But I wasn't going to offer that up. Let them assume what they would.

"I'd like to keep you here for observation. At least for another hour."

I glanced at Bijou. When she nodded in encouragement, I relented.

"Will you stay with me?" I asked.

"I'm not going anywhere."

I could tell she was upset, clearly trying to wrap her head around what happened. I knew the feeling.

"I'll be back shortly," the doctor said before slipping out.

Feeling the need to reassure Bijou that I was fine, I motioned her over, then shifted so there was room for her on the mattress.

"Come here."

Her beautiful green eyes locked on my face, and I thought for a moment she would decline my request, but then she was crawling up with me.

I shifted once more when she reclined, ensuring her head was resting in the crook of my shoulder. I curled her closer, pressed my lips to her forehead.

"I'm sorry about that."

Her soft laughter was like a balm to my soul. "You shouldn't be apologizing."

Inhaling deeply, I let her scent wash over me. I loved the way she smelled, though I couldn't quite pinpoint what it was.

Perhaps perfume. Maybe soap or shampoo. Whatever it was, I longed to breathe it in.

When her hand rested lightly on my stomach, my muscles tightened from the touch. Placing my free hand over hers, I held her close to me, content in a way I'd never been before.

There was still a strange sensation within me. Something wasn't quite right. Like two magnetic poles warring, trying to fight to overrule the other.

Taking a deep breath, I closed my eyes and prayed whatever it was would pass quickly, because this ... being with Bijou ... was the only thing I'd wanted since the day I saw her in the dining room.

The absolute only thing I wanted.

OBSIDIAN

I remained in the hallway to the infirmary when Penelope opted to head back up to the mansion. Apollo had given her the information as he knew it—Oliver having a seizure, being brought down by Reidar at Bijou's request, looking over the male and finding nothing to indicate what had caused it. The healer's explanation had eased her mind, and she'd been eager to get back to Ari'el since Oliver was with Bijou.

That was all good and fine. I didn't mind the fact that

Apollo had sugarcoated his observations in an effort to keep Penelope calm.

However...

Get your ass down here now, I projected to Michael.

A second later, there was a flutter of sound, then the male appeared, looking both curious and wary.

Michael glanced at me, peered around, eyes swinging back. "Based on your tone, I suppose this isn't an invitation to the morning meal."

I turned to face the archangel. "What's going on with Oliver?"

Michael turned, as though looking into the room. "Well, right now he's holding the female vamp—"

"That's not what I mean, and you know it."

The male turned back around and sighed. "Honestly, I don't really know. I suspect Khari and Oliver are warring at the moment. The vampire's been repressed, and the female is his mate. I suspect he knows this and he's asserting his dominance."

"Is Oliver in danger?"

Michael shrugged. "I've never had this happen before. Khari's always been a docile passenger in the human vessels he's occupied. If I had to guess, Bijou's his trigger. He wants out, and he'll do what's necessary to make that happen."

"So you're saying Oliver's prominent? The human is repressing the vampire?"

"No." Michael's face grew serious. "Though he doesn't understand what he is, Khari's fully in charge of the human vessel. Those readings the healer's getting are those of the vessel, nothing more."

"He's in there," came a voice from behind Michael.

Apollo appeared.

Michael and I turned toward him.

"The human. I can sense his soul. And Michael's right. The vampire's conflicted right now. And he's short-circuiting the vessel. Hence the seizure."

And *that* was what I had suspected Apollo was keeping from Penelope.

"How is it you sense Khari, but I don't?" I inquired.

Apollo's gaze shifted to Michael, clearly looking for him to answer.

I waited, gaze darting between the two males. Someone would answer me or we would fucking stand here all day.

"It doesn't matter," Michael finally said.

"It does mat—"

"Look," Apollo stated firmly. "We can stand out here and hash out the why and how of our existence, but it's not going to solve the problem."

I studied Apollo. "The problem being *what*, exactly?"

"The fact that Khari's growing more irritated being confined," Apollo stated firmly, his voice lower than before.

Son of a bitch.

"Where's Kaj?" I asked, though I knew neither of them would have the answer.

"I'll get him," Michael said before vanishing.

I turned my attention to Apollo. "I assume someone's made you aware of what's going on?"

The healer's pale blue eyes leveled on mine. "I've detected him before. In the other vessels Khari has hitched a ride in. But never has he attempted to free himself. I agree with Michael. Bijou's his trigger. He's trying to bond with her, but he's trapped by the human. I hate to say it, but as long as they're in each other's presence"—he motioned toward the door—"as long as their affections are building for one another, there's the potential for this to get worse. For the human vessel."

"How do we stop it?"

"Short of restricting them from seeing one another, I don't see how you can. And even then, it's possible Khari's made enough of a connection that he'll get violent. If that happens, he'll incinerate the vessel. The vampire's strength, even in his current state, is far more powerful than the human. If Khari believes you're keeping her from him, there's no telling what he'll do."

"He's on his way," Michael said when he flashed into existence.

Sure enough, the doors at the end of the hall opened, and Kaj came strolling through, his eyes narrowed, black eyebrows pitched low.

"What's going on?"

Apollo gave the vampire the high-level details of what transpired. When he got to the part about Khari becoming uncivilized because he was attempting to bond, I thought I would have to stand between Kaj and the healer.

"Get her out of there," Kaj demanded.

"That's probably the worst thing we can do right now," Apollo said firmly. "As her father, you have that right. At least, I assume you do. But there is a serious risk of you sending Khari into a frenzy."

"So what are you saying?" Kaj's gaze shot between the three of us.

"He needs to be moved to his proper vessel," Michael answered. "It was bound to happen sooner or later."

"You planned this," Kaj accused.

Michael smirked. "No. Actually, I did not. However, if I'd known this would happen, I could've helped this situation along a long time ago."

Kaj snarled, and I did insert myself between the vampire and the archangel.

"Do not goad him," I warned Michael. "You purposely piss

him off, you have to deal with the consequences." I turned back and addressed all three males. "I understand this is an impossible situation. However, that human vessel in there … he's Penelope's brother." I held up a hand to cut off Michael. "Regardless of whether they share the same blood. She sees him as her brother. Under no circumstances can we allow the vampire to extinguish the human. I want both of them to come out the other side intact. Understand?"

Apollo was the one to speak while the other two males faced off with death glares.

"I'm going to monitor him for a while. And I can insist Oliver come down to have his vitals checked for the next couple of days. Provided he remains stable, that'll buy you some time to figure this out."

"In the meantime," Michael said, speaking directly to Kaj, "I suggest you keep him and your daughter apart."

"No," Apollo barked. "Do not interfere. I'm warning you right now, he's—"

"A bonded vampire," I snarled. "You do not come between a bonded vampire and his mate." I squared off with Kaj. "And you … I get that you're her father, and I can't imagine this is easy for you. But honestly, tell me you wouldn't lose your mind if I were to keep you from Acadia."

The male snarled, his upper lip pulling back from his fangs.

"Exactly my point. Just the thought of it isn't something you can comprehend. The same's going to be the case for the ten-thousand-year-old vampire hopping a ride in the human. We do, however, need to come up with a plan. And for that to happen, we have to explain what's going on to the others. Including Oliver."

Once more, the healer spoke up. "That's the last thing you want to do. There's already conflict in that vessel. It's best to keep him out of the loop for as long as you can."

I wasn't in agreement, but I also wasn't a healer. I had to trust Apollo knew what he was talking about. The end goal was to get Khari out and to keep Oliver alive. If we had to go this route, so be it.

"This is ultimately your responsibility," Michael told Kaj. "I've told you what I need, and you've given me your terms. I'm not sure what you're waiting for."

Kaj's thick brows arched, but he kept his mouth shut. Probably not a bad thing.

"We'll reconvene tonight," I told them. "But we have to come to a decision then." I locked eyes with Apollo. "Let me know if anything changes with him."

As I walked away, I couldn't help but wonder what Michael had gotten himself into this time.

And more importantly, how we were all going to come out the other side. In one piece.

30

KAJ

After leaving Obsidian and the others, I made my way through the mansion, heading up to the second floor, beelining for Acadia's room. I had no idea whether she was there or not, but I had to find her, had to see her.

I felt slightly out of control, a bit off-kilter. It had more to do with the fact I was losing my grip on what was going on. Nothing I could do or say would change the outcome of what was spiraling out of control. Khari, Bijou, Oliver. None of it made sense, and I knew no amount of thinking about it would help.

With a quick rap on the door to announce my presence, I barreled through, closing it quickly behind me.

Leaning against the door, I took a deep breath in, let it out. In, out. Again and again.

"Kaj?" Acadia stepped out from the bathroom, a white towel wrapped around her, shielding her nakedness from me, her long, thick hair hanging down to her waist.

I stared at her, unable to form words thanks to the crazy that had kicked off in my brain. There was no reining it in. Not yet.

"What's wrong?" she asked as she came closer.

Realizing I was beginning to hyperventilate, I motioned her toward me.

She didn't hesitate, closing the distance, her eyes wide, concerned.

I pulled her into my arms, holding her tightly and burying my face in her neck. I breathed her in, allowing that familiar scent of cherry blossoms to soothe the chaos, to settle my nerves.

"You're scaring me," she whispered.

"I need you," I replied, not quite sure in what manner I meant.

"I'm here, Kaj. Whatever you need."

Right now, this was what I needed. To hold her. For whatever reason, it was the answer. The longer I stood there, my female pulled in tight to my body, the better I felt. Not necessarily calmer because I wasn't sure anything could ease the bedlam in my brain, but I felt a bit more grounded.

Before I realized what I was doing, I had begun tugging at the towel that concealed her. Acadia eased back enough to allow the plush cotton to be pulled away, leaving her naked in my arms.

Better.

Definitely better.

My hands slid over her smooth, warm skin. Her back, her ass, her hips. I consoled myself with the feel of her even as my body heated, anticipation building, my cock thickening. I wanted her. I had always wanted her. I would always want her. And I realized, I was bound to her. Heart, body, soul. She owned every piece of me despite the fact I'd yet to claim her. It didn't necessarily matter.

Soft lips pressed against my neck, causing me to tilt my head back, skull meeting the wooden door. Those lips began a slow glide over my skin.

"Relax," she whispered, her lips continuing their trek as her hands worked beneath my T-shirt, forcing the cotton higher until I pulled it over my head.

Then those lips were moving over my collarbone, my pecs. Acadia teased my nipples with gentle licks, and I found I was actually relaxing, the stress from earlier melting away, replaced by a heat that consumed me.

I cradled her head with my hand, holding her so she continued to do that ... that wicked thing with her tongue. My other hand dropped to my jeans, freeing the button, lowering the zipper. I reached for my cock, stroked it while she kissed and licked, teased and provoked. My female knew exactly what to do to rock me to my core, her smooth hands beginning to wander while her mouth inched lower, gliding down over my stomach as she started to her knees.

"Wait," I groaned, lifting my head and meeting her eyes.

I could see the surprise and the confusion in those amethyst orbs, but I didn't say a word, simply took her hand and led her into the bathroom. I willed the water on in the tub, then stripped off my remaining clothes, watching her while I did. Acadia's body was a work of art, all rounded curves and smooth, sleek skin. Her dusky pink nipples were hardened into points, beckoning my tongue.

As the water filled the tub, I took her hand once more, led her into it. Rather than let her sit in the water, I urged her onto the side of the tub as I went to my knees.

"Let me taste you, *balisra*."

Her eyes heated as she spread her thighs, allowing me to position them so I had room to shoulder my way between them. As I neared her glistening sex, I inhaled deeply, breathing her in. I loved the scent of her arousal. It spoke to the beast within, the animal emerging, eager to mate, desperate to claim.

Acadia shifted, leaning back against the tiled wall as I pressed my face between her thighs, nuzzling the soft skin, my lips grazing her.

"Kaj..."

I answered the plea that didn't fall from her lips, licking her gently, then more firmly, gliding through her slickness, teasing, exploring. Every time I grazed her clit, Acadia whimpered, her hips rocking forward as though she needed me right there. Using my fingers, I parted her slick flesh. As her breaths grew more labored, I relented, taking and giving at the same time. I devoured her, my tongue and lips feasting on her, licking, stroking, fucking. I focused on her taste, let her sweet moans fuel me.

Come for me, balisra. *Come in my mouth.*

Acadia cried out in response as I thrust my tongue as deep as I could, plunging into her again and again. When her hands cradled my head, holding me there, I worked her more, teased her ruthlessly. And when she cried out my name, her body bucking against me, I held her in place, refusing to relent. I made her come twice more before I got to my feet, gripping my cock roughly. Her eyes opened, her mouth following suit as I planted one palm on the wall and guided my erection between those sultry lips. Acadia's eyes closed as she took me in her mouth. Her hands shifted to my thighs, and I nearly lost it when she began drawing energy from me.

Fearful I would hurt her, I let her lead, watching as she

bobbed forward, taking me deep in her throat. Again and again she sucked me, the heat of her mouth an exquisite torment that I never wanted to end.

ACADIA

I hadn't expected Kaj to show up at my door, but the moment I saw his face, I knew what he needed.

Not necessarily sex, per se. But he had certainly needed the intimacy we shared. And this worked for me. Not once had he ever made me feel as though he was using me to sate an urge. How could I feel that way when he plied me with such overwhelming pleasure? Now it was my turn, and I wanted this to last forever.

Beneath my palms, his thighs trembled as I sucked him deeper than I ever had before. He wasn't guiding me, wasn't pumping his hips. No, Kaj had handed over the reins, allowing me to be in control. It was rare for him to do so, and I knew the only reason he did was because he trusted me. The same as I did him. Together, we were safe, protected, and loved by the other. We were whole.

"Acadia..."

In my mouth, I responded in his mind.

"Oh, fuck ... *balisra*."

Spurred by his words, I released his thighs and curled my

fist around the thick base of his erection while I worked my mouth on him. I wanted to taste him, to drink him down. I loved the way his erection pulsed on my tongue, his breath soughing in and out of his lungs as he fought for control while knowing it was futile.

Suddenly, his hand was in my hair, gripping roughly, holding me in place as he thrust forward, nearly choking me. I breathed through my nose and drank him down as he came.

He all but crumpled to the floor of the tub, his arms reaching for me, pulling me in with him. Luckily, it was a large tub, big enough to hold his enormous body even if said body displaced the water, bringing it higher over us.

"Inside you..." he rasped. "I just need to be inside you."

I straddled his hips, allowing him to pull me against him as I seated myself on his erection. Dragging out the delicious feeling, I worked myself down slowly until he was fully inside me.

Then I relaxed against him, my face pressed to his neck, my breasts crushed against his chest, the warm water covering us both.

"This..." His arms banded around me. "This is all I ever need."

Neither of us moved, relaxing. It was strange to have him inside me without friction, but I knew that would come with time. The fact that Kaj wanted to be one with me was something I'd gotten used to long ago. I remembered the first time he made the request, pulling me onto him as we lay in his bed. I'd fallen asleep like that, woken some time later when I felt him moving, his body tending to mine, offering a pleasure unlike anything I'd ever known.

"I need you, Acadia."

"I'm here," I assured him.

"No. I mean ... I need you at my side. From now on. I don't want to move forward without you."

A sigh of contentment escaped me. "I'm here," I repeated. "Now and always. I'm yours, Kaj. For eternity."

"Do you mean that?"

I didn't answer right away, wanting to find the right words. But I'd never been good with words. Sharing my feelings didn't come naturally, but I trusted no one more than I trusted Kaj.

"You hurt me when you left me," I told him, keeping my voice low, my cheek on his shoulder. "Those first few days you were gone ... it nearly killed me."

His hand slid over my back, warm and comforting. "I hated leaving you, but I had no choice."

I knew that now. I knew that he'd left the mansion to get back to his father. He'd been too late to save Kardobahn or the others. There were times when I felt guilty, as though I was responsible for that. Kaj had stayed a few extra days because I'd asked him to. If he had left when he'd first mentioned it, perhaps his father would still be alive.

"It wouldn't have mattered," he said, clearly reading my thoughts. "I wouldn't have left, Acadia. It took everything I had to walk away."

"I missed you so much," I admitted. "During the day, I couldn't sleep because I missed the warmth of your body against mine. My heart broke, Kaj. I've never felt anything like that before."

He pressed his lips to my forehead. "I won't leave you again. I swear on my life, *balisra*. I don't want to spend another day or night without you."

I wanted to believe that. Truly. Every molecule in my body seemed to gravitate toward this male. I thought about him endlessly, worried about him, feared for him. He'd long ago buried himself beneath my skin, become the most important thing in my world. I wasn't sure that was appropriate because I'd always longed to be an independent female, despite the fact my entire race was at the mercy of angels. Sometimes I feared I was trading one duty for another, but then I thought about how happy I was when I was with Kaj. No, not even with him. Thinking about him, loving him, and yes, even fearing for him. He'd become a part of me at some point in our history, and I couldn't imagine the rest of my life without him in it.

"I have to talk to Obsidian." I'd been putting it off, and I knew it had to be done. "I'll speak with him tonight."

"If you don't, Acadia," he whispered softly, "I will."

"No," I said urgently. "I will. I promise."

"And then you'll spend the rest of your days in my bed, the rest of your nights nearby."

It wasn't a question, but I answered anyway. "I don't want to be anywhere else."

Kaj's hips shifted and rolled, his erection moving inside me, thickening as my muscles clenched, the friction making my skin prickle. His head turned to the side, his mouth brushing over my ear, then down to my neck.

"Stay just like that," he whispered. "I'm going to bite you and I'm going to make love to you at the same time."

A shiver of warmth curled in my belly as the gruff rasp of his voice stroked my senses.

I angled my head to give him better access to my vein, but I didn't move otherwise.

I was aware of his fangs as they sensually scraped my skin once, twice... I inhaled sharply when he pierced me, my inner muscles clenching on his sex. The rough growl that escaped had my body tightening. And then he was feeding from me while he gently rocked his hips, pushing in deep, retreating a fraction. Deep again. Over and over, I let the euphoria overwhelm me.

The water in the tub began lapping at the edges as Kaj's movements became less rhythmic, the friction driving us both higher until I couldn't refrain from coming. The orgasm rolled through me, gently at first, then growing stronger as he punched upward, driving in deeper than I thought possible.

Before I had drifted back down from that incredible high, I was aware of him lifting me, our bodies still joined. Kaj wasted no time carrying me into the bedroom, moving over me, and finishing us both off as the last tether of his control snapped. I let him overwhelm me, the orgasms free-flowing as he slammed into me again and again. Our eyes met and held, and in those moments, as he rocked me to my very core, something shifted between us.

Our future was on the horizon, the winds of change blowing in our direction.

And for the first time, I didn't fear what they might bring. Above all else, I knew Kaj would take care of me. He would love me, he would protect me. And in turn, I would prove to him I was as strong as he believed me to be.

A deep, dark growl sounded as Kaj's lower body drove forward one final time. He pulsed deep inside me, his orgasm triggering another. And as I let it wash over me, I gave myself over to him. Completely.

31

Saturday, April 14, 2018

ACADIA

———

Pressure.

There was so much pressure on my chest, I wasn't sure how my heart would survive it. Never in my existence had I ever felt this sort of tremendous pain. Though I knew rationally that there wasn't anything doing harm to my heart, it certainly felt as though someone had taken the organ and was squeezing.

Kaj was leaving.

In fact, he was wandering through the mansion, saying goodbye to everyone else because I refused to see him. I could hear his voice down below, and I wondered how he could sound so strong, so unaffected, when here I was, my chest ready to implode from the agony.

Kaj was leaving.

My mind was overloaded with memories of the past six months. The day he arrived, injured, dying. Obsidian saving him. All the days that passed before he awoke so I could see those beautiful green eyes peering back at me. He'd been so vulnerable, yet he had trusted me implicitly to care for him, to nurse him back to health. And the past couple of months, when he'd been fully recovered, our bodies coming together to celebrate the emotions we invoked in one another, the love that had developed though neither of us spoke of it.

Kaj. Was. Leaving.

I felt as though I was being abandoned all over again. The difference was I didn't remember the first time because I'd been only a few weeks old when I was brought to the orphanage, my parents taken from this world. Part of me wished I wouldn't remember this day, could avoid this unbearable pressure sitting firmly in the middle of my chest.

Come morning, I would go to bed alone. I would wake up without the warmth of his body next to mine, the reassuring sound of his breathing, the brilliant light in his eyes that I'd come to cherish seeing each and every night.

Alone.

Although the house was full of angels, I had never felt more alone than I did in that moment. And Kaj was still down there, still talking, laughing, joking. Seemingly okay with the fact he was going to walk out the door and never look back. I wasn't sure I would ever see him again.

I wanted him to stay. That was all there was to it. I wanted him to love me enough that he didn't walk away. It wasn't in the cards, I knew that. He had responsibilities to tend to, a life dedicated to others, the same as mine. I couldn't help but think that if he loved me enough, he would refuse to leave me. In fact, if he loved me even half as much as I loved him, how could he walk away?

The sound of footsteps coming down the hall drew my head up from the pillow I was clutching to my chest. When I woke up tonight, I left his bed and came back to this cold, lonely room I shared with two others. They had been kind enough to give me space, but it wouldn't have mattered. I was still alone.

"Acadia?"

My heart squeezed in my chest at the sound of his voice.

Forcing my head up, I took one final look at that handsome face, hoping I could memorize his features, keep him with me long after he was gone.

"Please don't go," I heard myself say, the words coming out tormented.

I instantly saw the pain reflecting back at me. He was hurting as much as I was, but it was difficult to see past my own sorrow.

"I would if I could," he said softly, not making a move to come into the room.

I swallowed past the lump in my throat, but it only induced a sob that ripped from me. Pain racked my entire being, my muscles tensing, my chest tightening as the devastating ache consumed me. I didn't even want to think about what it would feel like once he was out the door. He was still here, and I was overwhelmed by pain. When he was gone...

"Come with me, balisra," *he whispered.*

"I can't." I honestly wished I could. It was the only thing I'd ever wanted aside from my freedom from this servitude that kept me chained to this mansion, to the angels. Although the idea of leaving Obsidian was painful, it was nothing compared to the misery I felt now.

"I will come back for you."

My eyes searched his face. I was looking for the truth in those words, but I saw none. He was placating me. Perhaps he was hopeful it would be true, but I knew deep down he had no intention of coming back. Why bother leaving in the first place?

"We both know that's not true," I told him, dropping my gaze to the pillow.

"Acadia—"

I clenched the pillow in my fists. "Please go," I bit out, another sob breaking free. "Just leave, Kaj."

"Please, Ac—"

"Go!"

His deep exhale and the sound of his footsteps leading away from the door tore the last shreds of my sanity.

I fell over, giving in to the tears.

KAJ

lthough it killed me, I forced myself to walk away. The tightness in my chest grew the more distance I put between us. I hadn't meant to hurt her, but if it was any consolation—which it wasn't—I was hurting just as much.

By the time I made it down the stairs, everyone who'd come to say goodbye had dispersed. The only one remaining was Obsidian, and there was a wealth of knowledge in those silver swirling eyes.

"Take care of her for me," I said, the words pushed out past the emotion threatening to strangle me.

"I will. I promise you that." The male clamped a hand on my shoulder. "Do what you need to do. She's safe here. It'll take some time, but she'll move past this."

I wanted to tell him I hoped that wasn't the case, but I wasn't that selfish. Deep down, I wanted Acadia to mourn the loss of what *we had the way I would. Though she didn't know it, I had imprinted on her. She was the only love I would ever know. Didn't matter how many lovers I took in the future, none would ever touch that part of me that belonged to her. Then again, I didn't intend to ever take a lover again. I would gladly spend the rest of my days abstaining, rather than bear the touch of another female.*

"Keep in touch, will you?" Obsidian said firmly. "Keep me in the loop."

"I will," I assured my friend.

"And if you ever need anything, I'm just a phone call away."

I nodded. "Thanks. For everything. I'm not sure I can ever repay you for saving my life."

"I'd do it again in a heartbeat."

I believed that. Obsidian was a rarity in this world, a true friend.

Forcing my shoulders back, I put one foot in front of the other. I had to get out of there. I could smell Acadia's tears, hear her almost silent sobs, and it was tearing me to shreds. But I had to get back to my father. There was danger on the horizon. Mirakel had told me as much. We would always be at war with the demons, and it was my duty to protect the ruler of the race. As much as I wished my needs and desires could be put first, they could never come before the greater good.

"Take care," Obsidian said as I stepped out the door and into the night.

"You, too, my friend."

When the door closed, I remained where I was, staring up at the second floor, wishing I could see her one last time. I knew it wouldn't matter. I would still be leaving here a broken and shattered male. Didn't matter that I was stronger than I'd ever been; I was no longer whole. There was a piece of me missing, a piece I'd gladly handed over to that female for safekeeping. I had a part of her with me, too, I knew that much. But it wouldn't make the distance any easier to bear.

I was leaving my heart behind, back in that room, back with that female.

As I peered up at the dark window, I spoke softly. "I will come back for you, balisra. I don't know when, and I don't know how. But I will come back."

I had to believe that.

Otherwise, there was no way I could've walked away.

32

BIJOU

"How are you feeling?" I asked Oliver when I stepped into his bedroom.

It had been nearly seventy-two hours since Oliver had that seizure. Since then, he'd been taking it easy, and I had appointed myself as his caretaker.

Not that he needed one. He seemed to be doing just fine, proven by the way he leaned back in the recliner, dropping the game controller as he stared at the frozen image on the screen.

"Better now." His voice was even and smooth, as though he hadn't a care in the world.

I smiled, couldn't help it. "Why's that?"

Those lovely brown eyes shifted to me, raking over me from head to foot. "I think you know."

Ever since Oliver's seizure and his subsequent stay in the infirmary, I had been spending more time with him. I wasn't sure if it was for his benefit or mine, though. According to Apollo, Oliver was fine. The doctor insisted on checking in with him every few hours, but aside from that, he didn't put any restrictions on him. As for Oliver, he was listening to me, taking a couple of nights off from work and resting.

Still, I wished I knew what had caused that seizure. No one seemed to know. Or if they did, they weren't sharing it. I suspected Apollo was hiding something, but I couldn't quite put my finger on what it was.

"Come sit with me?" Oliver requested.

Realizing I was still standing near the door, I relaxed my shoulders and moved over to join him. I had intended to take a seat on the small love seat, but my direction shifted when Oliver held out his arm to block me.

"Here." He moved over, opening some space for me to sit next to him.

Laughing, I glanced at the small space he was giving me. "I'm not sure my butt's that small."

He patted his thigh. "Then sit here."

As much as I wanted to argue, to tell him we were moving too quickly, I knew that was merely a cop-out. An excuse because I was still worried about him, afraid I would do something that would trigger another seizure, and the next time...

His hand curled around my wrist, pulling me toward him. Before he toppled me off balance, I twisted, allowing him to pull me down into the chair with him. I was draped across his lap, my legs dangling over the armrest, my back partially against his chest, partially against the other armrest.

"Much better." Oliver sighed, then tapped the button that had the chair reclining, forcing me to lean into him.

"What are you doing?" I asked when he lifted the game controller.

"Finishing my game. What does it look like?"

Smiling, I stared up at him because I couldn't see much else. His arms surrounded me, his attention on the television once again, and he seemed completely content for me to be sitting on his lap.

What the hell, I thought, letting my head rest against his shoulder.

Another sigh escaped him and I put my hand on his abdomen.

The sounds of the game did little to distract me from the steady thump of his heart near my ear. While he played, I let my thoughts drift to our previous conversations. No matter how hard I tried to relax, my brain kept coming back to one thing. That darkness I had sensed within Oliver. We'd never talked about it, though I had always intended to bring it up, to see if I could dig deep enough to figure out what it was he was hiding. Based on everything he'd shared with me during our time together, I didn't think he knew he was hiding something. Perhaps because of my heightened senses, I could practically hear it, a steady echo of something within him.

"What's it like to feed?"

My head jerked up as I tried to look at Oliver's face. "What?"

The game controller settled on my thigh, his attention turning to me. "To feed. What's it like?"

"What do you mean?"

He shrugged. "What does it ... taste like?"

"I..." I honestly didn't know how to answer that. I'd never really thought about it before. Probably because it was a necessity, not something I did for fun. "Blood is blood, I guess."

"So it tastes like copper?"

I frowned. "Copper? No. It's ... um..." Wow. How did I explain this? "I guess there's a richness to it. And everyone's tastes different."

Oliver's head shifted back so he could look directly into my eyes. "Would you feed from me?"

I made a move to sit up, to get off his lap, but Oliver's hand curled over my hip, holding me in place. He wasn't rough, and if I tried, I would've easily broken his hold, but I stayed where I was because I sensed he was serious.

"I can't live on human blood. You know that."

"Will it hurt you?"

"No."

"Does it taste different than other blood?"

"I don't know," I admitted. "I've never tasted human blood."

I held his stare, searched deep in his eyes, attempting to see where he was going with this.

"Please."

My gaze shifted to his neck, to the pulse I could hear thumping steadily.

"Oliver..."

"Please," he whispered.

"Okay," I heard myself say.

Oliver didn't move, his eyes still steady on mine.

I reached up, cupping his face as I shifted in his lap, bringing my mouth toward his neck. I would've offered to take from his wrist, but I didn't want to. Despite my hesitation, I had a strong desire to feed from him, to taste him, my curiosity likely spurred by his.

"Relax," I urged, bringing my mouth to his neck as my fangs elongated, my upper lip pulling back.

Oliver moaned softly when I pressed my lips to his skin, and it was then I realized how intimate this was. He wasn't a

Fae, nor was he merely a blood source for me to survive on. No, Oliver's blood would do nothing for me, which made this more intimate than anything I'd ever done before.

"Bite me," he ground out.

Shocked by the command in his tone, I pressed my fangs to his skin then sank into him as gently as I could.

He hissed, his hand tightening on my hip. I couldn't ask if I was hurting him, and I only hoped he would let me know if I was.

The instant his blood hit my tongue, I noticed something different about his taste. It was familiar, almost. Which was odd because I'd only ever fed from vampires and Fae. The first time I'd taken from Madok's vein, I had noticed the difference. He didn't taste like vampire.

But Oliver did.

"Don't stop," Oliver moaned, pulling me toward him. "Please don't stop."

I wasn't sure I could've if I'd wanted to. As I latched on, sealing my lips to his skin, I drank him down. His soft moans were erotic, making me want to continue even though I feared I would hurt him. I had no idea how much blood a human could spare.

"Bijou ... oh, Christ..."

Oliver's hips jerked beneath me, and I felt his erection.

"Oh, fuck ... you have to stop," he warned. "I'm ... *asyra*... Christ, I'm coming."

Before I could pull from his vein, Oliver's hips bucked again. I allowed him to finish before I jerked my mouth from his neck, sealing the wounds quickly.

"What did you call me?" I asked, my voice nothing more than a breath of air. *Asyra* was a word from the ancient vampire language. It was a term of endearment, one I knew no one here had ever used before. Yet he'd spoken it, even enunciated correctly. How? Where had he learned that word?

His brown eyes met mine briefly, but before he could respond, they rolled back in his head, his body convulsing once more.

"Shit!"

ACADIA

"Do you have a moment?" I asked when Obsidian came down from the sunroom.

It wasn't that I'd been stalking him, but I was waiting nearby in hopes I would have a chance to speak with him alone.

"Of course," he said, motioning toward the darkened office on the main floor.

I led the way inside, the lights coming on when I willed them to. Obsidian joined me, then closed the door behind him.

"What's on your mind, Acadia?"

The idea of this was simple. Now that I was here, now that I was supposed to come up with the words, I wished I'd walked on by when I saw the male approaching me.

You can do this. The words were a mantra in my head, had been for the past half hour as I waited patiently for Obsidian to be finished. I *could* do this. I would.

Squaring my shoulders, I stopped pacing, pivoting to face the enormous angel.

"I'm going to simply get this out there," I said quickly. "Before I lose my nerve."

After all, I had spent the better part of the last two days trying to come up with the appropriate way to relay this to Obsidian. My official conclusion: there wasn't one. The only thing I could do was put it out there and hope for the best.

He nodded, then perched on the edge of the heavy wood desk that sat in the center of the space.

"I'd like to be relieved of my duties. Feeding the *fiestreigh*." I swallowed to wet my dry throat. "I'm not trying to shirk my duties by any means, and I'd be more than willing to perform other duties, even work alongside the *heurosp* if that's where I'd be most helpful. I just..."

When I peered up at Obsidian, I noticed he was smiling.

"What?"

His eyes softened. "Acadia, despite popular belief, you are not a prisoner here. Nor have you ever been. Not in my eyes. We appreciate you more than you'll ever know, but not once have we ever seen your contribution to this war as a requirement."

I wasn't sure what to say to that. I had never felt like a prisoner, but I knew all too well what was required of me. According to God, at least.

"You love him," he stated.

"More than anything," I admitted.

"Have you told him as much?"

I shook my head. "Not in so many words, no. It's like ... when those words come out, it'll be official. No turning back." I sighed. "I fear revealing too much of myself." I realized how it sounded and quickly continued. "Not to him. I think Kaj knows deep down. It's more ... I know what's at stake. Where my duties are concerned."

"Understandable." Obsidian's head tilted. "But he loves you. And he's willing to do whatever's necessary to make you happy."

"That's the problem," I blurted. "I don't want him to do anything because of me. I know about Michael's proposition. Kaj let me read his mind. Michael wants him to resurrect the original vampire in return for freeing the Fae."

It was just like Michael to manipulate a situation like that. Hanging something like that over Kaj's head ... he was a noble male. He would do what was right for those he cared about. Which made this doubly unsettling.

"It makes sense that he'd want to do that," Obsidian said. "But I don't think you have the whole story. It's not solely about freeing you. The vampire race is at risk. Kaj has to make a decision for his people, but the scales are weighted because he knows it will benefit you as well."

It pained me to know that Michael would use me against Kaj.

"Trust me. You're not the only one worried about this domino effect Michael's set in motion. I don't know what'll happen to us once the Fae are freed," Obsidian said, his tone reflecting concern. "Not that I'd want it any other way."

I hadn't thought about this from his perspective. Without our blood, the *fiestreigh* wouldn't be able to survive here on Earth. Fae blood was their life source, the means to their survival. It not only allowed them to survive, it provided a homing beacon so they could be monitored, one of the Almighty's prerequisites for allowing them to come to Earth.

"We won't leave you," I said, taking a step toward him. "If that's what you're worried about. It's more than duty for us as well."

"Those are the chains that keep you here. That's simply fact, Acadia. I would never force anyone to remain here. That's not how I operate. Nor do my brothers. But there's no denying you're a necessity for us. Without the blood of the Fae, the angels wouldn't be capable of remaining here."

Not unless they'd found their *amsouelot*, anyway. Obsidian and Eclipse were safe because they had their own life source now. The other warriors, as well as the *fiestreigh*...

"They could feed from the angels Michael's providing to the trainees," I said.

"True. They could. And they will if it comes down to it."

"Do you think Michael's considered that?" I asked. "He's the one who made the proposition in the first place."

Obsidian smiled. "I honestly don't know what goes through that male's mind. But yes, I'd like to think he has our best interest at heart."

One would hope, but like Obsidian, I didn't know what spurred Michael's decisions. I had never completely understood him.

"Kaj has a huge undertaking ahead of him," Obsidian continued. "And he's going to need you at his side. He can't go this alone."

"He's not alone."

"He feels as though he is."

I hadn't considered that. With so many people around, I assumed he had more help than was necessary. Between the Zenith and the *fiestreigh*, there were a number of males willing to stand at his back, to protect him should it come to that. But it helped to explain what he'd told me the other morning when he'd come to my room. He had openly admitted to needing me at his side.

"Perhaps now isn't the time to worry about myself," I said softly.

"Then when is?" Obsidian stood tall. "Acadia, you've fulfilled your duty to me, to my brothers, to the *fiestreigh*. Do we still need you? Absolutely. And not for your blood. We need you because you're a vital part of this family. Don't ever forget that. If you're asking me to release you, then I do. Consider yourself free to go to the male you love, to stand at his side, to help him when he needs you most. It may seem like things are quiet right now because they are. We have no idea what's going on, where the demons have disappeared to, but I'm not going to believe they've vacated forever. We've seen this before. They will be back. And when they return, we will be ready for them. All of us. No matter our role."

"Thank you, Obsidian."

"You don't have to thank me. I'm forever grateful for what you've done for all of us. You might consider your duty punishment, but I see it as a blessing."

I would've hugged him if it weren't for the fact my touch would cause him tremendous pain. Instead, I curtsied low, showing my gratitude and respect for the male I'd come to see as family.

"Now, go to your male," he said with a chuckle. "Let him claim you the way he needs so he can get his head back in the game. We need him as much as we need you."

Feeling lighter than I had in ... well, possibly ever, I spun around and hurried out of the room.

No sooner had I stepped into the hall than I heard the chaos.

"Someone help! Get Apollo!"

It was Bijou.

Obsidian's heavy footfalls sounded behind me. "You get Apollo," he instructed. "I'll go up there."

"Of course." On bare feet, I took off toward the infirmary, down the stairs, past the bar, beyond the war room.

I slammed through the doors that sealed off the medical facility.

"Apollo!"

The male came sauntering out from somewhere, his dark brows lowered. "What's wrong?"

"It's Bijou. She's calling for you. From the second floor."

The male nodded, then disappeared.

I followed suit, vanishing and reforming on the second floor. The door to Oliver's bedroom was open, Obsidian standing just inside.

"You should probably get Kaj," he told me when I peeked my head in to see Apollo tending to Oliver.

The human was sitting in a recliner, his body convulsing.

"Acadia. Now."

I nodded, then took off running. Knowing I couldn't materialize in the Lair because of the titanium that secured both residences, I settled for making my way on foot.

As I ran down the hallways, I briefly wondered why I needed to get Kaj.

Then it hit me.

I came to an abrupt halt as I stepped into the tunnels that led from the mansion to the Lair.

Oliver.

The original vampire.

"Oh, my God."

33

KAJ

I rubbed my eyes, trying to maintain my focus on the computer screen in front of me.

Not an easy feat considering I fucking hated this shit. Emails. Questions. Concerns.

What the fuck was I supposed to do about all this? It wasn't like I could simply shoot off a quick *Sure, let's do that* or *Hey, let's get together and chat more about it.* There had to be a precedent set, right? And where would I go to visit with these people making the requests? Not like I could show up on their doorstep and say, "Hey, I'm the Alpha. Want to chat?"

Nope.

Kardobahn had handled the task with grace and authority, but he'd also had an army of support. There had been significantly more Zenith, an abundance of *vestrahn*, plus office staff and helpers galore. I had never really considered all that my father had done, all the trips, not to mention the risks, that he took. It had been my responsibility to lead the Zenith, to protect the Alpha. And I'd spent all my time focused on that, ignoring the minutia of Kardobahn's responsibilities.

The very same responsibilities that now rested firmly on my shoulders.

Had I known it would come down to this one day, I would've spent more time with my father, learning the ropes.

Huh.

I hadn't realized until just then that I wanted the responsibility; I wanted to lead the race. All this time, I'd considered it a burden, something forced upon me without my consent. But somewhere along the way, the shoes had started to fit, and I realized I didn't want to pass the buck, so to speak. I didn't want Khari to rule our species. Not because I suspected the original vampire wasn't capable—although that was certainly in question, considering where the male had been for the past who knew how long. No, I wanted this for myself. I wanted to matter in the grand scheme of things. This was my place in the world, and it was the first time I'd accepted it.

My gaze refocused on the computer screen. So how did Blāz expect me to respond?

Sighing, I was about to flop back in my chair when the doors to my office flew open, Acadia stumbling inside.

I was on my feet in an instant. "What's wrong?"

"I don't know. It's Bijou and Oliver. Something's ... wrong."

My blood froze in my veins. "Is she hurt?"

Acadia shook her head. "Oh, God. No. I'm sorry. I shouldn't have said it like that. Not her. She's fine. It's Oliver... He's having another seizure."

Fucking great.

Just what I didn't need, that fucking ancient vampire getting antsy.

"Obsidian told me to come get you."

Realizing she was out of breath because she had run over here, I moved around my desk and pulled her into my arms. "Is Apollo with him?"

"Yes."

"Then there's nothing we can do. Not immediately. So take a deep breath, then we'll head back over."

She nodded, then leaned into me, her lungs working overtime.

I brushed my hands over her back, wishing her hair was down so I could stroke through the fine, silky strands.

Just her touch relaxed me, washing my brain of the stress and chaos stimulated by all those emails. Some fucking Alpha I was turning out to be. Couldn't even tackle my inbox.

"Better?" I asked when she pulled back and smoothed the bodice of her gown.

"Yes. Thank you."

I smiled, not sure what she was thanking me for.

"Let's head over there."

As I took her hand, Acadia nodded.

When we stepped out of my office, I saw Kidel sitting at the dining room table.

"Find the others. Bring them to the mansion."

The male's eyes shot up to me, his expression turning serious. "Absolutely, *phaal.*"

Because I didn't have more details to relay, I continued on with Acadia at my side.

I had to slow my roll to ensure my female didn't have to hurry. As we made our way down to the tunnels, I realized how I enjoyed the simplicity of this. Walking hand in hand with the female I loved, heading off to take care of some pressing issue.

Yes, I definitely liked this whole being-needed aspect. For so long, I'd felt alone, putting one foot in front of the other. I'd spent my entire life taking care of others, ensuring their safety. Now it was my turn to lead, and my desire to do so was compounded by the fact I had the support I needed. I had the four males I trusted most to back me and the female I loved more than life at my side. And with my daughter close, I felt as though I could tackle any task presented to me.

"I spoke to Obsidian," Acadia said softly, her words washing out the sound of my heavy footfalls on the hard-packed earth at my feet.

Because I heard the underlying meaning in her words, I stopped, turning so I could look at her. My eyes searched her face, trying to read her, to figure out what she was telling me.

A smile pulled at her mouth, and I released the breath I didn't realize I was holding.

"He's given me his consent," she said softly.

Warmth filled every crevice of his body, heating me from the inside out.

"I want to be at your side, Kaj. I want to spend the rest of my days in your bed, my nights working alongside you, supporting you."

So much emotion filled my chest, I thought for a minute I would explode. To hear those words from her mouth... They made me feel invincible.

Hell, it took everything in me not to drag her back to the Lair, to lock us in my bedroom so I could claim her appropriately. It was the only thing I could think about. I didn't want to waste another second, to risk her changing her mind.

Unfortunately, there were more pressing issues to deal with. Namely, an unruly vampire soul hell-bent on staking his claim on a female.

I leaned in and kissed Acadia. Just a gentle sweep of my lips over hers.

"Is something wrong?" she whispered.

"Nothing, *balisra*. Absolutely nothing."

I would find myself eating those words a few minutes later when we emerged into the chaos that was Angel Central.

OLIVER

W hat the holy ever-loving fuck?

I had no idea what the hell was going on, but seriously. This shit had to stop.

Now that the convulsions had ceased, I was attempting to get my head on straight. Not easy to do when there were so many people staring at me like I'd just appeared from another realm. All those eyes raked over me as though they were searching for ... shit, I didn't even know what they were looking at but it wasn't comforting.

The bright flash of a light in my eyes had me wincing. Once more, when Apollo shifted that brain-piercing beam into my other eye.

"What's going on?" Bijou asked, her voice soft as she spoke to the doctor.

Apollo sighed, and that didn't sit well with me, either.

Something was happening, and I got the sense the angel knew something he wasn't sharing with the class.

"I want to keep an eye on him for a little while." Apollo's attention swung to me. "You want to go downstairs?"

"Not really, no." Not to mention, I didn't want to be someone's guinea pig, and that was what I felt like.

"Maybe you should," Bijou suggested.

"No." I didn't mean to be curt with her, but right now, I had no intention of being led around by the nose while they tiptoed around me.

"What brought this on?" Apollo asked, though the question didn't seem directed at me.

I thought back to the moment Bijou's fangs sank into my neck. The feeling had been surreal. An overwhelming sense of euphoria had consumed me. Hell, it had been so good I'd come in my fucking jeans without touching my cock.

Just the thought had my cock thickening once more. Which was completely inappropriate considering those who were in the room. Obsidian, Penelope, Kaj, Acadia, Bijou, Apollo. And yes, I was almost positive that was Amethyst standing near the door, the other doctor probably curious as to what was sending my brain into chaos. I was curious, too. Whatever it was, it felt... God, I didn't even know how to explain it. There was a strange feeling inside me, as though there was a battle brewing.

Like the first time, it felt like something was emerging, attempting to push beyond the realm of my body. Whatever it was, it didn't want to be bound, held captive. Or at least, that was the sense I was getting, which was absolutely crazy, I knew. Probably best not to voice it. Last thing I wanted was a straitjacket.

Shifting in the leather recliner, I attempted to sit up

straight. My efforts failed me. My body was weak, my muscles refusing to coordinate.

This was fucking ridiculous.

"Are those ... puncture wounds?"

Yep, that was Kaj's voice, and he didn't sound at all pleased by the acknowledgement.

Of course, I didn't respond because I wasn't about to get into it with Bijou's father. What happened between Bijou and me was our business. We were both consenting adults.

"Bijou, I'd like to speak with you. Alone." Kaj's words were a demand, not a request, and the intensity in them sparked something dark within me.

"No," I said, but the voice that came out of me sounded nothing like my own.

Evidently, everyone thought so because all eyes shot to me.

"It's all right, Oliver." Bijou's soft tone and gentle hand on my arm settled the strange darkness inside me. "I owe him this much. But I won't be gone long."

I met her pretty green eyes and finally nodded.

"Please stay with him until I return," she told Apollo before slipping out of the room.

I watched her go, and when she was out of my sight, there was a strange churning within me. A disconnect, maybe? Like a piece of me had shifted, rearranged like puzzle pieces working their way into the overall picture. So freaking weird.

"So, hit me with it, Doc. What's the prognosis?"

Apollo's pale blue eyes leveled on me. There was concern there, definitely. But there was something else.

"What aren't you telling me?"

Before the angel could answer, there was a flutter of wings. A second later, Michael appeared.

I jumped back, my body slamming into the recliner. Why

the archangel always scared the shit out of me when he did that, I didn't know. But ... *fuck!*

"Not yet," Michael told Apollo.

The doctor nodded, but I wasn't sure if it was agreement or resignation.

"I think it's best if we move you to the infirmary," Amethyst said, speaking up for the first time since she entered the room. "I'd like to get you hooked up to some monitors. At least until we can get you stable."

Stable? I was stable.

My gaze shot from Amethyst to Obsidian, over to Penelope, on to Apollo, and finally settling on Michael.

No sooner did I meet the archangel's strangely swirling eyes than I began to vibrate again. A second later, my body was convulsing. Not long after that...

Pitch. Fucking. Black.

MICHAEL

Hmm.

Interesting way for the human/vampire to greet me, that was for sure.

Not that I expected a warm greeting by any means, but come on. A seizure?

A bit extreme, no?

With a heavy exhale, I stepped back while Apollo and Amethyst did whatever it was they needed to do.

"I don't think your presence is comforting to him," Obsidian noted.

Yeah, well. I had that effect on people, now didn't I?

"Move him to the infirmary," I insisted, not bothering to look at Obsidian or Penelope when I made the decision.

Expecting a rebuttal from the female, I steeled myself for an argument. When one never came, I forced my eyes over to Obsidian's *ereswa*. She looked sincerely concerned for her brother. And from what I could tell, she had absolutely no idea what was going on. Which could only mean Obsidian hadn't bothered to share the ... interesting news with her yet.

I glanced up at Obsidian. The quick shake I got in response said he didn't want to go into it now, either.

Fine.

"Can I come with you?" Penelope asked the healers as they discussed moving him.

When they called for someone to bring a gurney up, I took that as my cue to make an exit. I wasn't surprised when Obsidian followed me into the hallway, then down a few doors to the library. Meant I was about to get an earful.

Without haste, I stepped into the elaborate room filled from floor to ceiling with literature in every size, shape, and form. The door closed behind me.

"What's the plan?" I asked, figuring I would launch right into my reason for showing up.

"That's not my decision to make," Obsidian grumbled.

I pivoted to face him. "It is if you want to keep Penelope's human alive."

"Are you controlling this?"

Dropping all sense of levity, I met the male's stare head on. "Not at all. I'm going to assume the healer's accurate when he said Khari is seeking his mate. Now that he's found Bijou, he's acting as all bonded males do. He's looking to keep her safe."

"She is safe."

"Perhaps. But they've been going through a little tiff. Now that things appear to be progressing..." I turned toward the windows, peered out as the moon shone high in the sky, brightening the world beneath it. "He prompted that feeding. I think he's uncovering his true nature."

"How much longer do we have?"

Turning back to Obsidian, I shrugged. "No idea, honestly. Like I've said, Khari's never had this issue in the human vessels. But he's also never been in close proximity to his mate."

"I have to tell Penelope."

I nodded. That much I understood. As for how the female would take it, that was anyone's guess.

"I hope you see how fucked up this is." Obsidian's tone reflected his disdain for the situation.

"While I tend to take heat for my decisions, know that I don't make them lightly. I get that no one understands what prompted me to encapsulate the original vampire in a human vessel, but I assure you, it's been for his safety."

"Did you have to choose my *amsouelot's* brother?"

"Technically, he's not related." I held up a hand. "But yes, it was calculated. I used that human vessel for a reason." I waved my arms to encompass our surroundings. "Everything I do is for a reason, Obsidian. I needed Khari to be returned to the vampires, but I also needed him separated for as long as was necessary. It might not be obvious now, but he's critical to the race's survival. I was protecting them."

"Why?"

"Because it's my responsibility to protect the humans, too."

"Then why was the original vampire sentenced to elimination in the first place?"

Ah. I should've expected that question. And, technically, I had, only I'd thought it would come from Kaj.

"Let's just say Khari's not your average vampire. When he was created, my father was looking to create a being that would supersede your abilities. As you've probably noticed, he used my mold for their creation, but since he's got drastically more abilities than I, he made some modifications. At the time of Khari's creation, the world wasn't ready for that. However, I knew one day it would be. So, I tucked him away for a bit."

"A bit?" Obsidian snorted. "How long's it been? Nine thousand years?"

"Give or take." I exhaled heavily. "The vampires have proven beneficial over the years, and I knew one day they would require the full abilities of the original. More importantly, he'll be vital in getting through this shitstorm my brother has initiated."

"The shadow beasts?"

"There will come a time when our limits are tested," I told Obsidian, hating that I had to admit that. I'd always hoped to be one step ahead of Lucifer, and in doing so, I'd underestimated my brother.

"When?"

"I honestly wish I knew. But until that time, my objective is to fortify the species created to protect the humans. That's all I'm capable of doing."

Obsidian exhaled heavily. "I'll talk to Kaj. Figure out the best way to proceed."

"I suggest you don't wait much longer. Khari will survive,

of that I have no doubt. I cannot say the same for Oliver Calazans."

With that parting shot, I vanished myself back to Heaven.

For now, it was out of my control, and there was nothing I could do but sit back and watch.

34

KAJ

I stepped out of the shower, snagged the towel from the bar, and ran it over myself before tossing it into the hamper.

I stared around the bathroom, taking it all in for the first time since I'd moved into this room. It reminded me a lot of the nothing-special room I'd maintained at the Seattle camp, back when I was leading the Zenith for my father. Simpler times, I figured. Back before I was forced into the role of Alpha.

Shitty job I was doing of it, too. Even I could acknowledge that as I met my own reflective gaze in the mirror above the sink. The only efforts we'd made were when Mirakel and Blāz had gone to speak to the noble families, assessing their oldest male offspring to see if they were worthy of training to become the elite. They'd gone one step further, bringing the males and females into the training center for assessment.

Then there was the ongoing investigation into Darko, the male we believed a traitor. Unfortunately, it wasn't as simple as eliminating him because he was an asshole. We needed proof before we could take him down. But take him down, we would.

Aside from that, I'd spent more time attempting to stabilize my life than to provide any sort of rule to the vampires.

I couldn't help but think about Oliver, about what was transpiring. The ancient vampire was attempting to surface, clearly sick of being repressed inside a human for centuries. According to Apollo, the vampire wouldn't remain much longer. He was getting stronger, in large part due to his feelings for Bijou, his need to claim her. And from what the healers had explained, it wouldn't be long before the human vessel was incinerated from the ever-growing powers of the vampire. They needed to separate the two and they needed to do it soon.

The question was, what would happen when Khari emerged? When he was no longer bound to the human vessel? Would he move into the role he was created for? Taking over the species, casting me aside?

A month ago, I would've said more power to him. Now ... well, I was no longer willing to step down unless I knew the race was going to rally. If I was expected to resurrect the male, I damn sure didn't intend to let him destroy the efforts of my father. No, maybe I didn't step into the role as I should have, but I was certainly moving in that direction.

Perhaps Khari would be a better leader.

It didn't matter, I decided. I was not stepping down. I would not hand over the reins to another, forgo the rare opportunity presented to me so I could stand at the right hand of the male who would one day mate my daughter.

Sad thing was, although I knew where I belonged, I was still up in the air about so many things. It was like I was a mix of bubbles in water, moving about, never settling. I needed to settle so I could get to work, focus on what was important. Plus, I had my daughter's well-being to consider.

I sighed heavily, forced the thoughts from my mind. They would hold until nightfall. At that point, I could address them all.

Not bothering with clothes, I went to my bedroom, willing the lights off behind me.

I came up short in the doorway when my eyes landed on the female kneeling on my bed. She was naked, her dark hair hanging down over her shoulders, the long strands discreetly hiding her naked breasts.

All thought fled. All my worries, my fears disappearing completely. The only thing that mattered was this female.

I hadn't expected to see Acadia. Ever since I left her back at the mansion a few hours ago, I expected to be accompanied by nothing more than the cold chill in my bones that remained whenever I wasn't in her presence. Sure, she told me she had talked to Obsidian, that she wanted to move forward, but she hadn't mentioned what her immediate plans were. And with so much going on, I assumed we would continue to take things slow.

I took a moment to drink in the sight of her. Not only the delicious curves of her naked form, but the image she presented in my bed.

"What are you doing here?" I asked, hoping it didn't come across negatively.

Her amethyst eyes lifted to my face, and a smile formed on her luscious mouth. "I am here to give myself to you. Completely and wholly, I am yours, Kaj. Provided you will have me."

My breath lodged in my chest when she bowed before me, the long line of her spine arching as she rested her forehead to the mattress, her arms reaching forward as though for me.

Mine.

As I moved toward her, Acadia remained where she was, her face tucked downward. I could do nothing more than bend over her, my lips gliding over her spine as I covered her with my body. Though we were both naked, it wasn't necessarily a sexual moment. However, it was uniquely intimate.

I trailed my hands over her waist, her hips, gripping firmly because I was so overwhelmed by her presence, I wasn't sure what to do next. I remained just like that for a couple of minutes, inhaling her sweet fragrance, absorbing the warmth of her skin, listening to her breathe. I'd never known true peace before Acadia, and to have it now...

Forcing myself up, I took her hands in mine, then helped her to sit upright. I brought her knuckles to my lips, kissed them one at a time as I met her gaze, held it.

"If I join you on this bed, I'm going to claim you," I warned. "There is no going back from this."

To my surprise, Acadia took my hand, urging me to accompany her. As I placed one knee on the mattress, she lay before me, her head resting on my pillow, hair spilling out around her. She was so... There were no words in any language that could do her justice. This female was absolute perfection. She was *everything*.

Leaning over her, I took her lips, attempting to hold back the urgency I could feel pulsing in my veins. I wanted to slide into the heavenly warmth of her body, to bring us both the ecstasy we often found in one another's arms.

Only, I wasn't ready for it to be over.

So rather than mount her like the animal I was, I eased onto my side, my lips still fused to hers, my hand beginning a slow exploration over her smooth skin. I started at her neck, drifted down to her chest, dipping between her breasts. I ventured lower, my palm spanning her belly, sliding farther until I reached her cleft. Rather than tease, I reversed my movements, returning to cup her throat as I thrust my tongue inside her mouth, mimicking the movements I would soon make with other parts of my body.

Heat from the fire merged with the warmth generated by our bodies. When my fingers trailed over her the second time, my mouth followed, pressing kisses as I inhaled her sweet scent. This time I paused to suck her nipples, teasing the nubs with my tongue while Acadia's fingers ran through my hair. Every so often, she would grip me firmly, holding me in place before releasing. I took my cues from her, loving every inch of her.

When I made my way between her thighs, I repositioned so her legs were draped over my arms, my mouth melding to her hot core. I took my time, pushing her to the brink but never over. I loved those sweet moans, the way her fingernails speared my scalp as she attempted to bring herself to orgasm against my intruding tongue.

"Kaj..."

She was right where I wanted her.

"Don't move," I instructed, pushing up onto my knees.

Time slowed as I admired her. Every beautiful inch. My fingertips swept over her soft, smooth skin. I had no need to memorize her because I had done so long ago.

Her eyes shifted to me as I lifted her left leg, cradling her foot in my hand. My lips trailed over the delicate arch, up to her ankle, slowly inching higher. I paused, my mouth hovering over the vein that ran to her foot. When our eyes met, I pressed my lips to that spot, stroked her with my tongue.

"Yours," she rasped, as though she knew what was coming.

Without warning, I pierced her with my fangs, drawing from the vein only briefly before sealing the wound. Her eyes widened, her chest rising and falling more rapidly. It wasn't pain that increased her respiration. Desire. I could practically taste it.

"That's just the beginning," I warned.

Acadia nodded, a plea in her beautiful eyes. She wanted this, I could sense it.

I did the same with her other leg, kissing her small foot, working higher, piercing the vein on that side. After sealing that wound, I trailed a path of kisses up her leg, once more toward the juncture of her thighs. This time I paused, placing one soft kiss, then pierced the femoral artery, drinking from her in long pulls. I sealed that wound, then performed the same maneuver on the other side before sealing her flesh with my tongue. It was a necessary ritual, marking her as mine, taking from her in every way. With every puncture, I took only small amounts of her blood before sealing the holes while she watched me, her breaths labored, her desire building.

I performed the same near her breasts, on each of her wrists.

When I made my way to her neck, I was panting, as was she. My cock was rock hard and desperate to find its way into her. I took my time, sinking my fangs into her jugular, first on the left, then the right. It wasn't to feed, as that would come later, so it didn't take long. Good thing because I was beginning to vibrate, my need for her overwhelming me.

My cock found the slick heat of her as I pumped my hips, sliding through her juices before angling for penetration. Before I slid inside, I met her gaze, held it. "I'm going to claim you, Acadia. There's no going back from this. You understand that?"

She nodded, her back arching in invitation. "Claim me, Kaj."

The soft rasp of her voice had me pushing my hips forward, filling her, stretching her. I took my time, rocking forward, retreating. And when I was fully seated within her, I took her hands, linked our fingers, and pinned her to the bed. I didn't rush, pleasuring us both for long minutes as I allowed her body to acclimate to the intrusion.

As the energy shifted between us, my hips began thrusting in earnest as I eased my weight onto her. I released her hands, sliding my arms beneath her back so I could balance without suffocating her. And when I was pressed against her from chest to thigh, I drove in hard and fast, as deep as I could go.

The scent was the first to emerge from my pores, a means of marking her. It would forever be imprinted in her skin, detected only by the males of my race so they knew who she belonged to.

"Kaj..." Acadia clung to me, her fingernails scoring my back.

The pain was an aphrodisiac, a reminder of exactly where I was, who I was with. What this moment meant.

I pushed into her again and again, faster, harder, deeper.

My fangs tingled with the need to pierce her. When it became too much, I shifted my mouth to her chest, directly over her heart. I met her gaze once more, noticed the slight nod of her head as though she knew exactly what I would do.

My fangs elongated, more so than they'd ever done before. Unable to hold back, I drove the sharpened points into her flesh, piercing the vein that delivered lifeblood directly to her heart. But I didn't drink from her. This time, I marked her as mine, merging with her as the venom possessed by male vampires shot into her bloodstream. Her body jerked, her sex clutching tightly as a knot formed at the base of my cock, locking me inside her. We were intimately joined in that moment, unable to separate as I came deep within her, claiming her while at the same time marking her as mine. Permanently.

By the time the venom was drained from me and pumped into her, the knot receding to allow movement, Acadia was writhing beneath me, her hands clutching my head, holding me to her as I retracted my fangs, sealed the wounds with a steady swipe of my tongue. Because of the venom that had passed through those punctures, they would be permanent, forever etched in her skin as a reminder to both of us.

And that was when I took her.

I shifted up onto my arms, hovering over her as I worked us both toward climax.

"Kaj!" Acadia's back bowed, her sex pulsing over mine as she came so beautifully.

Only then did I give myself over to another climax, releasing inside her, filling her, the ultimate marking of my female.

Satisfied in every way, I rolled, taking Acadia with me without retreating from her body. I draped her over my chest, ran my hands over her hair, and held her there. I was still rock hard, probably would be for a couple of days, because the urge to mark her over and over was triggered by the venom.

"I love you, *balisra*," I whispered softly in the language we were both familiar with, then in my own language I said, "*From now until eternity, I shall love only you.*"

"*And I you,*" Acadia responded in my language.

The fact that she'd learned it had my heart swelling as well as other parts of me throbbing.

She moaned softly, her body moving over mine. When she lifted her head and met my gaze, I saw she was smiling.

"Take me, *balisra*. Make me yours."

Acadia did exactly as I requested, making me feel like the most powerful male in the universe.

MIRAKEL

I knew when it happened.

I'd been sitting on my bed, trying to talk myself out of inviting Briony to my room. Over and over her words played in my head, my body hard and aching, my lips still tingling from being melded to hers during that one far-too-brief kiss we'd shared the last time I'd gone to her. And yes, I had apologized for my reaction, and yes, she had forgiven me. But after that, I hadn't been sure how to proceed, so I'd kept my distance. Emotionally, at least. Physically ... well, that was more difficult than not. I was still feeding from her, and while we managed to keep things platonic during those instances, I knew it wouldn't last much longer.

Right now, it seemed fucking impossible thanks to the goings-on taking place beneath this roof. Kaj had mated his female, officially claimed her.

Perhaps it was because Kaj's room was not all that far from my own, but I smelled his marking, sensed the male bonding with the female. There was no energy like with the angels. No, this was subtle, something that would only be picked up by vampires. Males from other species would sense something even if they didn't know exactly what it meant, but they would be deterred from the female. And while it wasn't a tsunami of energy, it was equally powerful, igniting the urge to fuck.

Damn good thing I'd held off on inviting Briony.

So why was I picking up my phone, pulling up her number, typing out a text?

Because I was an idiot. One who had no self-control when it came to her.

Do you know how many males I've been with? Zero, Mirakel. I have never taken a male inside my body.

There was no denying the rush that had threatened to level me when she'd admitted that. To know she'd never had another male inside her was a temptation unlike anything I'd ever known. The need to claim her had been so potent, the only thing I could do to refrain was to send her away.

I want to be with you. I want to know what it feels like to have your hands on me, your lips. Your tongue. I want to feel you move inside me.

Even now, as the words pierced my frontal lobe, I knew I couldn't call her to me. It was wrong on so many levels.

My thumb hovered over *send*. The text was already written —*Come to me, Briony*—but sending it would ultimately alter both of us.

I'd felt her desire, knew she wanted me. Only I wasn't sure she wanted me the same way. How could she? Briony didn't know the first thing about me. We'd fed from one another, but that was the extent of our interactions. The brief conversations we'd had were mostly contrived of my attempts to keep away from her.

It would've been so easy to take her up on her offer, to pleasure her body, but I knew I would want more. And I damn sure wasn't going to think simply because I'd imprinted that she belonged to me.

Didn't work that way.

The angels had it all figured out. Or, I figured, whoever was in control up there in Heaven. They had predestined souls, and once they came together, they wanted one another. Vampires weren't that lucky. Nor were Fae, I suspected. The only thing we truly had in common with angels was the fact that we mated only once, loved only one.

And Kaj had mated with Acadia.

I figured this was significant in some way. I was truly happy for the male, but at the same time there was a hint of jealousy. I wanted what Kaj now had. I wanted to claim my female, to ensure all other males understood she belonged to me and me alone.

With a heavy exhale, I tossed my phone on the bed and dropped back to my pillow, staring up at the dark ceiling. I began running through multiplication tables in an effort to shut off my brain and relax my body. I went so far as to purposely tense and relax every individual muscle from head to toe. By the time I got to my abdominals, I was interrupted by a knock on the door.

Figuring it was Blāz or Huracān there to gossip like women, I yanked the sheet over my lower half and shouted a half-hearted, "Come in."

The door opened, but it wasn't either male who had arrived.

"What are you doing?" I asked Briony, watching as she gently closed the door behind her.

Her brows lowered in what appeared to be confusion. "You asked me to come."

Glancing over at my phone, I groaned. I snatched it up, and what do you know? I'd sent the fucking text.

Great.

Just fucking great.

Briony was watching me as though I were a rabid animal seconds away from breaking its chain. And what do you know? I felt like one, too.

What was I supposed to do now? Send her away? Tell her it was an accident, that I didn't really want her here?

And what sort of asshole would that make me?

With a sigh, I sat up, ensuring the sheet remained over me, though I wasn't sure why I bothered. She'd already seen every inch of me.

I propped myself against the headboard, then motioned her over. "I've decided to feed."

She nodded politely, and if I wasn't mistaken, there was definite disappointment in her eyes.

When she approached the side of the bed, I intended to take her hand, to use her wrist. All those good intentions left the building when I inhaled her sweet scent. So, instead of taking her hand so I could pierce her wrist, I tugged her forward, shifted my legs apart, and patted the mattress.

"Like we did the other day." Yep, that was my voice all ripped to shreds thanks to the lust coursing through me.

Briony gracefully joined me, shifting her robes so they settled around her and over my knees.

I took deep, calming breaths as I eased her back against me, her back to my chest. I relaxed against the headboard but didn't do anything more.

"Is something wrong?"

"No. Just ... stay right there."

It took a minute for me to get myself under control, but I managed.

Mostly.

Instead of keeping my hands to myself, I brushed the wisps of her hair away from her neck as I stared down at the delicate column, watching the steady thump of her pulse. What I should've done was pierce her flesh and offer her my hands so she could feed from me. What I did was slide one arm around, pulling her head back against my shoulder as I pressed my fingers against her chin, angling her how I wanted her.

I leaned in, my fangs having emerged long ago. But rather than pierce her vein, I pressed my lips to her skin.

Briony moaned softly, relaxing into me.

I kissed her, sliding my mouth up and down, toward her ear, along her shoulder.

"Briony..."

The hand that wasn't holding her chin found its way to her chest, then slipped lower, separating the folds of the robe until her breasts were revealed. She had nothing on beneath the burgundy silk, her ivory skin as creamy as I remembered from the first time she'd revealed herself to me.

As I unwrapped her like a present, I watched my hand move over her skin. It was as though I was observing someone else cupping her heavy breast, rubbing her nipple between forefinger and thumb. And though that voice in the back of my head was telling me I was going to get burned, I couldn't seem to stop.

"Spread your legs," I urged, sliding my hand down her flat belly to the juncture between her thighs.

Briony's knees parted, falling open and exposing her sex. As a Fae, she was completely bare, her skin utterly smooth, no hair anywhere except on her head. My fingers homed in on their target, sliding through her slick slit. When she bucked her hips, I groaned softly.

"Move back," I instructed, shifting so I could get her neck closer to my mouth while my fingers continued to wander.

Her soft moans had my cock throbbing, but I ignored the damn thing.

"I'm going to bite you," I informed her as my fangs trailed

down her neck. "And I'm going to make you come with my fingers."

"Please…"

Figuring it was in our best interest for me to be at least somewhat distracted, I shoved my fangs into her skin, piercing the vein. As I took the first pull on her, I pushed my finger inside her, then retreated, coating the digit in her silky juices before thrusting inside her again.

Time became irrelevant at that point. I fed from her as I fingered her, spurred on by her softly spoken pleas and the decadent taste of her blood on my tongue.

Fearful I was going to hurt her, I finally pulled my fangs from her flesh, sealed the wounds, and then pushed two fingers inside her. I curled them upward, searching for—

"Mirakel! Oh … yes!"

Briony's sex squeezed my fingers as she came in my arms. I let her ride out the waves, my fingers still buried inside her tight sheath. Only when she was breathing normally did I pull them out and bring them to my mouth. My eyes slammed shut as her exquisite taste exploded on my tongue. It was all I could do not to move, not to roll her beneath me and mount her.

Somehow I refrained, but I did reposition so that we were flat on the mattress, me spooning her from behind, my arm draped over her, the sheet between us, ensuring I didn't do exactly what I wanted to do.

"Don't go, Briony," I whispered. "Let me hold you tonight."

Her hand covered my arm, squeezed gently. "I don't want to be anywhere else."

As I drifted off, I found myself hoping that was true.

35

MICHAEL

———

I didn't expect the Alpha vampire to emerge from his bedchamber, yet I had come here anyway. And here I was, sitting on the strange furniture in what I'd heard them refer to as a living room, waiting to see if, by some miracle, the male would come out of his room so we could address the pressing issue before it was too late.

Patience had never been my strong suit, but I had long ago learned to hone it when it came to my warriors. Those males worked on their own timeline, and they cared not whether I was appreciative. I sometimes wondered how they could stand to be idle for so long. Heaven knew it wasn't my favorite thing to do.

However, it was imperative that I speak with the vampire, find out what his intentions were. Now that Kaj had officially claimed the Fae as his own, decisions had to be made. There was no longer time to sit around and wonder what would happen next. We were running out of time, and if they didn't prepare, they would be caught unawares once again.

And not only because I feared Khari was getting restless, the male threatening to emerge regardless of the body he was inhabiting. If that happened while he was still ensconced in the human vessel, things were going to get ugly. However, that was the least of our worries.

My true fear lay in what they would encounter in the future. The attack that was imminent was going to make Eevuhl's breach look like a day at the playground. I only hoped they were prepared, and they were able to keep the fight away from the home front. It was the only way they would protect the child that would change everything. And for once, I wasn't referring to Ari'el, though she was most certainly at the top of my priority list.

I recalled Eevuhl's attack, seeing with my own eyes as Lucifer's demon charged forth with the intention of taking Obsidian's daughter. There had been only one thing to do, and I had met the onslaught without thought. Nothing would harm the babe. Not as long as my heart pumped blood in my veins. And if the other warriors had offspring, I would protect them the same, until my dying breath. However, as important as she was to me, Ari'el was not the child who would change everything.

I had lost all that mattered to me when my beloved *amsouelot* was taken from me. Lucifer had betrayed me in the worst possible way, dooming me to a hell of my own even though I resided in Heaven. Then Obsidian came along and gave me hope for the first time in forever. And though I would give almost anything to have my beloved Ari'el back in my arms, I knew that would never happen. Lucifer was nothing if not determined, and the male would keep her for the simple fact I still felt the loss.

Nothing could be done about that now.

And here on Earth, there were other things to worry about. Namely, the demons that were making a stronger presence with every passing day. The *impietans* were no longer our main concern. The humans turned into mindless, soulless idiots were but a tiny fissure in the overall crater that was breaking open in the fabric of humanity. The demons had begun taking over human flesh, choking out the souls that were housed there and assuming their lives. And with the vampire numbers dwindling, it was imperative that Kaj take a stand and protect his people. The best option I could see was to activate the original vampire, to bring Khari back to his former glory, because his power was what they would need in order to succeed.

A throat clearing had me looking up.

There, standing in the doorway, was the Alpha himself, wearing a pair of jeans he'd clearly tugged on as he'd left his chambers.

"Michael."

"Kaj." I didn't bother to get up, preferring to let the sofa hold the burden of my body. At the moment, I didn't have the strength to do much of anything else.

"Bring to me the written release of the Fae, and I will fulfill my end of the bargain."

I stared at the male, surprised but not at all disappointed by his decision. I snapped my fingers, produced the scroll with the Heavenly seal.

"Wasting no time, I see," Kaj said as he strolled forward to retrieve the sheet of rolled papyrus.

"There is no time to waste."

A light turned on, clearly by the vampire's will, as he broke the seal and skimmed the document.

"I have only one other condition."

Of course he did. "What's that?"

"You'll make the human immortal. That way Oliver can live out his life here with the angels, with his sister."

I hadn't expected the request, but I wasn't the least bit surprised. Kaj was a protector of others. It was in his nature.

"Done." I produced a quill, passed it over.

Kaj scrawled his name, then handed the paper back.

After reviewing the signature, I nodded. "As of now, the Fae are free."

Kaj lifted his eyes. "And their ability to procreate?"

I met the celadon-green stare.

"You owe them this," Kaj said stiffly. "They've proven their worth to your warriors."

Although Kaj's claiming had altered Acadia, rendering her fertile, the same would not be the case unless the other Fae were to mate with a vampire, so I had to consider it.

"I shall render them fertile," I told the vampire, "however, they will no longer be indestructible, merely immortal."

Kaj nodded. "I think it's a fair trade. And when they die?"

Ah. I should've seen that one coming.

"They must be given the opportunity of Heaven," Kaj insisted.

Because I knew I wouldn't get out of this one without reassurances, I nodded. "I'll ensure they're allowed in, provided they've met the same criteria as all others."

Kaj seemed satisfied with that.

"There's only one thing you'll have to contend with," I stated.

"And what's that?"

"Those who've been cast into shadows, trapped between Heaven and Earth..."

Kaj's eyebrows raised.

"They shall remain in the in-between until Acadia has freed them. All of them."

"And how will she do that?" Kaj asked, my tone concerned.

"Not for me to disclose."

"Never is," Kaj grumbled.

When no more demands came, I pushed to my feet. "Once Khari is resurrected, I will expect you and Obsidian to groom him for his role as Alpha."

"I've changed my mind about that," the vampire stated.

"Oh?"

"I'll be maintaining the position as Alpha."

"Just so you know, as the father of the female who will mate the original vampire," I clarified, "you will maintain the same abilities as the Alpha. And until the time they produce an heir, should Khari fall, you shall resume the duties as the Alpha."

"That changes nothing. I will continue as the Alpha. And should *I* fall, Khari can resume the duties."

I didn't need to argue because I trusted Kaj at the helm of the race. I'd always known he would make a phenomenal leader, above and beyond his father, even. I'd merely wanted the male to choose the position and not vice versa.

"Very well," I agreed. "You'll remain Alpha. Khari will lead the Zenith."

Once more, Kaj shook his head. "Huracān will lead the Zenith. Mirakel is my *adighrielin*. That's the way it will remain. Khari will integrate in, and we'll determine where he belongs as time goes by." Kaj stood tall, squared his shoulders. "And you understand I will not force my daughter into this mating. It shall be her decision."

Yep. Just as I'd thought. The male was the right person for the job. Not even an almighty archangel intimidated him.

"Understood." I was not worried about that. I was privy to

what had transpired between Bijou and Oliver—more accurately, Khari, though unbeknownst to her—up to this point.

"The resurrection will be done here," Kaj stated. "That way, the angels' healers can be present should the human male have issues."

"That is a reasonable request. Tonight."

Kaj shook his head. "I need a day to relay the information to my daughter and my mate, as well as my males. We shall undergo the resurrection on Friday, the thirteenth of March."

I had to give the vampire credit; he'd thought this through. Not to mention, he had brass balls to issue so many demands upon an archangel.

I held the male's stare. "I cannot reiterate the importance of this. Oh, but I should clarify one thing."

"What's that?"

"Should you fall, Khari will not be the one to rise as Alpha. Your heir will."

Kaj frowned. "My heir? Bijou?"

"Your unborn child."

Kaj inhaled sharply, his eyes widening.

"Fair warning, vampire, your child is going to change our very existence. The offspring of a vampire and a Fae ... not something the universe has ever encountered."

"What does that mean?"

"It is not for me to disclose, but it's the best I can do. He is the reason Khari must rise again. The child will need the protection of the most powerful being in the universe."

Kaj stared at me with so much hope in my eyes. "He?"

I nodded. "In the meantime, I shall continue to oversee the trainees. It's imperative their training commence without haste." I smiled widely. "Now you should proceed to get your female the food you intended to retrieve for her. I shall see myself out."

With a smile, I vanished, returning to Heaven.

I had much to do and not a lot of time to do it.

BLĀZ

"All right, just what the hell is going on?" I prompted when I made a pit stop in the infirmary.

Not that I wanted to hang out here, but, you know, shit happened.

And here I was.

But only because I was curious what was going on with the human, and well, Apollo seemed to be all up in that male's business.

"Excuse me?" The healer stepped out from the storage space where they kept all their extra shit.

"The human," I clarified. "What's with the seizures?"

"I'm not sure what you mean."

Oh, for fuck's sake. "Don't mess with me, Doc. I see it in your eyes. You know what's going on. Now spill."

"First of all, it's called doctor-patient confidentiality."

I barked a laugh. "Right. And next, you'll pass out your HIPAA pamphlet, right? Gimme a break."

There was a spark in the male's eyes. One that had me taking a step back as the healer neared.

"You're telling me you stopped by here to quell your curiosity about the human?"

"Why else would I be here?" I countered, hating that the healer had my number.

"Anyone ever tell you you're a shitty liar?" Apollo countered, still closing in on me.

"Unlike you, huh? Seems you're up to par on dodging questions."

I made sure to maintain eye contact as the male neared. And yep, that was a wall at my back now. Any closer and the doc was going to make a sandwich out of me.

Not that I was hoping for that or anything.

The instant Apollo's chest brushed mine, I inhaled sharply. Ever since that fucking incident in the patient room, I'd been trying to figure out just what the hell was going on between us. I'd half expected the healer to seek me out, ask for a bit of repayment. Tit for tat and all that.

Nope.

Not yet.

"You come back for more, Blāz?" Apollo taunted.

"More what?" I rasped through clenched teeth.

I grunted when Apollo's hand slid between our bodies, grazing my cock.

"At least he's hopeful," the healer whispered, his mouth now dangerously close to mine. "Would you like me to help you with that?"

Fuck, yes. "No."

The doc chuckled and the sound went right fucking through me. How was it the male could be that damn cocky and still be sexy? It defied logic. I had never been into arrogant males, yet here I was.

The lips that crashed into mine were hard and insistent and so fucking good, I was suddenly grateful for the stone at my back. Otherwise, I might've been on my ass, my legs kicked right out from under me.

By some strange stroke of luck, I managed not to topple us both as I grabbed for Apollo, jerking him closer, our tongues battling for supremacy. I didn't mean to touch him, shocked by the feeling as much as my desire to do it. But it was when Apollo nipped my lower lip that shit got real. That spark of pain lit me up from the inside out, gave me half the mind to go to my knees right here and show the sexy healer just what I was capable of.

"You won't hear me complaining," Apollo whispered.

I jerked back, my skull making contact with the wall. I glared at the healer as I rubbed my head. "Get outta my head, healer."

That hand that had grazed me a minute ago dipped into the waistband of my jeans, those deft fingers brushing the head of my cock.

"How about this head? Have any demands for me to stay away from it?"

What the fuck had I been thinking coming down here?

Oh, wait. I hadn't been thinking. Not with the rational side of my body, anyway.

"Say the word," Apollo growled.

"Not worried someone might see us?"

"Not even a little. You scared?"

Was I? I wasn't sure how to answer that question. I'd never much cared for exhibitionism, but it wasn't like I was opposed to it. When it came to sex, I took it as it came. But for some fucked-up reason, I didn't want to exploit whatever this was that was happening between us. The thought of someone seeing Apollo with my cock down his throat... Nope. Nuh-uh. And it had nothing to do with me worrying about someone learning I was gay. That shit was public record.

NICOLE EDWARDS

No, for some dumb-ass reason, I had the strange notion to keep this between us. The only person I wanted watching the healer taking me deep in his throat was me.

I was so lost in my head, I didn't even realize Apollo had unbuttoned my jeans, lowered the zipper.

"Not here," I snapped.

Apollo glanced both directions, then pinned me with those pale blue eyes. "Scared?"

"No." I met that stare. "Possessive."

That seemed to shock the healer, because Apollo took one step back, his hands falling to his sides.

"Scared?" I shot back using the doc's own word.

Apollo's blue eyes narrowed as though he wasn't sure what to make of this. A second later, he shook his head and turned away.

"See yourself out, vampire."

I remained where I was, fixing my jeans as I watched Apollo disappear around the corner, back where he'd come from. I was half tempted to go after him, but I'd seen that look. Apollo thought this was all fun and games.

Wasn't it, though?

Oh, for fuck's sake.

36

ACADIA

———

I awoke to the sound of the shutters lifting.

I opened my eyes, scanning my surroundings. The first thing I realized was that I was not in my room.

Then the memories of early that morning came flooding back. Instantly, I tugged the blankets down as I peered at my chest. The puncture wounds over my heart had healed; however, they were still visible. I brushed the markings with my fingers and smiled, wondering if I felt different. I had the moment Kaj had pierced my heart. There had been a strange elation that flooded me when his *sonavex* had filled my veins. I hadn't asked Kaj what the mating entailed, but I'd done a bit of research. There wasn't much documented about the phenomenon, but I'd learned enough to have an idea.

Yet I'd been overwhelmed. In a good way, of course.

And while I could've asked him to lay it out so I would understand, I hadn't felt it necessary. I trusted Kaj with my life, knew he wouldn't do anything to hurt me. Even now, as I thought about what happened when he pierced that artery, I wondered why some referred to it as venom. Perhaps there hadn't been a better translation for it.

The smile was still planted firmly on my face when I forced myself out of bed. Kaj had woken me earlier to let me know he had some things to take care of, but that he would meet me for the evening meal at Angel Central.

As I retrieved my gown from the floor, I glanced around the space. Kaj had recently moved rooms because he said the other one was getting some updates. It made me wonder if he was actually going to decorate. That room was the very room I had nursed Kaj back to health in so long ago. Only now it lacked the color and decor that had once brought it to life. Or I thought it did. That could've changed in the past week or so, but I doubted it. From what I'd gathered, Blāz was fortifying the space for the Alpha. When Kaj was explaining it to me, he referred to it as a panic room.

For some reason, that made me think of steel panels and concrete floors. It didn't sound all that homey. No more than this room. As it was, there wasn't anything personal within the space, and the thought of living in a protected area only made it feel colder. I doubted Kaj cared much since he simply occupied it physically. If we were to share a space, which I assumed we would, I wanted it to be welcoming and cheerful.

A task for another day, I supposed.

. . .

An hour later, having returned to my room within the mansion, I had showered and made myself presentable for the night. Something had compelled me to wear red, a color I'd often forgone because of how bold a statement it made. But it suited my mood this evening. I wasn't sure what it was, but I definitely felt different. Perhaps not physically, but emotionally for sure. As though I'd been made whole after all this time.

When I made it to the main floor, I heard a cacophony of voices coming from the dining room. There was only one I was seeking out as I neared the open doors.

"Acadia?"

My heart beat faster as I turned toward the male calling out to me from the kitchen. I turned to face him, unable to hide my smile.

Though he was dressed similarly to how he usually was— head to toe in black—Kaj looked resplendent. Then again, I'd always found him utterly beautiful, but this evening, he stood out even more to me.

Kaj offered his arm, so I slipped mine into it, allowing him to lead me into the dining room. I could feel the eyes shifting in my direction, monitoring me like something was different. I offered a smile to all familiar faces sitting at the tables, filling the space. For a moment, I was confused as to what was going on, but then I noticed them.

"Oh." My hand came up to my throat as I stopped before the four males kneeling on the floor just inside the dining hall.

Huracān, Blāz, Kidel, and Mirakel. The enormous males were bowing, steel daggers gripped firmly in both hands, the tips of the blades pressed into the hardwood flooring.

"Rise, warriors," Kaj instructed.

All four males got to their feet. The daggers were sheathed, and all eyes lifted.

"What's going on?" I whispered, though I knew everyone heard.

"They're welcoming you as their queen," he said softly.

Ah. Well, I was no one's queen, but I wasn't going to say as much. I had a lot to learn when it came to vampire tradition, and the last thing I wanted to do was offend them in some manner.

"At ease," Kaj told them before glancing over at me. "Shall we eat?" Kaj nodded toward the table where Obsidian was sitting, his hand on Penelope's chair, the female beside him with Ari'el in her arms.

"I'm not sure that's appropriate," I whispered to Kaj, refraining from telling him I was but a servant in this world.

"Sit," Obsidian urged, as though he'd heard my thoughts and wasn't pleased by them. "Within these walls, we are and will always be family, Acadia."

When Kaj pulled out my chair, I settled into it, not sure where to look, so I let my gaze land on Ari'el, who was sleeping soundly in her mother's arms. It wasn't that Obsidian had ever treated me lower than him, but I had always been aware of his status. Although I had fed him for centuries, I had never shared a meal with him. Not like this. In the breakfast nook, yes. In the kitchen, sure. At the dining room table ... never. And I was more than aware of Kaj's status in the hierarchy, so it made sense because he had claimed me that I would sit with him.

Still, this felt awkward.

Voices sounded from behind me, causing me to peer over my shoulder to see who had joined us. The *heurosp* were entering the space, heading for Obsidian and Eclipse first. But it wasn't the servants who had my heart missing a beat. It was the way Bijou had entered the room and come to an abrupt halt.

Kaj must've sensed her because he also looked back. Only then did Bijou smile and come forward.

Rather than go to her father, though, she came over to me, stopping at the side of my chair.

"If you'll excuse me," she said kindly to Obsidian and Penelope, then took my hand.

Not sure what was going on, I got to my feet, watching the young female closely.

The next thing I knew, I was being pulled in for a hug. I immediately embraced Bijou as was polite.

"Congratulations," Bijou said softly in my ear.

"Thank you?" Yeah, it came out as a question, but I was confused. "How did you know?"

Bijou pulled back and met my gaze. "His scent is all over you."

I lifted my hand, sniffed my forearm.

Bijou chuckled. "You can't smell it, but vampires can." She released me. "Congrats, Dad," she said, patting him on the shoulder and heading across the room.

When I sat, Kaj reached for my hand, lifted it to his lips.

"Do they all know?" I whispered, feeling a bit like a spectacle.

"The males, yes. They're quite aware that you belong to me now."

Perhaps it really was time for me to do a bit more research into this whole vampire mating thing.

KAJ

So I probably should've warned Acadia before she came down. Honestly, I didn't expect my males to react that way, but I greatly appreciated the gesture. For what it was worth, it helped solidify my decision to embrace the role as Alpha.

As the food was brought forth and consumed, I relaxed as the others in the room did. Everyone went back to their normal routine, shoving food in while they chatted amongst themselves, laughing at jokes, teasing each other, and enjoying this brief moment before the night got underway. It was a routine I'd always admired, the sharing of meals, the opportunity to catch up and stay caught up with the goings-on around us. I even hoped one day to introduce a similar tradition for the *kirlesgun*, once the regime was in place, the positions filled.

When Michael told me Khari would be taking over as leader of the race, my first reaction was relief. I enjoyed leading the Zenith because being a fighter was what I knew, what I was good at. Despite my best efforts, I knew I would never be the leader my father was. I had no desire to sit behind a desk and snap orders, create laws, and solve the problems of those who couldn't solve them for themselves. I wanted to be on the front lines, where I could be beneficial.

In the same regard, I felt as though I had something to contribute, and the longer I thought about it, the more I realized this was an opportunity I had to embrace. Not for myself, necessarily, but for the entire species, the males and females I wanted to protect, to nurture. I'd thought about Bijou and her future. I wanted her to live in a world that was safe for her to traverse, and the best way to ensure that happened was to have a hand in it.

But what etched my decision in stone was Michael's reference to my heir. If the male was to be believed, Acadia was pregnant with my child. Our child. A male. The news had shocked me to the roots of my soul, but there was absolutely no disappointment. The opposite, in fact. The idea of having a child with the female I adored ... it only added to this sense of peace, even if it made me panic at the same time.

There was time to fall apart later, though. Right now, I had shit to do, people to talk to, decisions to make.

Of course, I knew it would take time before I could get everything in order. I had enough challenges to deal with. Namely, relaying to Penelope that the brother she'd known all her life was, in fact, not her brother. He was a ten-thousand-year-old vampire who needed to be separated from the human vessel he'd been residing in for the past twenty-eight years.

The mere thought of being the bearer of that disturbing news had me pushing my plate away, wiping my mouth with my linen napkin, and depositing it for removal.

As I sipped coffee, I realized Obsidian was staring at me.

"You wanted to talk to me?" the angel asked.

"I do." I glanced at Penelope and Acadia. "I think it's best if the four of us went somewhere more private, if that's all right."

"I'd like Eclipse to join us," Obsidian stated.

"Of course." I didn't care who was there to hear this, provided the news didn't get back to Bijou until I had a chance to discuss with her personally. Though this particular conversation—relaying the information to Penelope—wasn't something I looked forward to, I knew it needed to be handled first. After Oliver's sister knew what was happening, I could share the news with my daughter.

Penelope, clearly surprised by the request, glanced over at

Obsidian, then down to the babe in her arms. "I'll have Josie take the baby."

Josie being the Fae who'd been appointed as the child's nanny.

"I can take her up there," Orianna offered. "If you don't mind, of course."

Penelope smiled at her sister-in-law. "Of course not."

Orianna beamed brightly, clearly pleased to spend time with the child.

Obsidian downed the rest of his coffee while Orianna and Penelope got to their feet. "We'll meet in the conference room on the third floor. I've got a few things to take care of first."

I nodded. "We'll be up in a few minutes."

When the five of them left, I turned to Acadia. She had been staring at her coffee mug for the past few minutes, as though she had no idea what she was doing there.

I shifted my position, turning in my chair so I was facing her. "I need to share something with you."

Her beautiful amethyst eyes bounced over my face, and I could see a wealth of uncertainty.

Reaching into my back pocket, I retrieved the paper I'd folded up and stuck there before I left our bedroom. I passed it over to Acadia.

Her eyebrows lowered as she took the papyrus paper from my hand, her delicate fingers unfolding it. When she began reading, I watched her face. Truth was, I wasn't feeling all that confident about what I'd done. Not because it wasn't the right thing, but because I hadn't considered how Acadia would feel about it. We'd briefly discussed it when she'd entered my mind and read my thoughts, but no further.

When she looked up at me, there were tears in her eyes.

My muscles tightened, fear trickling in my veins. Those

tears could mean anything—good or bad—and I wasn't about to get my hopes up.

"We're truly free?" Her words were so soft.

"Completely." I held her stare. "He's also lifted the infertility. However, while you're still immortal, your people are no longer indestructible. It was a compromise on his part."

When her tears began to fall, I quickly cupped her face, wiping the wetness with my thumbs. I figured now was probably not the best time to share the news about those trapped in the in-between.

"Please tell me these are happy tears, Acadia."

"They are." She nodded, smiled. "I promise."

"I'd like you to go with me to talk with Penelope. Obsidian and I agreed we would deliver the news to her together."

"About Oliver?"

"Yes."

Acadia wiped her eyes. "Of course I'll go with you."

While I was grateful to have my female at my side, I wasn't looking forward to the next part. I wasn't one to ever anticipate drama, but there seemed to be a lack of it right now. Surely something was going to blow up in a big way. The question was when.

T he answer, apparently, was today.

I stood in the third-floor conference room with its big table and office-like decor while Penelope lost her shit.

Like, seriously, lost. Her. Shit.

Needless to say, she hadn't taken the news well, but then again, did I really expect her to? It wasn't every day you learned that the male you thought you were related to turned out to be some random child who'd been placed in your family because an archangel had manipulated it to be so. Oh, and on top of that, that male you considered a brother ... he had a vampire inside him.

"He's not my brother?"

"Biologically, no," Obsidian explained, clearly having gotten all the deets from Michael.

"And you're telling me ... the guy I've known my whole life is the original vampire?"

"Camping out in Oliver's body, yes," I confirmed.

"So when we talk to him ... who are we speaking to?"

"That's the part I'm not exactly sure on," I told her. "I believe when Khari emerges, he'll maintain all of Oliver's memories."

"Meaning my brother will be what? An empty husk?" Her golden eyes were brighter than before.

I shot a quick look at Obsidian.

The male shrugged in response. He looked as lost as I felt.

"I want to speak to Michael," Penelope insisted. "Right now."

Obsidian turned away from her, probably summoning the archangel for his female.

Personally, I didn't care to be in attendance for this part. It was hard enough having all those eyes pinned on me, waiting for me to bring forth some more disturbing news.

Before I could come up with an excuse to leave, there was a flutter of wings and Michael appeared, his strangely swirling eyes darting over every face before coming to rest on Obsidian.

"You rang?"

Though the female was a good foot shorter than the archangel, she stood tall when she marched right up to Michael and squared off with him.

"What have you done?"

Michael frowned. "I'm sorry?"

"My brother."

As though a light went on in his head, Michael's eyes drifted away from her face. "Coulda warned me."

Penelope didn't seem to realize he'd spoken. "Why him? Why did you pick Oliver?"

I could've told her it seemed incredibly obvious. In fact, twofold. It was Michael's way of keeping an eye on the female who would eventually mate Obsidian as well as keeping ties to the original vampire.

Of course, Michael being Michael, he didn't answer her question. Or he tried not to. Right up until Obsidian came to stand behind Penelope, his hands curling over her shoulders.

"I thought it was the best place for him," Michael said on a sigh.

"You knew who Obsidian's mate was?" Acadia asked.

Wow. Good question.

"I might've taken a peek."

"But those lists are supposed to be sealed," Obsidian argued.

"They are."

Clearly not concerned about that, Penelope cleared her throat, drawing all attention back to her. "What happens to Oliver when you separate him and the vampire?"

Right to the point. I knew I liked her.

"He'll be the same as he is now."

"You mean physically," Obsidian stated.

"Correct. Physically, he'll remain human." Michael's gaze shot to me. "Immortal, of course, but still human. Mostly."

"And his memories?"

"Well, technically..." Michael's eyes shifted around the room once more. "Those aren't his memories. The human has been repressed."

Penelope's eyebrows shot downward. "So what? He won't know how to walk or talk if you retrieve Khari?"

I wondered if anyone else noticed her use of *if* not *when*.

"He'll retain all his motor skills. And more than likely, some of the memories will still be embedded. He simply won't know how to retrieve them."

"And Khari?" I had to know what we would be dealing with.

"He'll possess all his memories from every vessel he's been in."

"So he'll be confused?" Acadia asked.

"It might take him some time to get oriented."

"How much time?" I inquired.

"I honestly don't know."

"I can't believe you did this," Penelope said, her tone rich with defeat as she turned toward Obsidian, burying her face in his chest.

"Why? Because I chose the male you were raised with as the vessel? Would it be so impossible to understand if it were a stranger? Would you even care?"

Penelope spun around to face him. "But you didn't pick a stranger. You picked my brother."

"He's of no relation to you," Michael said calmly. "You were both merely raised to believe otherwise."

For a second, I thought Penelope was going to incinerate the archangel with a glare. He must have thought so, too, because Michael took a step back and held up his hands in the universal sign of surrender.

"What if I don't agree with this?" Penelope prompted. "What if I refuse to let you ... take out the vampire?"

Michael's gaze shot to me, which had Penelope looking over as well.

"Then it's highly possible my race will die out." I didn't

bother to tell her that Oliver would likely die because Khari was insistent.

The pain that was triggered in her eyes made me like her all the more. She wasn't a selfish female; that much was a given. I'd been around her enough to see she had a pure heart. Which explained her reasons for wanting to protect Oliver, even if he wasn't related to her by blood.

"When?" she asked, her voice softer and a tad wobbly.

"Friday," I told her. "I've requested Khari's body be brought here so we can have your healers available for the human should it be necessary."

She nodded, then turned to Obsidian. Their eyes met briefly before she stepped around him and left the room.

I hated that this had to be done, and I would've argued for more time, but in the grand scheme of things, I did have to put the lives of my race over that of a human vessel. Not to mention, we were in a race against time to save said vessel.

It wasn't the perfect answer, but it was the only one I seemed to have.

Which meant, resurrecting the original vampire was inevitable.

PERFIDIOUS

While the vampires and angels were dealing with their own crisis, I was but a few miles away, reaping the rewards of my actions.

"Come here, gorgeous," I crooned to the female standing before me.

After I introduced my Fae to the shadow beasts, I noticed a significant change in their demeanor. It was quite possible they didn't completely trust me, but they did hold me in high esteem. So much so, they were still congregating within the mountain, more being drawn here every night. It wasn't every day, after all, that a demon came into possession of a Fae, and they were all eager to see her.

Yet here she was.

"How may I serve you, my king?"

I watched her, admiring her beauty while assessing the minute details of her reaction to me.

Since shedding the last human husk, I hadn't bothered with another, choosing rather to maintain my demon form. And over the course of the past five days, I found I preferred it this way. I had missed being myself. There was a freedom to be had when one wasn't ensconced in the vessel of another.

"Kneel before me," I instructed.

Asmia was naked, as had been the case since the meeting with the shadow beasts. I preferred her this way. Not only did it give me access to her body, it kept her vulnerable to me, something I enjoyed immensely.

Not that she cared. That was the one thing I'd noticed about the female, she didn't seem to care one way or another about anything. It was as though she were merely a vessel for me to use however I saw fit. And use her, I had. Many times, including in front of the shadow beasts, I had claimed what belonged to me. I'd taken her in whatever manner that struck my fancy at the time, and she was always willing, bending this way and that, never fighting me off as I penetrated her, using every one of her orifices for my pleasure.

Admittedly, I would've preferred to get some sort of reaction from her. Perhaps a mirroring desire of some sort.

However, I'd known from the beginning that she wasn't here because she wanted to be here. Asmia was here because I demanded it, and I decided that would have to do.

Before me, Asmia went to her knees, bowing her head and placing her hands on her thighs. She'd become rather adept at that position, as though she preferred it because it allowed her to keep her distance from me. Without eye contact, I had no idea what she was thinking. Then again, I wasn't sure she was thinking at all. It was as though she'd disappeared inside her own head, her body the only thing available to me.

And that was starting to piss me off.

"Look at me," I demanded.

Her black eyes lifted to my face, her expression as blank as her stare.

I took my cock in hand, stroked myself, watching for any reaction. Nothing.

I recalled the way Seraphina used to lick her lips with greed when I touched myself like this. That demon was always eager to get me off, to worship me however I saw fit. I couldn't help but wonder what had happened to her. Eevuhl had taken her with him when he left, and now that Eevuhl was dead, I wondered if Seraphina was still here on Earth or if she'd been taken back to Hell.

No one seemed to know anything about what happened to Eevuhl, either. Nothing was coming out of Hell right now. Not a peep.

"Stand up," I barked.

I continued to stroke myself as Asmia gracefully got to her feet, her long, lithe body giving away nothing.

Hmm.

Perhaps I'd gone about this all wrong. Controlling her mind, forcing her to submit... Without meaning to, I had created something that merely performed for me. What I wanted was the female I'd fallen for.

I smiled as I got to my feet. "Turn around."

Asmia turned around.

"Bend over."

She did.

I stepped up behind her, planted one hand in the center of her back, and used the other to guide my cock between her thighs.

Before I rammed myself inside her, I leaned over her, placed my mouth beside her ear.

"Sweet Asmia. I think it's time we take this to another level."

I was looking for some sort of reaction, so very tempted to release the hold on her mind. Something held me back. Not yet. I wanted an audience. Yes. The shadow beasts deserved to witness this. Soon.

Very, very soon.

37

PENELOPE

I didn't understand.

I never would.

Didn't matter how many times I tossed it around in my head, no matter how many angles I attempted to view it, the fact of the matter, the brother I thought was my twin was in fact... Well, he wasn't my twin, I knew that much for certain. The rest of it was a bit of a tangled mess.

A soft knock sounded on my bedroom door seconds before it opened. I looked up to see Obsidian standing there.

"Mind if I come in?"

Some semblance of a smile formed. "It's your bedroom, too."

"I figured you needed some space."

No, what I needed was an explanation that made sense. Or

better yet, if I could wake up now from this truly messed-up dream, that would be fantastic.

Continuing my efforts to wear the hardwood thin, I paced across the room, past the foot of the bed, over to the bathroom doors. I pivoted, returned.

"I guess in a way, it does explain why I've always felt a disconnect with Oliver," I mused, still trying to make sense of this. "Everyone always asked about our twin bond, which we've never had. Now I know why." I shook my head. "Because he's not even related."

Obsidian took a seat on the love seat, crossing his ankle over his knee. I glanced at him, smiled to myself. He was enormous. To the point it was amusing to see him sit on that little couch. To a normal-sized person, I figured the furniture wasn't all that small. However, with his six-foot-ten-inch frame, it looked as though it belonged in a dollhouse.

Returning my attention to the problem, I kept moving. "And maybe it's part of the reason he's always been so angry. I mean, if Khari is aware of what's happening to him, that he's been trapped for centuries, you can't really blame him for being pissed." I continued my trek. "But I don't understand why Oliver has to be left with no memories. Some poor boy's been repressed for twenty-eight years? Has he any idea what's been going on? And even if he did, will he have memories of what's happened to him?"

I knew Obsidian didn't have the answers just as he knew I wasn't expecting any. I just needed to talk it out, and I appreciated that he understood me so well.

"What if the original Oliver emerges ... pissed off, too? What do we do then?" I stopped, turned toward Obsidian. "Or what if Oliver's scared because he has no idea where he is or what's happened to him?"

"Then we help him," my *reuthet* replied as though it were

that simple. "The human boy was brought to your parents to raise. Therefore, he's still your brother. Regardless of whether it's biological."

He had a point there. "So we help him," I echoed. "We bring him into this family like we would anyone else."

"It's up to you whether you let him know he's not your brother," Obsidian said. "You could share all your memories with him, of the times you had with him."

I nodded. It made sense. Only it would take effort to dig out the good ones. For as long as I could remember, Oliver had hated me. Or so it had seemed.

"What about Khari?"

"He's not really our problem," he replied with a casual shrug of his shoulder. "However, we're here for Kaj, so we'll help however he needs us."

"Who requested Oliver be made immortal?" I asked.

"Kaj. Completely his idea. He said it was about the only thing he had to offer you, so he wanted to ensure you wouldn't outlive your brother."

The notion had tears prickling my eyes. Though I knew Obsidian and Kaj were extremely close, I hadn't spent much time with the vampire. These days, I didn't spend much time with anyone except for Ari'el and Obsidian. They kept me plenty busy.

Exhaling heavily, I walked over to Obsidian. When he held out his arms to me, I settled on his lap, wrapping my arms around his neck and burrowing in close. I loved him so much, more than I ever expected to love anyone. These past few months had been chaotic, but I wouldn't trade them for anything.

Well, maybe this whole Oliver debacle. I could've happily lived the rest of my life without my brother being inhabited by a vampire.

Shaking off the thought, I tried to focus on something else.

"Do you know if Eclipse and Orianna have decided to build a house for Elizabeth?" I asked, relaxing into his warmth.

"They're leaving the decision up to her." He pressed his lips to the top of my head. "I think for the first time in a long time, Elizabeth's at peace."

"I hate that she lost a child, but yeah, I can see how the not knowing would've been so much harder. I think it's good she's taken to Bijou. Sort of a surrogate daughter in a way."

"Speaking of Bijou..." Obsidian's hand began to gently rub my back. "Kaj told me she's to mate Khari."

I lifted my head. "Does she know this?"

He shook his head.

I sighed, dropped my head again. "In my opinion, Michael made a mess of this."

"That he did."

And I would've hated the archangel if it weren't for the fact he had single-handedly saved my daughter's life. Had he not intervened when Eevuhl attacked the mansion, chances are good none of us would be here now. And since that evil demon had come for Ari'el, I figured he would've disposed of me once I'd given birth. A chill ran down my spine the same way it did whenever I thought about it.

"I want to be there," I told Obsidian. "When they do whatever they do to return Khari to his body."

"Of course." He kissed my head again. "Oliver will need you."

I wasn't so sure about that, but I would be there anyway.

Just in case.

OLIVER

"Hey, Em," I said in greeting as I stepped into the kitchen.

"Good evening, sire. I mean ... Oliver." The smile she gifted me was like the sun, I thought as I made my way over to the refrigerator. "How are you feeling?"

"Better." And it was mostly true. I felt immensely better once those damn healers stopped poking and prodding at me. They'd been reluctant to let me leave the infirmary, but thankfully, they'd eventually grown tired of my constant pestering and sent me on my way.

"I saved you some waffles," Emily told me.

"With whipped cream?"

Her smile widened. "Of course. And strawberries."

I honestly wasn't sure what I'd done to deserve Emily's kindness, but I couldn't deny I looked forward to our daily interactions. In a, you know, completely platonic manner, of course.

"Has anyone seen Bijou?" Kaj called out as he strolled into the kitchen.

"I believe she's in the pool, sire," Emily said kindly.

The vampire's eyes shot over to me, and I fought the urge to duck my head. It wasn't that I was scared of him... Okay, maybe a little. More so that I had a hard time looking him in the eyes after what transpired between Bijou and me in the sauna a while back. That one moment in time was forever imprinted in my mind, and I knew I could live to be a hundred, and I would never forget it. It even overshadowed my memory of Bijou feeding from me. And that incredible experience had resulted in an orgasm. Along with another seizure, but hey, it was worth it.

Kaj offered a curt nod, then headed toward the entrance to the pool, which was off the hallway to the garage.

"May I warm your meal for you?"

Emily's kind voice had me jerking my attention away from the vampire and back to the task at hand.

"That would be great. Thanks." I glanced in the direction Kaj went. "I'll be back in a minute, Em."

"Sure."

Why I was compelled to follow, I didn't know. Probably had a lot to do with all the secrecy I'd sensed going on. Something big was underway, but it seemed no one at Angel Central was aware of the details. Which meant it was a vampire issue, and I couldn't deny I was curious. I tried to blame it on my feelings for Bijou. I simply wanted to make sure she was okay. That was all it was. Really.

I peeked around the corner to see the thick glass door to the pool area closing. I glanced over my shoulder, ensuring no one was keeping tabs on me, then made a beeline for the door. I wasn't sure what I would do when I got there, but again, I couldn't stop myself.

It took effort, but I kept my feet light as I moved down the hallway. The last thing I wanted was for Kaj to catch on to the fact I was attempting to eavesdrop. As I approached the door, I stopped far enough back to see inside, but not so close that Bijou or Kaj would see me standing there. I watched as Bijou emerged from the pool, her beautiful body clad in a black one-piece that showcased every glorious curve. She accepted a towel her father held out for her, swiped it over her face, then wrapped it around herself as he spoke, her full attention on him.

If only I had supersonic hearing like the rest of the people in this place. Then perhaps I could listen to what was causing her to furrow her brow at her father. When her hand went to her throat, I sensed her shock. Some strange instinct had me wanting to burst through that door and run to her rescue. For some reason, I'd grown unusually protective of her lately. Ever since we attempted to rekindle our friendship, we'd grown closer. I had been leaning on her, and she seemed content to take care of me as the healers attempted to identify what was causing my seizures.

Unaware I was doing it, I rubbed my chest directly over my heart. Whenever I thought about Bijou, about where this seemed to be going between us, there was a strange ache that took up residence there. I found I wanted to go to her, to take her in my arms, hold her until whatever problem she was facing could be resolved. Then I wanted to keep her safe for the rest of … well, my life, since it would be significantly shorter than hers.

Which brought me full circle once more. It didn't matter how much I cared for her or how I hoped things could progress with us. It wasn't like it would matter in the long run. We weren't meant to be together, clearly. Humans and vampires weren't meant to co-exist, and biology had dictated that.

Suddenly, Bijou was wrapped in Kaj's arms as father consoled daughter.

Feeling like I was intruding on their private moment, I spun on my heel and headed back to the kitchen. I schooled my expression as I joined Emily, who was currently piling mounds of whipped cream on top of the Belgian waffle. She must've noticed me there because she smiled again.

"Almost ready."

"Perfect. I'm starving."

As for whether I could choke it down, that was yet to be seen.

It didn't matter how good it looked; I got the feeling it was going to taste like cardboard.

Everything did these days.

BIJOU

"But ... how?"

I knew I'd heard my father's words, knew my brain had processed them, yet I couldn't seem to make sense of them.

Oliver Calazans was the original vampire?

Or rather, the original vampire was stuck inside Oliver's body.

In what universe was that even possible?

"I sensed it," I whispered. "I sensed a darkness inside him."

Kaj pulled back and peered down at me.

"Is that Khari?" Or was it the human that had been pushed down so Khari could take over?

"I don't know," he said softly. "I wish I had the answers."

470

I wished *someone* did. According to my father, no one seemed to know the logistics, and it sounded like that was the question of the hour. Everyone wanted to know what would happen once they were separated. Would Khari emerge knowing what was going on? Would Oliver retain his memories?

More importantly, why was I the last one to find this out? The way he'd laid it all out made me think he'd been chewing on it for a while. And yet, despite all that Kaj had waylaid me with, I knew my father was holding something back. I probably should've questioned him, but it was obvious he was having a hard time dealing with this as well. Probably not fair for me to pelt him with more questions.

"Wait." I met his eyes. "Does Oliver know?"

Kaj shook his head. "Because of the seizures, we've decided to hold off telling him as long as we can."

"You can't do that," I countered hotly. "He deserves to know."

"Even if it kills him?"

I stepped back, the words coming at me like a slap.

My father exhaled as though he was exhausted. "Look, I don't like it any more than you do. I agree he deserves to know. But in his current state, it's a risk we're not willing to take."

"We?"

"Me, Obsidian, Penelope."

I sadly wished I'd been included in that list.

"For the time being," he said, his eyes locked with mine. "I'd prefer you to remain here. Once we have a better understanding of where we stand with Khari, it's likely I'll have you move into the Lair."

I nodded, not because I understood his reasoning but because it no longer mattered. I was content where I was now that I had made up with Oliver. We were growing closer, and the thought of leaving him didn't sit well. Especially not now. I intended to remain by him through ... whatever was going to happen.

A resurrection. Wow. It still sounded strange even as I tossed the word around in my brain, and that was saying something considering I had seen plenty of strange in my life. But this...

Kaj gave my shoulder a gentle squeeze before he headed toward the door to the house.

"Oh, and Bijou?"

"Hmm?" I pivoted to face him.

"Thank you."

I frowned. "For?"

"For accepting Acadia."

That pulled a genuine smile from me. "I'm happy for you both."

He stopped, stared at me. "Really?"

I nodded. "I think you're good for each other."

His eyes brightened, and I could tell that meant a lot to him.

When he left, I remained where I was, staring at the spot he'd vacated. I wasn't surprised when I scented the bonding that morning. In fact, I'd been anticipating it. Despite the fact that they were dealing with whatever issues plaguing them, I knew Acadia and Kaj were meant for one another. How that worked, I had no idea. I'd never even heard of the Fae before I arrived here, much less heard of a vampire mating one. However, I figured as long as they were happy, I was, too.

Not quite ready to go back into the house, I made my way over to the hot tub. I tapped a few buttons on the screen mounted to the wall to get the jets blowing, dropped my towel, and slipped down into the warm water.

As I got comfortable, I realized I was staring at the door to the sauna, memories of that night with Oliver flooding me.

Had that been Oliver? I wondered. Or was that Khari who had offered me relief from the overwhelming heat plaguing the mansion at the time? I still recalled the way he'd worked me with his mouth...

Okay, enough of that.

No way was I going to sit here and relive that erotic encounter. It didn't matter if that was Oliver or Khari. It had been a mistake, one I was moving beyond now that I was back to being friends with Oliver.

Or was it Khari?

I groaned softly. So freaking confusing.

The thoughts spurred others, though. Such as, was that the reason I was attracted to Oliver? Because he had the soul of a vampire? I'd never been attracted to a human before, so it was a reasonable conclusion.

What if I was attracted to Khari when he emerged?

Was that even possible?

Closing my eyes, I dropped my head back and decided now was not the time to worry about stupid stuff like that. A male's life was about to be altered in unimaginable ways.

I seriously doubted his love life—Khari or Oliver—was going to matter once it was all said and done.

38

KAJ

F riday the thirteenth was a human superstition, not one claimed by vampires, but it seemed fitting for what was taking place today.

The past couple of days had gone by in a blur. I had shared the details of what was going on regarding Khari with the vampires. As much as I knew about it, anyway. Obsidian had tackled filling in the angels who needed to know, and Acadia had wrangled in the Fae to give them the good news associated with them. If I heard correctly, there was a party scheduled for the near future—postponed until Asmia's return—to celebrate their freedom. I hoped we could come through for them in that regard, too, but things still weren't looking good on that front.

Unfortunately, the same could be said for this. There would

be no party taking place today, but I hoped like hell there wasn't going to be a wake instead.

As I walked through the tunnels to the infirmary beneath Angel Central, my entourage and I remained quiet. Mirakel, Blāz, Huracān, and Kidel were pulling up the rear, not a single one of them making any remarks. No jokes, no questions, just breathing as we walked to what would ultimately outline our destiny.

Acadia had gone ahead to be with Ari'el, having offered to stay with the baby in the event something were to happen. She was more than capable of ensuring the baby's safety, and Penelope trusted her probably more than anyone else.

When we reached the doors leading to the medical facility that separated the two residences, I took a deep breath as I placed my palm on the scanner, my eyeball in front of the laser, then said the magic words to allow voice recognition to release the locks.

The doors swung wide and—

"Is that a … coffin?" Blāz asked, his cough clearly covering up a laugh.

"Seriously, Michael," I grumbled. "A fucking coffin."

"Seemed suitable," the archangel said as he stood guard over what I assumed was the body of the original vampire beneath the wooden lid.

"Fuck you," I retorted. Coffins were part of the myths humans had made up long ago about the undead, fanged creatures who drained the blood of their human victims.

I was not a fan of human storytelling.

"Are you fucking serious?"

The shout came from one of the rooms dedicated to the treatment of patients, the voice familiar and respectfully upset.

For fuck's sake. "You haven't told him yet?" I shook my head. "I don't see this going well."

"You can't sedate him!" Michael called out from behind us. "He has to be awake."

I briefly wondered if this would be painful for the human. I hoped not. Considering all the male would have to deal with going forward, he had enough on his plate. The least we could do was make sure he didn't suffer.

The doors on the other side of the clinic opened, and three big males came through. Magnar, Valterri, and Reidar strolled forward, shoulders squared as though they were prepped for battle. Eclipse appeared behind them, his eyes wary as his ears perked to the shouting coming from the room.

"No one thought to tell him before now?" Eclipse asked. "Poor fucking human."

Oh, we'd thought about it. We simply hadn't done it.

It honestly was a shitty move, but I wasn't going to pretend to know how to deal with a situation such as this one. Had we told Oliver, there was the risk of the human bolting when no one was looking. Or doing something equally stupid. And on the flip side, it could've triggered Khari, causing the vampire to incinerate the vessel.

"So, what's the plan?" Eclipse prompted, his attention on the archangel. "You chant or something to draw him out?"

I glanced from Eclipse over to Michael. "Good question."

The archangel smiled. "It's pretty simple, really. I will channel your energy along with my own to draw Khari out of the vessel and into his body."

Ah, yeah. Simple. I clearly remembered what happened when Obsidian channeled the archangel.

Fucking hell.

The door to the room opened, and Apollo stepped out, Amethyst at his side. The healers walked over, nodded at the newcomers.

"He okay?" Eclipse asked.

Apollo shook his head. "Can't blame him, though. He wants to talk to Penelope alone, but Obsidian won't leave the room."

I didn't blame the angel. A mated male did not put his female at risk if he could help it.

Apollo peered around me. "Is that a coffin?"

"Little party joke," Blāz answered. "You know Michael."

Eclipse chuckled, clearly amused.

"We do need to prep the body," Amethyst noted. "And I'm not comfortable keeping him ... in there."

I had to assume she was referring to the coffin. I had to agree with her. No telling what Khari might do if he came awake in that damn thing. I knew what I would do and it wasn't pretty.

The doors at the end of the hall opened once more and Bijou appeared.

Son of a bitch.

"Get him ready," I instructed the others as I headed toward my daughter. "What are you doing down here?"

"I want to be here," she said, her tone already insistent, as though she expected me to argue.

She knew me too well.

"I don't think that's a good idea."

"Well, I do," she countered. "Oliver's my friend."

More shouting came from the room behind us, drawing Bijou's attention.

"Is that him?"

"They just told him the good news," Eclipse offered, his voice ringing with what sounded like both concern and amusement.

Bijou's hand went to her mouth, her eyes filling.

"Maybe you could go talk to him," I suggested, though I wasn't sure what the fuck I was doing. Honestly, I would've preferred she stay somewhere else while this was going down. Since no one knew what to expect, I would've felt better knowing she was safe. Preferably in another hemisphere. At the very least, surrounded by the *fiestreigh*, who would go to battle if something were to come at us. Namely, an ancient fucking vampire.

My daughter's watery gaze met mine and she nodded.

Because I could not risk Oliver going apeshit on Bijou, I led the way. I rapped my knuckles on the door, opened it, and stuck my head in.

Oliver's face was a brilliant shade of red, his hair sticking up as though he'd been pulling on it.

"Bijou would like to see you."

Almost instantly, the human's eyes calmed. "She would?"

I stepped into the room and allowed Bijou in behind me.

"Could I have a few minutes alone with him?" she requested.

"No," I stated firmly.

"But we'll step out," Penelope said softly, her arms hugging her middle as though she was attempting to hold herself together. "I love you, Oliver. I hope you know that."

The human grunted.

"Pretend I'm not here," I told them when it was just the three of us.

I stepped back against the door, crossing my arms over my chest.

"Dad. Give us a minute," Bijou demanded.

"I'm sorry, I—"

"He won't hurt me," she insisted aloud, then projected *He can't hurt me* into my head.

Being a vampire, she was far stronger than the human, but that didn't mean—

"Leave us, Dad."

I met the human's gaze. "Don't you dare hurt her."

"I would never," he said, his voice nothing more than a gravelly whisper.

Because I wasn't going to win this one, I decided to give in.

But I would be outside the door.

Just in case.

BIJOU

Once my father stepped out, I tried to come up with something to say, anything that might make this easier.

Considering I still hadn't come to terms with it, I wasn't sure if that was even possible. It pained me to see Oliver like this, so distraught, so anxious. Not that I blamed him for what he was feeling. I had no idea what they'd told him, but I suspected Penelope had laid it all on the line.

Wringing my hands, I took a step forward, closing the gap between Oliver and me. When I moved closer to the bed he was sitting on, his legs dangling over the side, I reached for his hands, taking them both in mine.

He stared down at them for the longest time, his body trembling.

"Look at me," I said firmly, though I wasn't sure who I was talking to, Khari or Oliver.

For the past two days, ever since my father waylaid me with the news, I'd been thinking about my interactions with Oliver. No matter which way I sliced it, I found it hard to believe that Khari wasn't the one I'd been talking to all this time, the one making the decisions. I recalled taking his vein, remembered thinking he tasted familiar. Not human but vampire. Of course, I'd never tasted human blood, so there was every chance humans simply tasted like vampires, though I doubted it.

Then I thought about the darkness, that shadow I could sense deep within him. Because there were two souls in there, I figured that was the soul of whichever was being repressed. How that was even possible, I didn't know. But at that point, I'd given up on attempting to make sense of it. It didn't. That was all there was to it.

But now, here, as I stood before this male, it was the male I'd been interacting with that I wanted to connect with. Oliver, Khari, it didn't matter much to me. That was the one I'd gotten close to, the one I'd alienated, made up with. Whoever it was, I wanted him to remain intact. One way or the other. Ultimately, Khari was the one who had to let Oliver go. He had to emerge and leave the human intact, even if we didn't know what shape Oliver would be in when it was all over. It wasn't ideal by any means, but the human deserved this.

When Oliver's golden-brown eyes lifted to my face, I stared deeply into them. "I know you're scared."

"Terrified," he whispered.

"But we will get through this."

"We?"

"Yes. We. You and me. We're friends, right?"

"We were." Oliver swallowed hard. "At one time."

"We *are*," I corrected. "Yes, things got complicated, but we were finding our way back, right?"

He didn't respond, but I realized he was calming down, as though my presence was what he'd needed.

"And we're going to keep right on doing that," I told him. "Once we're through this, you and I will pick up right where we left off."

His eyes flashed, as though there was a hint of light within them.

"I'm not going to leave your side. I promise you that. No matter what, I'll be here through it all. And when it's all said and done, you're going to look into my eyes and know that I'm going to help you through this."

Oliver nodded.

"Trust me," I said softly.

Some of the tension drained from his fingers, but he kept his hands in mine as we remained there, face-to-face. I didn't know what would happen when it was all said and done, but whoever looked at me after, whoever sought my gaze when they awoke, I would know who I'd fallen in love with. Human or vampire, it didn't matter. My heart cared naught.

"Are you ready?"

He shook his head but forced a smile. "You'll stay with me."

"I'll hold your hand the entire time."

Again, something lit from behind those eyes, and I wondered who it was.

Clasping my fingers with his, I turned toward the door, but Oliver pulled me back. When I pivoted, I was almost nose to nose with him.

He leaned in and pressed his lips to mine in a sweet, reverent kiss.

"Just in case."

I smiled. "It's not necessary. It'll be fine. I can feel it."

Granted, that wasn't the truth, but I didn't know what else to say. Truth was, I could feel nothing. I was pretty much numb, overwhelmed by what was happening here. My heart ached for Oliver and Khari because the future was unknown for both of them.

"Are you ready?" I forced a smile. "They're waiting for us."

Oliver hopped to his feet, then allowed me to lead him out of the room.

The halls were barricaded on both sides by a wall of males, both vampires and angels, there to ensure Oliver didn't make a run for it.

Pretending they weren't there, I kept my fingers twined with his and walked over to the empty gurney. The one next to it was draped with a sheet, and though I couldn't see him, the body beneath was enormous.

I swallowed hard, then stepped back so Oliver could get in position.

His hand trembled again, and my heart broke for him. Regardless, this was the end of something huge and the beginning of something monumental. Human and vampire would go their separate ways, to emerge not as one but two, their souls untethered.

"Look at me," I urged as he paused. "Keep looking at me. No matter what."

His eyes were glassy, but he was holding back his emotions by sheer force of will.

"We don't care about any of them," I told him, standing as close to him as I could get. "They don't matter right now."

"Can I see him?" Oliver asked, nodding toward the sheet-draped gurney.

Michael was the one who came forward, revealing the enormous vampire. His eyes were closed, his long hair tucked beneath his head. I couldn't help thinking he was well-preserved for being so ... dead.

Oliver let out a shudder, then eased onto the gurney. I

stood between both gurneys, turning my full attention to Oliver, his eyes locked on mine.

I maintained eye contact as he reclined.

Somewhere behind me, I heard them speaking. Familiar voices discussing what was going to happen next. I blocked them out, kept my attention fully on the male in front of me.

"Bijou?" My father tapped me on the shoulder.

Still, I didn't look away. "What?"

"You can't be touching him."

"Too bad," I said. "I'm not letting him go."

There were more voices, a couple of them raised, but I was locked with Oliver in that moment.

"We will get through this together," I whispered. "Stay with me."

His Adam's apple bobbed in his throat, his brown eyes steady on mine as though I were his lifeline.

"Stay with me," I repeated, swallowing past the emotion choking me.

As stoic as I was being, I knew it was only for him.

Whoever he was.

OLIVER

I expected to wake up from this nightmare any minute now.

No fucking way was I seriously laid out on this gurney, about to have a vampire's soul ripped out of me. No matter what they told me, I couldn't even fathom having the soul of a vampire inside me. It was ludicrous to think that.

In fact, it was all absolutely ridiculous. My mind could not process how this was even possible. Maybe I was the vampire, maybe I wasn't. No one seemed to know anything aside from the fact there were two souls taking up residence inside my body. A human and a vampire, having co-existed for twenty-eight years.

Nope. Nuh-uh.

Then again, someone had shared the news with Penelope that we weren't blood-related. So, at least we had part of the story right. The sane part of it. Yes, I was adopted, born some-time in the vicinity of Penelope's birth. We shared just enough features to be passed off as brother and sister.

What had surprised me most was Penelope's genuine concern for me. She was angry on my behalf and that… I hadn't known what to do with that. After all the shit I'd put her through, she was standing behind me in this.

Maybe this was my sister's way of getting rid of me. It wasn't like I'd been a good brother to her. In fact, I'd been a shitty one. Never had I felt close to her, but then again, I had known all along that I wasn't her brother. Not in the biological sense. My parents had dropped that little bomb when they separated, back when my mother ran off with a man-child. I didn't think they meant to traumatize me, but they were both so self-involved, it simply happened.

Of course, I'd done some research on my own, and the only thing I was able to determine for a fact was that there weren't any pictures of Penelope and me together for the first few weeks of our lives. Every single one I found was of us individu-ally. How could parents of twins not take pictures of their babies together? They couldn't. And that was when I realized they were telling the truth. The pain that it had caused ... well, it was the very reason I'd taken to being mean to her. I had been jealous. Angry and jealous.

Initially, I pretended it was possible that Penelope was the one adopted. I never actually thought it was logical, consid-ering Penelope resembled our mother the most. But how had I ended up with them? How had I been the one Michael selected, the infant he supposedly stuck the vampire in?

God, even thinking about it was ludicrous. This was not happening.

For a brief moment, I considered making a run for it. I doubted I would make it all that far before they dragged my sorry ass back here and forced ... *this*. Whatever the fuck this was.

No. I couldn't run. Not when Bijou was with me, looking at me with those lovely green eyes.

A quitter I was not.

Unfortunately, they'd stolen my will with their revelations.

Now, as I stared into Bijou's beautiful eyes, I prayed that whatever happened in these next few minutes wouldn't take her from me. I hadn't expected her to show up, and when she did ... well, some of the chaos faded. As though her presence was all I needed.

Bijou squeezed my hand, her other hand brushing my hair back from my forehead.

"Are you ready?"

"No." I would never be ready, but that was beside the point. "But let's get this over with."

"I need your hand."

I lifted my right hand, the one Bijou wasn't holding.

"The other one." Kaj glanced at Bijou. "Trade."

She did, releasing my hand and taking the other, easily draping it over my chest as she held onto me from where she stood between both gurneys, the same as Kaj.

Not sure what the vampire intended to do, I offered my hand to Kaj, but I had to wait until Michael instructed the vampire to remove his shirt.

Getting weirder and weirder here.

Once he was shirtless, Kaj took my hand, clasped it firmly, a tight squeeze that would ensure I didn't lose my grip.

Fantastic.

"You might want to close your eyes for this," Kaj said softly, but turned away from me, his gaze landing on Bijou standing directly in front of him.

My attention shifted back to Bijou. She was still looking at me, as though waiting for my gaze to return to hers.

No, I would not be closing my eyes.

A soft smile pulled at her mouth, but I could see the concern. She knew no more than I did about how this would go, but she was willing to remain with me because she knew I needed it.

"Everyone else needs to move back," the archangel said as he stepped up behind Kaj.

I blocked them out of my peripheral vision, focusing solely on Bijou. I was vaguely aware of Michael's wings expanding, stretching out, and curling around all of us, almost touching Bijou but not quite.

"Close your eyes," Bijou insisted. "And focus on my touch."

I didn't want to close my eyes. I wanted her face to be the only thing I saw. If I were going to die right here and now, it was the only thing I wanted to take with me wherever I was going. Heaven would be preferred, but with the life I'd led, it really could go either way. Perhaps my time here, working with the angels in their war against demons, was enough to get my ticket punched. Then again—

I inhaled sharply when warmth traveled up from the hand Kaj was holding. It moved quickly, consuming my entire body until I felt it in every molecule. Warmth turned to heat. Heat morphed into an inferno. I tried to cry out, but my voice didn't work. Bijou was speaking, but I couldn't hear her. I began to tremble, first my legs, then the rest of my body.

It was the lightning bolt that speared me that had my back bowing, my eyes breaking away from Bijou as a fiery blaze erupted from somewhere within me.

Everything went black, and I thought for sure I was dead. No Heaven, no Hell, only darkness.

As I lay there, surrounded by nothingness, I wasn't sure how much time passed. Minutes, hours? Millenia? Forever, maybe.

However long it was, it was a lifetime that I was consumed by agony that tore through every nerve ending. Just when I thought my head would explode off my body, the pain disappeared, and I could breathe again, but that lasted only seconds before another bolt crashed into me.

"Fuck!" I roared, the word booming out of my lungs, my body slamming into the gurney as though I'd been dropped from a cliff.

A flood of sound shot into my ears, but there were no words being spoken. I had no idea what I was hearing, but I kept my eyes closed and focused.

Breathing. Those were breaths being taken. There were fourteen heartbeats—no, make that fifteen, not counting my own.

Something beeped, a steady sound that was oddly soothing. Feet were shuffling on tile. Air was being blown from somewhere, the sound a soft rasp in my ears.

I was aware of a hand holding mine. Only one now, and it was small but strong.

Taking a deep breath, I tried to crack my eyelids, but it took a minute, as though they were glued together. When they split open, light beamed in.

"Too bright," I grumbled.

A second later, they dimmed.

It took a moment for my pupils to adjust, and when they did, I looked up to see Bijou. She was still standing beside me, only she'd moved. Instead of being on my left, between the gurneys, she was … no, she was still between the gurneys but now on my right. Weird. Her eyes were darting from me to someone else. Back and forth, clearly waiting for something.

"You didn't leave me," I said softly, though my voice sounded strange to my ears. Deeper, more resonant.

Her eyes landed on my face and remained there. "I didn't leave."

And that was a damn good thing because Bijou's face was the only thing that made sense.

Considering this—

I patted my chest with my other hand.

—was not my fucking body.

39

KAJ

———

"Holy. Shit."

Yeah, I thought. What he said.

No doubt about it, all eyes in the mansion were on Khari as the ancient vampire went from a stone-cold corpse to ... animated. Not that he was moving all that much, but still. He was most definitely breathing.

Those who weren't here physically to observe the resurrection were likely monitoring on the many cameras that spanned the space, because I could hear a wealth of rumbling coming from not too far down the hall in the war room.

"How're you feeling?" Obsidian asked, his voice soft, as though he didn't want to risk inciting the ancient vampire.

How *was* I feeling? As Michael said would happen, I'd

transferred the archangel's energy directly into Oliver. But what the damn winged asshole hadn't told me was that the fucking ancient vampire's soul was going to pass right through me after a short pit stop in my body. *That* I had felt. And if I never again had to feel the presence of another being within me, it would be too fucking soon.

"I'll live," I assured my friend, though a quick peek downward was in order. You know, just to be sure.

Yep. Still intact.

"And him?" the angel asked, nodding toward Khari.

That was a damn good question.

Khari's eyes were open because every so often, I would see him blink, so I figured that was a good thing. Being that it was the intended result and all. The ancient vampire had returned.

And there he was. Resting comfortably on a gurney that looked a bit rickety beneath six feet ten inches, three hundred some odd pounds of ten-thousand-year-old vampire. I couldn't help wondering how Michael had kept the body preserved, but it appeared he'd done a damn good job of it. Khari was likely in fighting shape even all these centuries later.

Of course, no one knew whether he was capable of standing, but hey, we had to start somewhere.

Apollo was the first to step forward, his attention on the human lying completely still.

Yep, and opposite Khari was Oliver Calazans. What was left of him, anyway. The human's eyes were closed, his arms lax at his sides, but his chest continued to rise and fall with even breaths.

"What's the word, Healer?" Eclipse prompted, moving to stand beside Apollo.

There wasn't a word spoken as Apollo began checking Oliver's vitals: heart, lungs, pulse, temperature. All the good stuff.

A few minutes later, we received a nod, though I didn't know what it meant.

"I need to move them both to rooms," Amethyst noted.

Good idea? No, probably not, but it made more sense than continuing to congregate in the hallway.

"I'm staying with Khari," Bijou stated.

Confused, I walked over to my daughter. It was then I noticed the male was definitely awake.

Holy fuck.

Those eyes were ice blue and pinned on Bijou. His canines had descended, longer than any I had ever seen.

"He'll need to feed," Mirakel noted, his voice traveling from behind me.

Ya think?

"Can we borrow one of the Fae?" I asked Obsidian.

"No," Bijou insisted, her gaze locked on Khari. "Not unless he chooses to. Is that what you want?"

Khari shook his head ever so slightly, those arctic eyes never shifting from Bijou's face.

"I'll feed him," she whispered softly.

"No." It was my turn to put my foot down. "Not in his current condition. We can't risk him killing you by taking too much."

"He won't."

"No," I repeated. "And that's final. And not only am I saying this as your father, but also as your Alpha. Right now, he needs to be assessed."

Bijou's head snapped in my direction, her eyes spitting fire. I could see she was gearing up to pelt me with whatever was on her mind—and I suspected it wasn't pretty—but Apollo spoke up first.

"We have blood on hand. We can give him that until he's steady. Then we'll decide how to proceed."

I ground my molars together.

Bijou nodded at the healer, returning her attention to Khari. "That's fine. For now. They're going to move you," she told the vampire. "I'll be right here with you. But you have to remain calm."

The vampire nodded.

I had yet to hear him say anything more after he'd acknowledged that Bijou had stayed with him. I could only assume whoever had been prevalent in Oliver's body had been successfully transferred to Khari since he recognized Bijou. Granted, he sounded nothing like the human, his voice far too deep. As for what he remembered, that was still the question of the hour.

And until Oliver came around, we really didn't know what we were dealing with.

"I'd like you to give us some space," Apollo announced. "I'll allow two guards. One vampire, one angel. That's it. The rest of you can head out."

I glanced over at Huracān, nodded. The male responded in kind. He would stand guard for now.

"Reidar, you stick around here. I'll have you relieved in a couple of hours," Obsidian stated.

There was some murmuring as the others began trickling out, all of them headed into the mansion. Probably going to gossip for a while about the shit that had gone down.

"And you"—Obsidian pointed directly at Michael—"you'll stay here for now. Should something happen, it's on you."

Michael opened his mouth, probably to add some smart-ass comment, but then closed it just as quickly, offering a nod of compliance instead.

"I expect updates hourly," Obsidian told Apollo and Amethyst. "Both on the human and the vampire."

"Same for me," I noted.

"Hey, boss?" Blāz said as I began walking back toward the Lair. "I thought maybe you'd want to meet Leilana."

"Who's that?" I asked, head down as I moved forward.

"The female we interviewed to be your assistant?"

Oh, right. I recalled Blāz mentioning her.

"Did you hire her?"

"Not yet, no."

"But you think she'll be a good fit?"

"I do."

"Then hire her. Get her here. Let's get a move on this." Those damn emails weren't slowing, and I figured they would only increase once the word got out that Khari was alive. Which was another task she could handle. Draft something to go out, something that made a little sense, maybe.

Christ. There was so much to do, and I wasn't even sure where to start.

I stopped, spun around.

"Where're you going, *phaal*?"

"To get my female," I said. Because right now, I suspected she was the only one who might possibly be able to calm the chaos in my head.

ΛCADIA

I was sitting in Ari'el's room, holding the sleeping baby as I rocked the little one.

I'd been in here for some time, though I wasn't sure how long. From the other side of the door, I heard Penelope pacing the room. Part of me wanted to go to the female, to assure her all would be fine. Offer platitudes, spew words that held little meaning because, truth was, no one knew the outcome. However, I'd opted to keep my thoughts to myself, to allow the female to pace the floor to expend some of her restless energy.

"I have a feeling your uncle'll be just fine," I whispered to the beautiful child. "He's strong. Like your mom."

As I stared down at the baby, I wondered whether one day I would have a child of my own. I'd always wanted one, though I'd spent no time in the presence of children. That had never stopped me from fantasizing.

Of course, that was all I'd been capable of doing because I was infertile thanks to God's punishment of my race. According to Kaj, Michael had relieved us of that punishment, but was it really true? Only time would tell, I figured.

There was a soft knock on the door, drawing my attention.

"The Alpha's here to see you," Josie whispered, peeking into the room.

I nodded, overwhelmed with worry. Had he come up here to find me because he wanted to see me? Or because something had gone wrong?

I got to my feet, ensuring I didn't jostle the tiny bundle in my arms. I settled Ari'el into her crib, keeping a gentle hand on the infant's belly until she settled. Once she was peacefully at rest once more, I hurried out of the room and into the small hallway that led back to the third-floor living area.

Kaj was pacing, hands in his pockets, chin resting on his chest, clearly deep in thought.

He must've heard me because his head instantly lifted and he redirected, coming right for me.

"Is everything all right?"

"For now, yes."

"And Oliver?"

"The healers are looking him over. Same with Khari. Both are alive."

The relief I felt nearly had me staggering.

Luckily, Kaj was there to hold me, pulling me into his strong arms, securing me against his body.

"I'm so glad."

"We've got a long road ahead of us," he said softly. "Who knows what it'll bring."

"And Bijou? How's she taking this?"

"She stayed with Khari."

I pulled back, peered up at Kaj. "And how do you feel about that?"

A small smile pulled at his mouth. "I don't think I have much of a say."

"You're her father, Kaj. She'll listen to you. You just have to speak to her logically. Leave the emotion out of it."

"Easier said than done."

Oh, how I knew that to be true. Life, no matter how it was laid out, who you were surrounded by, or even the gifts you'd acquired, whether material or in the manner of people, was never easy. Perhaps because humans, angels, vampires, and especially Fae tended to make it more difficult. I didn't know. However, over the past fifteen hundred years, I had learned to take things one moment at a time. Not even a full day at a time. A moment. A single breath. That was the only way I found I could make it through.

It was immensely easier now that I had Kaj to lean on.

Someone created specifically for me. But that didn't mean it would be rainbows and unicorns.

"Blāz wants me to meet the female he'd like me to hire as my assistant," Kaj said softly. "Would you do me the honor of joining me in that meeting?"

I pulled back, peered up at him. "Me?"

"I'd really like your opinion."

I wasn't sure what to say to that. No one … absolutely no one had ever asked me for my opinion before. I'd given it, sure, because that was in my nature. However, I'd never had it requested. The feeling that swelled within my chest was unfamiliar, completely foreign, and it filled me with a warmth I hadn't expected.

"I'd like that," I admitted. "Very much."

"Perfect." Kaj stepped back, retrieved his phone from his pocket, and tapped something out. When he tucked it back away, he was smiling. "Shall we?"

When he offered me his arm, I smiled, sliding mine through.

"How's Ari'el?" he asked as we headed for the stairs that would take us down.

"She's perfect." I grinned, warmth infusing me as it always did when I thought about that precious child. "She's getting bigger every minute."

Together, we made our way down two flights of stairs, through the main hall. We continued on, chatting about the mundane. Kaj would ask a question, I would answer. It was a warm conversation, and it felt surprisingly … normal.

Even the thought made me smile. I'd honestly never considered what normal would feel like. Up to this point, my normal had consisted of being the blood bank for an army of angels. Now, I was mated. To a vampire.

It was a ridiculously pleasant feeling to acknowledge that.

By the time we stepped through the doors of the Lair, my cheeks were hurting from smiling so much.

"Where's Blāz?" Kaj asked Kidel when we approached where he was sitting at the dining room table, his laptop open in front of him.

"He went to meet Leilana, drive her in."

"And Mirakel?"

"He went out to interview for the *vestrahn* position. We had five candidates Blāz thought would be good."

Kaj nodded. "We'll need them in place sooner rather than later."

"Of course, *phaal*."

I listened to the interaction between the two males. I noticed how Kidel dutifully paid attention to what Kaj wanted, even taking notes as though he might forget.

"At the top of the hour, I'd like you to relieve Huracān at the infirmary."

"Absolutely."

"Shoot me an update when you get there. I'd like your take on what's going on."

That seemed to please the vampire immensely, to be utilized for his opinions. Funny how such a minor request could change your status from simple employee to valued contributor.

"Let Blāz know we're in my office," Kaj concluded, taking my hand and leading me toward the other side of the residence, through the double doors, and into the enormous space they'd allocated for the Alpha's private workspace.

The fireplace had been tended to, the flames licking brightly, warming the room nicely.

"I'm starting to wonder what the point is in having those shutters," Kaj noted as he moved toward the entire wall of windows at the back of the house.

"It's a lovely view," I said, peering out at the grounds. "It'll be pretty as a picture once spring arrives."

Kaj smiled. "Thanks to the *dhira*, I'm unable to see."

Oh. I hadn't thought about that. I reached up and placed my fingers on his temples, slid them down, and let them fall back to my sides. "How about now?"

"Definitely beautiful," he rasped, but he never turned to look out the window.

I felt my cheeks warm with my blush. "I was referring to the view beyond the glass."

He chuckled, then turned away, his smile brightening. "I can't tell you how relieved it makes me to see out and not be met with total blackness. I understand Obsidian's reasoning, but it's a bit disconcerting for the rest of us."

"Consider it resolved," I offered. "I'll take care of it for the Zenith and anyone else you deem worthy of seeing."

His eyes shifted back to my face, and the warmth I saw in them melted me. I briefly wondered if that would always be the case. Centuries, even millennia in the future, would he still look at me like I mattered? I couldn't imagine the reverse being the case. What I felt for this male ... it had been building for so long. It almost didn't seem real.

A soft knock on the door behind me had me turning. Kaj offered his arm, and I gratefully took it as our guest stepped into the space.

"*Phaal*, I'd like to introduce Leilana Torvolyan, youngest child of Sir Markiel Torvolyan."

I was tempted to curtsy to the female, but I refrained. For vampires, only those who were considered noble were assigned surnames. All others simply had one single name. Which meant this young female was from a regal bloodline.

Leilana's eyes were wide in shock, and the moment they landed on Kaj, I feared the female was going to pass out.

"*It's an honor to be allowed in your presence, my Alpha,*" she said softly, speaking in the language of vampires.

While I wasn't exactly fluent, I'd learned enough over the past few months to keep up.

"No need for formalities," Kaj told the female. "I'd like to introduce you to my mate, Acadia."

Leilana shifted her full attention and curtsied respectfully.

"It's a pleasure to meet you," I said kindly.

"The pleasure's all mine," Leilana returned.

I considered the young female as she stood before us, clearly nervous to be in the presence of the Alpha. Her blond hair was pulled back in a tidy ponytail. Her pretty, round face had minimal makeup. Probably a couple of inches shorter than me, she stood taller thanks to the heels she wore. Her outfit was modern, though it seemed better suited for someone quite a bit older than her. The boxy jacket and calf-length skirt were a bit large on her small frame, as though she'd borrowed the clothes from someone else.

"Let's sit," Kaj prompted, motioning toward the seating area near the fire.

While I wasn't sure what this meeting entailed, I found myself oddly interested in participating.

For the first time in my existence, I felt almost ... necessary.

LEILANA TORVOLYAN

I f it were possible to be any more nervous, I had no idea how that would be.

Here, sitting before the Alpha and his mate, I felt as though I was about to plead my case to be allowed to live. The problem was, I had no words. Nothing that would make sense, anyhow.

"Would you like something to drink?" Kaj offered.

He was just so ... casual. It was oddly disconcerting.

"No, thank you. I'm..." I swallowed to wet my dry, scratchy throat. "Actually, I could use some water."

The Alpha smiled, then peered toward Blāz, the male who'd met me and driven me in. Good thing, too, considering I hadn't been able to see two inches in front of me.

"Blāz tells me you're a teacher."

I nodded. "Yes, sir."

It was obvious that he expected me to elaborate, but I found myself tongue-tied.

Boy, if my family could see me now. I was screwing this up royally, I knew it. The funny thing was, when I wasn't feeling intimidated by someone in power, I found it difficult to shut up. Always talking, sometimes to the point of aggravation. At least where my brothers and sisters were concerned.

Wouldn't know it based on this epic failure of an interview.

"Leilana?"

My eyes widened. Had I missed a question? Oh, crap. Not good.

"I'm sorry, sir."

"Distracted?" His expression reflected amusement.

Exhaling heavily, I forced myself to calm down.

"Why don't I give you two a few minutes?" Acadia offered as she got to her feet. "I'll bring drinks for all of us upon my return."

I nodded. What else could I do?

The female strolled out of the room, and I couldn't help but watch her as she seemed to glide over the floor. Had I not been looking at the hem of the dress, I wouldn't have noticed... "She's barefoot."

Kaj chuckled. "She is. I'm not sure Acadia owns a pair of shoes. She prefers it that way."

For whatever reason, that lightened some of the strain on my nervous system. To know the mate of the Alpha strolled around without shoes ... yeah, it helped. How, I didn't know, but I wasn't going to question it.

"I'd like to apologize, *phaal*," I told Kaj. "I'm not normally this nervous. But I've never been in front of royalty before."

"Don't consider me royalty," he said simply. "Trust me, when you've been here long enough, you'll see me as just another male."

I seriously doubted that.

"And call me Kaj. Unless we're in public. Then you can use your discretion."

I narrowed my eyes. "You're saying ... I ... I have the job?"

"If you'd like. I assume that's why you're here."

"Of course," I blurted. "It's just ... I thought you'd want to interview me."

He chuckled. "In case it's not obvious, that's not my forte. In fact, I'll look to you to handle that going forward."

A strange, giddy feeling stirred in my belly. I hadn't known what to expect from today, but this certainly hadn't been it. Oh, I knew I was qualified and all, but I figured I would have to jump through hoops to get this job.

"You should know this is new to all of us. Blāz, he's one of the Zenith. As are Huracān, Kidel, and Mirakel. With you in the mix, that's the extent of my support. Hell, we don't even have *vestrahn* yet. But I'm hoping you'll be able to rectify that in the near future."

503

I felt as though I should have a notepad.

As though he read my mind, Kaj shook his head. "Trust me, there's no need to write it down. I'm sure we'll go over it all again. The question I have for you is, when can you start?"

"As soon as you need me." I smiled. "And no, I'm not abandoning my current job. In the past couple of months, we've brought on a few additional teachers for our clan's school. They're aware of what my intentions are, and we've got a replacement. Considering the opportunity, my clan wasn't willing to let it pass me by."

He seemed confused by my statement.

"The Torvolyans have always been a big supporter of Kardobahn. We were devastated to hear of his death. When we learned that you had survived the attack and would be the reigning Alpha, my clan was quite pleased. There's a lot of respect for you, *phaal*. The only request my clan has is that they have the opportunity to get to know you better. Similar to the way your father interacted with the race."

He nodded, as though that made sense.

"I'm more than willing to help you build the *kirlesgun* so that you have the support you need. It's an enormous task, but I'm up for it."

"It'll require you to use that backbone you're hiding in there," he said, a smile on his face.

"Yes, I know. And I assure you, I will. I'm not easily intimidated, which is saying something considering how overwhelmed I am in your presence. But I figure with time, I'll get used to it."

Kaj nodded. "I hope so. There's a lot to do. Due to ... recent events, we don't have any more time to waste."

Though I wasn't sure what events he was referring to, I understood.

"When would you like me to start?" I asked, feeling far more confident than when I walked into the room.

"Considering there are probably three thousand emails that need tending to, I'd say as soon as possible."

"I'm ready when you are," I offered, smiling in return.

The door to the room opened, and Acadia appeared once more. Behind me ... wow.

"He would not allow me to carry the drinks," she told Kaj, smiling.

I swallowed hard when the male stepped into the space. He was the most amazing male I'd ever seen, but it was his gunmetal-gray eyes that captivated me.

"Huracān, I'd like to introduce you to Leilana Torvolyan. Leilana, meet Huracān. He's one of the few I trust with my life. Thank you, *balisra*," he said when Acadia passed him a crystal glass, then turned his attention to Huracān. "Leilana is my new assistant going forward. The full extent of her role is up in the air; however, she'll have plenty to do."

The male peered over at me and nodded kindly.

Kaj took a sip of his drink, set it on the table, then sat back in his chair. "Blāz mentioned you requested visits with your family. I have no issues with you leaving the premises. However, you will only do so with Huracān accompanying you. He will be your personal protection anytime you step free of the residence. No exceptions. As you can imagine, I have many enemies. I won't take your safety lightly. The two of you can work out how you want to handle your family visits or other trips away."

Personal protection.

Great.

I wasn't even sure I could *look* at the male, much less be alone with him.

Perhaps visits home weren't as important as I originally thought.

40

KAJ

After spending another half hour with Leilana, I was convinced she would do well in the role. Her initial bout of nerves had dissipated, and I felt confident she was up to the task of being my right hand when it came to interacting with the public and managing my day-to-day.

Granted, I had yet to introduce her to Mirakel, and since my *adighrielin* would be required to work alongside her at times, I did need to see how well they would interact with one another. But that could be dealt with at a later date. For now, I simply wanted to get Leilana settled into the Lair.

"When you're ready to move your things into the residence," I told her, "get in touch with Huracān. He'll handle the logistics."

Leilana turned to Huracān. "Would you provide me with your phone number?"

"When you're done with that, can you give her a quick tour of the residence?" I asked the male. "Then lead her back off the property?"

"Oh, wait." Acadia stepped up to Huracān. "Would you permit me to touch you briefly?"

I watched my female as she waited for his response. I couldn't help but smile at the way Huracān seemed to blush at the thought.

"Of course, *leaqua*," he said softly.

Acadia stepped up, placed her fingers on his temples, and slid them down. I noticed the move was more clinical than when she'd performed it on me, which again made me smile.

Huracān's eyes widened as he stared out the windows. "Wow. That's ... better. Thank you."

"My pleasure," she replied, then turned to Leilana. "It was a pleasure to meet you. I look forward to seeing you in the near future."

Leilana performed another of those antiquated curtsies.

"I'll see you soon," I told the female, then took Acadia's hand and led her away. "I'd like to make a trip to the training center, if you don't mind. Unless you have something more pressing. I don't want to take up all your time."

"I'm free for this evening," she said sweetly. "Though I will have to find something to fill my time with."

Her words had a bolt of heat slamming into me. "I can think of something."

Her laugh was a balm to my soul. "I don't think that's going to be possible. Looks as though things are about to get busy for you."

"Maybe. But I'll always make time for you, *balisra*. Always."

I squeezed her hand gently. "I'd like to have your things moved here if you're okay with it."

She chuckled. "I've already taken care of it. The *heurosp* assured me it would all be delivered before dawn. But I do have one request."

"Anything."

"Would it bother you terribly if I had the room redecorated? It doesn't quite feel like you."

"Us, you mean," I corrected. "And I wouldn't mind at all."

We continued through the tunnels, branching off in the direction of the training facility. Another few minutes and we were stepping into what was quickly starting to look like a usable space.

"This looks amazing," Acadia said. "I didn't expect them to be so far along."

"I think a couple of them have bets on which teams can get more work completed. A good challenge is always a decent motivator."

"Screw you, Arman," someone snapped. "I didn't ask for your help."

I cleared my throat, drawing the attention of four trainees who were in the process of finishing the kitchen.

"*Phaal*," Romer greeted. "We didn't realize you were coming by."

"Since I don't intend to announce ahead of time, you should keep that in mind," I told the male vampire.

As it stood, there were currently twenty-one of the original twenty-seven trainees remaining. Six—all angels—had been eliminated by Obsidian within the first three days of their arrival. I was content to say that six of the seven vampires Mirakel had hand-selected for the program were still there. And though there wasn't anything perfect about this, I was also glad to say they were making progress.

"Please, return to your work," I said, motioning with my hand. "We're merely observing."

"Of course, *phaal*," Romer stated, turning his attention back to the sink he was installing with the help of one of the angels.

While they worked diligently, I led Acadia through the space, checking out the new walls that had been erected. I had to admit, they'd accomplished quite a bit in a short time. From what I understood, all the sleeping quarters were completed, allowing them to alternate shifts, as Bijou had suggested. It seemed to be working, but not quickly enough for my taste. I knew that they needed to get moving with the actual training portion because we needed more boots on the ground, more competent fighters out taking down the demons who were hunting both humans and vampires. As long as they were here, installing sinks and walls, they were not building the skills necessary to be functional where they were needed.

However, I trusted Obsidian knew what he was doing. And since the Zenith had the *fiestreigh* to back them up, we were able to maintain a steady patrol of the neighboring cities.

Speaking of...

"Has there been any updates on Asmia?" I asked Acadia when we were heading back through the tunnels.

"No." The single word was laced with so much pain. "But Reidar is convinced she's nearby."

"And Taayin?"

"Obsidian has moved him back into the mansion, but they're still keeping him sedated," she said softly.

No sooner had we passed the entrance to Angel Central than my cell phone chimed. I snagged it from my pocket and saw a 911 text from Kidel, urging me to come to the infirmary.

"This way," I said, quickly turning around. Without waiting, I took off in a jog. I hated to leave Acadia, but I knew an emergency text was never sent unless something critical was going on.

We burst through the doors to the infirmary and came to an immediate stop.

There on the floor was Khari, his enormous body flopping about like a fish out of water.

"What the hell's going on? Is he seizing?"

Standing near the wall, her hand over her mouth, Bijou looked horrified as she watched Apollo and Amethyst attempt to hold Khari still so that he didn't hurt himself.

"One minute they were walking, the next he was on the floor," Kidel informed me.

"It's not a seizure," Apollo announced.

Then what the fuck?

Suddenly the vampire's body went stone still, his eyes closed, arms flopping to his sides.

"Khari?" Bijou rasped, taking one hesitant step forward.

While I wanted to hold her back, I found I couldn't. She'd been down here with the male since his life force had been returned to his body. Being a male vampire with a mate, I knew all too well what a male was capable of if someone attempted to interfere with his *nehadon*. And though I wasn't all that keen on the idea that Bijou was the intended mate for the original vampire, I couldn't simply pretend it wasn't the case.

My daughter went to her knees first, then shifted so she could lift Khari's head and rest it on her legs.

"Khari?" she whispered again.

Apollo got to his feet and strolled toward me.

"What's going on?"

The male healer's voice was low when he said, "I think that was him getting all his memories back."

My eyes jerked to Apollo's.

The male nodded, the same trepidation in his eyes that I felt.

"I've been keeping an eye on him for the past few hours," the healer continued, "and it's been like Oliver's entire personality transferred. I didn't notice anything different aside from the obvious. New body, different voice, et cetera."

Shit.

Why I thought the male would simply exist as he had, I wasn't sure. But it made sense that all those repressed memories would come flooding forward at some point. Ten thousand years' worth...

"Where the fuck is Michael?" I shouted.

KHARI

Christ Almighty.

What the fuck was happening to me?

I couldn't move, my body wracked with an immeasurable pain. Memories assaulted me, consuming me, dragging me into a hell within my consciousness. Not just years, but centuries' worth of images flashed through my head, never-ending.

Oliver Calazans.

David Cartwright.

Finley Knox.

Bentley Palmer.

Damion Hayes.

Dante Beltran.

Then more.

At one time or another, I'd shared the name and vessel of some ninety humans, but why?

The names were endless, the list going on and on as the memories of those humans ransacked my mind. I'd lived within them, shared a vessel with the human soul that had originally accompanied the body. Until Oliver, I had outlived the human husk, transferred into another when they shriveled up and died. But I remembered every single thing that had happened, remembered being alone in all of them, never finding true happiness, even though the experiences were infinite.

Centuries' worth of memories, people, places, things. It felt like they were frying my brain cells as they bombarded me. All the while, I felt a deep, disturbing anger surge within me. The need for vengeance. Someone had to be punished for what had happened to me.

"Khari? Come back to me, please."

Oh, sweet heavens. That voice. The soft rasp of her words was a balm to my soul. My vampire soul.

I wasn't human, even if most of my memories were comprised of those I'd inhabited.

No, I was vampire.

The most powerful vampire to have ever walked the face of the Earth. Sent here by the Almighty. Created to protect the very humans I'd interacted with, the ones I'd mistakenly believed I belonged with.

A soft hand slid over my forehead, brushing back my hair. Smooth, warm. Soothing. That was the touch of this female. My female. Bijou Courtenay. She belonged to me. I'd felt it even when I was trapped within the human male. I had wanted her with a passion that defied reason.

Another surge of power tore through me, my muscles tensing. I was powerful. So fucking powerful. Not only physically, either. This went deeper than the fibers of my physical makeup. The full extent of who I was slammed into me, a reminder of what I'd been long ago. Back before I was locked away in one corporeal prison after another, transferred time and time again.

I was free.

My eyes flashed open.

Bright light pierced my brain, and I instantly shut it off.

"What the fuck? Who turned out the lights?" someone grumbled.

"It's him," another voice said. "Khari's doing it. Give him a minute."

That was a voice of reason, one I actually recognized.

Kaj Courtenay. The Alpha.

But I could see nothing but the face above me, the beautiful radiance of the female my heart belonged to. The only one I trusted in the world.

"Khari." Her smile was as blinding as those fluorescents, but I had no desire to dim it.

In fact, it was the light I wanted to live by. Only her.

Those soft fingers trailed over my cheek.

"Where am I?" I asked.

"Darkness, Colorado," she replied. "In the mansion owned by the angels. You're safe here."

Safe.

That wasn't a word I was familiar with. For so long, I'd been anything but.

Though I hated to break the contact, I sat up, my body moving easily, my power fully charged, my strength unparalleled. Within seconds, I was on my feet, helping Bijou up, peering around at those who watched me as though I might spring at any moment.

I easily picked out the vampires, noted the angels. I cataloged the exits, let my senses expand to take in my surroundings. A mansion of great size and filled with a number of souls was at my back, tunnels leading to another. In one direction, there was another facility, filled with vampires and angels, these not nearly as strong as those who surrounded me now.

I turned to see my female standing beside me, her eyes full of... I wasn't sure I could pinpoint the emotion I saw there. But it wasn't fear, and that was the only thing that mattered. No, this female knew I would never hurt her.

Then I heard a familiar heartbeat, one I'd listened to for the past twenty-eight years. Turning, I headed in the direction of the sound.

"Khari? Leave the human be. He's not well," someone said.

I ignored them. Opening the door, I pushed it wide, stepped into the sterile room with its white walls and shiny equipment. A machine sat at the head of the bed, colored lines dancing over the screen, moving in time with the heartbeat I could hear.

Oliver Calazans.

This was the male I'd inhabited. The human I'd forced aside.

Stepping up to the male, I placed my hand on the human's forehead. Warmth traveled from me into the human husk. I would not allow the human to suffer. Not after what he'd done for me all these years.

That tremulous heartbeat strengthened, the pulse shifting into the normal range.

"It's okay," I told Oliver. "You're safe now."

With my hand on Oliver's forehead, I gave the human a

glimpse of the past, assured him he was where he was supposed to be. Then, because I could, I returned the memories, but stopped those that occurred right before he met Bijou. Those weren't Oliver's to have. Those would remain with me, where they belonged. No other male would know that sort of intimacy with the female. Only me.

"What are you doing?"

I shifted my attention to the door, to the female standing there. This was the one whom the human Oliver knew as his sister. Penelope.

"I'm returning him to you," I assured her.

She stepped forward, her eyes glassy with unshed tears. "Will he remember me?"

"He will now." Before removing my hand, I sent a sense of peace and well-being into the male, removing the anger and hatred he'd lived with for so long. Those emotions belonged to me as well. The human didn't need to be shackled with them.

Penelope moved closer, taking Oliver's hand in hers, holding it carefully as though the male might break.

"He'll wake soon." I met her golden eyes, saw the beauty that radiated within the human turned angel. Yes, Oliver was safe with her. She would care for the male she believed to be her brother.

"Thank you," she said kindly.

I nodded, then stepped back, turning for the door. I peered down at myself, noticed the baggy blue clothes I wore. They had to go. I needed something ... else.

When I returned to the main hall, I realized more angels and vampires had joined us.

Including the archangel.

I narrowed my eyes. "You."

I had to give the male credit, he didn't back down, didn't show fear.

"We have a lot to discuss," Michael said. "When you're ready."

Though I considered eliminating the male once and for all, I refrained. Only because Bijou was there. I had no desire to allow the female to see that side of me.

"I'll find you when I'm ready," I told him. "Until then, I suggest you stay out of my way."

All eyes shot to Michael, as though they expected him to smite me where I stood. He wouldn't. No, the archangel needed me too much for that. Not to mention, I was far more powerful than Michael, though it seemed no one knew that except for me and the archangel.

I shifted my attention to Bijou. "I'd like to go to my chambers now."

She nodded once, then peered over at the Alpha. Something passed between them, then the male nodded.

With that settled, I held out my arm for the female. She stepped forward, sliding hers through mine as though that was exactly where she was meant to be.

Of course it was.

But I got the feeling it was going to take some time to show her as much.

ACADIA

T hough I sensed there was nothing to fear from the ancient vampire, I couldn't help but wonder how long that would be true.

Like Obsidian, the male was enormous, towering over everyone around him. But I could sense a power within him that was stronger than anything I'd ever encountered. I wondered if the others could sense it, if Khari even knew what he harnessed within him.

As though the male heard my thoughts, those ice-blue eyes shifted to me.

"*Leaqua*," he said softly, bowing slightly.

When he stood, his eyes returned to mine and held for the longest time. I didn't look away. I couldn't. There was something in his gaze that drew me in, as though he had something he needed to say to me.

Whatever it was, it seemed to pass as his attention shifted to Kaj. "*Phaal*."

For the ancient vampire to acknowledge Kaj as his Alpha spoke volumes. And it seemed to settle the energy in the space. At least with the Zenith. They relaxed, though they maintained their positioning around Kaj and me, ready to protect us should it come to that.

Khari peered down at Bijou once more. "*Asyra*. Shall we?"

Bijou nodded, gripping his arm more firmly.

Next to him, Bijou looked so small, so delicate. Yet the way Khari was with her spoke to what was transpiring between the two. There was no denying the vampire recognized her as his mate. The way Khari looked at Bijou ... it was the same way Kaj looked at me. As though he were ready to slay dragons for her, to eliminate kingdoms, annihilate anything and everything that threatened to harm her.

"Now what?" Blāz asked, his question directed at Kaj.

"We let him get settled. Give him a few days to acclimate."

"I'd like to check on him," Apollo noted.

"That's up to him," Kaj told the healer. "He's not under my control."

I could only imagine how difficult it was for Kaj to accept that. Especially since the male was being protective of Kaj's daughter.

But things were most definitely changing, which meant we would, too. We would adapt, as we always had. Those who'd been sent here to protect humans would work together, moving forward, shifting as the world did.

I knew not what the future would bring, but I had to trust in those around me. They would do what was necessary. I had to believe that.

As I watched Khari and Bijou exit the infirmary, I had a feeling that male would play an integral part going forward. Sure, I knew what Michael had said, but it was more than that. I could *feel* it. As for what it was, I didn't know, but my senses were finely tuned, the world around me clearer.

Yes, everything was changing.

And for once, I didn't think it was a bad thing.

EPILOGUE

Two months later...

KAJ

───────

"It's about damn time," I said as Acadia and I followed Blāz up the stairs to the second floor.

In the past couple of months, the Lair had undergone quite a bit of renovation. Now that Acadia and Leilana were in residence, the decor had not been up to par. But the good news was, they'd allowed the Zenith to keep their recreation areas, so there hadn't been much grumbling going on. And truthfully, I didn't think anyone would complain that they'd replaced some of the hideous furniture with pieces that inspired relaxation with a modern touch.

"We finished earlier in the night," Blāz explained. "But Leilana insisted on waiting to show you."

I smiled to myself. Yes, I could see why she would've held off. From the moment I stepped foot in my office at the beginning of the evening, she had insisted we get through a couple dozen emails that required my response. Despite my efforts to push it off for another day, she refused to let me leave until it was done.

Good thing I liked the female. In fact, I was quite fond of her. From the moment she moved into the Lair and stepped into the role, Leilana had made drastic changes. With help from Mirakel and Blāz, she had managed to hire ten *vestrahn*, and as of two weeks ago, the *heurosp* had all returned to Angel Central to handle what they'd been destined for. With the exception of Acadia, only vampires resided within the Lair, and I was grateful. Not that I didn't appreciate the angels. I most certainly did, but there was something to be said about being surrounded by your own.

"Are you ready?" Blāz asked, a huge grin on his face.

I rolled my eyes. I'd been ready for months.

"Impatient, much?" the male teased, then choked on a laugh when I lunged for him. "Go. What're you waiting for? Go on in."

Frowning, I turned toward the door. For whatever reason, I had expected Blāz to give me a personal tour. That did not seem to be the case as Blāz backed down the hall, grinning like an idiot.

I turned the knob, surprised there weren't all sorts of locking mechanisms that would keep me out. When I stepped inside, I paused for a moment, confused. What had once been a bedroom was now a comfortable living space complete with sofas and chairs, a big-screen television. The entrance to the adjoining bath had been closed off, altering the space entirely.

"Welcome home."

Turning, I saw Acadia smiling at me from the doorway. She looked resplendent as always.

"How're you feeling?" I prompted as I moved toward her.

Her smile widened. "Perfect. Absolutely perfect."

Placing my hand on her flat stomach, I leaned down and pressed my lips to hers. "I'm glad to hear it."

Although I had heard Michael's revelation that Acadia was pregnant, I had kept that bit of information to myself. Mostly out of fear the archangel was wrong, and the last thing I'd wanted was to get Acadia's hopes up about a baby.

Turned out, Michael hadn't been blowing smoke up my ass. Acadia was, in fact, pregnant. Her symptoms had revealed themselves just a couple of weeks ago. Since then, Amethyst had taken a keen interest in what was going on. From what I could tell, they were trying to determine how the pregnancy would go. Considering there was a drastic difference between vampire pregnancies and Fae pregnancies, we were learning as we went. However, it appeared the child was going to go the way of the Fae and stay in its own personal incubator for twelve months rather than the six required by vampires.

And though we had quite some time before our child would arrive, I was excited by the prospect.

"So, what do you think?" Acadia asked, motioning toward the living space.

"It's private," I said. "Which is already a plus."

I was surprised to see that the decor was more along the modern lines. The simplicity of it was rather nice.

"There are three bedrooms," she continued, turning back the way she'd come. "Two of them are empty right now."

I chuckled. "No nursery yet?"

Acadia's hand slid over her belly as she beamed up at me once more. "I figure we'll do that together."

I definitely liked the idea of that.

"And our bedroom?" I asked, looking forward to breaking in our new space.

"Right this way." Acadia took my hand and led me farther down the narrow hallway to the door at the very end.

When she opened the door, I was not prepared for what I saw. More with the modern, simplistic decor, but the space was enormous, as was the bed.

"What do you think?" she whispered.

"It's lovely," I told her, turning toward her. "Almost as lovely as you are."

Truth was, I didn't care where I lay my head at night as long as this female was beside me. When it came to home, mine was not a place. It was her. Acadia was where I belonged.

"I was thinking we could have the morning meal up here," she said with a seductive grin.

That was something new, I'd noticed. In the past couple of months, Acadia had come into her own. I wasn't sure if something specific had prompted it—be it her freedom from servitude or her acceptance of her role amongst the Fae, or maybe even our mating or the pregnancy—but she had awakened. I hadn't thought it possible to love her more than I already had, but with every passing day, I found I did. She was my perfect complement, my very heartbeat, the love I'd never had the strength to hope for.

She was my everything.

I knew that as long as she was by my side, I could survive anything.

So much had changed in such a short period of time, but it was looking up. Neither of us was tied to our past; instead, we were bound to one another and this new life we shared.

Together.

MICHAEL

E verything was changing.
      Or maybe it was simply falling into place; I wasn't
      entirely certain. I'd put these dominos in motion long
ago, so it made sense that they were beginning to fall now.

But somewhere along the way, the game had changed. I could no longer wait for one piece to tip the next and finally settle. No, I needed to treat them as chess pieces because the stakes were too high. I needed room to maneuver. Although I'd foreseen some of what was taking place, there were a few scenarios that I hadn't anticipated. God's plan, maybe.

As I stood, staring out over the kingdom in Heaven, I decided on which piece to move. While the *amsouelots* were important, they would have to wait. Uniting the vampires and the angels was crucial.

And I knew exactly how to do it.

STAY TUNED

Are you asking where do we go from here? That's a great question. There is more to come, and yes, it's been a minute since I published this book, but I'm in the process of writing more. A lot more. I love this series, but it got started at the beginning of the COVID pandemic, and with life getting chaotic, I lost touch with my muses. I've spent the past few weeks re-reading the series so I can get back into it, and I'm excited about the direction it's heading. So please be patient. I promise not to leave you hanging.

If you enjoyed *Bound in Darkness*, please consider leaving a review.

Acknowledgments

While writing is a solitary task, it's not a completely solo project. Because of that, I'd like to thank those who've assisted in one way or another. As a side note, I received no compensation for these acknowledgments, so they are in no particular order.

As always, I have to thank my husband for putting up with me. This series has resulted in some rather intriguing conversations over dinner, and I have to say, I truly enjoy picking my husband's brain. We're about to celebrate 18 years of marriage, and I have to admit, I never thought anyone would put up with me for this long. I love you, Steven!

You, the reader: I am forever grateful for your support. If it weren't for you, I wouldn't be able to continue doing what I love. Thank you for reading, thank you for writing a review, and thank you for hopping on social media and telling your friends about the book. You're amazing like that.

TERMS FROM THE ANCIENT LANGUAGE OF ANGELS

Amnigh: intense desire, or mating heat, experienced between amsouelots.

Amsouelot: the soul destined for another.

Archsire and **Archdam**: angels who procreate specifically for angel warriors.

Ayreme: Term of endearment meaning my greatest love.

Dhira: the cloak of darkness initiated by warrior angels. Only angels and Fae can see through, disorients those who attempt to locate them.

Ereswa: loosely translates to the human term *wife*.

Gathenya: the sexual energy produced when angels mate.

Heurosp: an immortal human who works for the angels, managing the mansion.

Lintamair: ancient mating ceremony of immortals.

Neilloh: demon sent back to Earth from Hell.

Reuthet: loosely translates to the human term *husband*.

Sezari: term of endearment meaning sweetheart, baby.

TERMS FROM THE ANCIENT LANGUAGE OF VAMPIRES

Adighrielin: The Alpha's advisor, his right hand. The most honorable position within the Zenith, that which is the first line of defense to the Alpha.

Asyra: term of endearment, translates to *my heart*.

Balisra: term of endearment, translates to *my love*.

Cosrobol: blood whore; vampires used solely for feeding.

Dyrlom: honorific title for a male of same status

Kirlesgun: The current alpha's regime

Leaqua: Queen

Mielix zan: the process of identifying/imprinting on one's sexual mate.

Nehadon: vampire mate.

Phaal: king/alpha

Sonavex: the secretion injected into a mate by a male vampire upon claiming.

Tresmar: Honorific title meaning master, someone higher than.

Vestrahn: housekeeper, groundskeeper, those in service to others.

Angels of Darkness Hierarchy:

Lieterra: the right-hand of a warrior angel, tasked with tracking, doling out responsibilities, as well as performing as the warrior's assistant.

Ladeare: highest rank within the fiestreigh, responsible for soldiers under him.

Fiestreigh: the legion of angels assigned to the Angels of Darkness.

Ritarro: a position held by a Fae. It's the equivalent of a handmaiden and a coveted role.

Demon Hierarchy:

Trielair: the three demons who oversee the demon factions: Eevuhl, Mizuhree, and Aguhnee.

Mesonneir: the level of demons beneath the trielair. Equivalent to lieutenants.

Impietan: a human turned demon by a mesonneir.

About the Author

New York Times and *USA Today* bestselling author Nicole Edwards lives in the suburbs of Austin, Texas, with her husband, their two fur babies, and the youngest of their three children, who has threatened never to leave home. When Nicole is not writing about sexy alpha males and sassy, independent women, she can often be found with a book in hand or attempting to keep the dogs happy. You can find her hanging out on social media and interacting with her readers - even when she's supposed to be writing.

NicoleEdwards.me

facebook.com/Author.Nicole.Edwards
instagram.com/nicoleedwardsauthor
tiktok.com/@nicoleedwardsauthor
bookbub.com/authors/nicole-edwards
threads.com/@nicoleedwardsauthor

CONNECT WITH NICOLE

I hope you're as eager to get the information as I am to give it. Any of these things is worth signing up for, or feel free to sign up for all. I do my best to keep each one unique and interesting.

NIC NEWS - If you haven't signed up for my newsletter and want notifications regarding preorders, new releases, give-aways, sales, etc., then you'll want to sign up. I promise not to spam your email; you get to pick exactly what you want to receive.

RAMBLINGS OF A WRITER BLOG - My blog is used for writer ramblings, which I am known to do from time to time.

NICOLE NATION - Visit my website to find exclusive content you won't find anywhere else, including Sneak Peeks, A Day in the Life character stories, exclusive giveaways, cards from Nicole, and join Nicole's review team.

NICOLE NATION ON FACEBOOK - Join my Facebook reader group to interact with other readers, ask me questions, play fun weekly games, celebrate during release week, and enter exclusive giveaways!

NAUGHTY & NICE SHOP - Not only does the shop have signed books, but there's fun merchandise, too—plenty of naughty and nice options to go around.

BY NICOLE EDWARDS

AUSTIN ARROWS
Rush
Kaufman

BRANTLEY WALKER: OFF THE BOOKS
All In
Without a Trace
Hide & Seek
Deadly Coincidence
Alibi
Secrets
Confessions
Bounty
Off Course
Chain Reaction
To Have and To Hold
Missing Pieces
Smoke and Mirrors

MISPLACED HALOS
Protected in Darkness
Salvation in Darkness
Bound in Darkness

OFFICE INTRIGUE
Office Intrigue
Intrigued Out of the Office
Their Rebellious Submissive
Their Famous Dominant
Their Ruthless Sadist
Their Naughty Student
Their Fairy Princess
Owned

PIER 70
Reckless
Fearless
Speechless
Harmless
Clueless

PRIMAL INSTINCTS
Chase (Volume 1-3)
Capture (Volume 4-6)
Claim (Volume 7-9)

THE JAMESONS OF COYOTE RIDGE
Hot Chocolate Wishes
Rough & Dirty

BY NICOLE EDWARDS

THE WALKERS OF COYOTE RIDGE
Kaleb
Zane
Travis
Holidays with the Walker Brothers
Ethan
Braydon
Sawyer
Brendon
Curtis
Jared
Hard to Hold
Hard to Handle
Beau
Rex
A Coyote Ridge Christmas
Mack
Kaden & Keegan
Trey
Rafe
Violet

STANDALONE NOVELS
Unhinged Trilogy
A Million Tiny Pieces
Inked on Paper
Bad Reputation
Bad Business
Filthy Hot Billionaire
RULE

www.ingramcontent.com/pod-product-compliance
Lightning Source LLC
Chambersburg PA
CBHW030842030726
47495CB00005B/1331